PALM TREES
IN THE STORM

A NOVEL
BY GENA WEST

Hasmark
PUBLISHING
INTERNATIONAL

This book comprises 91,000 words and was written entirely by Gena West

This is a work of fiction. The characters in this book are purely fictitious and any similarity to actual persons, real or imagined, living or dead, is purely coincidental and not a depiction of genuine relationships or events

Copyright © Gena West 2025

The right of Gena West to be identified as the author of this work has been asserted by her in accordance with the Copyright, Designs and Patents Act 1988

An audiobook version of this book, narrated by the author, is also available for purchase

ISBN13: 978-1-77482-339-2
ISBN 10:1-77482-339-X

All rights reserved. No part of this publication may be reproduced, stored in a retrieval system, or transmitted in any form, or by any means, electronic, mechanical, photocopying, recording or otherwise, without the prior permission of the copyright owner.

Hasmark Publishing International

With much love,
Genax

To everyone who supported me
along this journey – thank you!
You know who you are.

The Rising

Of branches splintered, scattered wide

A tempest's fervour gathers pride.

The brooding sky erupts with rage,

In tandem strikes the lightning stage.

Majestic palms bow then relent,

Defying storm without dissent.

Resilient to their bark and core,

Unyielding roots grip deep and sure,

A dance with Nature's matador,

They lean, but know they'll rise once more.

PROLOGUE

Independence and Stilettos

Click clack. Click clack.

The strident, staccato sound sliced through the growing stillness of Kilburn's high street. The once bustling area now lay quiet, wrapped in a heavy blanket of midnight silence. That was the problem with stilettos; their blatant disregard for subtlety or surprise. Their echo a constant drum beat, giving away her every step, betraying any attempt at stealth.

"Bloody things!" she muttered under her breath, and unceremoniously kicked them off. She broke into a steady run, casting furtive glances over her shoulder to ensure he wasn't still following. Her hurried exit meant she hadn't bothered to switch back to trainers and the rough pavement under her pounding, bare feet underlined her desperation. What had driven her to work in that dodgy venue? Pride and necessity, that's what. The pay was good, her rent was looming and she refused to crawl back to her father. No way. Her independence displayed a quiet rebellion against parents who had 'disowned' her for not following the expected path.

She zigzagged to avoid a rancid pile of roadside rubbish, its overflowing contents spilling into the street, with rummaging rats scurrying among the debris. Her pace quickened.

Click clack. Click clack. Even without those treacherous heels, the echo haunted her frantic thoughts.

The club – if one could call it that - was just a twenty-minute walk from her house, but at this hour it felt endless. She calculated if she really legged it – sprinted for dear life – she could be home in five. Her breath came in quick, sharp bursts as she wriggled the trembling key in its stubborn lock, sneaking one last panicked glance behind her. Empty.

Nobody there.

Relief flooded her as she latched the door, mindful not to wake her housemates. The silence was comforting yet unnerving. She leaned against the door exhaling a shaky sigh. It was nothing. As usual. Still, that gnawing sensation in her gut persisted, a whisper of unease, hinting she'd missed something – something important. A telltale sign, which had eluded her because she was distracted by his hands. They were enormous.

That ugly flashback surfaced; a memory from nearly a decade ago, when she'd felt a similar, unsettling disquiet, but had been too young to understand its intuitive warning.

PALM TREES IN THE STORM

CHAPTER 1

Longing to Belong

"**O**uch!"

Mikey flinched as Mother's bunched knuckles connected with the top of his head. He massaged his scalp, wincing, while Jessica fought to suppress a smirk. That'll teach him to snigger, she thought, regaining her precarious pose on tiny tiptoes. Despite her gratitude that her family was generally too polite to openly mock her, Jessica couldn't ignore the obvious lack of faith they had in her talent. Except for their long-standing houseboy, whose heartfelt claps always felt genuine. Did that count?

A sudden silence filled the room as the trusty generator's steady hum died, taking the comforting cool of the air-conditioner with it. The creak of window louvres being adjusted signalled her show had come to an abrupt end. She quickly bowed, then planted one foot behind the other and surrendered her knobbly knees to a curtsy. Her brother's stifled cough suspiciously resembled a snort, and Jessica's heart sank. *I shouldn't have bowed*, she chided herself. *Girls curtsy, Jessica!*

The scattered, tepid applause that followed did nothing to alleviate her growing self-doubt, or recapture her childlike confidence.

"Ah, well done, my dear! That was... nice." Her father's lone offer of praise rang sincere, yet this paltry acknowledgment of her efforts gave rise to a familiar sense of despondency. Even at age five, she grasped the word "nice" was distinctly noncommittal; a term devoid of true endorsement. Sokari Brown just as quickly vanished from view; his bearded face obscured by yesterday's newspaper. Jessica felt invisible.

Her mother, Edith, bore the strain of tried patience, as though her daughter's performance was just another task to tick off her endless list. "Hmm," she mumbled distractedly, before turning her ire to the staff. "Which of you people forgot to top-up the diesel, eh? In this unbearable Accra heat!" Kissing her teeth in annoyance, she strutted from the stuffy living area, disappearing down the dim hall into the kitchen, babbling baby perched on her hip, and whiny twins clinging to her legs like limpets.

As her spectators dispersed, Jessica's scrawny, nail-bitten fingers

CHAPTER 1 — LONGING TO BELONG

picked miserably at the ruffles of her pink tutu. Certain she'd performed the moves with precision, she squeezed her brimming eyes shut and visualized the exact exquisite routine of that elusive prima-ballerina on their large, black-and-white television.

Two years passed, yet time seemed frozen for this budding ballet dancer.

She swallowed hard and scrutinized the expressions of her audience. The entire clan had gathered to watch, including both parents, which Jessica conceded was something of a veritable feat nowadays. For they, unlike many couples she'd observed, hadn't succumbed to the casual indifference typical of disenfranchised long-term partners, but were still prone to frequent and embarrassing public displays of affection. It's no wonder they'd spawned a whopping eight children! These two couldn't keep their hands off each other and, even now, when they should be enthralled by her impassioned performance, she noted a distinct lack of focus. While they perceived having multiple children as an African symbol of prosperity and great fortune, such generosity seldom extended to regular, demonstrable tenderness toward their brood.

An odd moistness blurred Jessica's vision when she overheard her hero whisper to his wife the oft-quoted scripture, "Go forth and multiply!" then grew wistful as she observed them fall into fits of giggles like carefree youngsters; an inside-joke that never failed to delight them. Theirs was a party of two and they invited no-one; not even their offspring who gazed at them in wonder.

Although not singled out, the scene made Jessica's heart ache with the feeling of being excluded from their private world, one where children were an afterthought. Acutely vulnerable on her make-shift stage, she glanced at her siblings. shuddering at the notion of being indistinguishable, one of many, earmarked for nothing particularly remarkable; born simply to exist.

Unseen.

Someone (probably Kofi) had drawn the curtains for her impromptu performance and this self-taught ballerina balanced high with her arms afloat, elbows rounded awkwardly, nervously awaiting her parents' acknowledgement. With a deep breath, she twirled, her chocolate-brown limbs gracefully arcing as she spun in the air. This was her grand finale, and she ended with a (now-perfected) curtsy, arms outstretched.

Silence.

It suffocated her, filling the room with the weight of ordinary, dismissive labels. Nice. Amateur. Good effort. Words with decidedly ordinary overtones. Words she would come to associate with failure.

Her parents continuing hushed conversation in their native tongue, earmarked their oblivion to her closing bow. Jessica's shoulders drooped in defeat, her spirit shattered, until one loyal set of hands started clapping. Slowly, the others joined in. Eyes glistening with gratitude, she met Kofi's gentle gaze. But the moment was fleeting; Edith's stern glance at the unpressed laundry prompted him to resume his chores. But Jessica noticed he was smiling.

CHAPTER 1 — LONGING TO BELONG

The household disintegrated, and she sniffled as another wave of self-pity enveloped her. All she wanted was recognition for her talent. Was that too much to ask?

Kofi caught her eye, lowered the iron, and waggled his browless forehead in a clumsy attempt to elicit a laugh. She sought a smile, but it quickly crumbled. "He wasn't even paying attention!" she spluttered.

The kindness in the houseboy's empathetic gaze triggered tears in hers, and she slumped in a heap of despair. He spoke; his broken English ringing with the wisdom of an Oxford graduate.

"Master... he just come now-now," he tried to explain her papa's behaviour. "Make you no fear, Miss Jess. Mi sef sabi clap. Eh?"

She gawked at her motionless feet, wanting to scream that Kofi's applause didn't count – only her dad's did. "I'm going to be famous," she garbled incoherently, clutching at the thin threads of this fast-fading fantasy.

Kofi paused, an impossible stack of bedding and clothing effortlessly propped in his sizeable hands; emphasising that they were far too large for his almost effeminate build. Jessica tried not to stare. Instead, she rose from her dejected spot on the polished parquet, hotly conscious of her polka-dot panties atop the precarious pile. Kofi was watching her.

He licked his full, dry lips and repeated with undying devotion, "I go clap-clap forever!"

Her bottom lip quivered, and she nodded her thanks, before bolting to her room as the tears spilled over.

She scaled the top bunk with ease and flung herself against its soft pillows, clutching her black Barbie, a cherished gift from her father's travels. His import/export business often took him away, and when home, her mother monopolised his time. She liked the fact he always returned bearing gifts and that each child took turns to tug at Daddy's shoes as he lounged on his special leather recliner following a tiresome day; that in those moments he'd express genuine fondness and probe them about their dreams and aspirations.

But today was different. Frustration tugged at her, despite having just done what she loved – danced in front of everyone. The day had started badly. Because mere minutes after her father's arrival that dusty harmattan morning, she'd found him already engrossed in a chess game with Mikey.

"But it's my turn!" she'd protested, more to herself than to anyone in particular, her feeble cry lacking the indignant conviction of one who's telling the truth. She knew she was acting spoilt, that her assertion wasn't accurate, but desperately willed it to be so. Her words were barely audible, and nobody was listening.

As she watched the scene of parental love, her heart tightened with jealousy.

"What will you be when you grow up, huh?" Her father's baritone warmth filled the room and his fingers gave a playful squeeze.

CHAPTER 1 — LONGING TO BELONG

She stilled herself, straining to catch Mikey's mumbled reply.

"I dunno. Maybe a doctor, or lawyer." He shrugged.

"That's my boy!" her father responded in a tone tinged with pride, much to Jessica's surprise.

Couldn't he tell Mikey would say *anything* to appease him? "See, Dad, he's doing it again. He looks bored." Her stance was proudly petulant.

Sokari Brown didn't pay her much heed, except to lift a dismissive hand, shooing her away. Not one to raise his voice, this gesture denoted chastisement for begrudging her eldest sibling his turn. An aggrieved Jessica stormed straight to her sister Freida, ever the ready-listener.

"It makes me so angry, Fifi. Why does Daddy waste space on him when he doesn't care?" Resentment trembled through each word. For her, these special interactions were a lifeline. How incomprehensible that it could be treated with such nonchalance.

Freida marked the page she'd been reading with a hairclip and laid her novel on the pillow. "I don't think you should complain, Jess; not when you get to perform for us this afternoon." Jessica's expression remained crestfallen, so Freida added, "Hey, we all look forward to our days with Dad, even Mikey – in his own way. He's seventeen, not seven. Maybe he feels too old for this sort of thing, but he still needs it."

Now, lying in bed post-performance, Jessica was mulling over Freida's wise words. Perhaps she *did* get her fair share of attention, after all. And yet, the idea of a mundane existence haunted her. She heaved herself from the bunk with a sigh, as the dreaded dinner bell rang, her cue to re-enter the family dynamic. When you were one of eight and your dad travelled a great deal, your turn didn't come around that often.

Not that they starved her of love. Far from it. Besides, her brothers and sisters never complained; seemingly satisfied with the crumbs of affection sprinkled their way once or twice a month. Compared to her schoolmates, she was indeed fortunate (or so her mama reiterated).

Alas, these grumbling thoughts proved stronger than her resolve to mask her sulk, and caused Mrs Brown to suck her teeth in irritation. "Jessica! Are you pulling another long face? *Ah-ah*! See this ungrateful *pikin*! Can't you be content with what you have, eh?"

This record on repeat listed how she lived in a big house, constantly had food on the table, wore decent clothes, and such. How could she possibly want more?

But she did want more. She wanted the whole darned loaf of bread! She needed a fully-present, uninterrupted hug that lasted more than a fleeting second. And those were very scant indeed. In the Brown household, there simply wasn't enough bandwidth to spread across so many children. Yes, theirs was a life secure in structure and habitat, but seldom in emotion. Jessica had soon come to realise that it isn't easy to stand out in a crowd. Yet, as an unwitting member of that rare breed of Nigerian-living-in-Ghana, she stood out at school; her distinct accent setting her apart in ways she

CHAPTER 1   LONGING TO BELONG

preferred it didn't. The girl who sounded nothing like her peers. A girl longing to belong.

PALM TREES IN THE STORM

CHAPTER 2

The Good Times

Summer 1989 was memorable in more ways than one. It began with the promise of her eighth birthday, a milestone Jessica awaited with uncontainable excitement. She traipsed around with a perpetual grin and not even her mama's intentional tugs on her delicate, stubborn afro could dampen her giddy mood. Seated cross-legged at her parents' feet, her heart was an explosion of candyfloss – light, pink and impossibly sugary – brimming with more optimism than she'd felt since turning five and graduating from nursery. No longer a baby, she was now in "big girl" territory, capable of having proper conversations with her beloved papa. Oh, how she adored her father, with his huge, hearty laugh and gentle hands.

She could recall resting in his lap, quizzing him on subjects she couldn't quite understand. Not their typical interaction because that day he'd indulged her curious mind without reservation, as though he had oodles of time for her.

"How come people call you 'Chief', Daddy?"

"Well, my father – your grandpa – was chief and, when he died, I became chief."

"Oh," she marvelled, "Chief of everyone? Like everyone in the world?"

"No, darling." He chuckled, pressing a kiss to the top of her head. "Chief of our compound in Buguma."

"Bu-gu-ma," she repeated with childlike reverence. "Is that where we're from? What's a compound?"

"Yes, it is!" His voice swelled with pride and he took her small hand in his. "You're asking all the right questions, eh, my clever Jessica." His eyes gleamed as he shared tales of the Kalabari people from Rivers State, Nigeria. Oh, how she loved his stories! Now she possessed enough maturity to appreciate historical facts, he injected great detail into his account. No longer peppered with cute childish anecdotes, it contained concrete information an eight-year-old might comprehend. Sokari spoke of their ancestors with such passion, painting vivid pictures with his words, making her feel connected to a rich and proud history.

CHAPTER 2 — THE GOOD TIMES

"Nigeria comprises many different states and tribes. We hail from Rivers, descendants of the Ijaw, inhabitants of the oil-rich Niger Delta."

Jessica twisted to take in her father's enlivened expression.

"We Kalabaris have an impressive cultural heritage. I think we boast the best local delicacies in the whole Federal Republic!" He winked at his wife as he proclaimed this broad statement.

Edith Brown smiled in agreement, then gently prodded her daughter's head back into position. "Yes-oh! Our boiled yam and fish stew is unbeatable, abi?" Her voice was light and teasing.

Her husband chortled, "Especially when prepared by a *Kalabari* beauty, eh?"

Edith giggled, and Jessica did, too. She relished this banter, particularly when she was a part of it.

"*Na-wah-oh*, Sokari Preye," her mother's voice became playful. "What will I do with you?"

Jessica turned to regard them once more.

"What will you do *without* me?" Her father laughed, and they gazed at each other, eyes twinkling.

"Daddy, I always meant to ask…" she began hesitantly. "How come you and I are both 'Sokari'? What does our name mean?"

His tone oozed indulgence as he responded, "Ah, are you ready?"

She bobbed her half-plaited head, savouring his undivided attention.

"The name Sokari Preye Brown. Hahaha," he laughed in sheer delight. "My parents tried for several years to bear children, but… nothing." A clap of his palms provided the requisite drama. "Then one day…tada!" He spread his arms wide. "Here I was! A blessing from God after they nearly gave up hope."

"A real blessing, huh?" her mum interjected.

"Yes-oh," her father agreed. "You see, in Nigerian culture names are often a reflection of circumstances surrounding a child's birth. My middle name Preye means 'gift'. Sokari, which means 'God's sworn intent' applies to both sexes." His voice filled with gratitude. "To them, Sokari Preye Brown was a covenant gift from God, their only child."

Jessica gesticulated to egg him on.

"And as for our last name…" He shrugged. "Way, way back… many moons ago, our forefathers had early interactions with European merchants and slave traders, so European names are a common feature in the Kalabari Kingdom. We traded countless things with these *Oyinbos*, including names. And *that's* how we got ours, 'Brown'."

Her father's description of his heritage made Jessica feel connected to her roots in a way she hadn't before. His tales transported her to the place of his upbringing, Port Harcourt (or the garden City of PH as he fondly referred to it), near his hometown of Buguma. In PH, he met Edith, a young girl from Abonnema, also within Kalabari-land. She became his

CHAPTER 2   THE GOOD TIMES

closest friend and, subsequently, his bride. He was twenty-two and she nineteen when they wed.

Life as a lone child made Sokari keen to start a family and determined to sire a veritable brood. Edith conceived soon after their wedding and for thirteen consecutive years, or so it appeared, was either nursing or pregnant. One of seven pregnancies bore them a set of twins, resulting in eight children. They dubbed it their 'mini-tribe', and Edith's fertile womb symbolised a significant source of pride for the Browns.

"Ok, we're done. You're now birthday-ready, my daughter," the fecund matriarch of the mini-tribe announced, using a narrow-toothed comb to smooth the coifed edges of her handiwork.

"Thanks, Mummy." A tad irritated by the untimely interruption Jessica shuffled to the side to allow her mother to rise. She glanced at her father to signal he could continue. This part describing the children had always been her favourite.

Their eldest son, Michael, was prone to tears due to his dreadful colic, so it came as a relief for the couple to welcome the gurgling, smiling David into the fold. Then emerged Freida, their unnaturally stoic first daughter, who seldom cried. With older siblings to show him the ropes, James, a typical happy-go-lucky fourth child followed. Jessica was next, then the twins – Anita and Evelyn – who had non-identical features, but were completely interchangeable character-wise. Jessica found them eerie.

The last-born, Jeremy, was the unexpected one, conceived even after they'd tied Mrs Brown's tubes. Tubal ligation should prevent an egg journeying from the ovaries through the fallopian tubes, and block sperm from travelling up to the egg. But not in this instance. Edith got pregnant and, thereafter, Mr Brown would refer to his seed as "super sperm" and to Jeremy as their miracle. (This account was delivered in such matter-of-fact, biological terms that it left no room for embarrassment.)

Jessica Sokari Brown was the fifth child of the family. Inspired by her bubbly nature as a new-born, (she loved this bit!), Chief Brown gave his second girl a middle name that matched his. This made Jessica feel singled-out and special, cementing their father-daughter bond in her eyes.

She cherished memories of times he sneaked her the biggest, most succulent mango of the pile – all perhaps in her over-active mind – moments she clung to as proof of his favour. Their house was filled with laughter and the smell of roasted corn and plantain. Her birthdays were extra-special, marked by her favourite dish, *Akara*, made from peeled beans formed into a patty and deep-fried. Yummy!

But the most glorious of days were those she spent making sun-baked mud pancakes and clay teacups for her doll's house. How she loved to frolic in the dirt! To Jessica's delight, her younger sisters sometimes joined her game of make-belief. All the while, the garden's towering mango trees stood as sentinels, laden with ripe, juicy fruit and offering branches ready

CHAPTER 2 — THE GOOD TIMES

for climbing.

Fridays were crowned by eight loaves of freshly-baked bread from the popular "Eat All Bakery", and individual tubs of Planta margarine which, according to the daily TV ad was "hard to resist for any young family in the know." It was a treat they eagerly anticipated, with each child lost in the creamy, buttery taste of their private loaf. Her brothers devoured theirs almost instantly, and the twins would start with one, then the other (they shared everything)! Freida invariably savoured hers, and Jessica, more like her brothers, found herself staring at it with longing. Excruciating. Yet, it was all part of the cherished ritual.

The Browns were a happy family, or so it seemed.

But shadows crept into their utopia. Jessica hadn't fully recovered from the shock of Kofi's sudden departure earlier that month. The pain still lingered especially with Mother's frequent outbursts about his betrayal.

"I can't believe that thankless wretch disappeared after ten years of service. We treat him like family and he just ups and leaves with some bogus excuse? Didn't even wait to say goodbye! Huh! Dreadful ingrate!" Edith's voice was thick with anger.

Jessica bit her lip, casting glances at her older sister, then at her feet. Her mum continued, oblivious to her discomfort.

"Honestly, these staff can be so ungrateful!" Mrs Brown ranted.

Freida leaned in, her voice urgent and reassuring. "It's been weeks,

Jess! Try to forget it – forget him."

Jessica scowled at the memory, her mind racing as she swivelled and stalked towards her bedroom.

"Ah! It seems that girl became antisocial the minute she turned eight." Their mother's comment echoed after her retreating form.

Jessica's only response was a fleeting glare followed by a defiant slam of the wooden door. The resounding thud reverberated throughout the house like a shout of rebellion.

CHAPTER 3

Serendipity

There it was again. Failure. No matter how hard Jessica tried to become invisible, she remained painfully conspicuous. If shrinking into her chair could save her from being picked on, her body would have melted into the wood. Instead, the more she sought to hide behind her desk, the higher the likelihood *she'd* be chosen to answer the question.

"Jessica? In which year did Columbus sail to The Americas?"

The lanky adolescent squirmed in her seat, her voice a whisper. "In... f... 1492." She dreaded opening her mouth – dreaded speaking. It led to teasing, and she hated being teased. Teasing made her stutter, which brought on *more* teasing.

"Sorry, yang lady, I didn't catch dat. *Which* date?" Mrs Amanfo's eyes scanned the room, noticing the smirks beginning to form.

Jessica cleared her throat, keeping her focus on the teacher's dress collar and bracing herself against the impending ridicule. "In 1492 Columbus sailed the ocean blue." Her tone was defiant, daring them to laugh at the single line of poetry that had somehow taken the edge off her nerves.

Mrs Amanfo clapped her hands with delight. "Beautifully put, Jessica! Very good. Class, you'd do well to memorise dat little rhyme. Clever strategy to rememba de date."

Jessica's gratitude swelled at the teacher's praise, but quickly deflated as the classroom erupted into giggles. Mrs Amanfo silenced them with a reprimand. "Quiet! Wat are you laffing at, Ebo?" she barked at the boy who had guffawed the loudest. "Stop your nansense at once! Wan more sound and off to the headmaster you go!"

As the gong chimed for recess, Jessica grimaced. Being defended made things worse. Exiting the room, she steeled herself for what was sure to follow.

"Hey, you! Rich girl… what are you looking at?"

"This isn't for foreigners. Go away!"

These taunts had become all too familiar. Trying to fit in, Jessica chased after a misdirected ball and tossed it back to a circle of girls who

CHAPTER 3 — SERENDIPITY

promptly ignored her. She plonked herself on a balding patch of grass along the side-line, her mind a frolicking field of fun. If only she belonged.

Math class was another battle zone. The mere sound of her pronouncing 'seventeen' in her monotonic 'correct' way, devoid of the local Ghanaian sing-song lilt, triggered brazen mimicry from her schoolmates. Despite clenched fists and burning cheeks, Jessica remained silent. But a fleeting sympathetic smile from across the room startled her. It was barely noticeable, but unmistakably there. Was it from the beautiful Deborah Pariwa? Jessica's heart dared to hope.

"She's the most popular person in class!" Jessica later declared to her bemused older sister. "If I'm kind to her, she'll notice me, right?" she postulated.

The truth was most days, the school heroine sauntered across the playground with nary a glance in her admirer's direction, acknowledging neither her existence, nor the obvious overtures of friendliness. Deborah's enviable poise and popularity granted her power, and she seemed to revel in it.

"Yes, but she doesn't even clock you, so just leave it." Freida's advice was pragmatic.

"No. *Everyone* wants to be her friend. Even the *teachers* like her," Jessica insisted.

But each passing day of unattained friendship mirrored the abundant lack of recognition she felt at home.

A serendipitous opportunity came knocking one sweltering afternoon, as Jessica waited patiently in the stands of the sports field. The air prickled with humidity, and the rickety awning had long shunned its duty to provide respite from Accra's scorching sun.

She wiped a sweaty temple with the hem of her jersey and hollered to her teammates, "Go, go, go!" squinting for a better view of the match.

And that's when she spotted it: that indiscriminate, tell-tale sign of early womanhood which had left its distinct stain at the rear of Debbie's shorts.

The latter, blithely unaware of this unwanted blemish to her pristine image, merrily bounded up and down, her braided ponytail swishing left, right. Left, right.

Jessica froze, transfixed. "Erhmm…" she half-called, then stopped herself. No, she needed to warn her before the others noticed.

Consumed by her mission to protect, the young athlete vaulted over rows of folded chairs and raced for the court, pulling off her blue smock as she ran.

Landing in front of an alarmed Debbie, she panted, "You… you have something on your shorts."

"I what?" Debbie looked confused.

Jessica glanced nervously at Coach Anneka who regarded the schoolgirls with some impatience. "Come on, you're our star player. Your team needs you!" the coach urged.

"Just a minute, Coach!" Jessica insisted, thrusting the garment at

CHAPTER 3 — SERENDIPITY

her idol, Deborah Pariwa, whose expression remained blankly bewildered.

"Why...?" Debbie peered at the garb as though it were a dirty rag.

"Put it on," Jessica instructed before reaching up. "Here, let me..." She placed it over the other girl's head, ignoring her wide-eyed protests. "Trust me."

Debbie slipped reluctant arms through the coverall and pulled it over her slender hips, her narrowed gaze demanding an explanation.

Donning a countenance of sympathy, Jessica offered in a whisper, "Your period. Mine came five weeks ago, so I know how it feels."

"Oh! How embarrassing!" Debbie muttered, her face flushing.

Laying consoling fingers on Debbie's cocoa-butter-smoothened arm, Jessica squeezed reassuringly. "Don't worry. I don't think anybody saw. Go. I'll take your place."

"Thanks!" Debbie started to walk away, then turned. "It's Jess, right?" she asked, her eyes more a smile than her lips.

Jessica twinkled; delighted Debbie knew her name.

"Thank you, Jess." Deborah planted a kiss on Jessica's stunned cheek and scurried off.

"Hey! Miss *Naija*! Are you playing, or what?" the tetchy team captain yelled.

"Yes, yes. Coming!" Jessica shook off her daydream of a lifelong liaison with Debbie and bounded into the game, shining with renewed hope.

This unexpected event cemented their alliance, and the two girls became fast friends, marking a dramatic turn in Jessica's popularity at school.

⁓

Two Years Later

Jessica's group skipped along the dusty road toward the main junction, their spirits high after Games Practice. She had chosen to dismiss her driver, enjoying the carefree ease of walking with friends. Her eyes widened when they stopped for local ice-lollies by the roadside.

"Chale, let's buy *poki*. I'm thirsty," someone suggested.

"*Poki?*" Jessica giggled. "What's that?"

"Oh, Jess! You *paaah*, you're so green. Try some."

"Well, my mum won't…"

"*Kai! Mama-ba*. Are you a baby? Have it – it won't kill you!"

Jessica grinned at Debbie and shrugged in a flash of uncharacteristic recklessness.

The seller was fanning herself with a crumpled, oil-stained newspaper, her expression one of weary boredom, unbothered by the drooling, slumbering infant strapped to her back.

Jessica cringed, then signalled, "And for me, too. Thanks." Chuckling as the girls applauded her, she tried to repress residual reservations about ingesting such vivid redness.

Giggles and shared stories made the fast-melting ice-lolly even

CHAPTER 3 🌴 SERENDIPITY

sweeter and more thirst-quenching.

～

As her twelfth birthday loomed, the Browns encouraged Jessica to host a proper party. Self-conscious about serving *Akara* at the party, she worried her image-conscious classmates wouldn't appreciate the traditional fried bean dish.

A fat purple notebook lay open before her, pen poised to jot festive ideas. Thick and cloth-bound, with five-hundred blank pages, it was an early gift from her sister. *"Darling Jess, Happy 12th Birthday! Make this journal your constant companion. Listen to your heart and trust it will guide you. Love always, Fxx,"* Freida had inscribed.

"Aww, Fifi, thank you. I adore it! I'll take it everywhere… tell it everything!"

Jessica jotted Debbie's name at the top of the guest list, adding 'BFF' beside it. Best-Friends-Forever! she thought with a smile. The once unattainable classroom queen had declared herself deeply indebted to Jessica ever since their serendipitous bonding on the netball court as ten-year-olds. The two had become inseparable.

Even menstrual advice was bandied between them, but Jessica's own discomfort was a fresh agony today and she groaned to her mother.

"Mum, I can't… I'll give school a miss today. It's PE and I've got cramps."

Edith Brown's chuckle was dry. "Cramps? Pele, oh. But no.

You shall go."

"Ugh! That's not fair, I…" Jessica began.

Edith looked unperturbed, her stalwart stance on menstruation and any accompanying pain was unyielding. "Listen, *every* woman has periods. They're uncomfortable, but shouldn't prevent you from doing anything." Her lips twitched. "Hmm. Wait until you give birth, hah! *Then* you'll know what cramps are. This is nothing, *O'jare!*"

Jessica gritted her teeth and implored, "But can't you write a sick note? My classmates hate me as it is."

Mrs Brown scoffed, "Your classmates, eh? They're jealous because you excel at everything. My dear, just carry on!"

"But they'll tease me."

Edith's tone hardened. "They *tease* you? Huh! Bullies! I thought you were over all that? Ignore them and just carry on, you hear? Besides, you have your siblings and… what's her name?"

"Debbie," Jessica prompted, eyes brightening.

"Good. So, you don't need anyone else."

॰॰॰

Debbie flicked her ponytail over a shoulder and bent to lace her shoe. "It's tomorrow, right?"

"Yep. My first real party." Jessica beamed at her friend.

The El Wak Stadium loudspeaker boomed, "Ladies and Gentlemen,

CHAPTER 3   SERENDIPITY

boys and girls, welcome to our end-of-season National Athletics Championships in Accra. If you won your heats and qualified for the finals, please make your way to the red area."

"That's you," Debbie prompted with admiration.

"I know." Jessica suppressed a nervous giggle. "Feels weird to be twelve and competing with fourteen and fifteen-year-olds." She pouted self-consciously.

"*Almost* twelve. Anyway, you're the fastest girl at school, so go kick some ass!"

They hugged, and Jessica bounded off.

Moments before the relay competition, she overheard her teammates chatting and moved closer, wanting to join the camaraderie. Her smile faded when Elsa, Jessica's biggest (and often mean-spirited) rival, turned to face her and began chanting the word "*Wotiabon*". Jessica peered at the other girls, deciphering from their body language that this was an insult of sorts. She crossed her arms with furrowed brows. But, the rhythmic chant, "*Wotiabon, Wotiabon*", grew menacing as more followed suit. She would later learn that whilst "*Wotiabon*" literally means "smelly hair" in Twi, (the native tongue of the Akan people of Ghana), its metaphorical imagery insinuates your thinking is not intelligent. Your head stinks, you have stinking thinking, therefore you're unintelligent. They were just being cruel.

Elsa upped the ante by jeering, "Smelly-Sweaty-Stinky," whilst punctuating each syllable with a finger jab at her pony-tailed head. Jessica reeled in horror. Them mimicking her accent was one thing, but outright abuse was another. These were her teammates and they were supposed to be running a race together in a few minutes!

She glanced wide-eyed at Debbie, who refused to meet her gaze. Left drowning in a torrid wave of embarrassment, she sneaked surreptitious fingers to her scalp, then pretended to pinch her nose. Nothing. She smelt nothing untoward. "What are they talking about?" her mind screamed, mortified by the possibility that her propensity for excessive perspiration might justify the name-calling.

Then the unimaginable happened. Deborah also began pointing, mocking and laughing out loud. It was the most crushing sound Jessica had ever heard; that her trusted friend, whom she'd saved from certain shame two years earlier, could turn against her now.

Tears streaming, she swivelled on her heel and sprinted – out of the stadium, up Burma Camp Road, past '37' towards Airport Residential, exhausted by the time she arrived home. She felt betrayed. Beaten. Had missed the tournament, but didn't care.

She never wanted to run again.

"What's wrong? Are you crying?" Her eldest brother Michael glanced up from his bowl of *Eba and Okra*, while sucking his sticky appendages with gusto. He regarded his breathless sister with moderate concern. Jessica wasn't surprised to encounter him at the kitchen table. These quick breaks from medical school were his chance to savour their mother's legendary cooking.

CHAPTER 3 🌴 SERENDIPITY

She wiped her tear-streaked cheeks with the back of a hand. "They… I didn't race."

"What d'you mean, you didn't race? Wasn't this your big event? I wanted to catch an earlier flight from Lagos to be here to watch my favourite sis. But lectures ended at 11:30 … hey, hey, hey, what's that face? What happened? Come. Sit. Tell me, eh?"

"They mocked me, Mikey. Called me names. I… Even *Debbie* joined in."

"And who's Debbie?"

"My best friend," she sniffed.

Mikey's eyes narrowed. "Are you saying your *best* friend ridiculed you?"

"Uh-huh."

Mikey used the clean fingers of his left hand to lift his sister's trembling chin. "Jess, anyone who laughs at you in front of others is *not* your friend! She's probably secretly jealous of you. Otherwise, this *Debbie* would've jumped to your defence."

That much was now apparent. Jessica nodded, glad to have bumped into her soon-to-be-doctor-brother on her tearful dash to the sanctuary of her room. She was sure this blade of betrayal would carve an indelible scar and forever alter the course of her life.

She cancelled her celebrations, settling instead for the usual family-only gathering with cake, candles and *Akara*.

To compound matters, Freida departed for boarding school the next day. So preoccupied had Jessica been with the tournament and her party-planning that she hadn't noticed the packed suitcases in the corner of their shared bedroom, until it was too late.

"What are these? Fifi? Are they yours?" She could sense panic rising within her.

Fifi stopped what she was doing and walked over, her features filled with regret. "I wanted to say something. I *should* have, but didn't dare ruin your birthday and…"

Jessica kicked the suitcase nearest to her, ignoring Fifi's raised eyebrows at her childishness. "But it *is* ruined! You *leave* tonight and I had no idea!"

Freida sighed, lifting and dropping her arms in a gesture of defeat. "It wasn't… they thought it better to keep hush. I'm sorry, Jess."

Jessica chewed her lip. "I can understand *them* not telling me, but *you*! My only real friend." Her voice broke. "What will I do without you here? You're the only one I t-talk to!" she stammered through uncontrollable sobs as she picked up the purple journal from the dresser. "So *that's* the reason you gave this to me. B-because you knew you were leaving. It explains why you've been s-s-so nice to me!"

Freida reached to hug her inconsolable sister, then decided to leave her be. She had a plane to catch.

The days that followed were a blur. Jessica suffered from the hitherto unknown sentiment of missing someone; an all-encompassing "sick" sensation right in the pit of her belly, which was eventually diagnosed

CHAPTER 3 — SERENDIPITY

as more than mere emotional despair. It was the dreaded Typhoid Fever.

Sokari Brown explained to the doctor on duty that his daughter had apparently been ill-advised by friends with more robust stomachs; that her curiosity had prevailed against better judgement. The local street vendor had likely made the ice-lollies under unsanitary conditions and poor Jessica paid the price. Nyaho Clinic, the private hospital in their neighbourhood, admitted her. They administered Ceftriaxone, an injectable antibiotic treatment, and put her on an intravenous drip for nutrients and rehydration. She almost died.

Through a haze of feverish hallucinations, she glimpsed the naked anxiety in both parents planted by her bedside, her faithful mother praying under her breath and her sturdy father staring ahead with his arms clasped. The room reeked of antiseptic and something else. Vomit?

A bespectacled, ageing physician entered and spoke in hushed tones. Jessica couldn't strain to listen, but the relief on their taut faces told her the worst was over. By the point of her discharge a week later her clothes swamped her frail body.

This unexpected illness, coupled with the horrible incident with her schoolmates, was the deciding factor for Mr and Mrs Brown.

"We have no choice, Edith. The minute she's stronger, we'll send her, too."

And so it was, that strings were pulled and hasty arrangements made.

After Freida's departure and the sports ground humiliation, the thick, purple journal became a ready confidante and Jessica diarised her experiences with daily diligence, imagining her intuitive inner cries of wisdom as its responses.

Dear J, I've had a horrid, few weeks. Never been sadder or sicker. Thought Debbie was a friend for life. But look what she did. I prefer not to be here anymore. When Fifi telephoned last night, I refused to speak to her. But I'm glad I'll see her soon. Boarding school, here I come!

CHAPTER 4

England

"**D**on't over-pack, my dear. You'll need new clothes anyway." Edith squinted at her second daughter. "Your flight's on Friday, so you have the weekend to get organised. It is well."

Jessica acknowledged her mother's words with a perfunctory nod, but said nothing.

Friday came, and despite anticipating a pit of dread as she prepared to leave her siblings, something strange happened. Relief washed over her like a wave, carrying her away from the confining safety-net of their structured upbringing.

She felt like a bird released from its cage, her spirit soaring as the plane lifted off the tarmac; not nervous about this unknown future, but exhilarated by the prospect of reuniting with her favourite sibling. All those Enid Blyton books she'd avidly devoured depicted English boarding schools as idyllic, akin to the fictional 'St Clare's' and 'Malory Towers'.

Oh, she couldn't wait to gobble up midnight feasts and meet genuine friends – true allies who'd never betray her like Judas-type Deborahs.

"Oooh, somebody's getting spoilt," remarked Sue, the custodian assigned to minors, her eyes twinkling with amusement.

Jessica felt obliged to explain, "I don't normally travel first class, but I guess my near-death illness frightened my parents. Plus, it was my birthday…"

"Well then, be sure to enjoy yourself!" Sue didn't pry further.

Dutifully, the eager traveller shunned sleep and relished movie after movie, immersing herself in the wonderful realm of make-belief.

"Fancy another drink, young lady?"

"Errhmm, yes please… and some popcorn if you have any."

Jessica delighted in the luxury, hugging the soft blanket closer, picturing the five siblings she'd left at home.

The flight landed at 06:20, and her chirpy chaperone ushered her through immigration into the uncrowded baggage area. As they moved towards the exit, Jessica clutched the trolley tighter, her heart pounding with anxiety.

CHAPTER 4 ENGLAND

"You alright, love?" Sue was peering at her.

She nodded, her steps faltering as they approached Arrivals. A heavy weight of uncertainty pinched her lips into a thin line. But the butterflies in her stomach evaporated the second she saw Fifi standing on the other side of the passenger divide, an enormous smile on her face, waving as though her life depended on it.

All was forgiven.

The sisters hugged fiercely, squeezing the breath out of each other in sheer delight.

"Never scare us like that again, you hear?" Freida's voice was husky with emotion.

Jessica squeezed her again. Theirs was an unspoken agreement.

The following three days were a flurry of activity. New uniform, check. School bag with emblem, check. School boater (that's a funny type of hat), check. Name labels for clothes, check. Mufti (which means home clothes), check. Tuck box, check. Train ticket, check. The list seemed endless, but Jessica ticked off each item with eager anticipation.

Boarders were instructed to arrive on Monday 6th September between 14:00 and 17:00, so the duo caught the 11:02 train from St Pancras, and embarked on their two-hour thirty-minute journey to St Ignatius' Church of England School, in Darley Dale, Matlock, Derbyshire.

"What's your impression, so far? You seem to have settled in nicely after only five weeks."

Jessica bobbed her braided head at Matron. "I have. It helps that my sister's here, too. In the Upper Sixth. We're used to being surrounded by relatives, so…" She shrugged.

Matron's ruddy cheeks rose and her eyes crinkled. "Ah, indeed. I know Freida. Smart lass, that one! Skipped the Lower Sixth Form altogether. I remember hearing you're from a household of *eight* children? That explains it. You're doing alright. Keep it up!" She slapped Jessica square on the back, leaving her feeling chuffed. **Maybe her large family was a plus after all.**

That night, she smiled as the housemistress bade them goodnight. Their hushed conversations after 'lights-out' were most entertaining, and Jessica started chatting the moment the door was securely shut.

"Gwen?"

"Hmm?"

"Thanks for helping me this morning with… you know."

"Sure. Still surprised you had no clue." Gwen **sounded bemused**, and a couple of girls chuckled. "How was it? Comfortable?"

It was too dark for them **to observe** Jessica's twiddling thumbs as she blinked rapidly in response to their mirth. Years of teasing had left

CHAPTER 4 　ENGLAND

her expecting the worst. She tried to sound nonchalant. "Yep, didn't notice it. So practical, especially for PE. Thanks, again!"

"Yeah. Gwen's our go-to for everything," squeaked Gwen's side-kick, Julia.

Another dorm-mate piped up, "So are you saying they don't use tampons in Africa?"

Jessica braced herself for more laughter, but none was forthcoming. "Dunno. They probably do. Africa's massive, after all." Careful not to appear patronizing or defensive, she added, "Back in Accra, nobody openly discusses such things, and the idea of shoving anything up your fanny is horrendous. I knew about tampons, but never considered them an option." Their silence told her she had their undivided attention. "My sister Freida says it reminds her of a plughole and refuses to follow that route." She sniggered self-consciously. Was she divulging too much? But her roommates were enthralled, so she continued, "It made movement class liberating, literally."

The girls giggled and chatted far beyond midnight.

Emily Dunn, the Director of Performing Arts at St Ignatius, greeted her students with a quick synopsis of her background: "I'm thirty-ish," she began with a wink. "Some say I was an eminent performer destined for fame. But alas, life got in the way. Today, my hopes rest on you ladies, which is why I teach with such fervour." With a disarming grin, she continued, "Many moons ago, I accepted a lead role in the hit musical, 'Cats,'" a distinct murmur spread through the class and she raised a hand to silence them, "but discovered I was with child during costume fittings, and that was that. The moral? Avoid getting pregnant if you want a stage career."

Jessica was captivated by this confident, yet self-effacing, woman. Despite her winning smile, she gleaned something akin to regret in Ms Dunn's eyes.

"Ok, so you've heard my story. Now, your turn. Each of you share." Ms Dunn looked directly at Jessica, as though sensing her intrigue. "You. What's your story? Why the performing arts?

A cloud of shyness overcame Jessica and her gaze darted around the room. It'd been so long since she'd buried that dream, and the thought of voicing it out loud felt too vulnerable. Everyone was staring. She scratched her forehead. "I-I've always loved to dance, and would like to, again." She swallowed, the snickers from Ghana haunting her, but none came. They were waiting.

"So, you've danced before?" Emily Dunn prompted gently.

"Just at home. Not since I was eight." An almost forgotten surge of shame resurfaced.

"And why did you stop?"

Jessica's amber pupils dilated and she froze, biting her lip. She wasn't

CHAPTER 4 ENGLAND

inclined to share *that* story. Ms Dunn cocked her neck, gave a small nod, then addressed the class. "Alright. Who's next?"

Jessica exhaled and stared at her trembling hands, relieved to have been let off the hook.

Emily Dunn had a special rapport with her students and an uncanny ability to pinpoint their strengths and weaknesses. "Don't overthink it. Just trust your body to deliver. Stop doubting yourself! It shows in your moves." "Relax into the flow. Yes, that's perfect. Stretch your arm out, long and graceful. Much better."

Jessica's challenge lay not with Ms Dunn, but with the formidable Madame Juliette Travers, Head of Dance. This former prima ballerina prided herself on spotting and honing talent. However, she had prematurely concluded the young African's talents lay elsewhere.

"*Regarde toi.* You do not have a dancer's body. It's not... classical." She shook her head disparagingly. "More for a runner, or sports person. But definitely not for ballet. *Non!*" Emitting a dramatic sigh, she added, "*Alors*, Emily likes you. So, *voila*! I've cast you as the prince. *That's* a lead role. You should be grateful." She tutted and turned to address someone else. Dismissed.

Jessica wished the ground would swallow her whole.

That night, she sneaked to the Senior Boarding House and tapped on Fifi's door.

"I think she hates me, Fif. She's only ever seen me in Movement; yet has already decided I'm no good!"

"Has she said that you're 'no good'?"

"Well, not exactly, but the role she gave me isn't fit for a 'proper' dancer."

Freida perched on the edge of her bed massaging her temples. "But how can she tell without seeing you dance? You're not making sense, darling."

Jessica scowled. "Hmph, the 'Prince' is hardly the most sought-after part!"

"At least you've got one, J! Quit grumbling. Give it your best shot, and who knows? Maybe you'll prove you deserve something better next time." Freida sounded irritated, and Jessica noticed the study papers strewn around.

She sighed and gave her sister an impromptu hug. "Your exams! I forgot. Sorry, Fif. Good luck tomorrow!" She crept to her dormitory with newfound resolve. She would show Madame Travers she *was* a real dancer.

⁓

"And one, and two, *relevé*, and hold… and five, and six, and seven, *plié*. Jessica, point those toes and circle and up! Come on! Lift your arm *up*. And seven and eight. *Et voila! Bon,* Ladies. Ok. We're finished for

CHAPTER 4 ENGLAND

today. Tomorrow, we work on the *finale*."

Once Madame Travers left the studio, Emily Dunn approached the budding ballerina stretching her stiff limbs. "So, how're you finding it? Still love to dance?"

Jessica's face erupted with enthusiasm. "Oh, yes! But I have so much to learn." She winced. "Those other girls… they're amazing!"

"They've been training since they were *four*." Emily didn't sound impressed. "Stop knocking yourself, Jessica. You're a fast learner. Your natural rhythm and aptitude for movement should hold you in good stead. Follow your instincts. Keep an open mind. And don't be too quick to dismiss Madame Travers as the enemy – she's excellent at what she does, and her critique might bring out the best in you."

"If you say so."

The school production took place in Matlock Town Hall and, to Jessica's surprise, her performance received what some might call positive feedback.

"I told you!" Ms Dunn said triumphantly. "You not only possess natural talent, but have this regal air about you. The show was a whopping success!"

The local paper described it as "ground-breaking," awarding Jessica Brown a mention as "the most princely of the cast."

Still, Jessica longed for accolades like "charismatic and mesmerizing", or "gifted dancer"; something that distinguished her from her peers, for Pete's sake! As it stood, she felt grossly underutilized and largely unnoticed.

Desperation made her seek advice from her toughest critic.

"Madame? May I ask you a question?"

"Go ahead." The French woman sat on the corner of her desk with arms folded.

"Do you think… given the success of the production… I could pursue a successful future in dance?" Jessica hurried on. "That it's possible for me to become world-famous some day?" She paused, battling self-doubt and craving reassurance.

The instructor pursed her rouged lips in that unique francophone manner, eyeing Jessica from top to toe. "*Mais, oui*, of course. You can pursue this 'future in dance'. *Pourquoi pas?* But to be *successful?*" She snorted and scrunched her nose. "You'll need to stop, and I mean *stop*, eating like a pig." Her keen gaze grazed Jessica's form once more, staring pointedly at her solid thighs, before returning to her stunned features. "*Non*. The tree trunks must go!"

If Jessica could blush, she would have. She wanted to be angry, but was too shocked by the woman's directness. *Tree trunks?* After the encouraging reviews from the newspapers, this critique was a harsh blow. Mostly because it felt true. No wonder she'd been cast as the prince! Dancers are typically lean and lithe, but Jessica knew she possessed the explosive thighs of a sprinter and was naturally bottom heavy. *Princely!* Hmm.

CHAPTER 4 ENGLAND

That evening, as the excited chitter chatter of over three hundred schoolgirls filled the dining hall, she idly pushed her food around her plate. Ironically, they'd been served pork pies for supper and she'd normally wolf hers down, then ask for seconds. But not today. Today, the very name 'pork pies' reminded her of Madame Travers' words: *Stop eating like a pig!* Jessica eyed her schoolmates, tucking into their meals with gusto.

Suddenly, she raised a hand. "Excuse me, Miss?"

"Yes?" The meal attendant's gesture was one of impatience. "Go on then!"

Jessica didn't bother to shove her chair under the table, but rushed to the bathroom and locked herself in the nearest stall, all the while thinking, "I'll show them. I will become the dancer I know I can be."

She plunged two middle fingers down her throat, gasping as her eyes stung and flooded in resistance to the deliberate choking. Within seconds, she'd expelled every morsel of thigh-enhancing piggy pork pie.

CHAPTER 5

I'm Different

Jessica's determination to succeed was fierce – like steel forged in fire. With each disciplined move and every painstaking effort, she carved her form into a physique deemed aesthetically perfect. Matron's scrutiny, however, was relentless.

One afternoon, she pulled Jessica aside, her voice laden with concern. "I've noticed you're losing a great deal of weight, young lady. Should I be worried?"

"No Matron, I'm fine," was Jessica's hasty response.

"Are you?" She peered over the top of her rimmed spectacles. "Hmmm!

There's talk of you frequenting the lavatory at mealtimes." Her piercing gaze swept Jessica's whittling form and Jessica shifted uncomfortably under those watchful eyes.

"Be careful," Matron warned.

"Yes, Matron," Jessica mumbled as their eyes met. She knew full well her secret habits were dangerously close to being exposed.

Matron's eagle-eyed appraisal should have been the wake-up call Jessica needed. But she was already in freefall, pounds dropping off, aided by intense workouts and habitual trips to the loo.

Slithers of pale, yellow moonlight slipped through the blinds, casting narrow beams across Jessica's bed. She snuggled deeper under her duvet, ready for a night of perfect slumber, but winced when Constance's high-pitched voice pierced the darkness.

"Hey, where's your sister now? Bet you miss her."

"Freida's at Uni in New York," Jessica answered, fighting a yawn.

"So, you're on your own and can do whatever you want." Her dorm-mate giggled.

"Yep, I guess. Listen, Connie, I really need to sleep," Jessica pleaded.

"Why? What's happening? Is life that hectic?" Gwen chimed in.

Jessica sighed and sat up. "Yeah, I've got tons on."

"I bet you do! Everyone's still raving about your last performance.

CHAPTER 5   I'M DIFFERENT

That was brilliant," Gwen said with admiration.

"Thanks. And now Ms Dunn has booked so many recitals for me." Jessica's voice wavered.

And I'm scared, she could have added, but didn't. Earlier that day, she'd told a surprised Emily Dunn that she was "not ready for Saturday's show." But the truth lay in her unhealthy obsession with Madame Travers' opinions and the battle with her insecurities. Her oppressive thoughts, fuelled by a relentless need for perfection, gnawed at her.

On Saturday, she was riddled with self-doubt; the prelude to a poor performance. She stepped on stage and transformed into her five-year-old self; eager to prove her prowess, yet faltering. Much too focused on eliciting the approval of her audience, she cringed as she took her final bow, her mind pleading for any accolade, whilst kicking herself for each misstep.

It came hurtling towards her with razor-sharp precision, gathering momentum as it whizzed through the silence. Wham! It hit her. Hard. **Right in that tender spot between her ribs.** The solar plexus. She expelled a gasp of excruciating inner turmoil, unable to thwart the misguided ball of twisted disappointment that assailed her. She had failed. This movie was on repeat: month after month, year after year. Yet she was never prepared for how it made her feel. Like a failure.

All she needed was the cover of a toilet cubicle to purge her anguish. She rushed blindly to the nearest bathroom and sunk to her knees. The violent expulsion of that blasted Mars Bar she'd earlier devoured quickly followed.

After a quick rinse of her mouth, she crept from the loo on stealthy feet, keen to avoid being accosted by anyone. But as it happened, Madame Travers (of all people) was lying in wait, laden with unsolicited advice. Instead of being critical, the former ballerina explained, "The truth about ballet is it matters not that you got it right a hundred times in rehearsal, Jessica. What matters is now – that's all your audience sees. Each movement, each misstep forms their judgement – applause or indifference. But you must never give up mid-performance. Jamais! Remember, with every eight count comes another chance to start over and prove yourself worthy of the applause."

Jessica was moved by the unexpected empathy in Madame Travers' voice. "Thank you, Madame. I promise I shan't disappoint you again."

"Non, ma petite danseuse. The important thing is you do not let yourself down."

Jessica dabbed the corner of her eye. If only they knew quite how often she did let herself down.

"That's it. Lift that leg higher… beautiful! You've mastered this."

Madame turned to update the department head after the lesson, and Jessica eavesdropped on their conversation, catching snippets.

CHAPTER 5 🌴 I'M DIFFERENT

"... wonderful to see such diligence and dedication. And she has actual skill. But even more special is that... unique vulnerability, clothed in supreme strength. Mon Dieu! It makes her irresistible."

Emily Dunn shone with pride. "Oh, I plan to make damn sure she is irresistible."

Their praise felt suffocating to Jessica. They both turned to regard the fourteen-year-old, whose body already resembled a woman's, albeit lean and toned, with a firm rounded bottom – a legacy of her African heritage. Jessica averted her gaze, grabbed her water-bottle and bolted from the studio.

In the changing cubicle, she frowned at her figure, wishing her leotard wouldn't hug her quite so tightly; that she could fade into the background like the pale silhouettes of the other girls.

Dear J, I wish I could change the way I look. Madame T says my 'form is much improved', which means I'm not fat anymore. She's kinder now, but I'm not happy. The others aren't forced to try as hard. It's so unfair. Constance and Gwen say having a bubble-butt is cute, but what do they know? They're as skinny as rakes, both of them! What if my shape means I'll never be a ballet dancer?

Ms Dunn's next announcement was a lifeline. "From Monday, we're shifting our focus to contemporary dance," she said, meeting Jessica's eye. "Your unique physique is an asset. Use it."

And Jessica did just that.

Thereafter, her impassioned performances evoked comments such as, "Stunning!" "Her poise and elegance belie her obvious athleticism and strength." That line was her favourite. She still liked to think of herself as an athlete (but without the thunder thighs).

"Play to your strengths," Madame would reiterate, and that mantra became Jessica's beacon. Once the lights hit and the music began, her soul came alive. As she channelled every ounce of her being into the choreographed routine, inhibitions rolled away. Madame's squinted gaze would widen with pleasure, and Jessica knew she'd found her calling.

※

"… Happy birthday to Jessie, Happy birthday to you!"

Jessica, Matron and a handful of girls were in the Common Room. They chanted, "Hip, hip, hurray!" as she blew out her fifteen candles.

"Only another week, then school is o-verrrr!" Gwen announced, and everyone cheered.

Jessica avoided Matron's watchful gaze as she dutifully nibbled a forkful of cake. "Erm, Ms Dunn's waiting for me in the studio…" she muttered and pushed the saucer aside. Her words trailed off and with a sheepish grin she scurried away.

Come September, her gruelling schedule resumed.

"Are you certain you're getting ample rest, Jess? You seem tired,"

CHAPTER 5   I'M DIFFERENT

Ms Dunn noticed. She reached for the phone on her desk. "Perhaps we should cut back on your commitments."

"No, no! Please, don't do that, Miss. We've found the perfect balance with my schoolwork and dancing. But… exams are coming up and I guess the pressure's getting to me," Jessica confessed.

"How so?" Emily probed. "Your teachers have no complaints."

"It's not them. It's my dad. His expectations are… that I excel."

"And you will. Our indicators show that you'll pass easily," Ms Dunn reassured her.

Jessica snickered, "Passing isn't the issue, Miss. It's passing with flying colours, as Dad puts it. That's what worries me." She recalled her recent conversation with her father.

He'd questioned her career ambitions, scoffing when she explained it didn't involve traditional subjects like Mathematics, English, Science or History. "Have you ever met a dancer who earns enough, huh? Dance as a hobby, for fun… but… ah ah, please!" He tutted with disapproval.

Arguing with him was pointless. Chief Brown was a force to reckon with, and there'd be no winning this battle. Forget that she didn't wish to blindly follow the Brown precedent of A grades and distinctions. "I'm different," she declared to her journal. "I wish they'd see that!" But she knew she couldn't disappoint her father. She craved his approval and burning the midnight candle, fitting studies into every available moment, was her only choice. She wouldn't quit dance, and academic mediocrity wasn't an option in her family.

※

"I did it! It's a miracle!" Jessica spun around in circles in the Accra living room. It was 10th August 1997, GCSE results day; exactly a month after her 16th birthday and she was floating on a cloud of joy. "I can't believe this!" she squealed, clutching the results slip. "3 A's (one in Theatre Studies, of course), an A, 4 Bs and a C. Well… a C in Physics, which I absolutely detested, so it doesn't count. Ooooooh!" She did another gleeful pirouette, smiling triumphantly at her twin sisters.

Anita, ever the pessimist, offered her unsolicited opinion. "A 'C' isn't anything to be proud of, though. Is it?"

Jessica froze mid-spin and glared at her infuriating younger sibling. "Pfff! Listen, Miss know-it-all, it's a wonder I passed the subject at all, given how much I hated it! Shut-up if you can't be nice."

"Daddy won't like it! Daddy won't like it," the teenage twins chanted, whilst shaking their heads in tandem!

Pushing aside her flicker of worry, Jessica scowled, "Just mind your bloody business, you two!"

To her immense relief, her dad said little about the 'C' grade. He seemed satisfied she'd upheld the Brown name and caused no social disgrace. Ever since she'd left for boarding school, her parents had become more demonstrative, even giving her a hug – a step up from the usual pat on the back.

CHAPTER 5   I'M DIFFERENT

"Congratulations, darling. You've done well!"

Jessica's heart grew warm and fuzzy.

Dear J, today marks the happiest moment of my life! I pulled it off and now Dad will surely support my dreams.

Later that morning, one of her old classmates paid a surprise visit with an invitation to a post-results party that night.

"Thanks!" Jessica smiled at Ebo. "You didn't have to deliver it. Could've called." She stared into his brown eyes. He's grown quite handsome, she mused, remembering his buck teeth and loud laugh.

Ebo grinned back, confirming that braces could indeed achieve the impossible. "Just making sure you got it! Now you'd better come."

Jessica flashed her brightest smile. "Surprised I haven't bumped into you before – I visit every Christmas and Summer, you know."

Ebo looked embarrassed and shrugged. "Yeah, I heard. But… well… you left Accra so suddenly. We assumed maybe you weren't interested in hanging with us. I was kinda mean to you, sometimes," he added ruefully.

"Ah." It was Jessica's turn to shrug. "No biggy – we were so young." She gave him her grown-up pout. "I'm cool." By this point, she had convinced herself their betrayal was thoroughly behind her. She was **in England and on the fast track to becoming a star. Nothing else mattered.** Besides, this was her chance to bid farewell to her former life. "I'll be there."

Ebo looked relieved. "Great! A lot of the gang are still here, then most are heading to England for A levels. I'm going to America."

"Nice. My sister Freida is studying medicine there."

"Are you planning to join her?"

"Nah. Too many opportunities in London."

"Eeish! Like what?" he asked, intrigued.

Jessica's face lit up, then dimmed. "Well, the Royal Academy of Dance is one of the best, and I hope to gain admission this autumn."

"Wow! That sounds impressive. So… why the long face?"

"My parents. I still need to persuade them of the 'merits' of my choice."

Yes. One more hill to climb.

CHAPTER 6

Reunited

Alone in the room she used to share with Fifi, Jessica twirled before the full-length mirror, her heart thumping with anticipation. "How surprised they'll be when they see me," she thought, a surge of pride swelling within her. No longer the *"wotiabom"* or smelly haired tomboy they once ridiculed, she was now a vision in a silvery-white silk dress that skimmed her newly-accepted curves.

Grinning with satisfaction, she ran her palms along her body, smoothing out any wrinkles. One final touch of shimmery lip-gloss and a quick dusting of translucent powder rendered her armour complete. She threw a nod of approval to the gorgeous young woman peering back at her, then flicked off the light and headed for the door.

The assembly hall pulsed with trendy tunes she and her friends listened to in England. How snobbish of her to imagine it might be otherwise. Frankly, the DJ's playlist was glorious! In an instant, she found herself positioned on the disco floor, her hips and torso gyrating and undulating to the beat, with a crowd rapidly converging around her and merry Ebo at the forefront.

When Ebo's hand snaked around her waist, she flinched and slapped it away. Her celebratory mood didn't extend to being touched by a boy. Expertly squirming her lithe body away from his, she resumed dancing. Ebo, dejected, shrugged and walked off. She ignored him. Nobody could ruin this rare moment of glory. In her element, the stress of the past few months dissipated with each twist and turn as the reality of her positive exam results sunk in.

The song ended, and Jessica leapt from the raised platform laughing and soaring on adrenaline, thrilled at the sight of her spectators visibly succumbing to her charms. Every time she assumed centre-stage, she became irresistible, a far cry from the gawking girl she once was. Chuckling again, eyes alight with sheer joy, she sauntered towards the bar.

Then she saw her.

She was unprepared for the jungle of emotions that assailed her upon seeing Deborah Pariwa that evening. Debbie, clad in a plunging leopard print jumpsuit accentuating her enviable cleavage, shimmied over to the drinks counter. Jessica paused, sipping her punch, and their

CHAPTER 6 🌴 REUINTED

eyes locked.

Dear J, Debbie looked genuinely sorry for what she did to me four years ago – we didn't even have to speak. All this while, I imagined I hated her, but not in the slightest.

Without a word, the girls hugged, and that encounter marked the rekindling of their bizarre friendship.

For the remainder of her trip, Jessica basked in the company of her former best buddy. They frequented beach parties, devoured spicy fried plantain known as *Kelewele*, danced to spectacular Afrobeats, and chatted far into the night. Deborah's tales of losing her virginity and other teenage escapades sounded so… delicious, especially to an intrigued Jessica who'd never given boys any consideration until recently.

With no homework or deadlines to manoeuvre, Accra appeared more vibrant. The adult-like Debbie seemed positively inclined to have fun, showing Jessica the coolest spots in town, and sharing the most outrageous, quirky stories. It was like finding a new friend.

One humid evening, they lounged at the poolside of the Labadi Beach Hotel, amidst tropical landscaped gardens, both smothered in lavender-infused mosquito repellent and feeling rather grown-up. Deborah noticeably perked up when two young men approached, thrusting her ample chest forward, arching her back and presenting her perfectly cultivated, lopsided grin. Jessica giggled, amused by her friend's flirtatious antics, or maybe the sparkling wine had unduly heightened her senses. Whatever the case, she figured that 'Desirable Debbie' had one up on her. She sniggered at the thought of her newly-coined nickname, wryly acknowledging it as the probable truth.

Except… Jessica squinted coyly at the guy named Jason who kept angling to catch her eye… he looked the more handsome of the pair, and her heart gave a brief flutter. She sneaked a glance at Debbie, who appeared pre-occupied with the second fellow.

"So, I didn't get *your* name," Jason murmured, his hot breath tickling the spot behind her ear.

Feeling emboldened, she parted her lips to respond, but Debbie's high-pitched titter drowned her out.

"Hey! Why are you troubling this *small girl*? She's from *Abrochi* and not interested in you bush boys!"

Jessica gasped at her friend's rudeness and watched the guys disappear as swiftly as they'd materialised. She couldn't see the funny side, though Debbie was doubled over laughing.

"Hey! Why did you do that? He was cute. What if I *wanted* to talk to him?" Although she generally had reservations about boys, Jason's appreciative gaze had made her tingle.

Debbie's face twisted with scorn. "Oh, please! He wasn't right for you, anyway. Don't worry. Your chance will come."

Lying in bed that night, Jessica experienced a resurgence of the age-old niggle that she was lacking somehow. Funny how, despite her

CHAPTER 6 — REUINTED

accomplishments, this intoxicating association with Deborah both uplifted and demoralised her in equal measure. Still, she was glad they had reconnected.

"I love London! Weeeee!" Debbie threw gleeful hands in the air as she cavorted on the bare mattress.

Jessica chortled and acknowledged, "With Freida gone, it's great having you here, Debs."

"Ah, yeah, how is she?"

"Busy with medical school. Haven't chatted to her in a while. But…," she shrugged.

"But at least you have meeee," Debbie squealed at the top of her voice, leaping off and planting a kiss on her cheek. "I'm your new sister."

Jessica laughed and trotted behind her bestie to the kitchen.

"Great that we've got this place to ourselves for another week." With relish, Debbie licked the last traces of yoghurt from her spoon, then crunched the empty tub before lobbing it into the large silver dustbin. "Hey, how did your try-out go? I bet you wowed them!"

Jessica chewed her bottom lip and shook her head. "Not sure. Gave it my all, but… can't tell with these people. There were six of them just staring at me. Very daunting." Debbie rinsed her grubby fingers and gave her friend a hug. "You'll be fine. I know it! You always are."

"Well, either way, I'll find out tomorrow."

"So, let's get this straight." The president of the Royal Academy of Dance was an austere man whose grave countenance appeared permanent. He liked to state the obvious. "Your initial plan was to acquire a Diploma of Higher Dance Education to qualify you to teach others. But you've switched to an advanced course to support your bursary application. Correct?"

Jessica nodded, her throat dry as the Sahara. Mr Ribbit squinted, and raised a brow. All neck and no chin, his anxious features were clustered together beneath slick grey hair. He expected her to present a convincing case, but she was damned if she knew what to say.

"Erm, I've choreographed minor school productions, and understand that an effective instructor must grasp all aspects of dance and execute the moves flawlessly," she said, taking a shaky breath and tried to gauge his expression. It revealed nothing, so she admitted, "To be honest, Sir, I chose the teacher-training path to appease my academia-obsessed Nigerian parents, who've never allowed me to make my own choices." Her speech was gathering pace now. "My skills as a dancer don't impress them. Yet, this will always be my first love. It's what I'm good at. Anyway, since they've withdrawn their support, it no longer matters. I'm on my own now." She exhaled and stared at her feet.

Mr Ribbit scribbled furiously on his notepad, remaining mute and leaving her on tenterhooks. Minutes later, he glanced up, his scraggly hands clasped in a thoughtful prayer position, index fingers drumming a silent rhythm. Jessica cringed, certain he was preparing to deliver a disappointing verdict. But then he grinned – gums, no teeth.

"I appreciate your passion. Although I observed from the audition your alignment can be…" He grimaced, and Jessica's spirit sank.

"… somewhat amateur," he continued, "but you're here to learn. I've seen worse! Plus, you aren't quite seventeen so still eligible for a grant."

Jessica exhaled and braced herself.

"We've seen such cases before – you know, parents who fail to comprehend what we do here at the academy and remain summarily unimpressed by any achievements beyond the realm of pure academia."

The nervous applicant breathed a sigh of relief. "Yes. Mine believe there's no substitute for a 'good education'. They'd prefer A Levels or, better still, that I got a degree. But I want to dance. Nothing else."

The dean stood. "Young lady, candidates such as yourself are indeed the intended benefactors of these bursaries. It would be our pleasure to offer you a full scholarship to cover your tuition."

Jessica's soul soared with gratitude as she reached her sweaty palm across the desk to grasp his. "Thank you, Sir. Oh, Mr Ribbit! I promise, I won't let you down. I'll work so hard. Thank you!"

"You'll need to," he warned, his demeanour serious again. "We don't tolerate any slacking here at RAD."

Exiting the dean's office, the aspiring ballerina did a quick victory hobble in the corridor, pumping her fists in glee, "Yes!" she whispered excitedly, before rushing home with her wonderful news.

"Now all that remains is for me to find a job," she declared triumphantly.

CHAPTER 7

His Hands

"Click clack, click clack…

…was the jarring echo of her frantic flee from that Kilburn nightspot, each step propelled by sheer panic; sprinting as though her existence depended on it. Her treacherous stilettos disregarded any notion of stealth as they click-clacked against the asphalt surface.

The tumultuous events that led to this terrifying moment replayed in her mind with crystal clarity.

"After the copious amounts we've poured into your education!

You're telling us you want to… what? *Dance*?" Edith Brown spat the last word as though it were an insult.

Jessica's father, usually so jovial, wore a mask of disappointment, and he shook his head.

"Such frivolous ambitions are incongruous with our African culture, Jessica. Nobody will take you seriously. We didn't send you to England to squander your future. I assumed you'd outgrow these childhood dreams. No, it's not acceptable."

"What your father is saying is we *do not* condone your choice of career. You hear? So, if you choose to remain in England…"

"But this is everything I yearn for," she protested, turning to her dad with a desperate plea in her eyes. "Daddy, all I've ever wanted is to dance. And I'm good at it!"

Edith shot a warning glare at her husband. "Sokari, don't even *think* about giving in!"

Sokari Brown sighed, shaking his head. "Uh-uh, Jessica. As your parents, we know what's best for you. It's out of the question."

Emboldened by desperation, the fifth Brown offspring summoned all her teenage indignation and righteous sense of independence, catalysed by several years at an English boarding school, and blurted, "Well, it isn't *your* decision! It's *my* life, and I'll do as I please. You can't force me. I…"

CHAPTER 7 — HIS HANDS

"Jessica!" Her father's harsh tone cut through her rebellious words. He held her gaze for the longest moment before added quietly, "Alright. As you wish. You're on your own."

And just like that, her fate was sealed. She stayed in London, applied for the scholarship at RAD, and her father withdrew his financial support. This forced her to secure part-time work to cover her expenses. The search for a job was grueling, and when her savings had dwindled to nought, she finally landed waitress duties at a local establishment.

One evening, the sleazy Irish manager called her into his "office" – a shabby, dimly lit room by the fire exit, replete with an old couch, peeling wallpaper, flickering light bulbs, and the lingering stench of fish'n'chips, and stale cigarettes.

"Hello lass! They tell me youse a dancer." His triple chin wobbled as he spoke, chubby fingers resting idly on his beer belly.

Jessica nodded cautiously, not certain who he meant by "they". Probably Jimmy, the bartender. He was the only person she chatted to in that dingy hole. She scrunched her nose.

The aptly named Mr O'Leary elaborated, "Well, I've been tinkin 'bout adding a 'lil colourrr to this place – especially now we've got you 'ere, eh?"

She tried not to gag. He couldn't be slimier, she thought miserably. But she needed this position. And a smile goes a long way.

"So, how 'bout it, then?"

How about *what*? He'd still said nothing concrete.

His beady pupils were dilated as he clarified, "We'll offer ye more and you'd only have to do four 'lil 15-minute shows – an hour, tops."

Realisation dawned on her. "Oh. Ok. Sure. Would I be required to… uh… continue serving?"

"Nah. Yer crap at it, anyways. By the looks of ye, youse much better with yer body, than yer hands."

No, he hadn't actually verbalised that, had he?

Mr O'Leary was already reaching for a clammy handshake to seal their deal. "Right. That's settled then. Plus, I'll give ye double. Ye start tomorrow."

Dancing was far superior to waitressing, Jessica reasoned. Besides, only a fool would reject double pay.

On the third evening, a drunken patron stumbled towards her, his breath reeking with alcohol. He belched and slurred, "Aye, lassie! Come 'ere. Wanna see ye up close and personal."

A cold shiver snaked up her spine. Keeping her gaze professional, she reminded herself not to make eye contact for too long and never to venture into the crowd. These men scared her, but their tips paid her bills.

A month into her new role, she spotted him again in the audience, the man whose eyes bore straight through her skin-tight top and lycra

CHAPTER 7 — HIS HANDS

pants. He had a presence that unnerved her, a look of raw desire she recognised as lust. He wore that same glazed expression she'd first encountered when she was but a wee lass. A look that frightened her.

After her final bow, she grabbed her coat and duffle bag from beneath the bar, waved at Jimmy, and dashed towards the exit. From the corner of her eye, she saw the man rise. She quickened her pace.

Click clack, click clack.

Even within the safety of her abode, she couldn't shake the menacing echo from her mind. The man had ridiculously large hands that evoked unsettling memories of Kofi. *His* appendages had been enormous, too. They'd all cracked jokes about it, including her father.

"Kofi, my boy, you should be a carpenter with paws like yaws! Hahaha!" Sokari Brown's hearty roar at his own joke would elicit a corresponding chuckle from their trusted helper. It was Kofi's automatic response.

"Yes, Sah, Master!" he'd say good-naturedly, before carrying on with household chores. But the tic in his jaw had always made Jessica wonder whether he was secretly annoyed by the teasing, given the considerable disproportion of his generous extremities to his slight, somewhat effeminate build.

Shivering at the memory, she pressed the handset against her ear, glad for the distraction of speaking with her sister, Fifi.

"Thank goodness I reached you on time. It could've been much worse! But why now, after so long?" Fifi's voice was filled with concern.

"I dunno… I suppose I can't figure why he did it," Jessica reflected. "And I never asked… what drove you to search for me that night?"

"Oh. Mum," Freida admitted. "She told me that, as the oldest girl, I was responsible for you when she wasn't there. I took it to heart, I suppose."

"Lucky you did. Imagine, Fif, he must've… hated us. Constant teasing would piss *anybody* off and the size of his palms made him seem… kinda freakish."

"Yes, plus imagine *his* life. Sure, he enjoyed living in the house, but he was largely uneducated, and was… what… twenty-four? With no exposure to girls, his hormones must've been raging. It's no excuse, but it couldn't have been easy for him."

"Maybe you're right. Maybe he *was* a half-decent guy who experienced a period of temporary insanity." Jessica sighed and lowered her voice. "But… um…I think it's affected me somehow, Fif. Everytime I meet a man who seems a tad strange, or has ginormous hands, or tries to catch my eye – eewww!" She shuddered. "Tonight, I was convinced a dude from the club followed me."

"What?! Are you serious?"

"No-no, it turns out he didn't, but I keep getting these ludicrous

CHAPTER 7 — HIS HANDS

panic attacks… you know, since…" She trailed off with a tremor.

"Hmmm. You might need to see a therapist, Jess."

"No!" Jessica declared with more vehemence than intended. "Talking about it with you is enough. I'll be fine. Eventually."

"Ah." Freida's voice held a note of humour. "So *that's* why you're calling this late. What time is it there, anyway?"

"Nearly 2 am…"

"2 am?! Jess, why were you wandering the streets of London at this ungodly hour? You crazy?"

"No. Just working. Plus, it's only a few minutes from home and I need the salary…"

"Stop! Listen to yourself. What are you – a hustler? What sort of place is this? Not…"

"As if!" Jessica snorted. "I'm not *that* desperate or stupid. No, it's a normal club where they play music. I dance to entertain the punters – nothing dodgy. And it pays well."

"*Cchheeewww!* I'll tell you who else 'pays well' – our father!"

"Fif…"

"No, listen! They're worried. I spoke to mum, and she says they haven't heard from you in like a month."

"Yeah, I'm busy fending for myself, aren't I?! They could call, too."

"Huh, Jess! Do you hear yourself?! We're dealing with African parents here. Have some respect, *ah-ah*. *You* pick up the damn phone. Please, *O'jare!* Wouldn't it be much easier to just swallow your foolish pride and get Dad to pay?" Freida huffed. "Anymore 'dodgy' situations and I'll report you myself."

When Jessica replaced the receiver, she reluctantly readied herself for bed. Sleep, as usual, eluded her. But she lowered her lids regardless, bracing herself for the inevitable assault…

CHAPTER 8

Kofi

The nightmare was no ordinary bad dream. It wasn't some disturbingly realistic hallucination that rattled her awake, her heart pounding with anxiety until she reassured herself that it was "just a dream." No. This was crippling; a brutal, vivid replay of actual events, dragging Jessica back to a past she wished to forget. Not some figment of her imagination, but the haunting truth.

She was a child again, living a privileged yet claustrophobic existence in Accra. Days were spent earmarking low-hanging, ripe, succulent tropical fruit on laden trees, and playing *Ampe* – the Ghanaian version of hopscotch – with her sisters. Life had been idyllic, until a certain incident, that forever became the centrepiece of her nightmares, shattered it.

In the dream, there stood the young African girl, gazing at her reflection. Too skinny, by far, with the arch in her lower-back quite pronounced. Still, her irises were a luminous amber, and not the dark brown hue which often typified her skin tone – a feature even her mother's friends described as pretty.

"If only I had Diana's complexion," she mused aloud, picturing the light-skinned American TV celebrity she idolised. Daily, Jessica stationed herself before the screen and mimicked the dancer's movements, dreaming someday she, too, could be a famous prima ballerina.

Initially, the dream always began with her dancing gracefully, executing the moves with precision. But it inevitably morphed into her tripping or stubbing her toe, triggering disdainful murmurs from her kin – except for their gracious houseboy, Kofi, who reserved a ready smile for Jessica and would stop whatever he was doing to applaud her.

"Well dan, Miss Jess!" he'd exclaim with great exuberance, encouraging her parents to follow suit. But their forced enthusiasm never fooled her. Young though she was, she understood the distinction between sincere acclamation and obligatory praise.

"Thank you, Kofi," she'd say, grinning, her eyes darting to her father, seeking his approval. She'd glimpse the ghost of a smile on his

CHAPTER 8   KOFI

face, a stark contrast to Kofi's jaw-splitting beam.

Kofi's genuine interest in her made him easy to trust. Besides, her parents fed and clothed him, and allowed him to reside in the spare suite of the outer-house, rather than in the Boys' Quarters as was customary for domestic help. Treated more like family than a servant, he had earned a special place in her heart. Plus, Kofi always egged her on with effusive commendation.

"…. *Eiiiii*, Miss Jess, amazing! *Woaye adee, papa*! Well dan!"

"If you *sabi*, make you *gimme* private show. *Chale! Ah for clap well-well*, Miss Jess!"

His interest energized her, and she proudly revealed, "I've been practising a new routine… Can I show you on Saturday?"

"Of course!" he responded with a nod and a wink, lifting his palm for their habitual high five before returning to his meticulous ironing of her father's shirts. Jessica floated to her room, leaning against the door with a smile. An audience, no matter how small, was all an aspiring performer could ask for. She awaited Saturday with bated breath.

Saturday came, signaling date-night for her parents, TV binge-watching for her brothers, and playroom boredom for the younger siblings and their nanny. Freida may as well have pasted a do-not-disturb sign on her forehead – so engrossed was she in her novel!

Jessica donned her white leotard and satin ballet slippers, then tried to pin her hair like a pro. However, she gave up after several unsuccessful attempts by her clumsy eight-year-old fingers and uncooperative thumbs.

None of her relatives noticed as she shuffled past, and the familiar feeling of being unseen underlined her renewed sense of gratitude for Kofi's attentiveness.

She stepped into the darkness surrounding the main house and shivered despite the humid heat. How she loathed the dark! The sing-song of chirping crickets seemed magnified amidst the cacophony of night sounds. Jessica drew a tremulous breath before venturing further into the unwelcome blackness at the rear of the garden. She scurried across the croaking grass to the outhouse, running on tip-toes to avoid arousing the excitable nocturnal frogs.

Kofi had left the entrance to his quarters unlocked, so she slid in as quickly as possible, knowing he'd have sprayed the premises against eager mosquitoes. A wave of delight surged as she surveyed the make-shift stage with strung Christmas lights, creating a theatre-like atmosphere.

"Oh. This is perfect, Kofi!" she exclaimed, seeing his self-conscious grin.

"Ah, Miss Jess, *you sef bi serious dancer oh*!"

Though she suspected his words were motivated by kindness, it made her feel valued. She handed him the cassette to slot into the tape recorder, then danced with all the fervour and passion her tiny body could muster. Every ounce of her swelled at the melody of his applause, and she imagined herself standing before multitudes, instead of a lone

CHAPTER 8 KOFI

houseboy.

The infectious enthusiasm of this audience of one made her throw her spindly arms around him in appreciation. He returned her affection by continuing to press against her even when she attempted to pull away.

Jessica cleared her throat, not wanting to wound his feelings. "Errhmm, I need to leave now. But thank you. Can you walk me to the house? Please? It's dark…" Her tone was tentative and she tried to wriggle free, but Kofi tightened his grip. She felt a hardening between her thighs. Alarmed, she struggled to shove him aside, but couldn't match his superior strength.

"Heh, Miss Jess, why *you dey* push me? *You no like me?*" Kofi sounded strained and his nostrils flared.

She blinked in bewilderment. "I… yes, of course I do. But… I want to go back."

A glance at his glazed pupils confirmed her friend had become a predator. She was his prey. It reminded her of those wildlife films on National Geographic, the ones that depicted an animal intent on mating. The creature sometimes resorted to violence to have its way. Her larynx contracted with fear. Although not fully comprehending, she sensed the danger. His left forearm maintained its vice-like restraint on her frail form as his massive right hand snaked underneath her leotard, finding its soft, innocent target and causing her to yelp in pain. Before he could smother her cry, she screamed and kicked with all her might. But Kofi was already on top of her, suffocating her with his taut body.

Then a sound – *whack*! Kofi whimpered and rolled off, Freida towering over him, eyes blazing with fury, clutching a massive mango stick weapon.

"Are you alright?" she directed at Jessica, but kept her gaze on her sibling's assailant, biceps twitching as though inclined to strike him again.

"Yes, I'm fine," the younger girl whispered.

"I searched for you everywhere!" Freida admonished. "Didn't you hear me calling?"

"No, I was… dancing. I…"

"You were *dancing* for *him*?"

"He… he asked me to." Jessica couldn't understand how it had gone so wrong.

"He what? You what?" Freida's look of incredulity turned menacing as she prodded Kofi with the stick. "So, if I hadn't come, what would have happened? What the hell would've happened, huh? Kofi?" Sheer disgust twisted her face. "After all these years? I've known you since *you* were *my* age. *Ten years,* Kofi – and *this* is how you repay us?"

"Please, Miss Fifi. Sorry. *Make you no tell. I dey fear*. Master… he sabi kill me. *Mepa wo Kyɛw*. Please, *abeg*."

Jessica rose to shaky feet. Such a close call. The spasms in her body felt involuntary. Never had she seen Freida this furious. Kofi remained crouched on the floor; huge, pleading eyeballs already watering in contrition.

CHAPTER 8   KOFI

Her sister acted older than fourteen, and her voice had turned deathly quiet.

"Shame on you. I ought to summon my brothers, right now. And I guarantee, you wouldn't leave this place alive. But we're not animals. So, I will give you a chance. *Stand up, pack your things and disappear.*"

"Thank you, Miss Fifi." Kofi scrambled to his feet, nodding.

"And I swear to God, if you *ever* do return, I'll ensure my father has you locked up for life! Now, *get out!*"

Freida wrapped a protective arm around Jessica's boney shoulders and ushered her back to the house, heading straight to the guest bathroom down the hallway by the kitchen. Locking the door, she whispered brusquely, "Show me! Did he hurt you?"

"He touched me. Hard. And when he lay on top, I couldn't breathe. But you came, and… oh, Fifi, I was so scared."

Freida squeezed Jessica in a tight hug. She was shaking. They both were. "Me too. Thank God I arrived in time." She paused. "Has he ever…?"

"No. Never. I thought he was my friend, Fif." Her voice sounded small.

"Hmmm! What a snake!" The murderous mien reappeared in her sister's eyes.

Jessica grasped Freida's shoulders. "Promise me, you won't tell anyone, ever! Please, promise me, Fifi." Adrenaline and terror had crystallized into salty tears of shame that muffled her plea.

Freida pulled her closer. "It's horrific, what just happened to you.

I promise it'll be our secret."

CHAPTER 9

En Pointe

J essica woke up utterly spent. The recurring nightmare was taking a toll on her.

She yawned deeply and crawled out of bed, her cramped body unwinding from the tight foetal position it had assumed during sleep, and headed straight for the bathroom.

"Hey, who's in there?" she called, rubbing her stiff neck. She could feel the urgency mounting.

"Yeah, well, you'll have to wait. I'm in the shower," came the muffled reply from behind the locked door.

"Aargh!" Jessica exhaled, pressing her knees together in discomfort.

Charlotte, their fourth housemate, walked past and commiserated, "One loo makes no sense. Let's do a rota; that should help?"

Jessica could only squeak in response, "I just need to pee."

Living with a group of girls was mostly fun, though she preferred the easy West African banter she shared with Deborah.

"Chale, wetin you dey cook?" Debbie would enquire, poking a wooden spoon at whatever was simmering in the pan.

"Eiyee! Give it here!" Jessica would grab the utensil in feigned indignation, using her hip to shove her friend aside. "Wait until I'm done. *Then* you can taste."

Laughing, Debbie would lounge against the kitchen table, flipping through Cosmopolitan magazine. "We should go out tonight," she'd pronounce with a mischievous glint in her eye. And they would. Again, and again.

Before long, Jessica couldn't imagine life without Deborah.

〜

"I still can't believe you're here, Ms Dunn."

"Emily. Please. We're no longer at school." Her former teacher smiled warmly. "I always planned to return to London, and you being here is a strong catalyst."

"I'm flattered," Jessica said, swallowing nervously. "I realise you quit teaching for this. Which means I *must* succeed."

"You *will* succeed," Emily stated in a tone that brooked no argument.

CHAPTER 9 — EN POINTE

"I'm thrilled with how many performances we have scheduled already. Next week is crucial. There'll be tons of reporters and we need to make a solid impression."

Debbie who had been washing dishes and eavesdropping, moved closer, drying her hands on a tea towel. "What's this about the media?" She turned to Jessica with a raised eyebrow. "*Chale*, d'you think you're prepared for that? Those people can destroy anyone who's not ready, oh!"

"She's ready!" Emily snapped, sounding sharper than usual. "This isn't time for uncertainty, Jess. Please don't listen to anything negative." She shot a forbidding glance at Debbie.

"Hey, sorry I spoke. Your superstar comes home most days with battered feet, that's all. I'm only trying to help!" Debbie lifted both palms in a gesture of mock apology and swanned from the room, hips swaying.

Once Debbie was out of earshot, Emily expressed her concern. "Are you sure you trust that friend of yours? There's something… off… about her."

Jessica shrugged, trying to appear nonchalant. "Oh, she's just different. You'll love her once you get to know her."

Emily snorted and mumbled, "I doubt that! And what's this about your feet?"

"It's… nothing. Just… they push us hard and I find pointe practice a little tough on these flat African extremities," she joked, though her laughter didn't convince her former teacher, who insisted, "Show me… come on, I want to see."

With a groan she removed her socks, and Ms Dunn yelped in horror. "Goodness, what happened? You call *this nothing?*"

"I…"

"Sshh. I taught you better, Jessica Brown! Your body is your instrument. If it breaks, that's you done."

Jessica looked crestfallen. "I know. But I've struggled with bloody pointe work forever."

Emily sighed. "Maybe your housemate is right after all. We must fix you before we can even contemplate presenting you to the public." She rose with a huff and retrieved a large bowl from the cupboard. Filling it with water and adding ice, she instructed, "Ok. In with them."

Jessica gingerly dipped her sore toes into the icy basin, her preparatory inhale soon becoming a gasp of shock as the biting frost enveloped her feet. Initial pain gave way to infinite relief. Ms Dunn was a genius! Oh, how she needed this. The lesson earlier that day had all but crippled her, and may have persuaded her to quit if not for her commitment to Mr Ribbit's scholarship. She longed to express her own style rather than endure the coaches' persistent reminders that ballet is the essential foundation for every dance student. *Blah, Blah.* Jessica had reached the end of her tether.

The main instructor at the Academy, Monique Dubois, made Madame Travers appear tame by comparison, and Jessica's resolve wavered under her scrutiny. Dubois didn't mince her words and often pushed students beyond their endurance.

"This isn't some pathetic high School performance – I need *real*

CHAPTER 9 — EN POINTE

dancers." "There's no room for mediocrity. Either you pick up the pace, or get out!" "*Mon Dieu!* How pitiful that someone so beautiful up top can be so ugly from the waist down. Point those toes, dammit!" "Give me length… more… *more* and lift. And ho-o-o-*old*."

When it became impossible to balance *en pointe* for a fraction of a second longer, Jessica held her breath. Any moment now, and…

Thud! Down she went. Oh no! It couldn't be more embarrassing. *Miss Brown was first to crumble.* Ugh! She imagined the whispering and didn't dare glance up to witness twelve pairs of eyes on her – judging, mocking, telling her she wasn't cut out for this. Could it be true? After all, here she was soaking her inflamed feet in icy water. But gruelling as it was, she was darned if she'd ever give up!

~

Jessica's deep exhale made her exhaustion palpable as she plonked herself on the giant Salvation Army sofa in their open-plan reception.

Charlotte brought over a pot of freshly brewed tea. "Want some?" she offered with a sympathetic smile.

Jessica shook her head with a weary yawn. "No thanks. This training at RAD's killing me, I swear."

"Yet, you enjoy it!" Charlotte perched on the fake marble counter, legs dangling.

"I do, but it's so laborious." Jessica sighed, then added, "I s'pose the encouraging thing is I *am* getting stronger. Plus, Emily's incredible. She's known me for ages, yet her belief in my talent is unflinching. Such an ego-boost."

"Of course, she believes in you. She's your manager, isn't she?" Charlotte said with a simple shrug.

Jessica liked Charlotte. She was friendly and showed genuine interest. "What about you? How are things?"

"Oh great! I'm off to visit my folks this weekend, which'll be nice. You quit your job at grimy O'Leary's, right?"

Jessica grinned with relief. "Yep. Thanks to all these lucrative contracts."

Debbie walked in that instant and asked, "Did I hear something about *mullah*?"

Jessica giggled. "Nobody mentioned money, silly. But, since you've brought it up, guess what?" She looked from one girl to the other with suspense before clenching her fists in glee. "I got that position at BMG. I'm soooo excited!"

"Wow. As their new in-house choreographer? That's awesome!" Debbie exclaimed.

"Amazing!" Charlotte agreed.

"It's because of that West End role. You're now a frequent feature in the press, y'know," Debbie added.

Jessica beamed and nodded. "Yes. It's finally coming together."

CHAPTER 10

Boys

Debbie's favourite topic of conversation was sex, and Jessica found herself both amused and captivated by her tales.

One evening, as they sat braiding each other's hair, Debbie was recounting the story of the boy she had given her virginity to. Jessica hadn't the foggiest recollection of the mixed-race school stud that Debbie described. Maybe he'd joined after she'd left, or maybe… he'd never existed? The thought flitted across her mind, but she dismissed it quickly.

Whether a figment of her imagination or not, Debbie's depiction was so vivid that it left Jessica salivating by its conclusion. He sounded… what was that word again… delicious!

"Remember, I mentioned prom night when he couldn't take his eyes off me?" Debbie boasted. "I saw him watching me dance." Her smirk bordered on triumphant. "I groove almost as well as you, you know."

Jessica grinned at the back-handed compliment. "So, what happened next?"

"He ditched the chick he was with…" Deborah explained, her fingers deftly intertwined in a braid. "Hah, you should've seen her face – she looked so annoyed! Then, he started walking towards me…"

"No waaayyy! What did you do?" Jessica exclaimed, twisting her half-woven head to get a better view of her friend.

"*Chale*, I also moved towards him. We met in the middle and kissed." Debbie's voice had risen in pitch, excitement evident.

Jessica's mouth widened in surprise.

"Just like in Mills & Boon. It was a-m-a-zing. Tongues and all." Debbie giggled. "He tasted of mango and beer."

"Yuk!" the word escaped before Jessica could stifle it.

Debbie shot her a sharp look and yanked a few strands in retribution.

"Ouch, Debs!" Jessica winced, swiveling her head to avoid any more painful tugs on her sensitive scalp.

Debbie continued, sounding mildly irritated. "I meant *sweet*. Like mango! He tasted sweet."

"What happened next?" Jessica asked in a more encouraging tone.

"He led me behind the hall…"

"Ah yeah, where people used to sneak and smoke by the sheds?"

Debbie nodded, eager to continue. "He pushed me against the

big Neem tree and started stroking my thigh." She chortled, back in sterling form, ever the effusive storyteller. "I was wearing this seriously tight dress, which showed off *everything,* and he kept saying, 'Debs, you're so pretty. So beautiful'…"

Jessica studied Debbie, whose gaze had drifted into the distance as her slanted lips curled to meet prominent cheekbones in a self-satisfied smile.

"And…?" Jessica prodded; the story too juicy to end prematurely.

"He shoved my dress all the way to my waist. He was panting."

"Were you nervous? How did you…?" Jessica pouted, trying to picture the scene.

"Nervous? Huh!" Debbie dismissed the idea. "Not at all. In fact, I touched him too and…"

"Nooooo!" Jessica sounded incredulous.

"When I unzipped his trousers, it popped out. So huge and hard and I pressed my body against it." Both girls burst into laughter.

"You bad girl." Jessica teased, trying to suppress memories it stirred in her mind. "And then it happened?"

"Yes! That's when we did it. Soooo *amazing*!"

Camaraderie overtook them and the unfinished tresses were long forgotten. Jessica admired her friend's boldness and knowledge. She noted that this repeat account of Debbie's no-longer-a-virgin story was considerably more explicit than before.

"Wow, Debs, you know so much! I would have been clueless if it were me."

"Well, it wasn't you." Debbie stroked her breast in a sensual, absent-minded caress. "But I'm sure your time will come."

Debbie's condescension stoked Jessica's self-doubt. Notwithstanding her provocative dance moves, she remained utterly naïve about boys and sex. Her physical intimacy was limited to interpreting music, accentuating rhythm, and evoking emotions for an audience – a role she had mastered on stage, but not in real life.

Recently, she'd been feeling quite discombobulated. The reason? A man. One whose massive hand had held open the closing doors of the lift when she was running late for a meeting at the record company. She turned to offer her thanks, only to find herself staring into impossibly green eyes, their piercing intensity softening into a gentle smile. Words stuck in her throat and she quickly looked away, internally chastising herself for her rudeness. "Say something, Jess!" She pictured her mother's dismay at her glaring lack of manners.

He broke the silence. "You seem in rather a bit of a hurry," he remarked, amusement rather than judgement in his clipped English accent.

She relaxed. "Yes, I might be late… erm four please."

He obliged and leaned against the lift door. He's going to fall out, she thought, as she continued to gape at this handsome giant of a stranger, drawn by the magnetic pull of his captivating gaze.

"Don't worry, I'm accustomed to being stared at," he said, breaking the silence again.

Her cheeks flushed with the heat of embarrassment, and she stammered, "Sorry, I…"

He raised an enormous paw to dismiss her apology. "No need. Six foot six is rather difficult to ignore." His smile was ridiculously charming, and her legs did a spastic wobble.

"No, it isn't… it's not… oh!" Jessica fumbled for words; trying to explain it wasn't just his height that had her flustered. Bizarrely, despite his over-long hair, half covering his sticky-out ears, and his ultra-thin lips sketched into a permanent grin, she found him dead gorgeous – unconventionally so. Everything about him was large, including his hawk-like nose, but to her, he was perfection personified.

"It's your…," Jessica began.

The lift dinged at the fourth floor. Saved by the bell. He moved aside, and she stepped out, aware he was right behind. Her pounding heart did a full somersault in her chest as she snuck him a questioning glance.

"This is where we hold our meetings, so it appears you and I are headed to the same one." His smile oozed warmth.

She smiled back.

For an entire hour, those green eyes bore into her, preventing even a modicum of concentration. His name was William Armstrong-Bell, and he was the most sought-after executive in the industry, handling the band that had commissioned her choreography.

Feeling out of her depth, she regretted not accepting Emily's offer to accompany her.

On the tube ride home, she couldn't shake his presence. "William Armstrong-Bell," she whispered, enjoying the sound of it. Jessica Armstrong-Bell – Oh, gosh! Had she said it out loud? She peeked at the other passengers, embarrassed.

Stop being pathetic, she scolded her giddy heart. You're so childish, Jess! He probably doesn't even remember your name.

CHAPTER 11

First Love

"Oh, Emily! It feels incredible, but maybe it's all in my head!"

"Goodness! Who's become a love-struck puppy?" Emily laughed as she reached for the phone. "Hello?" Her expression shifted to one of surprise and she mouthed, "It's him!"

Jessica's lips parted, her brain resuming its unhelpful, monotonous chant, "William-Armstrong-Bell-William-Armstrong-Bell".

"Yes. I agree. She is extremely talented, and… absolutely. A real stunner, too!" Emily winked at her protégée, who was wringing her nervous hands. "Well," she surmised as she replaced the handset, "It appears a certain young man can't get you out of his mind, either."

Despite his evident interest, subsequent meetings with William were an exercise in restraint. He was friendly, yet often hurried off, perhaps to avoid the seductive intensity that simmered between them. Each encounter was a slow-dance of emotions that left Jessica stuttering and perplexed.

Dear J, he makes me giddy. Not sure why, but I get an actual tingle in my body. Haven't told Debs cos she'll laugh at me. Besides, he's 25 or 26, so probably not interested in a seventeen-year-old, anyway. Ohhh, but I totally fancy him!

"*Chale!* If you weren't my sis, I swear, I'd be jealous."

Jessica gave her buddy a playful shove. "What are you talking about?"

Debbie's response was wide-eyed. "What…? Are you serious? Everyone's singing your praises. You're a sensation! Look!" She pointed at an article in the newspaper. "Jessica Brown… blah, blah… aha! Here. '… has secured several contracts to work with artists signed to Arista/BMG and is touted as the youngest choreographer on their roster. Currently in the home stretch of her studies at RAD, she's looking forward to its completion so she can focus on her career.' *Eiiish*! Life is good for you, *paaah*!"

"Thanks, Debs! I've been lucky, and I'm so grateful to Ms Dunn."

CHAPTER 11 — FIRST LOVE

May 1999 – 18th birthday – Guest List.

Debbie was oohing and aahing while examining Jessica's notebook. "Wow! I can't believe you've hired the Roof Gardens for your shindig. And are these *celebrity* names I see here? Who's William?"

"Ohhhh," Jessica squealed. "The guy I mentioned, remember? I invited him and he said *yes*!"

"And that's a surprise because…?" Debbie's tone was dry.

Jessica shrugged. "Dunno. Didn't expect it. Oh, Debs! What shall I wear? I need to get my hair done." She fingered her braids, her expression dreamy.

On the night of the party, Jessica ascended to the rooftop venue with a heart hammering in her heaving chest. Whatever Debbie was blabbing about fell on deaf ears. All she could think about was whether William would show up.

On that balmy evening, Jessica's crimson, backless dress highlighted her smooth, velvet skin. The stylist had crafted big, soft curls pinned to the side of her neck, and her sensual lips were stained in matching rouge. Debbie half-complimented, "If not for your large, innocent brown eyes, you'd look like an alluring temptress!" Jessica appreciated the endorsement.

The way William's jaw dropped when she stepped out of the lift suggested he was indeed captivated by her charm. He moved towards her in a trance, and suddenly, they were alone amidst the 65,000 square feet of private roof gardens. Everyone around them ceased to exist.

"You look divine." His mouth hovered before brushing her cheek, and the heat emanating from him was palpable.

She gave a shy smile. "I'm glad you came – wasn't sure you'd accept."

"Oh?" He sounded surprised. "Why would you think that? I was pleased to receive your invitation."

She studied him. "You're different tonight."

"I am?" Green eyes twinkled. "How so?"

The room seemed to grow warmer. "I don't know… more… approachable?"

He laughed and drew her close. "Let's dance, shall we?"

Her body melted into his embrace; happy to be held. He exuded strength. Hours ticked by as they immersed themselves in each other's essence, talking and laughing and dancing and chatting some more. What a far cry from our usual awkward dynamic of stilted conversations and polite nods, she mused.

More at ease, she scolded him, "For months, I presumed you had zero interest in me. Imagining it was all in my head." She nudged him playfully.

William grinned. "Just a tad old-fashioned. Wanted to wait till you 'came of age'." He kissed her fingertips.

Jessica gazed at him, charmed by such unusual gallantry, and it crossed her mind that her father might approve of William Armstrong-Bell.

CHAPTER 11 — FIRST LOVE

"But we had almost zero communication," she chided gently.

He stroked her chin with the back of his long fingers, murmuring, "If only you knew how I felt… I-I've never experienced this." His Adam's apple bobbed as he spoke. "Didn't dare scare you away."

They were holding hands. She squeezed his. "Well, you've got me now."

Despite the ramped-up-music, they remained ensconced in their private vacuum, surrounded by foliage and greenery, illuminated by flickering candles, their enlivened faces kissed by the moonlight. And his mouth. Lips of pure heaven.

This was perfection.

The party ended at 2 am, and he offered to drive her home. Debbie insisted she'd take a taxi instead.

"But that's silly, Debs – just come along – he's offering."

"No, you go," she mumbled, unpersuaded. "Three's a crowd…"

Jessica noted her friend's terse smile before she walked away. She turned to William, her gaze apologetic.

He shrugged and prompted, "Ready when you are."

They stood toe to toe in the lift. Her heart sang as she slid into the leather seat of his sports car, suddenly nervous. As though sensing her discomfort, William placed a gentle hand on her knee, his eyes sparkling.

"I'm merely driving you home," he reassured, his deep voice

calming. "So, where to, Madam?"

"Kilburn," she replied, her white teeth gleaming in the dark.

Their goodnight kiss was tender, nothing more. He was holding back; she could tell. A rare gentleman, indeed!

The following morning, the birthday girl still basked in the thrill of the night before. It seemed surreal. She headed straight for Debbie's door and lifted bunched knuckles, then decided against knocking; choosing instead to potter around the kitchen, humming to herself as she made coffee and toast. She was in such a good mood!

In her journal, she wrote, *I feel complete. Yet all we did was kiss.* She tapped her pen against her nose, unable to keep still. *No, what we shared was more than a mere kiss. Deeper. Less fleeting. It was…* she swallowed and stared at the page before her…… *Indescribable. I think I love him, J.*

When Debbie emerged from slumber, still groggy from the remnants of excess champagne, Jessica plunged in, eager to share her excitement.

"Chale, I'm amazed that the guy I dreamt of all year not only came, but spent the whole evening with me and even drove me home." Her eyes turned hazy. "Plus, he wants to see me again."

"Good for you," Debbie replied coolly, focusing on pouring a cup of coffee. "So *that's* your excuse for abandoning me!"

Oblivious to her housemate's chagrin, Jessica continued, "When

CHAPTER 11 · FIRST LOVE

we kissed, it was... oh! This feels like love."

Debbie's unexpected sneer stung. "Oh Jess, grow up!" she snapped. "It was only a kiss. How can you even think you're in love with him? So childish and ridiculous. Next, you'll be telling me he's your 'soul mate' or some other corny, pathetic declaration." She shook her head in clear derision.

What a killjoy. Jessica promptly changed the subject, kicking herself for confiding in Debbie.

Dear J, you'll never believe what happened. Kensington Roof Gardens claims someone has already covered the full bill. Imagine that?! I said it was impossible. I figured maybe Dad paid because it's my birthday. But, no. It was William – unbelievable! William Armstrong-Bell. He says it's his gift to me. How sweet! I tell you, J, this guy is amazing. Debbie doesn't agree, but I know he likes me... A LOT.

CHAPTER 12

William

William Armstrong-Bell shifted from his position across the candlelit table to settle on the banquette with a husky murmur, "I prefer you close."

Jessica slid her fingers through his. "Me too."

He smiled at their interlocked hands. "I do believe, Miss Brown, you have me quite besotted. Head-over-heels, in fact." The sugar-laden desserts placed before them went unnoticed. "But I…" he kissed her with each word, "must–woo–you–properly."

"Oh?" She gazed at him with a shy smile.

"Uh huh, I suspect slow and steady's best with you." He nuzzled her nose, and she snuggled closer. "Tell me more about your fascinating Kalabari heritage, and those juicy, overhanging mango trees," he prompted, tucking into his trifle.

"Mmm, I like how you pronounce 'Kalabari'," she teased, spooning a mouthful of the tempting calorie-bomb, before pushing it away.

"Kalabari," he stated again, and they both giggled.

"Now, your turn. You're an only child… and your parents, Sir Michael and Lady Armstrong-Bell…" Jessica paused, "Gosh! They sound rather forbidding…" She searched his face, but saw no sign that her observation was correct.

Instead, he chuckled. "Not at all! Though, I'm fairly certain my upbringing wasn't half as colourful as yours. Don't fret about this weekend, darling. They'll adore you!"

However, as the day to meet-the-parents drew closer, Jessica's nerves grew tighter, leaving her in dire need of a sympathetic sounding board. Keen to give the still-disgruntled Deborah some space, she telephoned her sister and delved into a heartfelt exposition of her extreme fondness for this dapper Englishman.

"It's as if I've known him my entire life. I totally love him, Fifi; he's kind, makes me laugh and is sooo handsome and…"

"Does he love you back?" Freida sounded protective.

Jessica hesitated. "Well, I think he does, though Debbie says until

CHAPTER 12 WILLIAM

a guy sleeps with you he can't possibly be into you."

"What? Downright rubbish! That girl's bad news. I tell you, Jess, don't listen to a word she utters. Follow your instincts. Besides, he wouldn't be taking you to meet his parents if he wasn't serious. Just be yourself and they'll love you. Plus, no rushing into anything, you hear? If he loves you, he'll respect you."

"Not sure, Fif. What if I'm a terrible judge of character? With men…you know. I mean, I trusted Kofi and look what happened."

"Stop. You were a *child*. And he was a sick individual. *Please*! This is different. Heed your heart. You're *not* a poor judge of character."

Sunday came and, as they drove to Suffolk, Jessica's anxiety dissipated somewhat. She observed William seated behind the steering wheel of his E-Type Jaguar, a sports classic he named Flora, and spoke to, as though it were alive.

"Common Sexy," he'd cajole, "A nice, smooth ride, that's what we need today, ok girl?" Then he'd stroke her bonnet before hopping in. And Jessica would laugh every time.

He had explained to her, when she'd first met Flora, that this XK120 was by far the best-looking Jaguar in existence and he'd never encountered a car whose alluring good looks were backed up by its performance. Flora was his one idiosyncrasy, and Jessica loved him for it.

Flora took a little over two hours to transport the love birds to the estate, allowing enough time for William's historical account, and Bell

Manor was truly as magnificent as described. Jessica absorbed every minute detail.

The Grade II listed home, tucked away in its own cul-de-sac, boasts fifteen bedrooms, each designed by a proud Lady Armstrong-Bell; eight of which centre around Bell Hall, a dramatic, double-height gallery with a vaulted ceiling, gigantic stone fireplace and stained-glass windows. Its glorious, lavish grounds are every country lover's dream, with rugged woods and wildflower meadows, carefree and abundant, which progress into a pristine and manicured garden as one draws nearer the primary residence. To the left of the mansion, there's a heart-swelling romantic swan-filled lake, depicting something out of a fairy-tale. The rear has a huddle of rural outbuildings and stables, a reminder of the surrounding, family-owned 4,500 acres of farmland.

Years at boarding school had made Jessica partial to the English countryside. She gazed around with contentment, taking in the green fields, hedgerows, trees, and distinct fragrance of farm animals. That unique blend of pleasant and earthy – the aroma of nature. Not everyone finds it pleasing, she considered with amusement, but for her it evoked powerful, positive memories and she gladly breathed in the clean air, tinged with a hint of horses and cowpat. It made her happy.

William grinned as he pulled up the circular driveway to the imposing house, unexpectedly bathed in welcoming sunlight. The exterior of the main building itself mightn't be described as beautiful, but it was damned impressive, and the sight of the liveried butler standing in its oak entrance added to the aura of grandeur.

CHAPTER 12 — WILLIAM

The Armstrong-Bells were in the Blue Drawing Room, so-called because of the gigantic painting hanging along the length of an entire wall so vividly blue one couldn't help but stop and stare upon entering. It had taken the artist a whole year to complete and been in the family for generations. Jessica tried to peel her attention from its bewitching allure and focus on the tall, striking couple who glided towards them.

"Father, Mother..." William sounded formal, but there was no mistaking his delight. They embraced with affection. Then Sir Michael turned to Jessica, who'd been standing awkwardly by the door.

"Goodness! You're rather a bit of a surprise!" His tone was unabashedly forthright without apology or prejudice; a mere observation acknowledging that their son hadn't forewarned them his girlfriend was not Caucasian.

She smiled at Sir Michael, recognising this as his way of welcoming her.

The older gentleman beamed back, adding conspiratorially, "Stunning, too, I dare say!" He winked at his son, as though to suggest, "Well done, Lad!" then took her by the elbow and guided her to the settee. Jessica flashed William's mother an uncertain smile, abundantly aware she hadn't said a proper hello. Philippa Armstrong-Bell's countenance was polite, but green eyes of steel told another story, revealing where William got his intensity. She swallowed and sat, relieved when her beau left his mother's side to join her on the two-seater. She avoided Philippa's scrutinizing stare.

"Don't worry," Will whispered, and wrapped a protective arm around her. "She can be pretty intimidating."

Lunch was less ceremonial than their surroundings suggested, granting Jessica new insight into William and his relatives. They'd lunched on the terrace by the lake and, despite having staff to hand, his mother had done much of the serving herself, declining Jessica's offer of help. Whilst the relaxed affair put her at ease with his dad, she hadn't cracked his mum yet. His family were strangely similar to hers, with their light banter and uninhibited laughter, giving her the distinct impression Sir Michael and Chief Brown might get on very well indeed.

That evening, Jessica squirmed away when William's kisses grew passionate. He cocked his head inquiringly. "Something wrong?"

"I'm a virgin," she blurted as an opener.

He squinted and pulled her closer. "I gathered you were, darling, the second I met you. What's this about? Hey?" His face wore that you-can-tell-me-anything look she'd grown accustomed to.

She picked at her nails. "I-I was nearly raped when I was eight." There. She'd said it.

"You were… what…? By whom? H-how?" William seemed taken-aback by her unexpected confession.

Jessica told him of the trauma she'd experienced as a youngster. As she recounted the story of Kofi, William's face reflected a mixture of empathy and fury.

"Thank God your sister barged in when she did. That… that man should be shot!" he exclaimed heatedly.

CHAPTER 12 🌴 WILLIAM

Jessica's amber gaze brimmed with tears. "I wanted to tell you because, well… I might be damaged."

"*Damaged*? How? Darling, it wasn't your fault. You were a mere girl and of course you trusted him."

"Yes, but it's made me… frightened. Of *that.*" She stared at his huge hands, and swallowed.

William's eyes became dark green pools of intensity as he clutched her shoulders. "I promise you, Jessica Brown, there's nothing to be afraid of. I'd never hurt you. We'll take it slow."

She clung to him, drawing comfort from his strength. "I stopped dancing after that. It put me off boys and… then came the nightmares…"

Will nodded thoughtfully. "I understand." He raked his hands through his hair. "With any luck, the fact you can now talk to someone… to me… may mean you're ready to leave it behind, at least."

Jessica gazed into his eyes. "I feel safe with you. This has been eating me up, but telling you… demystifies it. It could've been worse!" She shivered at the horrible prospect.

"You were so young. Impressionable. Such a brutal attack on your childlike trust!" He looked angry.

"Afterwards, I withdrew from everything."

"You poor thing. What did your folks say?"

"I never told them." She shrugged. "They assumed my anti-social behaviour was due to hormones, or whatever." Her brown eyes held his green gaze. "I've always been wary of men. Until you."

Dear J, William and I are going to Accra for Christmas, so he can meet M&D. He's on a work trip at the moment, and I miss him sooo much I think I could explode. He says he misses me, too. This is such bliss. I hope our kisses never end. Want them to go on and on. I want more…

Dear J, ok, this is it. I've decided to do it with William. He repeatedly stops himself, but I genuinely wish he wouldn't…

Dear J, I am ready…

Dear J, today I became a real woman.

Deborah walked into the kitchen sporting a more open countenance than she'd favoured in weeks, so Jessica laid down her pen with a smile, inviting conversation.

Debbie's excitement was tangible. "Remember I told you about Pete?"

Jessica did a quick mental recap and nodded. Pete was a boy doing A-levels with Debbie, and she'd spent months preening to catch his attention.

"Well, he finally asked me out!" she trilled, twirling in a Debbie-style pirouette with her chest thrust forward, emphasizing how impressively buxom she was. She then cupped her prized assets with both hands and teased, "How could he resist these juicy melons?"

CHAPTER 12   WILLIAM

Now, this resembles the girl I know, Jessica thought with a grin. "Oh Debs, you paaah, you're crazy!" she declared with an affectionate chuckle, slipping into the Ghanaian lingo which had always helped cement their bond.

Deborah leaned closer and whispered. "*Chale*, Jess, we actually went all the way. It was painful, but I really fancy him, and…"

"What do you mean, painful? I thought you said…?" Jessica threw her a quizzical look. "So, was this your first time?".

Debbie's expression crumbled and she seemed at a loss for words. "It… I…," she stammered.

Debbie, who'd always boasted about her sexual prowess, looked vulnerable and Jessica laid an empathetic hand on her shoulder and assured, "No biggy, darling, I was a virgin too, until recently."

Debbie shrugged off her hand with a frown. "Of course, it's *not* my first time! It hurt only because Pete is so large." Her glare dared any challenge of her statement, and Jessica deemed it wise to simply nod.

She noted with relief that her friend responded with a smile which even reached her eyes. Maybe she'll quit making lame excuses to avoid me, Jessica pondered. I'd better not ruin this moment of reconciliation by calling her a liar. What does it matter if she invented those sexual escapades? She's clearly insecure, like me. She exhaled the breath she'd been holding captive from the moment Debbie had appeared. So much had changed for her since July, and journaling isn't the same as telling a living, breathing soul; especially one she regarded as her best friend.

Eager to carry on their conversation, she succumbed to the powerful urge to share.

She described how close she and William had become; how he treated her like the most special person to exist in his world. I'm no longer unseen, she mused, remembering the countless days in her childhood when she felt voiceless, simply one of many, indistinguishable from the rest.

And to top it off, he was ever the gentleman, albeit passionate and horny as hell; yet possessing an admirable degree of self-control which allowed him to stop "before it got out of hand". He said he wanted her to be "ready" and would wait until she was.

"So romantic Debs. I mean, who does that nowadays?"

Debbie gave an incomprehensible grunt.

Jessica continued, "I realise you two haven't ever taken to each other, and our being serious means *we* spend less time together. But this guy… Oh, Debs! When it happened, I wasn't nervous in the slightest. Strange, but I am so relaxed with him. He's gentle and… he knows what to do to make me…," she sighed, leaving her remarks hanging.

Debbie was silent, her eyes narrow slits. "Wow, you're acting like you're in love." She sounded almost accusatory.

Jessica ignored her tone and gushed, "Yes! I love him, Debs. I truly do. Like we… I don't know… were made for each other."

She glanced sideways at her friend, expecting a barbed comeback.

But Debbie stayed speechless.

CHAPTER 12 — WILLIAM

Then she responded, "Of course he makes you feel… amazing or whatever. He is *older*, and older guys know what to do."

Her tone smacked of disinterest and quashed any compulsion Jessica felt to disclose more than that tiny tit bit.

Writing it down was like reliving a sensuous, sweet seduction of the senses, with the memory of that night still so vivid she could recall each minute detail, as if it had just happened. She closed her eyes and his arms were holding her. He was declaring his feelings, and his voice trembled as he spoke. Jessica pressed her body against his and nestled into his neck, drinking in his musty, manly scent; the tickling, tingling roughness of his stubble. She loved the way he felt. The way he smelled, the touch of his hands, the intensity of his gaze.

She could drown in him.

CHAPTER 13

To become a Woman

They were in his home – one of those enormous mansions by Holland Park, six stories tall with both an indoor and outdoor pool.

"Wow!" Jessica spluttered when he first showed her around. "How very Nigerian of you!" She giggled.

"Oh?"

"*Two* pools?" she chortled, "Reminds me of ostentatious *Naija* houses on Bishop's Avenue in Hampstead. Minus the gold faucets."

William laughed. "It is rather much, I suppose. I grew up here, though – been ours for yonks! Having both allows us to enjoy year-round swimming, given the unpredictability of the weather." He pulled her close and rubbed her nose against his. "Besides, the garden pool makes for superb Summer soirees."

"I'll bet it does!" Jessica's gaze was appreciative. "So, you're here alone? Your parents don't…"

"No. They're based in Suffolk and keep a London pied-à-terre, so I get this entirely to myself." He shrugged dismissively.

"I can't imagine how that must feel. Being an only child… alien concept for me."

"Hey, don't be fooled. I'm not lonely – the chef and housekeeper live here too."

"*Chef?* Hahaha. So, where are these culinary skills you boast of?" she teased, giving him a playful prod in the belly.

William chuckled. "Yeah, I cook a mean boiled egg when I'm allowed in the kitchen."

She giggled and wandered through the house. Yes, it was excessive for single occupancy, but in the perfect location, with tasteful decor. Not the typical bachelor pad, she concluded with relief.

The punctilious staff were available but discreet and, having served the young couple a scrumptious dinner of seared monkfish in Lemon Parsley butter with Rosemary Potatoes and Broccoli, Chef Lee had evidently disappeared, leaving them alone in the conservatory. They'd

CHAPTER 13 — TO BECOME A WOMAN

both declined his offer of dessert, tempting though it was, opting to share a pot of mint tea instead. Jessica had read about the benefits of mint after a meal... it helps with digestion and um... her thoughts were rambling and her left leg wouldn't keep still.

William's twitching nose confirmed he too was apprehensive, and she swallowed the lump in her throat as he led her into the adjoining living area. When he guided her onto his knee, she noticed that his gaze seemed greener, somehow. She wrapped her arms around his neck and purred with contentment.

"I love you, Jess!" he declared, his voice husky with emotion. "You're my everything and I... I want to spend the rest of my days loving you."

Her head was spinning. It felt so right. Every fibre of her being was alive, and she kissed him with passionate fervour. Unaware of undressing him, or of him disrobing her, time stood still in seductive, slow motion. She was both partaker and spectator as each magical moment unfolded. A fuse was lit within her and yet she was a fly on the wall, watching and absorbing each detail like it was happening to someone else. Surreal.

Parting her thighs with gentle hands, his eyes never once left hers as he lowered his body. Her heart was beating so fast she was certain he could hear it. He didn't enter her at once, but slid up and down in a slow rhythm, his manhood teasing and probing until she thought she would burst. He took her in his mouth, one nipple and then the other and, when he kissed her, she spread her legs even wider, in full submission. It was as though they were moulded together.

～

Four months had elapsed since Jessica's 18th birthday, and the trajectory of her story had taken a real turn.

Dear J, I can't believe it! Will proposed today at Sunday brunch!! Rather than our usual Bloody Marys, he ordered Champagne, and I teased, "Oooh, somebody wants to celebrate," and then I saw it sparkling at the bottom of the glass; a huge diamond solitaire set in platinum – simple and perfect. At first, I could only stare, thinking the bubbles had created an illusion – that my eyes were deceiving me. Oh J!!! He asked me to marry him and I said YES!

"You said what?!" Freida exclaimed.

"Yes!" Jessica repeated ecstatically.

"Wow. That happened fast, Jess. Are you sure?"

"Absolutely! I *totally* adore him, Fifi. I'm very sure."

"Ok, but don't you think it's a little rushed? How well d'you know this guy?"

"Well enough!" Jessica rebutted. "Must you *always* be the voice of caution? Not everyone can be like you and Yinka; dating for three whole years and still no talk of marriage. I *want* to marry this man, Fif. Plus, he accepts me for who I am."

"Ok then. Congratulations. I'm happy for you! And by the way, Yinka and I *have* discussed marriage – it just isn't the ideal moment with

CHAPTER 13 — TO BECOME A WOMAN

work and everything."

Jessica hung up with a triumphant twirl. *Ah! My life is the epitome of true happiness. This is how it feels to become a woman.*

"Eight months to go," she said with a contented sigh.

"There's still the more pressing issue of meeting your parents," Will stated solemnly.

"Aww, how adorable that Daddy's approval is so important to you. Frightfully old-fashioned," she teased.

"Essential!" William countered. "I *must* ask your father for your hand. Wouldn't be proper to do otherwise."

She chuckled. "But you've already asked *me*, and I said yes!"

"That's not the point, darling. It's 1999, so naturally I asked *you* first, just to be certain." He grinned boyishly. "It's a symbolic gesture – shows respect and proves my intentions are honourable." He bent to kiss her forehead.

"They are?" She winked, rising to hug his waist and draw him close. "I'm convinced you've met my parents before! You seem to understand precisely how to win them over."

William laughed and tickled her. "Hope you're right!"

She giggled and squirmed away from the mock-wrestling she knew would follow. She'd earlier told her mum about the serious boyfriend she was bringing to Ghana for Christmas. Edith Brown had asked a million-and-nine questions and, satisfied her child's integrity was still somewhat intact, was excited to meet the young Englishman.

At 19:55 on December 18th, as they disembarked the aircraft, the unique warmth and familiar, delicious soupy smell of Accra enveloped Jessica. At nearly 90% humidity, she'd stepped from the cool staleness of rancid six-hour cabin-air into a pot of steamy moistness, and marvelled at how it always hit her smack in the face, no matter how often she'd experienced this moment.

Mr Mensah, their household driver of fifteen years, was beaming like a Cheshire cat when he glimpsed Jessica gliding down the gangway towards the exit. He inadvertently straightened his shirt (a recognisable hand-me-down from her father), before raising an arm in a salutary wave and she smiled with genuine warmth, pleased to spot his distinguishable face. He'd become almost part of the family, and they half-embraced before he took over the trolley with their bags.

"Hello Sah!" He nodded respectfully at William. "*Akwaaba*! Welcam to Accra!"

William grinned back, absorbing the excitable atmosphere, the bright clothing and lively voices. "They seem a jolly bunch, these Ghanaians," he mumbled to Jessica as he lifted a palm to decline yet another taxi ride on offer. "I do wonder how your family will react to me," he speculated out loud.

She looked at him quizzically.

CHAPTER 13   TO BECOME A WOMAN

"Well, you did say Nigerians aren't as approachable to strangers. They mightn't take kindly to this Englishman capturing their daughter's heart," he reasoned.

"Hey! They'll love you, silly, just as I do. You're looking forward to meeting them, aren't you?" She tucked her handbag closer under her armpit as they weaved through the thronging crowd of meeters and greeters.

"Of course. But, from what you've said, sounds like I should proceed with caution." William cleared his throat. He smiled, but his nose twitched as it always did when he was nervous.

Jessica pictured her parents, and felt her heart swell. Her three older brothers had joined Freida in America, and the only siblings who remained were her twin sisters and youngest brother. She was looking forward to seeing them all.

The drive to Airport Residential lasted under ten minutes. As the watchman pushed open the gate, William exclaimed, "Ah! An old, colonial house. How exquisite!"

Jessica placed a hand on his knee. "Daddy renovated it in the 70s."

Mr and Mrs Sokari Brown must have heard the car approaching for they were standing at the front door. The hug from her father was tighter than normal, and Jessica's eyes smarted with affection. Even Edith was unusually demonstrative, clinging for several moments after their initial embrace as if to reassure herself her fifth offspring was there in the flesh. *Wow! They missed me*, Jessica reflected to her diary. *They're getting soft in their old age.*

William was his usual charming self, and before long he had her mother eating out of his hand.

"What a lovely young man!" Edith whispered to her daughter. "Clearly comes from a good family."

Manners ranked high on her mother's list of priorities, and Jessica had already given it a tick on her mental checklist of Brown pros and cons. The only possible con might be William's age, coupled with the fact she was only eighteen, no longer a virgin, and he wasn't Kalabari. They hadn't yet commented on him being white, probably because he possessed an incredible ability to blend in, which rendered the colour of his skin redundant. It was what she loved most about him! That open, relaxed approach to life and ready willingness to try new things, without judgement; a genuine curiosity and respect for other cultures – it gave him a distinct advantage.

From Edith Brown's attitude, it appeared her mother knew she'd lost her virginity. Perhaps it showed in the soft lines of her face, or the way she arched her spine and leaned towards William whenever he was near. It was subtle and almost imperceptible, but nothing escaped that woman. Mrs Brown knew.

After two days of sleeping in separate bedrooms, the betrothed couple found themselves awake at the same hour in the dead of night.

"Oh, you gave me a fright!" Jessica blurted, startled to discover William at the kitchen counter, a glass of water before him.

"Couldn't sleep," He stated the obvious. His luminous green eyes

CHAPTER 13 — TO BECOME A WOMAN

and boyish expression made him look vulnerable. "I miss you." The heat in his voice was palpable.

"Me too," Jessica admitted. "I'm going crazy!" She slid onto his lap and noticed the rising evidence of his desire. Writhing her hips, she draped her bare arms round his neck. "This is an impossible situation, Will. Maybe we should make a quick getaway… to a beach resort in Axim. It's beautiful there. We could finally be alone…"

But William was already shaking his head. "No, darling. I came here to meet your folks." He grazed her nose with his. "I'll speak with your dad tomorrow."

The following morning, the men went to sit on the front porch after breakfast and Mrs Brown rose to give her love-struck daughter an unexpected hug.

"Welcome to the club, my dear," she said with a knowing look akin to admiration.

The days that ensued were a whirlwind of activity. Jessica shepherded William throughout the West African city, visiting her old school and the El Wak Stadium, where she'd run many a race.

"Perhaps we should venture out on our own," he suggested after a while. "I appreciate Mr Mensah chauffeuring us, but it'd be nice to do something original. Maybe hop on those painted mini buses I notice in town totally jampacked with people?"

Jessica's eyebrows rose in horror. "You mean *tro-tros*? Gosh! I've never even ridden in one. A local taxi is as far as I've ever ventured," she scoffed self-consciously.

"Ooooo, look who's sounding all uppity and spoilt," William teased.

"No, no, no, it's not *that*. I haven't… considered it." She frowned thoughtfully. "It isn't snobbery, or anything. Simply… things are different here."

"Darling, people are people. How different can it be?"

"*Different* doesn't signify better or worse, Will. Just different. We have money, they don't. It's… life."

"Hey, hey, no need to be defensive. It's not a criticism, sweetheart." William lifted her pouting chin. "Trying to understand, that's all. Besides, it might be fun!" He smiled disarmingly.

His smile soon transformed into a mien of mock horror as he found himself rammed against the sweaty armpit of a snoring labourer, whose head lolled back and forth in tempo with the bouncing tro-tro on the uneven road. William appeared to be holding his breath and Jessica stifled a giggle. His six-foot-six frame was no match for the stuffy interior of this popular mode of local transportation and, when they hopped off at Makola Market, he gave a loud guffaw at Jessica's I-told-you-so expression.

He feigned an exaggerated gasp for air. "I see what you meant, darling!"

"Serves you right!" she roared with laughter and linked an arm through his, glad they'd experienced it together.

They strolled through the hustle and bustle of the market, moving idly from kiosk to kiosk. Jessica smiled at the unknown, yet familiar, faces of

CHAPTER 13   TO BECOME A WOMAN

strangers; aware of the tremendous difference between the claustrophobic feeling of being squeezed between people on a small bus, and the liberating freedom of mingling amongst the crowds of animated sellers and buyers engaged in a battle of barter and wits.

"How much?"

"Fifty-five." The sing-song pronunciation of numbers peculiar to Ghanaians.

"Twenty." Stated boldly.

"*Eeiiii! Ah no sabi dat.* Forty-five." Sung, again.

"No, twenty-five." Also said in sing-song.

"Eeiiii, Madam, *you wan kill me.*" Slightly weary in tone, and with a tinge of desperation. "Terty-five. Last price." A final bluff.

"Thirty. And I'll take four."

"Oh, Madam! *Meda ase pii*! Tenk you!" Delighted gratitude.

And on it went.

"Wow!" William exclaimed as they moved along. "This barter thing is quite a skill."

"Exactly! And no-one does it better than my mum," Jessica added laughingly.

"I do wonder, though. With prices already so cheap, why try to beat them lower?"

"Cheap for *you*, maybe. But not the average person. Mum says a seasoned market-seller expects a good haggle. Otherwise, they clock you're a foreigner and will probably charge you double!"

William looked pointedly at his bare arm and shrugged.

They both chuckled and, at that precise moment, a vendor called out, "*Obroni!*" White man. And they laughed again. Jessica expected they'd hear many such calls in this vibrant epicentre of trade and commerce. William's skin made him stand out, rightly or wrongly, as someone with purchasing power.

The market place was buzzing. With the wide array of produce sold within it and its surrounding streets, you could feel your senses exploding with the smell of fresh beef and fish one instant, then surrounded by a bevy of colourful fabrics the next. Most noteworthy was the expectant mood of everyone there; even the odd stray dog appeared intent on striking a profitable bargain, hoping to be flung a morsel of meat scraps every now and again.

They journeyed back to the sheltered existence of the Brown residence in the relative comfort of a private taxi. Though the air-conditioning was faulty, the driver advised against lowering the windows on this dusty Harmattan day. The exhausted couple did so anyway, leaning against the cracked PVC seats with a contented smile.

Their fortnight in Accra flew by and 31st December 1999 seemed strangely symbolic, not just because it was the end of one millennium and the start of another, but because it marked an important shift in Jessica's relationship with her parents. For the first time in her life, she

CHAPTER 13 — TO BECOME A WOMAN

sensed they not only "saw" her, but respected who she was, notably her mother, who valued a 'good' marriage above all else.

"Jessica, this is when we bid farewell to the child you were, and accept the woman you are." Seeing the confusion on his daughter's face, her father elaborated, "Despite the odds, you've proven that you are talented, have forged a lucrative career path and made wise personal choices. All without our financial support. I'm proud of you. I think your future is bright, my dear."

Finally. Her biggest idol, her dad, had expressed his approval.

She was officially a woman.

PALM TREES IN THE STORM

CHAPTER 14

The Millennium

"The year two thousand. Sounds special, doesn't it?"

"A new millennium is special." Jessica enveloped her mentor-manager in a spontaneous hug. "And so are you! Look at all these incredible opportunities!"

Emily Dunn squeezed her talented protégée affectionately. "I must say, the media frenzy over your engagement to William is astounding!"

"I know. I hadn't realised we're such a newsworthy couple... it's mind-boggling. But I'm thoroughly enjoying it." Jessica chuckled, her eyes sparkling with excitement.

"And why shouldn't you? Darling, in our world, all publicity is good publicity."

༄

One morning, William awakened to find his lover and future bride already downstairs in the conservatory. She sat bathed in sunlight, coffee in one hand and notepad in the other, completely absorbed in her work.

"Goodness, you're up early!" he commented, perhaps more forcibly than intended.

Jessica squinted in surprise at his tone. "Hey, sweetie, I told you… remember? Got a rehearsal with that singer… Jason Devereaux… the blonde guy…"

Will plopped onto the seat across from her, his eyes narrowing. "Yeah. The young stud who can't keep his eyes off you," he sulked, his jealousy barely masked.

She gave him a brief, blank stare and kept scribbling.

"What are you writing, anyway?" He sought to inject enthusiasm into his tone, but failed miserably.

"Just fine-tuning a few moves for the video shoot. Woke up with some genius ideas and don't want to forget them." She grinned, her mind clearly elsewhere.

Will was silent for a moment, then reiterated, "I'm convinced that Jason guy wants more from you… you just can't see it."

Jessica scoffed, "Oh please. It's work – I don't even remember what he looks like." Will's expression remained petulant, and she added, "Anyway, I can't help it if *every* man finds me irresistible."

He finally grinned, more relaxed now. She stood to give him a lingering kiss on the lips. "Gotta dash, my jealous lover, or I'll be late."

He tried pulling her onto his lap, but she resisted, wriggling away and blowing him an air-kiss.

Truth be told, William's apparent discontent disturbed Jessica, as she shared with Emily after the shoot. But work was work. And she adored her work. She treasured the sense of freedom and unique power of holding an audience captive. She was born to do this. Surely William understood that? She scratched her head. You're being silly, Jessica Brown, she chided herself. He supports your career. It's early days and, naturally, he wants you to himself. The notion made her smile. My God, she adored that man!

The following evening, Will offered her a gift – a house key and an invitation to cohabit. This gesture of commitment thrilled her beyond measure, but her housemate's reaction to the news was unexpected.

"Isn't it enough he hogs you to himself most of the time? Must you move in with him, too?"

"Thought you'd be pleased for me, Debs."

Debbie folded her arms. "I am! But…"

"But you'd rather I didn't live with him?"

"Well, yes! I don't see much of you, as it is." Her voice was high-pitched with emotion. "We… we're supposed to house-share for at least another six months. And now, *this!*" She raised a hand to halt Jessica's interjection. "Yes, I know you'll continue paying your share of the rent, but that's not the same thing. Gosh, Jess, you're not his wife yet, and he controls you already!"

"He's not controlling me. You've got that wrong. He *loves* me – we're engaged. Besides, I've been so busy, it'd be much easier than shuffling back and forth to his place! I *want* to do this, Debs."

"Hmm. Whatever!" Debbie huffed with exasperation and stormed off.

Nonplussed, Jessica slid into a kitchen chair. Her friend had been so furious, but she felt certain of her choice. She loved William. As they were publicly betrothed and sleeping together anyway, she saw no reason to keep up the pretence of living apart. Plus, it might make him less upset by her early work calls. It made perfect sense.

So, on January 24th, 2000, the eighteen-year-old African ballet dancer took up residence with her English boyfriend in Holland Park.

CHAPTER 14 — THE MILLENNIUM

Spring soon arrived and lined the streets and pavements with cherry blossom snow.

"Stop looking so frantic, darling, the wedding isn't until after your birthday – still three months away!"

Jessica bit her lip. "Yes, but your mum's bent on taking over. I'd much rather we organise it ourselves."

Will regarded her thoughtfully. "Hmm, she *is* suggesting hiring the Millennium Dome for the reception…"

"Which is a ridiculous idea! First, because the place is ginormous and second, we'd prefer a more intimate affair, wouldn't we?"

William stroked her cheek. "It's a wedding, darling. Mother will insist on inviting every titled Brit to her only son's nuptials." He chuckled at her look of horror.

Jessica asserted, "Isn't it customary for the bride's family to take responsibility, anyway? This is becoming so awkward!"

In an unlikely turn of events, Mrs Sokari Brown came to the rescue.

"My daughter, I spoke with your father-in-law, Sir Michael. Such a gentleman!" Edith declared.

"And…?" Jessica prompted.

"As a token of goodwill, we've agreed to hold the ceremony in Suffolk at your in-laws' home. Your father will, of course, cover all expenses, and we will fly over to attend. Now, the matter's settled."

"So, it'll be at Bell Manor, meaning *Will's mum* is in charge of everything?" Jessica couldn't hide her disappointment.

Her mother's cheery tone resonated confidence. "Ah, don't worry, my dear. I conversed with her too. She was gracious enough to concede that no young bride wants her big day hijacked by her future mother-in-law. It is well."

As a peace offering, and to talk wedding business, Philippa Armstrong-Bell invited Jessica to lunch at Daphne's in Chelsea one Friday afternoon. After the initial ping pong of get-to-know-you-better chitchat, they discovered their ideas were not so dissimilar.

"I can understand why my William's smitten with you," Will's mother stated with a wry smile of acceptance. "Quite decisive, aren't you? With good taste too… hmmm… I think I rather misjudged you." She observed her future daughter-in-law with narrowed eyes.

Jessica's grin widened. "Thank you, Lady Armstrong-Bell. I…"

"Oh no, Dear. Please do call me Philippa," she interjected firmly.

"Absolutely not!" Jessica responded with genuine alarm. "I wouldn't dream of using your first name. It simply isn't done…"

Philippa gave a dismissive wave. "I appreciate culture and all that,

CHAPTER 14 — THE MILLENNIUM

but I must insist. It's either that or Lady Armstrong-Bell, which is a considerable mouthful, wouldn't you say? And I certainly won't have you calling me 'Mum'." She sounded quite horrified at the prospect and swiftly changed subject. "Besides, Michael and I have been discussing your… union with our son and… well, there's no delicate way of putting this. Are you two planning on having children?"

Jessica's reply was categoric. "Definitely. Why do you ask?"

Lady Armstrong-Bell leaned back in her chair, observing Jessica with care. She sighed, then stated in somewhat stilted tones, "Your children will be… well, you're coloured and… let's just say it's prudent to consider these matters. I'm sure you agree."

Jessica's heart sank. She'd suspected they didn't approve of her, but today made it crystal clear. Indignant self-regard demanded a response, so she uttered with quiet conviction, "I'm not 'coloured', but black. And we *have* considered it. Will and I adore each other and wish to spend the rest of our lives together — which *will* involve children. Loads of them, we hope! With mixed-race curly hair and gorgeous light brown skin. The best bits of both of us." She pursed her trembling lips.

Philippa raised a manicured finger to an arched brow and smiled stiffly. "Yes, of course. I'm sure they'll be beautiful. Happy to hear you've given some… consideration… to the matter."

Freida called later that afternoon, clearly excited for her sister. "How are the plans progressing? Were you able to book your dress fitting at Harrods?"

"Yeah… that's going fine…" Jessica sounded despondent.

"Hey, what's wrong?"

"I don't know. I mean… I had lunch with Will's mum and…"

"She isn't still angling to take over, is she?"

"No, not really. In fact, we got on well to begin with, but then she hinted that she's opposed to the idea of mixed-race children."

"*What?* She actually said this to your face?"

"Not in so many words, but yes! She mentioned it would be 'prudent to consider such matters' before having kids."

"Oh, please!" Freida scoffed. "The woman should *commot* with her racist views. Ignore her, *O'jare*! Such ignorance!"

"Exactly. And then she asked me to call her Philippa."

"Okayyyyy… and… isn't that her name?"

"Yes, but how could I do that?? Soooo rude. Mum would kill me!"

"Jess, Jess! There you go again – overthinking everything. The woman is English. You can't expect her to understand our tradition of respect for elders. How're you supposed to address her? *Aunty* Philippa?? Of course not." Freida was laughing and Jessica could see the funny side.

"I guess so. She insisted it was that or Lady Armstrong-Bell. So formal! Seems like there'll always be a barrier between me and my mother-in-law," she pronounced wistfully.

CHAPTER 14 — THE MILLENNIUM

"But, which do you prefer? What makes you more comfortable?"

Jessica pondered for a minute, trying to apply Freida's level-headed reasoning. "Lady Armstrong-Bell, I s'pose."

There was a smile in her sister's voice. "Well, there you have it."

~

Life soon became a busy balancing act between wedding planning and work commitments. Typical days comprised gruelling morning rehearsals, meetings with music video directors, the odd bridal appointment, and the task of prepping for scheduled shows.

On one such day, Jessica rose early and sat by the French windows with her journal – the usual routine. But this morning was different. For starters, she'd woken up lightheaded and queasy, and even vomited.

"I must tell Chef Lee," she murmured. "Perhaps it was the fish."

Settling in her favourite seat, she gazed into the garden. It looked picture-perfect; magnificent, in fact. Lit by the sunlight, a golden glow on the peeping daisies and a shimmer on the freshwater pond, the frogspawn glistened like mini moons. She couldn't understand why she felt the way she did. Bloody awful. She reckoned the most likely culprit was the sushi from the night before and shuffled to the cabinet, angry stomach growling. A spoonful of Andrews liver salts might help settle it.

By mid-afternoon, with sound and lighting checks only two hours away, she was nowhere near okay. She wanted to crawl back into bed.

As she rushed to the bathroom to vomit once again, a worrying thought crossed her mind.

Could it be? *Could* she be? It was highly feasible.

My goodness! Maybe she was.

CHAPTER 15

How do you make God laugh?

Jessica stared at the pregnancy test, the two lines glaring back at her, undeniable and immutable. She was pregnant. Every attempt to dismiss the fear only reinforced the inescapable truth.

"Oh, my God. How did this happen? What do I do now??" The words echoed in her mind, each one a fresh wave of panic. She felt a sudden swell of nausea and dashed to the bathroom, barely making it.

As she sank to the floor, tears mingled with the cold sweat on her face. How was she going to tell William? What about her parents? The thought of her mother's inevitable disappointment sent shivers down her spine. She retched again, the bathroom's walls closing in as her plans unraveled before her eyes.

"A pregnant bride is not part of our fairy tale," she murmured to herself, frustrated and scared. She loved William dearly and always envisioned a future with him, children included. But this timing; oh, the timing was all wrong.

Her phone rang, jolting her back to the moment. Freida's name flashed on the screen. Jessica hesitated before answering, her hiccups muffling her words.

"Stop crying!" Freida's voice was stern, but laced with concern. "Okay, you're pregnant. And so? Termination is not an option, so dry your tears and let's figure this out."

Jessica's sobs only got louder.

Freida softened her tone. "Listen, Jess, it is what it is. It's happened. And at least you're marrying him in two months."

Jessica sniffled. "I'm so s-sick, Fifi. Can't keep anything down. Bloody awful!"

"*Pele* oh! I'm sorry," Fifi sympathised. "These first few weeks are hard… it'll pass."

Jessica took a deep breath, trying to find calm. "I have to tell William – he's bound to notice something soon – what do I say? We didn't plan

CHAPTER 15 — HOW DO YOU MAKE GOD LAUGH?

this, Fifi." Her voice dropped to a whisper.

Her sister's tone became brisk and business-like. "You *inform* him. Plain and simple."

"But what if he…"

"What if he what?!" Fifi cut her off, seemingly irritated by the mere hint of any reticence on William's part. "It takes two, Jess! He won't blame you. Just tell him. Tonight. It'll be fine. No *wahala*, I promise."

The Nigerian pidgin-English word for trouble, *"wahala"*, brought unexpected comfort to Jessica. "I'll tell him tonight," she resolved. "But what do I say to Mum and Dad?" The paralyzing rush of panic threatened to resurface.

Freida didn't miss a beat. "They'll be thrilled to have a grandchild on the way. You remember their favourite quote?"

Both girls cleared their throats in readiness and recited in unison, "Go forth and multiply!"

The ensuing laughter dissipated some of Jessica's concerns, but thoughts of William's mother's disapproval still lingered. "And Will's parents? They won't be happy, especially his mum…" Jessica's words trailed off.

Freida sighed, resigned. "People don't switch sides, Jess. They just dig deeper into their bias. We don't want a reason to love; we want to justify our hate. She'll never change. Just leave it."

Jessica nodded in reluctant agreement, wiping away the last of her tears.

Dear J, Will was ecstatic when I shared the news – he'll make such a brilliant father! But what happens now? Doesn't pregnancy ruin showbiz careers?? The moment things start to go well for me, I get bloody pregnant!

Days later, whilst thumbing through old photos, Jessica stumbled upon a carefree image of her and Debbie and traced it with idle fingers. Staring at the reminder of those happy times, she felt a deep pang of regret for their strained relationship. It hadn't recovered since the previous summer when Debbie had adopted a frosty attitude toward her. Feeling a sudden urge to reconnect, she dialled Debbie's number. She could no longer ignore the mountain of dust that had accumulated on the fabric of their friendship. Now seemed a prudent time to shake out that rug, free any stubborn resentment lurking beneath the surface, be honest with each other and move on.

After a few rings, a familiar, almost cautious, voice answered. "Hello, Jess?"

"Hi. How are you?" Jessica asked, forcing cheerfulness.

"It's been a looong time." Deborah replied, her tone warming slightly.

"Yeah, been busy with Will and everything," Jessica said, attempting to bridge the gap.

Debbie's tone turned chilly. "Yes, I know."

CHAPTER 15 🌴 HOW DO YOU MAKE GOD LAUGH?

"Erm, I hear you're moving to New York in August?" Jessica ventured, looking for common ground.

"Yep. But I'll be around for the wedding in July," Deborah stated, with an edge. There was a pause, then she asked the question Jessica knew was coming. "Who's your maid-of-honour?"

Jessica cringed. "I-I've asked… um I'm keeping things simple. Won't even have bridesmaids. Fifi…"

"I see."

Jessica offered an olive branch. "Want to meet?"

Debbie mumbled, "I'd like that."

They met that afternoon at Giraffe, a restaurant Jessica secretly hoped would become her go-to place as a mother. On most Sundays, Jessica noticed women with pushchairs and fathers with babies strapped to their chests, heading into the family eatery for their weekend brunch. It looked ideal. Her glowing face radiated pure happiness as she entered.

The first few minutes were painfully awkward, but before long the girls had resuscitated their unique brand of camaraderie and were chortling with delight at each other's stories.

Despite limiting herself to tiny sips of orange juice, the added pressure on her pelvic floor caused Jessica to scurry countless times to the lavatory. This uncontrollable and very common unruly bladder impulse occurred one time too many, piquing Debbie's curiosity.

"Are you ok?" she enquired, a suspicious glint in her narrowed eyes.

Jessica tried to sound casual. "Umm, yes. Just a bit…indisposed."

Debbie's next words hit like a dart. "You're not pregnant, are you?"

Jessica's face froze, and her former housemate yelped in triumph. "*Eeiisshh*, I knew it!" she declared. "I thought there might be something amiss, but… couldn't be sure. You look different, though. Ha!"

Jessica divulged everything. "Incredible, isn't it?" she concluded with a small smile.

Her friend gawped at her, obviously taken aback. She'd been clutching at straws with her suggestion of pregnancy, and Jessica had fallen into the trap.

Deborah smirked, "Who would've imagined? Pretty Miss Perfect *pregnant*?! Wowww!"

Jessica's eyes darted around the restaurant, shushing her friend.

"Why, is it a secret?" Debbie half-mouthed, half-whispered, but with a little mischief in her eye.

"No, not really," Jessica countered. "William knows, of course."

"What did he say?" Debbie quizzed.

Jessica's face softened with love. "He laughed. A long belly *laugh*; can you believe it!" Her dreamy eyes moistened at the memory. "Then he hugged me and said I'd made him the happiest man in the world."

CHAPTER 15   HOW DO YOU MAKE GOD LAUGH?

She shook her head in wonder. "He reminded me of the joke, 'How do you make God laugh? Tell him your plans.' Get it?" Jessica chuckled. "And that was it. No big deal, or no *wahala*, as Freida always says."

"Oh, so Freida knows?"

"Yeah, she's the first person I told."

"What about your mom and pop?"

Jessica's emphatic head shake was a categoric no. "It's not the right time to tell them. You remember what they're like. Uh-uh! No way. I need to wait and see. Fifi says I won't start showing for another three of four months and by that point I'll be married."

"Wow! Everything always works out for you. Congratulations, Jess." Debbie rose and moved to Jessica's side of the booth to give her former housemate a hug. Their conversation drifted to lighter topics, but Jessica couldn't shake the feeling of being judged, even subtly, by her old friend.

Yet, she refused to let it affect her buoyant mood, and practically skipped home, the spring in her step reflecting the song in her heart. It seemed everyone she walked past smiled back at her. So contagious was her joy! So what if Debbie viewed Jessica's unplanned pregnancy as proof her life wasn't so 'picture-perfect'? Well, Jessica gloated to herself, it looks pretty darn picture-perfect right now. And I couldn't be happier!

Deciding to pop into Waitrose for a pint of milk and perhaps for that bar of chocolate she'd been craving, she was surprised to collide head-on into none other than Ms Dunn. Both women let out a startled yelp of gleeful surprise, before embracing each other.

"You've been on my mind!" Emily Dunn proclaimed as she hugged Jessica, before leaning back to study her. "To be honest, darling, I've been a tad worried since Friday – you looked frightfully off colour during rehearsal and I meant to call and ask. Everything ok?"

Jessica smiled into Ms Dunn's kind eyes.

"Oh, thanks… Ms… erm… Emily." She still wasn't comfortable calling her former teacher by her first name. "I'm doing fine…," she paused, her grin broadening, and whispered, "I'm… pregnant."

Emily's mouth hung agape. "You're… Oh! That's sur-prising news!! Goodness!" She was frowning.

Jessica's heart plummeted, and she squinted at her manager's crossed arms. She'd been expecting a more favourable response. "Thought you'd be pleased for me!"

Still stunned by the sudden announcement, Emily struggled to disguise her dismay. "B-but how? Why? What about your career? What's going to happen now?"

Jessica's eyes drowned in disappointment. "It wasn't planned," she sniffed. "But, regardless… I'm… we're happy." She sounded hurt and defensive.

CHAPTER 15   HOW DO YOU MAKE GOD LAUGH?

Emily took a concerned step toward Jessica in a visible attempt at recovery. "Of course, you are! And I'm delighted for you. Sorry, Jess, you took me by surprise, is all. Congratulations!" She pulled back after a brief hug. "How are you? They claim peppermint's good for the nausea."

"Yes, I've heard that." Emily's quick about-turn brought immense relief, and Jessica felt a renewed sense of hope. Her eyes glistened and she confided, "At first, I was so worried. But now… we're thrilled."

Emily Dunn gave her a tighter hug. "My granny always said children are a blessing from God," she added reassuringly, attempting to make up for her initial sourness. "And darling," she lifted Jessica's chin, "there's nothing to fret about. What happened to me needn't be your story. We'll make this work, don't you worry. You can have it all, my love. Remember that. You *can* have it all."

Jessica sincerely hoped she could.

CHAPTER 16

Let the cat out

"Why didn't you tell me you're pregnant?" Edith's demand dripped with disappointment and dared her daughter to deny it. Her voice shattered the morning tranquility.

Jessica's eyes widened, darting helplessly to William, who was ensconced behind his classic 19th Century oak desk. This impressive six-foot by four work-space, topped with green-tooled leather, seemed dwarfed by the gravity of their predicament. Sensing her distress, he set down his ballpoint pen and gave Jessica a blank, yet sympathetic shrug.

She clutched her face in dismay and turned her attention back to her irate caller, whose repeated question came louder the second time, if that were humanly possible. A roar.

"*Why didn't you tell me you're pregnant?*" The explosive outburst made Edith's fury palpable as it reverberated through the phone.

Who could have informed her? Jessica's mind was racing – obviously not William. And Ms Dunn would take any secret to her grave. The only other person… Oh, nooo, Jessica deduced with a grimace! Debbie!! Bloody Debbie must've told Mum.

She tried to sound outraged, to deflect her mother's anger. "Mum, who was it? Who told you? Debbie?"

When she got no response, she took a deep, calming breath and changed tactic, reasoning, "I would have notified you myself. I just… it wasn't the right time and…."

Her heart thudded, then almost stopped.

"Wasn't–the–right–time?" Edith Brown's scathing voice boomed each syllable. "What do you mean, it wasn't the right time? What do you mean by that?! Huh?"

Jessica swallowed the gigantic ball of debilitating fear that squeezed her throat dry, threatening to choke her into wordless submission. Her mother's wrath always produced this reaction. Ever since childhood, she dreaded it. And today was no different. Her mum might as well be right

CHAPTER 16 — LET THE CAT OUT

there in the room with her.

"What I mean is I've been so sick and confused and… I'm sorry, Mum."

Mrs Brown was silent. She wasn't making this easy. Jessica swallowed again and explained, "We didn't plan it… and when I started getting nauseous, I did tests and… wasn't sure whether to be happy or sad, or what to say to you and Dad."

"Shame on you, Jessica Sokari Brown. Shame on you! I had no illusions about you and your boyfriend… cavorting – that much was clear when you visited Accra – but how foolish can you be? *Why* allow yourself to get *pregnant* in this day and age? What were you thinking, eh? Imagine hearing such a thing from that girl Debbie!? What an embarrassment to be t-t-told our unmarried daughter is pre… p-pregnant… *Chineke God!*" She always stuttered when she got emotional.

Jessica sniffed. "I am so sorry. I didn't mean to embarrass you, or Dad…" Her voice cracked. "Debbie shouldn't have – she had no right to tell you. You should've heard it from me first. I'm sorry, Mum!" Jessica repeated.

Silence.

"Mum?"

Edith Brown finally spoke, her tone calmer, though still somewhat aggrieved. "I've never been more shocked in my life. But, as your father said, it could be worse." She sighed dramatically. "At least, the young man has already proposed marriage. I suppose that's something to be thankful for." Her mother's tone became more conciliatory. "And as for that Debbie, hmmm. Ok. It's ok. So now we know. I hope you're drinking ginger for the nausea, eh?"

Jessica's eyes flooded with relief and she nodded, forgetting her mum wasn't privy to her actions.

Her mother continued her attempt to rescue the situation. "And I suppose we should say *Tamuno imiete* – Thank God! At least my daughter isn't barren and we'll soon celebrate a grandchild."

Jessica beamed. "Yes. Like you and Dad used to say all the time: 'Go forth and multiply!'"

"Hey! Look at this cheeky girl!" Mrs Brown laughed softly. "*Nah true oh*. That's what the good book says. Go forth and multiply, my child."

After the phone call with her mother, Jessica dialed Debbie's number with a pounding heart and trembling hands.

"Hello?" Debbie's voice sounded groggy with sleep. It was a quarter to nine in the morning.

"How could you?" Jessica's voice quivered with rage.

"How…?"

"*Don't even try to deny it!*" Subconsciously, her tone mirrored her mother's, and she was now bellowing at Deborah.

"Oh…"

CHAPTER 16 — LET THE CAT OUT

"Oh? *Oh?* Is that all you can say, Debbie? You're aware of my parents' prudish rules! And you still went ahead and told them? What were you trying to achieve, anyway?"

William retreated from the room to give his girlfriend her space. Debbie remained silent, her breathing heavy. Jessica waited.

"I shouldn't have, Jess. I apologise. Please forgive me…" She seemed contrite.

Jessica refused to let it go. "But why? Why did you do it? I told you I needed to find the right time to tell them!"

"You did," Deborah admitted, "And I burst your bubble. It was your news to share, not mine. I just… I s'pose I felt… excited for you and… I'm sorry, Jess."

"Fine… ok. I guess there's no secret any longer."

After replacing the handset, she sat alone for a long moment, analyzing this turn of events. William re-entered and placed an arm around her.

"You feel betrayed by your buddy," he commiserated.

Jessica frowned and huffed, "Not sure she's *that* anymore!"

He winced sympathetically. "I have to agree there. Hard facts are undeniable, darling."

Dear J, can I trust Debbie? Why would she betray my confidence? Well, now M&D know. And as for Will's parents, maybe I should leave that up to him.

William believed in sharing information on a need-to-know-basis. His mother's implicit disapproval of their relationship, hinted at without full admission, informed his stance. Consigned to boarding school at age five, William's initial feelings of abandonment had morphed into a staunch independence shaping his adulthood. Their union required no parental endorsement on his side, and news of Jessica's pregnancy could wait until it was undeniable.

Dear J, William has arranged a ten-day trip to Bali for my 19th birthday. He says it'll be a perfect escape before the wedding.

"But my entire tribe arrives in London the week before, and we'll be in Indonesia?" Jessica's voice held a mix of incredulity and irritation. The proposition appeared even more ludicrous when spoken out loud.

"Your family's fine with it. I've already spoken to your dad. Plus, we return on the 12th."

"That's just *days* before the wedding!" Jessica exclaimed, baffled by his nonchalance.

"Exactly! We get back, go straight to the church, and any exhaustion you feel can be chalked up to jetlag. My parents won't suspect a thing!" William's confidence was unshakable.

Jessica stared at her husband-to-be. "Gosh! You're steps ahead of us all, aren't you?" she said, half-admiring, half-annoyed. "I'd pegged

CHAPTER 16 — LET THE CAT OUT

this trip as a spontaneous, romantic gesture." She pouted and assumed a miffed mien.

Will chuckled and hugged her. "Think of it as a final gift before we wed. You'll love Bali – it's beautiful."

In truth, Jessica hadn't realised how much she needed the break. The stress from moving house, the pregnancy, and subliminal tension with her future mother-in-law had taken a toll. Not to mention the craziness of her work schedule and learning to balance her demanding job with William's expectations. Yes, she was well and truly knackered.

And Bali brought the much-needed respite. They loved exploring the tranquility of its forested volcanic mountains, its iconic rice paddles, and the serenity of its gorgeous sandy beaches and coral reefs. At the resort, Jessica was particularly taken by the inspiring yoga teacher, Magdalena, whose quiet demeanour belied an unexpectedly exuberant personality. The woman was the epitome of pure contentment, virtually bubbling with inner joy, yet exuding a distinct aura of calm. It was clear she possessed a naturally fiery temperament, typical of some Latin women, but had cleverly channeled this energy into her practice. When Jessica expressed delight at having met her, the petite, dark-haired beauty embraced her like an old friend.

The couple returned to London filled with vitality, but overcome with nerves. Their wedding was in three days!

CHAPTER 17

According to Plan

The air hung with a cool crispness, the kind that hinted at imminent rain as Jessica rummaged through her closet, her mind awash with a blend of excitement and trepidation.

"They haven't seen me since I got pregnant," she mused out loud, her hands sifting through garments, pausing momentarily with each flicker of fabric. After much consideration, she selected a fitted pencil skirt that hugged her slender frame. A silk scarf found its way around her shoulders, a feeble attempt to mask her newly prominent bustline. Despite her best efforts, the mirror reflected a woman trying too hard to reclaim her old self.

William, always the calm anchor in their whirlwind of change, smiled reassuringly. "You look perfect. They'll be so happy to see you, Jess."

As the ornate clock in the opulent lobby of Claridge's chimed four, the Brown clan gathered for their daily ritual of afternoon tea. William embraced Jessica's parents with genuine warmth. "Lovely to see you again!" he beamed. "Excellent choice of hotel."

Sokari Brown's chuckle was as rich as the mahogany paneling that lined the hotel's walls. "Well, my dear son-in-law," he began, casting an indulgent glance at his wife, "we chose Claridge's of Mayfair for two reasons. First, its proximity to the attractive boutiques of Bond Street…"

"Where I have essential items to purchase," Edith Brown interjected, her grin mischievous.

"And secondly," Sokari continued, his eyes twinkling with delight, "because we are rather partial to their Afternoon Tea."

"Predictable," Jessica teased, her mouth curving into a smile as her father issued a theatrical smack of his lips.

"In fact, their variety of finger sandwiches, patisserie and warm scones served with strawberry conserve and Cornish clotted cream is second to none." Sokari declared.

"He's memorised the menu, oh!" Edith joked, her eyes dancing with affection, and everyone laughed.

CHAPTER 17 — ACCORDING TO PLAN

Will chuckled, joining in the lighthearted atmosphere that settled around them like a cosy blanket of contentment. "Sounds like a win-win for everybody," he remarked jovially.

"Indeed. At the behest of my dear wife, we gather here each day to partake in 'London's Leading Traditional Afternoon Tea'," Sokari proclaimed in a mock-formal tone.

David, Jessica's carefree, older brother, quipped, "Yes! We're all expected to attend this daily tea-party and no-one dares disappoint." Freida nudged him, stifling a giggle, even as the laughter rippled through the group like a wave, soothing Jessica's lingering anxieties.

Edith's eyes narrowed slightly as she appraised Jessica with the keen regard of an experienced matriarch. "You look well," she concluded, her tone both kind and probing.

"Thanks, Mum! Our holiday was glorious," Jessica responded, pinching her mother gently. The subtle exchange served as a reminder that, except for Fifi, her siblings were still in the dark about her condition.

Sokari leaned close with a reassuring squeeze. "All is good, *inate*? You hear?" he whispered. His Kalabari words were a balm to her soul.

"Thank you, Daddy." She tightened her hold.

"In two days, you shall no longer be called Jessica Brown," Sokari announced with an air of finality, the statement heavy laden with tradition.

Jessica felt a momentary surge of confusion and defiance, prompting her immediate rebuttal, "Of course, I will! Though I do intend to be Mrs Armstrong-Bell," she peeked at Will, "but I'll keep my maiden-name, too." Her dad smiled, and she continued, "Jessica Sokari Brown carries a certain gravitas and is an identity I shall guard with pride."

Her mother commended with a wistful smile, "Well said! I've always believed there's power in a name. Which is the reason your father and I were careful about the names we gave each of you."

William cleared his throat, a beacon of light slicing through the somber mood. "Alright then, my love. Introduce me to everyone."

With a grateful smile, his fiancée clasped his hand, happy for the change of subject. "You've met my younger siblings; Jeremy is sixteen, and Evelyn and Anita are seventeen, but act like they're twenty-seven!" She laughed at the playful tongue-sticking responses from the twins, and blew them a kiss.

"James is twenty-one and about to graduate from university. Fifi…" Jessica lowered her tone to a mock-whisper, "… is my favourite; twenty-six and a GP. Oh, and that's her boyfriend, Yinka, who's a dentist." She smiled as Yinka performed a theatrical bow.

"David, our fun-loving, number two, is twenty-eight. And, my eldest brother Mikey, the star of our family, is the one destined for greatness. He sets a high bar for the rest of us mere mortals," she finished, winking at Mikey, who winked back.

CHAPTER 17   ACCORDING TO PLAN

"That was pleasant," Will slipped off his jeans with a yawn.

Jessica echoed his fatigue, speaking through her yawn. "I'm pleased they got to meet you. Apparently, your mum's arranged for us all to spend the night tomorrow after dinner."

"So, I hear." His voice was tinged with amusement. "You know why that is, don't you?"

She rolled her eyes and wriggled out of her dress. "Oh, I know! She's worried we Africans will be late to the ceremony and can't take any chances."

Their laughter filled the room, a moment of shared intimacy. Jessica added with mock solemnity, "All perfectly planned. No room for error."

"Yep. That's my mother."

The following day's drive to Bell Manor was an ordeal. Friday's abysmal traffic tested their patience, compounded by Jessica's uncooperative bladder demanding frequent bathroom stops. By the time they arrived, nerves were frayed, camouflaged only by the excuse of jetlag. Indonesia's seven-hour time difference provided the perfect cover, just as William had predicted.

The Butler led Jessica to her room, and she collapsed onto the luxurious four-poster bed, sleep claiming her almost instantly.

༄

"Jess, Jess…" The call was growing more persistent. It wasn't a dream.

Jessica opened groggy, sleep-filled eyes to see Freida leaning over her, concern etched in her features.

"Hi," Jessica croaked, clearing her parched throat and stretching her stiff body.

"Are you ok? The maid mentioned she came to unpack your bags, but was afraid to wake you."

Jessica glanced at her watch, panic flaring. "Shoot! It's a quarter past six!" she exclaimed, tossing the covers aside. "Where's Will?" Her eyes were wide with urgency.

"He's in the Blue Room with his parents. The others are still getting ready," Freida replied.

"Oh! Dinner in forty minutes… aargh!" Jessica's voice trembled.

Fifi reached to steady her. "Which is plenty of time to get ready. No need for panic."

Tears welled in Jessica's eyes. "I'm so glad you're here, Fif!"

"Of course, I'm here, silly. Now you…," she streaked a thumb across her sister's cheek, "… go shower while I lay out your dress. The red one, right?"

CHAPTER 17 — ACCORDING TO PLAN

Jessica nodded and surveyed Freida's midnight blue, organza cocktail attire, and elegant up-do. "Gosh, you look beautiful, Fifi!"

Freida smiled at her younger sister and moved towards the walk-in wardrobe. "Thanks, darling. Your turn now. Remember to have fun. This happens once in a lifetime."

Jessica floated into the drawing room, resplendent in her off-the-shoulder, crimson frock.

"You seem re-energized!" William whispered, beaming at his intended as she moved to his side.

"Positively glowing!" David agreed.

Jessica's eyes twinkled, exuding its own special light. "I childishly want to feel like a princess at my pre-wedding dinner," she confided. Maybe this was a fairy tale after all.

As conversations buzzed around the candlelit room, she noted the synergies between her family and his. "Funny, how your dad and my brother share the same name," she observed. "'Sir Michael' sounds so different from 'Mikey'."

Her father proudly introduced Mikey. "Michael's the youngest consultant cardiologist in the State of California." He slapped his son on the back. "He's not yet thirty, but has his own medical practice in Beverly Hills!"

Duly impressed, Sir Michael spent a solid minute shaking Dr

Mike Brown's hand, whilst simultaneously conducting a line of rapid-fire questioning. Satisfied his daughter-in-law hailed from excellent stock, he redirected Mikey towards Lady Armstrong-Bell for her own interrogation. An unbeatable duo, Jessica marveled at their impersonation of two detectives working in tandem, enacting the precise, pre-rehearsed scene of a coordinated investigation. The Armstrong-Bells weren't taking any chances. They wanted to make sure their son was getting hitched to the right family.

Well, he's marrying me, she reflected with irritation. Not my brothers or sisters. Me. And once the wedding is over, we'll focus on living our lives, just us two, exactly as planned.

Jessica awoke early on Saturday, 15th July 2000, her heart fluttering with excitement.

Sunshine peeked through the gap in the curtains, casting a hopeful glow for promising weather. Summer in England could be so unpredictable. She glanced at the empty space beside her, feeling the ache of separation from William; a pre-wedding tradition her mum asserted would usher good fortune.

Freida's entrance elicited a giggle, her mock-alarm at Jessica's unflattering flannel pyjamas lightening the mood.

"What? They bring me luck!" Jessica defended, tossing her head

CHAPTER 17   ACCORDING TO PLAN

playfully.

Freida opened the drapes, sunlight streaming in, flooding the room with warmth. Outside, a symphony of chirping birds declared, "It's a beautiful day!" Even the leaves seemed to sway in agreement. Jessica felt giddy with happiness.

Standing by the window, Fifi's body was drenched in light, creating the impression of a halo. *My guardian angel,* Jessica thought, as she blinked and yawned.

"Didn't sleep much, huh?" Freida sympathised. "Not surprising after yesterday's looong nap."

"Gosh, Fif, I was so exhausted I figured I was ill or something."

"Not ill," Freida interjected, moving closer, "just more pregnant with each passing hour. That's how it goes, J. It's not a sickness you know." She gave Jessica's shoulders a reassuring squeeze. "Anyway, today's focus should be on enjoying every moment of your big day. **Mum's already up.**"

"She is?"

"Yep. Has completed her 'sanctification ritual', sprinkling holy water around the house to ensure God's blessings."

Both girls chortled.

"Mum's something else… but she means well," Jessica spluttered through laughter.

Freida added, "And now she's in the kitchen…"

"… busy doing mum stuff."

"Yeah. Doing her duty as Mother-of-the-Bride."

They fell silent for a moment.

Freida looked at Jessica. "What d'you say… shall we?"

"Yes, boss!" Jessica performed a military salute and followed her downstairs.

They were whispering by this point, to avoid awaking anyone.

"Thank Goodness, the morning sickness is over." Jess rolled her eyes at the memory.

"That would've been disastrous!" Freida agreed. "Imagine walking down the aisle… here comes the bride, here comes the *uugghhhh*."

Both girls fell about in fits of giggles, before remembering to lower their voices.

Edith beamed at the sight of her daughters bounding into the kitchen. All alone with her bible in hand, she appeared rather vulnerable. "So, you're finally following in my footsteps, eh?"

Jessica hugged her. "Yes. Getting married at nineteen like you, Mum."

Freida chimed in, "All she's ever wanted was to copy you and marry young."

Mrs Brown regarded her eldest daughter. "And what about you? You and Yinka cannot date forever."

CHAPTER 17 ACCORDING TO PLAN

The young doctor shook her head with a delicate laugh. "Nah, We're good Ma. Too busy for all that."

Edith tutted, unconvinced, but smiling. "Ok, Jessica Sokari Brown. It's time. I pray our Heavenly Father blesses you with the same luck I've enjoyed with your daddy all these years — that you have a wonderful life with William. I believe you will!"

Jessica believed it, too.

***

"Come on, Jess, it's 8:30!" Freida announced, moving to answer the knock at the door, and quickly stepping aside to reveal a flamboyant and rather effeminate man in his thirties, wreathed in smiles as he breezed in.

"Hello darrrling, ya ready t'look beeauuutiful?" He cooed with twinkling eyes.

Jessica liked him on sight.

"I'm Gareth… Gary. This is my assistant Charlene and… ah, there she is… 'Magic Meghan', right on time!" He moved towards a petite blond, who also had a helper in tow and was armed with a whole artillery of makeup ammunition. Gary air-kissed the magician on both cheeks, declaring, "This woman's a total genius, so don't you worry about a thing, darrrling. She'll highlight your best features and make you…" he raised his palms to invite his audience's participation, "…beeauuutiful!"

Jessica found his exuberance infectious, but Freida was observing this sudden invasion of the unexpected army of beauticians with some trepidation, perhaps wondering why a single individual would require so many of them.

Gary seemed to notice Freida's discomfort and immediately shifted gear, enveloping her with his charms. "And you… you must be the maid-of-honor, yes?"

Freida nodded, her lips parting in uneasy surprise at his accuracy.

Gary's voice assumed an authoritative tone. "Right! Youuuu…" he gently, but firmly, guided her towards the exit, "… go with Charlene, and…"

"Misha." Magic Meghan introduced her assistant.

"… and Misha," Gary continued. "They'll handle youuu and the bride's mother." He clapped his palms together to signal action.

Everyone had their marching orders and promptly advanced to their bases, leaving the excited bride with the main stylists. She could sense the invisible wand of Lady Armstrong-Bell orchestrating this entire performance. That woman's impeccable planning had proved impressive, thus far.

There was only one thing bothering Jessica, and she turned to address Meghan. "Errhmm, you do….?"

"Black skin?" the make-up artist pre-empted with a confident grin.

CHAPTER 17   ACCORDING TO PLAN

"Honey, don't worry. I can handle all shades and make your beauty shine!"

Jessica quelled her doubts and surrendered to the alleged magician's dexterous touch and, for the next fifty-five minutes, reveled in being primped and preened by this delightful pair. But one glance in the mirror evoked a piercing scream.

"What have you done?" She stared aghast at her pale reflection in horror. "It's dreadful!"

The mortified magician tried to placate her. "But see how your eyes…"
"I'm a *ghost*!" Jessica wailed.
Gary had rushed to fetch Freida, who came striding in.

"What's the matter… oh!" she snorted at the sight of her sister's phantom-like complexion.

Gary's breezy wave of a hand presented some wet wipes. Freida peered at the beautician, who resembled a helpless, thumb-twiddling ninny. Jessica's whitened cheeks twitched in the semblance of a smile. Had she not been the very subject of the faux-pas, she might have found the scene hysterical.

Freida's quick thinking saved the day. "Use Jess's own foundation," she suggested as they scrambled to fix the blunder. "You did a nice job with her eyes though," she conceded with a gracious nod, while scrubbing Jessica's skin clean.

Ever on cue, at precisely 09:35, there was another knock.

"That was close!" Freida muttered to a relieved Jessica, brandishing a final swish of the brush.

Gary stood back to survey their handiwork. Sufficiently satisfied, and having recovered from his near heart-attack, he resumed his role of General and strode to the door. Harry the Butler was standing there with Jessica's wedding gown in his sturdy grip.

Gary stretched out his arms, a human clothes hanger, and Harry gingerly draped the sheer garment bags over them.

It was time to dress the bride.

CHAPTER 18

The Wedding & Thereafter

Gary's flair for the dramatic was on full display as he seamlessly switched from hairdresser to fashion stylist. Jessica watched him with glee.

He unzipped the garment bag, unveiling the spectacular gown with reverent delight, gasping as he fingered the handmade creation. "Exquisite!" he declared, with the ardent fervour of a person in love with the art of design. "The cut, the lines… look at the finish. With *your* physique, divine!" He kissed the tips of his fingers for emphasis.

His enthusiasm was contagious, and Jessica's heart soared in anticipation. She felt like a true princess.

"Wait, I just need to… uh… pee… first," she said, hurrying to the bathroom with a giggle. Freida's practical reminder had saved her from a potential mid-vow disaster.

The dress flattered her figure perfectly, despite the weight loss from her early pregnancy days. "Gosh, I look older than nineteen…" she mused aloud.

"Gorgeous!" Gary effused, revealing the veil. One-and-a-quarter times the gown's length, it was fashioned from silk chiffon, with an intricate French lace border. Ethereal.

At 9.55am, Freida returned, joy sparkling in her eyes. "Oh Jess… You've been transformed into a goddess."

Jessica held back her own tears – she didn't dare ruin the carefully crafted work of art which was now her face – and hugged her sister as best she could amidst the voluminous fabric. Fifi handed over the bouquet and assumed her spot behind the bride, lifting the veil so Jessica could glide downstairs unencumbered, without tripping.

It was a sight to behold; a bridal vision of angelic innocence, alongside the quintessential maid-of-honour, adorned in vivid red.

"You peed, right?" Freida whispered, halfway down the stairs.

Jessica snickered and nodded.

CHAPTER 18 — THE WEDDING & THEREAFTER

Edith's eyes glistened as she watched her daughters descend with effortless grace. Clutching her hands together, she murmured, "*Tamuno imiete,* thank you, God!"

Chief Brown planted a kiss on his younger daughter's forehead, before proffering his crooked elbow for her to clasp. Jessica beamed at her father and reflected on how she'd always adored him. He was her ultimate benchmark for how a man should treat a woman, until William came along.

Her heart performed its usual acrobatics at the thought of her husband-to-be. She drew a deep breath and stepped outside into the welcoming sunshine.

Although the chapel was a mere five-minute walk away, Lady Armstrong-Bell had arranged a horse-drawn carriage. Photographers and journalists awaited their arrival, and the driver brought the vehicle to a grinding halt with a camera-worthy flourish, eliciting giggles from the bridal party.

"I'll see you in there!" Edith alighted first, adjusting her elaborate *gele* head-tie and offering the cameras a royal wave before confidently waddling into the chapel.

Sokari Brown wore his traditional Kalabari Chief attire – a full-length embroidered gown tailored from hand-woven fabric, topped with a crescent hat and the obligatory walking stick. Upright and proud, he assisted his daughter from the carriage. Flashbulbs popped furiously as

Freida adjusted the veil, then hurried into the church.

The Wedding March began and Jessica sailed down the aisle on her father's arm, taking in the sheer size of the congregation, absorbing the sea of stylish hats and fashionable ensembles, the tailcoats and balding heads. Everyone deemed worthy of an invitation had been invited, and it was a relief to spot the familiar faces of her siblings, a few friends from school, Emily Dunn, and even Deborah. The guests filled the small chapel to capacity and overflowing, with late arrivals relegated to standing at the sides.

The deep resonance of Chief Sokari Brown's rich baritone provided the perfect backdrop, injecting a much-needed boost to the mélange of nervously cleared throats and hesitant voices. Edith Brown was equally obliging, adding the occasional harmony to her spouse's ebullient melody. The outcome was flawless. Jessica glanced at her parents with a smile, knowing they'd always been partial to these popular Methodist hymns. They'd become a choir onto themselves, perfectly complementing each other and further accentuating their unity. As Sir Michael later acknowledged, their "enthusiastic contribution added a splash of colour to the otherwise bland ceremony".

The guests filed toward the large tent positioned by the lake, and Jessica overheard Lady Armstrong-Bell explaining, "I had my gardener cover this entire field with lavender. It keeps bugs away and smells divine!"

CHAPTER 18 — THE WEDDING & THEREAFTER

An unknown guest complimented, "How thoughtful of you! It's an enchanting sight, I daresay. Purple, interspersed with pockets of white and yellow daisies; you've created quite the folktale! Aren't you clever, Philippa!"

Her mother-in-law clucked with pride and Jessica smiled at her ingenuity. The day couldn't have been more perfect: even the weather was ideal. During the Champagne Brunch Reception, a euphoric Edith convinced her newly married daughter to perform their native *Tu Seki*, or shake-your-booty dance, as Jessica had always called it.

"Let's show them how we Kalabaris do it, huh?" She laughed and beckoned her other daughters to create a joyful booty train which William joined with gusto, reaffirming his position in his new family. Much to everyone's delight, at a well-timed moment Sir Michael attempted to join the human locomotive with his rendition of the *Tu Seki*.

This glorious day marked the beginning of Jessica's life as Mrs William Armstrong-Bell, and she prayed her fairytale would never end. The next morning, she awoke in William's warm embrace, elated yet disbelieving.

"That went well, right?" she murmured to her half-slumbering husband.

"Hmm," he grunted, lashes fluttering open for a nanosecond.

"Your mother deserves all the accolades. I must remember to thank her properly." She sighed and snuggled some more.

Later, as they breakfasted with the others, Jessica noted how the sun created lingering, dancing patterns on the pool, amidst the delightful sound of bonding laughter. It was perfection. She gave her relatives tight hugs before they clambered into their chauffeur-driven vehicles.

"I presume you two'll be off in a moment?" Sir Michael turned to his son. "Sintra, wasn't it?"

William shook his head. "Actually, Dad, we're staying put. Just got back from travelling, and… Portugal's only next door, so…"

"No honeymoon? That's surprising!" his mother noted, eyes narrowing as she looked at Jessica.

"Well, I *am* pretty tired after Bali. But, thank you for everything." Jessica said with genuine warmth, kissing her mother-in-law's cheek. "It was the best day!"

Philippa smiled graciously and returned the peck on her cheek. "Oh, you're quite welcome, Dear," she replied. "Turned out brilliantly, didn't it?" She looked pleased with herself.

Sir Michael chirped, "Yes, it rather did! I think it was terrific. Well done, darling!" he commended his wife, who swelled visibly at the praise.

Jessica was glad she'd said something. Everyone needs to be shown appreciation, no matter how self-assured they appear, she thought.

William could barely mask his eagerness to have his bride to himself

CHAPTER 18 — THE WEDDING & THEREAFTER

and Flora was already purring in readiness, awaiting their departure. Sir Michael moved to join his son by the car.

Lady Armstrong-Bell's knowing whisper caught Jessica off-guard. "You looked somewhat off-colour yesterday. Lost quite a bit of weight, too. Is everything alright?"

Jessica gasped at her mother-in-law's astute observation. "Oh, just nerves, you know…"

It was a blatant, but necessary, lie. This was William's secret to share.

⁓

A month later, Jessica was startled to find two strange men in the corridor. "Who… what are you doing here?"

"Sorry, Ma'am. We're the decorators. We'll stay out of your way." They dashed into the next room.

Jessica huffed in bewilderment and hurried downstairs. "Will, what's going on?"

"Hey, Sweetheart. Figured I'd get the nursery started." William beamed, tape measure in hand.

"The *nursery*? Will?! I'm barely out of my first trimester!"

"It'll help me feel part of this pregnancy. Gives me something to do," he admitted ruefully.

Two months later, at their official 20-week scan, William suggested,

"Not knowing the sex is romantic, but wouldn't it be practical to ask?"

"Eh!" Jessica nudged him playfully. "Choosing nursery colours, are we?"

William laughed. "Alright, romanticism rules."

The sonographer's reassuring voice filled the room. "The skull circumference and brain appear fine. Face, spine, heart… all good. Hear that strong heartbeat?" She smiled at the expectant couple.

Jessica tightened her grip on Will's hand, relief flooding her.

The sonographer continued, "Now, the other organs. See this black bubble here? It's amniotic fluid in his… or her… wholly intact stomach. And two kidneys… free-flowing urine…"

"Urine?" Jessica giggled in surprise.

"Yes, absolutely. Do you realise your baby has been doing a wee every half an hour or so for months? And here…" she pointed to the screen, "is its bladder, which is filling up this instant. See that?" She sounded excited.

Will's fascination grew with every detail.

"Ok, let's check arms and legs… fingers and toes. All measurements align with your due date," she was nodding with satisfaction. "The placenta is lying a little low, but nothing for concern at this stage. All the main aspects of your baby's development are normal. Congratulations, on a fully able-bodied baby."

CHAPTER 18 — THE WEDDING & THEREAFTER

They left the doctor's office elated by the reassurance that everything was fine.

"I secretly wish for a boy, but a healthy baby is what matters," Jessica revealed.

Will gazed at her with tenderness. "Hey, since you've got a recital on Saturday, let's not drive to Suffolk. We'll invite my parents to lunch instead."

Chef Lee had created a culinary masterpiece and was putting meticulous finishing touches to the dining area. It was unusually chilly for the first day of October, and the warmth from the fireplace made the high-ceilinged room more inviting.

Jessica's discarded garments lay haphazardly across their bed, and she scrutinised her form for the umpteenth time.

"Stop staring at yourself in the mirror, darling. You look fine!"

Jessica's expression was sullen. "What about these bulges!" she groaned, pinching at non-existent flaws. "What if I get too big to dance? Ugh! I'm dreading that! I remember being younger and *really* bottom-heavy. No, it's true. I had to work hard to become this. And now…huh!" she grimaced.

"Now what, Jess? You're pregnant, and gorgeous. The body bounces back, anyway. You'll have no trouble. Stop worrying. Ah… the doorbell."

Jessica watched William walk ahead, contemplating what he'd just said. She caressed her slight bump, so neat and compact it was nearly imperceptible, especially when she wore a loose enough outfit. No one in last night's audience would have guessed she was pregnant. But today was different – it was about showing off her bump to her in-laws, so a figure-hugging tube dress was the perfect selection. For good measure, she rested her left palm on her belly as she floated across the hallway to greet them.

Sir Michael's jaw hung agape as he studied his daughter-in-law. "Goodness, Dear, you're decidedly radiant today!"

Lady Armstrong-Bell's eyes narrowed as realisation dawned, and she inquired frostily of her son, "I suppose congratulations are in order?"

William shifted his stance.

Jessica strode to her husband's side and clasped his hand, a confident smile stretched across her features as she responded, "Yes! Thank you, we're thrilled." She looked directly at Will's mum as she spoke, and their eyes met and held for an uncomfortable second.

The older woman recovered with a fleeting grin. "Well, a child is always good news, regardless of the timing of its conception." She cast a pointed glance at Jessica's belly and added, "Congratulations, my dears."

Jessica accepted their perfunctory hugs and could see her husband

CHAPTER 18 THE WEDDING & THEREAFTER

looked relieved to share the truth.

"We found out just before the wedding," he gushed. "Kept it to ourselves until… erhmmm… until now, I s'pose."

His mother's keen stare and arched eyebrow emphasised her skepticism. "*Just before?*"

"Well, actually…." William faltered.

Jessica interjected, "Nine weeks earlier. I discovered I was pregnant in May."

Sir Michael laid a calming hand on his wife's arm. "Such wonderful news! Isn't it, darling?"

Lady Armstrong-Bell's vague nod conceded, "Yes, of course. You seem about… what, five months?"

"Yes, and we just completed the scan and are told the baby's growing fine." Jessica smiled again.

"Well then, this *is* cause for celebration, so why don't we move into the reception, which would be a great deal more comfortable, huh?" Sir Michael's tone was decisive and he led the way.

Twenty-five minutes later, the proud chef ushered them to their seats, and served a delicious Sunday lunch of Cardamom Roasted Leg of Lamb, with Rosemary Potatoes and Steamed Asparagus.

"I see your appetite's improved," Will's dad commented in his usual forthright manner, as he observed Jessica devour her third helping.

She laughed, not in the least bit offended. "My appetite's increased this last month, second trimester and all. Couldn't keep much down before," she explained.

"Well, you're glowing with it, my love." William was quick to support his wife.

"You'd better watch out," Lady Armstrong-Bell warned half-jokingly. "This thing they say about eating for two is a myth."

"I'm aware," Jessica admitted, laying down her cutlery and pushing her almost-empty plate away. She took a sip of water, conscious everyone was watching her. "I believe if I keep listening to my body, I can't go wrong."

"But are you? Listening to your body, that is?" Will's mother's tone turned serious. "Managing quite a busy schedule with regular performances means you're still jumping around that stage as though nothing's changed. Don't you think you should slow down, Dear?" She felt perfectly within her rights to admonish her daughter-in-law.

"The doctor says I can continue as long as I have the energy," Jessica countered, "and when that changes, I'll stop. I promise." Her voice had assumed an almost-childlike whine (which she hated, but couldn't help). "Dancing's my life! And I've really strived to get here. I know nothing else!" Her almond-shaped, amber eyes held a silent plea, willing her parents-in-law to condone her decision to keep working. "Last night, the audience gave me a standing ovation, which says something! Performing is literally the only thing that affords me some semblance of

CHAPTER 18 — THE WEDDING & THEREAFTER

normalcy. I mean, we didn't plan this, and my body's changing so fast I'm not sure how much longer I'll be able to continue, even after the baby. I don't want to give it up. Not yet."

"Ok. Your body, your decision," Philippa granted reluctantly. "Just be careful." It sounded like a warning.

Dear J, I must keep dancing for as long as I can. For my sanity. Besides, it's the only way to avoid getting fat!

PALM TREES IN THE STORM

CHAPTER 19

Busy Bee

"I hate that over-used turn of phrase!" William crossed his arms, and smouldered as Jessica threw on her coat.

"True, though. If it doesn't rain, it pours!" she quipped, a mischievous grin on her face. "Gotta run, darling. I'm inundated." Her lips grazed his, a fleeting touch of affection, before she scurried out the door, leaving a faint trace of her cherry blossom perfume in the air.

At the rehearsal studio, Emily stood by the entrance finishing up a phone conversation. "That was your husband," she confirmed. "He's concerned you're working too hard."

Jessica flicked a dismissive hand. "Why's he moaning? I'm in my element. He knows I love being busy. This is my chance to shine," she declared, effortlessly clicking her heels as she skipped into the practice room.

By November's end, Jessica's swelling abdomen had assumed torpedo-like proportions, making it impossible to take centre-stage. Yet her passion for choreography burned bright and kept her working into the night, much to Emily's chagrin.

"As your manager, I really must stop you. Go home, young lady." She glanced at her wrist, and grimaced. "It's late. You've been teaching this bunch for a straight four hours. If they haven't grasped it yet, it's unlikely they will tonight. Let's call it a day and pick up again tomorrow, ok?"

"Fifteen more minutes, Emily, they're almost there," Jessica insisted, a crazed glint in her eye.

Her mentor sighed. "You said that half an hour ago. William's going to kill me!"

"No, he won't. Stop worrying. He understands this keeps me sane. I *need* it. In a couple of months, I'll be done. Let me savour this while I can.

There was no arguing with her.

The frantic month of December carried with it a plethora of pre-

CHAPTER 19   BUSY BEE

Christmas shows and a packed social calendar. Jessica had enthusiastically ticked off each commitment.

William had lost his patience. "You're driving me insane, Jess. Our schedule's becoming ridiculous. It's a whirlwind! We can't attend *every* event, and you certainly can't continue to push this hard. You think you're invincible, but look at you – it doesn't make sense!"

She reacted as though he'd assaulted her. "Look at me? *Look at me?* What's wrong with me, Will? Tell me what's wrong with me!"

"Nothing, but you can't deny you do get tired – sometimes so exhausted you can barely stand straight. Why you'd endure this is a mystery to me. You are pregnant, Jess. You need to slow down."

"Pregnancy isn't an illness," Jessica retorted. "I'm not *sick*! Aarrghh!" she growled, tears of frustration spilling from her dejected eyes. "Besides, I'm damn good at what I do."

Will approached, arms outstretched, but Jessica sidestepped his embrace, her furious thoughts uncharacteristically slipping into Nigerian Pidgin. (Funny how the subconscious mind defaults to the language of your upbringing when anger has robbed you of the ability to reason.)

"*Commot, O'jare*! Leave me alone!! Nobody gets it," she grumbled, her voice quivering. "This is who I am and no-one understands."

William surveyed his nineteen-year-old wife with tenderness. "We're worried, darling. You *are* great at what you do, but that's not the point. Who you are is not what you *do*, Jess, but so much more than this! With a baby coming soon, you should rest." His green eyes shone in earnest.

Jessica stuck out her bottom lip in a sulk. "But the baby's not due till February," she reasoned.

"Yes, and February isn't as far off as you think. At 32-weeks it's a wonder you're still so active. Christmas is only a week away. Let's relax and enjoy it?" Will had been diligently attending every antenatal appointment, which kept him fully abreast of the developmental stages.

Relenting, Jessica murmured as she caressed her belly, "Okay, after the next session I'll hand over the baton, I promise."

William kissed her gently. "Thank you, my love. I know it's tough. But it's time to think of our child. Even *you* have to slow down. You're not superwoman – nothing to prove. Please let's relish this adventure together."

Dear J, I've been such a cow. Will's so understanding, but I get furious for no reason. Livid. The midwife says it's my hormones, but that's no excuse. Dancing helps me release frustration, and now I have to give it up. Really thought this would be easier. I'm truly not enjoying this pregnancy thing in the slightest and hate being so irritable.

"See, I kept my promise."

CHAPTER 19 BUSY BEE

"Yes, you did! And the production was brilliant. Well done! Plus, Christmas was great and I daresay you appear considerably happier."

"I am happy," Jessica acknowledged. "New Year is the perfect day for a walk." She slipped an arm through Will's, drawing him closer. Winter had stripped the trees of their foliage, lending a frosty dampness to the air. Her swollen feet tread silently on the muddy path.

William peered at her and offered, "You do look much better for it!"

"Huh!" Jessica scoffed, "I don't *feel* much better!" She pointed at her midriff. "It grew overnight – like a canonball between my legs. Shockingly uncomfortable!"

He rested a palm on her tummy and exclaimed as she yelped in surprise, making him chuckle at the exaggerated expression on her face. "That was some kick. Wow! Our baby's protesting that mummy's complaining," he suggested, and she laughed too.

Just shy of 34-weeks, these vicious baby boots, combined with painless Braxton Hicks contractions, were all normal. The obstetrician confirmed the head had descended into her pelvis, giving her lungs a break and easing her breathlessness. The reduced pressure on her stomach lessened symptoms of heartburn, which was mostly favourable news, except it had brought on that ball-between-the-legs sensation which made walking immensely difficult.

Jessica resumed her waddling, cursing each step under her breath. "How did my mother do this seven times? I'm clearly not like her in this regard."

"Oh, darling! You're doing fine," Will encouraged.

She grimaced and reserved further grumblings to herself. Honestly, she'd be hard-pressed to describe this experience with many positive adjectives. Its only redeeming feature was the phenomenal miracle of human life, which was the promised prize of every healthy pregnancy. Little else about it was pleasant. The baby was the only thing she looked forward to.

CHAPTER 20

False Alarm

Jessica scribbled the date *20th January 2001* in her diary, and wrote, *'approx 37-wks and baby could arrive any moment. Due = February 12th, but midwife says anytime from 38-wks is fair game. Also warned most first pregnancies continue beyond full-term and may sometimes require medical inducement (??) to coax baby to emerge from womb. Not sure I want that!'*

"Pfff." She blew out a silky breath and heaved her swollen form from the sofa. The phone remained pressed against her ear.

Freida was saying, "You've led such an active life I highly doubt there'll be any issues with this baby coming out. Inducement is unlikely."

"Hmm. My instincts point to a quick birth," Jessica agreed. "These Braxton Hicks contractions are getting stronger. I wonder how I'll distinguish between them and the real thing."

Freida laughed, "I'm sure you'll know when the time comes!"

Her pregnant sister snorted in disbelief, "Not so certain about that! Last week, right in the middle of the night I had such an intense contraction I swore I was in labour. Will grabbed our packed hospital bag, we dashed to Chelsea and Westminster only to be informed it was a false alarm."

Freida chuckled, "Oh, no!"

"Oh, yes! Returned home at 4 am, exhausted but unable to go back to sleep! Why do these things always happen at night?" she inquired wearily.

Fifi giggled again. "Sod's law, I suppose. Though, somehow, I doubt you've got long to wait."

Jessica cradled her huge bump, now positioned so low in her abdomen it was a wonder she could still move unassisted. She smiled wryly. "Mum will be so disappointed if this baby comes before she does."

"*Wahala*! She arrives tomorrow, right?"

"Yeah."

CHAPTER 20 — FALSE ALARM

"There's no chance of her missing the birth of her first grandchild. Imagine?!" Fifi chortled.

"I'd never live it down. The false alarm was inconvenient, but the best outcome, for sure."

Just five days after Mrs Brown's arrival in London, she'd already made a batch load of *Akara* following a special trip to nearby Shepherd's Bush market for the ingredients. Jessica didn't have the heart to reveal that her earlier symptom of a heightened sense of smell had unfortunately returned, hence her revulsion to the aroma of the fried bean patties. But, one bite of her favourite dish provoked an involuntary gagging reflex, and a corresponding tut from her mother.

"You should have told me, my dear!" she reprimanded, whilst sweeping the offending Kalabari treat away from sight. "Let's finish sorting out the baby's room," she added, referring to Jessica's recent compulsion to tidy, whereupon she'd spend hours folding and unfolding cute little onesies and doll-sized clothing.

"They're so adorable, Mum!"

"This sudden urge to spring clean is very common at the end of most pregnancies," Edith expressed knowingly. "It's your 'nesting' instinct kicking in. They claim it's not a scientifically proven phenomenon, but don't mind them! I experienced the same impulse with every single one of you. That child is soon to be born!"

Jessica gave her a tired smile.

"But you mustn't overdo it," Edith cautioned. "You should try to rest as much as you can."

"Yes, Mum, but I have to do… something."

"It's just your hormones telling you to prepare for baby busy-ness." She chuckled out loud at her own witticism. "Heh! *No be joke oh*! *Nah* serious matter. But that's why I'm here. To help you, eh?"

Jessica laughed, her mood lightened by her mother's jovial attitude and use of broken English. This will be fun, she thought. She had the greatest childbirth expert on hand to assist!

~

Jessica felt a strange, sharp twinge in her belly, something she likely would have ignored a few months ago. But now, with her pregnancy progressing unexpectedly quickly, each sensation commanded immediate attention. Tonight, the moon hung low and heavy in the sky, casting a silver glow through their bedroom window, as if to forewarn them of the tumultuous hours ahead. These were contractions. Not practice ones, but real, excruciating, son-of-a-gun spasms that threatened to rip her frame in two.

She nudged her slumbering husband, clutching her stomach as

CHAPTER 20 — FALSE ALARM

another piercing wave rippled through her, more intense than before. It was unbearable. How on earth did women do this?

William stirred immediately and turned to her, eyes widening with concern when he saw the glistening sweat on her brow. "Jessica, what's wrong?"

"I think… I think it's time," she replied, her voice barely above a whisper, betraying the fear she had kept tightly contained.

William quickly switched into his role of protector and provider. He leapt up, pulling on underpants and a shirt and jumper, then calmly helped Jessica into a robe and draped a cashmere shawl around her shoulders.

In between spasms, she gasped for breath and whispered, "Shall we wake mum?"

He shook his head. "No time, darling. We have to leave immediately. I'll send a car for her once we're at the hospital. Let's get you there." He clutched the ever-ready overnight case that had been packed weeks in advance – one of the few ways they tried to exert control over this uncontrollable process. Jessica leaned against him, and his racing heart mirrored the pounding in her ears as they hurried from the room.

They almost jumped out of their skins when they heard Edith's quiet voice in the corridor. "I couldn't sleep. Is it happening?" One glance at their taut expressions confirmed her suspicions. "*Nguania*, let's go!" She was fully dressed, clearly expecting this turn of events.

The drive to the hospital felt like an eternity and a blink all at once. Each contraction was a sharp reminder of the life-altering event about to unfold. Edith sat at the rear with her daughter, holding Jessica's hand and mopping her brow, while spewing Kalabari words of direction and comfort with every contraction. "*Nguania*, breathe slow and steady, *inate?*"

William dropped them at the entrance and rushed to park the car on nearby Hollywood Road. Mrs Brown took charge and immediately found an orderly to escort them to the Labour Ward. Once they'd checked in and strapped the expectant mother to a monitor, Edith pulled the nurse aside for a lengthy word, and whatever they were discussing seemed serious, for she appeared agitated.

"What was that all about, Mum?" Jessica asked breathlessly, feeling desperately thirsty and a tad dizzy. Will hurried to fetch her water.

Edith Brown feigned a cheerful countenance for her daughter's sake. "It's nothing, my dear. Don't worry, you hear?" Her attempt at a smile couldn't disguise her concern.

"Mum…?" Jessica's voice was firm.

The older woman hesitated. William had returned with a plastic cup and was observing them with a quizzical expression.

"I was telling the nurse…," Edith gestured towards a plumpish, brown-haired lady at the nurse's station. "I was advising her to keep a special eye on you because… I don't like the way your face looks."

CHAPTER 20 — FALSE ALARM

Jessica raised an eyebrow.

Her mother soldiered on. "It's swollen. Can you see that, William? Her face is swollen, right?" Worry had sharpened her tone.

William inspected his wife and grimaced. "Well, isn't it typical to experience swelling at this stage of pregnancy?"

Jessica found it difficult to keep track of their conversation. These blasted contractions were fast and furious; the assault on her body relentless!

Mrs Brown was speaking. "Some develop bigger noses, that sort of thing, but not *this*. Look! Even her hands and her fingers... they're swollen."

Their raised voices brought the medic to Jessica's bedside, and she'd clearly caught the tail end of the conversation. She gave a professional smile and reiterated patiently, "Like I said before, there's no need to fret. Your daughter's labour is progressing at a steady pace and is within the range of normalcy."

"*Normalcy?*" Edith Brown sounded angry. "Normal *keh*? Does this face look normal to you?"

"Well, I've never met your daughter before, so I have no idea what you'd classify as normal, but she looks perfectly healthy and..."

"Are you an expert?" She jabbed a finger aggressively. "Young lady, I have had eight children! Believe me when I say this is *not* normal.

Please, c-can we have a doctor check on her? Do some tests? I'm not sure… I-I…" Her anger suddenly dissolved into a wordless pool of helplessness.

Will placed a comforting arm around his mother-in-law. "I'll have a word with them, Aunty," he reassured her.

Will's quiet exchange with the nurse persuaded her to take a urine specimen and summon the obstetrician on call.

Dr Shah was a kind-looking gentleman, slightly balding, with a rotund middle section. His calm but urgent request for more tests sliced through their anxious reverie, a stark reminder of the fragility of their situation. He spoke in a plain, concise manner and was careful to include Jessica in the discussions. "Your urine sample shows traces of protein, and your blood pressure is a little on the high side. For anyone else it wouldn't be considered abnormal, but since your resting bp is naturally low it causes me some concern. Now, these factors in themselves may be attributed to you being in labour…," he smiled reassuringly at her, "however what perturbs me is the apparent fluid retention in your hands and face." He glanced at her legs. "And your ankles and feet, too."

William looked troubled. "So, what does this mean? Is everything ok?"

"Well, we've been monitoring your baby's heartbeat and so far, so good." Dr Shah turned back to Jessica. "You mention you've had limited movement in the past day or so?" He perused her chart.

She nodded as best she could, mid-contraction.

CHAPTER 20 — FALSE ALARM

The doctor added gently, "That might be because the poor little tyke is squashed in there and preparing to grace this big, bold world of ours!"

Jessica was quick to pick up on his choice of language. "Does that mean it's a boy?" she probed breathlessly. "If so, I'll name him Philip."

The physician laughed softly, "I didn't say that! Now, you relax and let's get this baby born."

Edith Brown did not join in the laughter. Instead, she frowned at Dr Shah. "But what exactly are you saying, Doctor? Is my daughter fine? Is my grandchild ok?"

"What I'm saying," his tone was careful, "is your daughter is suffering from pre-eclampsia."

"Eh!! Oh God! *Chineke*…"

The diagnosis of pre-eclampsia hit them like a freight train. Words like 'risk' and 'complication' swirled around them, as the sterile scent of the hospital mingled with their rising panic. Their hopeful anticipation had turned into a fog of fear.

"Yes," he continued, "and as she's in the midst of labour, we must let this run its course. Delivery is the only way to cure pre-eclampsia, so I'll administer an induction to speed up matters. If that doesn't work, we'll perform an emergency caesarian section. Bottom line, this child needs to be delivered as soon as possible." His gaze was serious, but empathetic.

"You're already eight centimetres dilated and we shouldn't have long to go, Jessica."

Jessica's insides clenched with dread. Her mind raced through the could-have-beens and what-ifs, the tension in her face a blend of agony and unspoken worry. What if something went wrong? She had a splitting headache and was in anguish. Every part of her wanted this to end. Eyes closed tight she willed it to be so. She found William's hand, gripping it with a strength that surprised them both.

"We'll get through this," he assured her, his voice steady despite the turmoil he must have felt inside.

There would be no waiting for nature to take its course – an induction was necessary.

As the drip was set up, Jessica clung to William, her lifeline amidst a sea of uncertainty. Before long she was moaning in agony from its effects. This was literally contractions on steroids, pulling Jessica deeper into a relentless cycle of pain and expectation! The hours of labour that followed were excruciating, a juxtaposition of physical endurance and emotional breakdown.

"Just keep breathing," Will urged, as he steadily rubbed her back the way they'd practiced over the previous six months of antenatal classes. They had dreamed of this moment, yet it was unraveling in ways they never could have anticipated.

The midwife was directing the process by giving clear guidance

CHAPTER 20 — FALSE ALARM

at each step. "Ok, now push, as if you're bearing down… good girl. It's crowning. That's it… yes!! The head's almost through… great… nearly there. You can do this, Jess. Don't stop. You've got this."

Finally, as dawn broke, casting a pale light over the room, Jessica pushed through the last contractions, her body exhausted but her spirit holding on to a fragile thread of hope.

The silence after the final push was deafening.

"The midwife turned to Will. "Would you like to do the honours?"

Jessica saw Will's jaw slacken as though in a daze. He was staring at their infant in the midwife's arms. Something wasn't okay.

His expression was wooden as he watched the efficient birth practitioner carefully cut and clamp the umbilical cord. Then he took a curious step towards her. Jessica swallowed. This didn't feel right. She could tell from Will's face as he peered closely at their newborn, and when he suddenly backed away with a look of absolute horror, Jessica felt the icy fingers of terror grip her beating heart.

Their baby boy was stillborn.

CHAPTER 21

Philip

Her wailing echoed throughout the ward; she was inconsolable.

Just a few short hours before, she'd felt her baby kick. The monitor confirmed a heartbeat! *What had gone wrong??*

She shifted on the hospital mattress. Her body sore. Bruised. Heaving sobs racked her beaten frame, exacerbating the agony. Not even William could penetrate the cloud of abject misery that enveloped her.

My heart is totally and completely broken, Jessica concluded.

The heartbreak had come swiftly, a dagger twisting and slicing through their world as grief crashed over them like waves on a broken shore.

This tragic event had shocked Edith Brown into a dumbfounded stupor, and she kept mumbling prayer after incomprehensible prayer in her native tongue. Fate had dashed her dreams of a gorgeous grandchild in one cruel instant, and she was apoplectic with anguish. Helpless in the face of her daughter's heartache, she could offer no rational explanation from her motherly pools of wisdom.

She explained she'd noticed the unnatural swelling of Jessica's extremities earlier that day, and by the time they'd arrived at the hospital, it had worsened. By then, it was too late. And the result? This disaster. How could she not have seen it coming? Or kicked a bigger fuss with that stupid, inexperienced nurse? Why didn't the doctor perform an emergency C-section? That might have saved her grandchild.

Once the midwife had severed and clamped the placenta, she'd rushed to summon Dr Shah to the scene. Together, they tried everything in their power to revive the stillborn, eventually giving up and accepting it was to no avail. Dr Shah regrettably confirmed that the late onset of pre-eclampsia had reduced vital blood flow to the baby, starving it of oxygen. They'd attempted to resuscitate baby Philip because they reasoned his death had happened whilst being squeezed through the birth canal,

CHAPTER 21 — PHILIP

which suggested an increased chance of him responding to their efforts.

In the end, it was William who'd let out a tormented cry to halt them. "Enough. Stop! He's dead." The blunt declaration stopped the flurry of activity bang in its tracks. And that was that.

William hung his head in a daze as Dr Shah laid a consoling hand on his hunched shoulders and commiserated gravely, "An intrapartum death is the most traumatic experience for you as parents. I'm so very sorry for your loss."

The midwife was staring at the grieving couple, seeking the proper words. "Would you like to hold your baby?" she asked tentatively.

William's body language suggested his first instinct was to decline, but when he saw a flicker of hope cross his wife's otherwise stony countenance, he promptly nodded. "Yes, please."

The nurse had swaddled Philip in a blanket and laid him across Jessica's chest. Jessica gazed at her baby boy with all the love and tenderness of a new mother, cooing and rocking him from side to side. William wrapped his arms around his wife as she cradled their infant, and the trio swayed to-and-fro for what seemed an eternity. Jessica's tears mingled with William's silent sobs. In that moment, their lives shattered and rebuilt in a framework of shared sorrow and unspoken promises. They held onto each other tightly, as if their combined love could somehow bridge the vast chasm of their loss as they held the lifeless form of their beloved son.

The childbirth practitioner cleared her throat, loath to interrupt this sacred moment, but it had to be done.

It proved difficult to pry the lifeless child from Jessica's clinging grip, and that was when she began to wail, "My baby… Philip… my Philip. My baby…," she sobbed as she repeated the name she'd only recently given their newborn. The heart-wrenching howl from the profound depths of her being sounded inhuman. Her hands tore at her clothes and she beat herself with her fists, as though to pummel the pain from her system. She couldn't survive this torture. It was too much to bear.

The obstetrician administered medication to control her hypertension and the distraught couple returned to their house in Holland Park, infant car seat empty and faces devoid of emotion. Drained. William, who'd been stalwart during the ordeal, crumbled the moment they were back in familiar surroundings, and looked grateful for his mother-in-law, who acted as something of a buffer between husband and wife. He preferred to grieve in private, and Jessica often heard him in the dead of night, weeping tears of hopeless abandonment in their master bathroom. He admitted that the indescribable sense of loss had come as a surprise to him; that he imagined men as rather removed from the reality of childbirth, but this harrowing incident had knocked from him every ounce of fortitude. She once crept into their ensuite to comfort him, and he'd said with great empathy, "If I'm feeling this dejected and heartbroken, what must *you* be going through?"

CHAPTER 21   PHILIP

But Jessica didn't want his pity. The doctor had cautioned them that pre-eclampsia was an unfathomable condition, largely inexplicable. Nonetheless, she heaped blame upon herself; she had continued to work well into her third trimester and hadn't heeded the warnings.

"I felt fine, Will. Perfectly healthy," she wept. "And when I got tired, I'd rest."

Not strictly true, but William didn't dare contradict her. "It wasn't your fault, or anyone else's. Just one of those things."

"But com… complications don't happen to someone like me. I'm only nineteen, for Goodness' sake. It doesn't make sense!"

Will took her hand. "Not in the slightest, but this tragedy could strike anybody, Jess. Researchers are still trying to learn more about what causes stillbirth. You can't blame yourself." He tried to reason with her, reminding her none of the prenatal appointments had picked up any issues with the baby or her blood pressure. He reiterated the doctor's comment that this had been a last-minute complication, negating the possibility of identifying it earlier, but Jessica maintained her stance of self-loathing.

Upon reading information in medical journals, they learned other contributory factors for stillbirth include women who've never given birth before, those younger than twenty or older than thirty-five, and black women. Apparently, black women are at higher risk compared to others.

This last finding elicited a disparaging tut from Edith Brown, who retorted, "Hmmm! Black women, *keh*?!" she kissed her teeth. "I wonder where on earth these *Oyinbos* get their research. Honestly!" She sounded unimpressed. Turning to her daughter, she stated categorically, "Listen to me. This terrible experience does not define your future, you understand? You will go forth and multiply when the season is right. You're young and healthy. Stillbirth is rare. Please! Don't believe any nonsense about *black women*. You need time to heal physically and emotionally, that's all. Just try again when you're ready, you hear?"

"But it's so difficult, Mum. I still feel pregnant. It's… it's these breasts. They're so sore."

"I know, my child." Her mother looked genuinely sympathetic. "They are producing milk with no release. *Pele oh!* Sorry."

"And I can't even take anything to stop it because of this bloody pre-eclampsia. So frustrating!" Jessica tucked her knees in a foetal position, hugging the cushion tighter.

"The doctor warned such medication would be dangerous. But it'll pass, my dear. This, too, shall pass." Edith Brown had regained her fire and faith, and her conviction provided some measure of comfort.

～

The funeral was a tiny affair – literally. The coffin was tiny, the hole in the ground was tiny, and there were very few people in attendance. Jessica had been adamant she wanted no-one there, but Mrs Brown

CHAPTER 21 🌴 PHILIP

persuaded them it was good karma to give this baby a proper send-off.

As they laid Philip Armstrong-Bell to rest, Jessica and William clung to each other and wept.

CHAPTER 22

Intervention

Edith Brown sensed her season in London had drawn to a close. Her gentle acceptance of the grieving couple's wish for solitude was immediate. Even William's mother had offered support, but they declined that too. Jessica and William craved isolation, a sanctuary for their all-encompassing grief.

Jessica loathed her post-baby bump and the relentless fact that she still looked bloody pregnant! Normally, a woman's uterus contracts after giving birth, assisted by a breastfeeding baby's sucking action. Her mother had often joked about 'natural liposuction' being God's way of ensuring the stomach shrank. But not for Jessica. Her swollen breasts, aching and engorged, hankered for a newborn to feed. The irony stung bitterly; she had been so fixated with returning to her pre-pregnancy physique, and now there was no baby. She was free to eat or starve without consequence. No new life depended on her nourishment. She could waste away, and it wouldn't matter!

The sting of irony wasn't the only bitter taste in her mouth – her throat was sore from a recent purge, and her eyes were shadows of red from all the crying.

William, on the other hand, devoured food in alarming quantities, attempting to fill an emptiness no meal could satisfy. The coveted six-pack once emblematic of his disciplined lifestyle had surrendered to a burgeoning belly. Jessica averted her gaze, suppressing judgement or repulsion, for despair was a shared burden.

Emily Dunn, aware of their private agony, gently suggested bereavement counseling. "I have an excellent recommendation for you, someone who helped *me*, in fact."

Jessica arched a weary brow. "What d'you mean, helped you? Did you lose…"

Emily nodded solemnly. "Yes. Twelve years ago. Eight months in utero." She pursed her lips briefly, before adding, "Few people are aware."

Jessica placed a hand over Emily's. "That must've been dreadful.

CHAPTER 22 INTERVENTION

I'm so sorry. At St. Ignatius you mentioned how your pregnancy altered your career's trajectory, but I didn't realise you'd *lost* your child?"

Emily gave a sad nod. "It was devastating. They had to induce me to deliver a stillborn baby. And Edwin, my ex, couldn't handle it. The tragedy destroyed our marriage. Without that counselor, I might never have recovered. She literally saved me. She could do the same for you."

Jessica rose and wrapped tight arms around Emily. "Thank you for sharing this with me." Her voice caught in her throat. "Somehow explains your reaction to my pregnancy; why you've been so protective."

The women embraced, one drawing comfort from the other.

William balked at the idea of counseling. "Nope. I come from steady stock and we Armstrong-Bells frown upon that sort of thing. Surely, we can handle the grief ourselves? Time heals, as my mother always says. We have each other, Jess. Our love will see us through."

"But darling, that's the point. An outsider brings objectivity. This isn't the moment for your stiff-upper-lip, British nonsense." Jessica, sitting upright in bed with an empty mug of chamomile tea, glowered at him. "Your fear of opening up is ridiculous."

William switched off his bedside lamp to underscore his refusal. "No. Absolutely not. Don't need anyone telling me what I should feel or do."

Jessica didn't respond. She shook her head in exasperation and turned off her reading light. The dark ceiling offered no answers as she finally succumbed to the escape of dreamless sleep, her only respite from the daily grip of conflicting emotions and doubt.

~

Dear J, it's been a month since we buried Philip, and I'm sinking further into an abyss of self-deprecation. I detest how I look, hate how I sound, and can't trust my thoughts. All Will and I do is cling to each other like lost souls. There's nobody who can provide the comfort we need.

Her sorrow crystallized as she penned these words, prompting fresh tears. It was a cathartic exercise, highlighting their descent down the slippery dark slope of co-dependent destruction. Hours later, she remained curled up on the settee, ballpoint in hand, overwhelmed by all she had to say. Amidst the backdrop of unexpressed emotions, she heard the ding of the doorbell and voices in the corridor which caused her to glance up.

Striding purposefully through the double doors was Freida, her smile unwavering. Fifi's arrival was a welcome intervention. Jessica catapulted herself into her sister's arms, clinging with the fervour of a starving child. Freida held her close, her silence potent with meaning.

William peered in, surprised to find the sisters standing in silent embrace; no tears, no words, no sound at all. A shadow crossed his face,

CHAPTER 22 — INTERVENTION

and he averted his eyes, perhaps feeling he was intruding on a deeply private moment. His dejected form underlined the immense loneliness welling up within him. Jessica ignored him, surrendering to the embrace, allowing her tension to dissolve. To an onlooker, it might have appeared almost spiritual and her husband stumbled while retreating, clearing his throat as he crept from the room.

The girls pulled apart.

"I'm worried about him, Fif," Jessica confessed. "He follows me around like a shadow, and he's becoming unhealthy."

"Hmm, look who's talking," Fifi chided. "You don't seem so great yourself. Are you even eating?"

"I have no appetite," Jessica replied bleakly.

Freida shrugged. "You still need to eat." Her eyes narrowed with empathy. "What's done, is done, Jess. You can't unscramble eggs. Just take it one step at a time. Before you know it, you'll feel normal again."

They sat facing each other.

Jessica's frown deepened. "I'm just so confused. Angry and sad and…" Her voice broke.

"And you mustn't beat yourself up." Freida grabbed Jessica's arm. "Promise me." She spotted the journal on the coffee table and pointed knowingly. "Writing will help you come to terms with everything. Look after yourself first or you'll be no use to William."

"But…" Jessica blinked back tears.

"No buts. He's a grown man… he'll pull through. Give him space."

After a stretch of silence, Jessica rubbed her blood-shot eyes. "How long are you staying?"

"Till Saturday. Five days is all I have."

"Gosh! They work you so hard at Weill Cornell. Thanks for coming, Fifi. I'd hate for you to jeopardize your tenure there."

Freida hugged her. "Family comes first. No question."

Freida's unexpected visit breathed fresh air into their sorrow-stricken environment. With Spring approaching, life felt slightly more hopeful. It's difficult to be surrounded by new blooms and budding flowers and remain miserable, Jessica thought. She mused over her sister's words: *happiness is a choice. It's about choosing how to live each day despite negative circumstances. Wallowing in misery serves no real purpose.*

Dear J, Fifi showed me a simple yet profound truth: We must move forward and live our lives. We're young and can try again. But not now. Not yet. Maybe someday…

Over afternoon tea, Emily Dunn revisited the idea of counseling. "It really helps to process the pain; compartmentalize it."

"I'm sure it does," Jessica agreed. "But as I mentioned, therapy isn't Will's cup of tea."

Both women laughed at the pun, lightening the mood. It felt wonderful

CHAPTER 22 — INTERVENTION

to laugh. Jessica was still smiling as Will walked into the conservatory.

"What's so funny?" He grinned and raised an eyebrow.

Jessica glanced at Emily, who stifled a giggle. "Nothing," she responded cheekily. "Just talking about you."

"Oh, really?" William smiled, catching their good humour. "Not sure I want to know, then."

Emily rose, taking their banter as her cue to leave. She whispered to Jessica, "I know you have a long hike ahead, but this is a great start."

Jessica felt it, too, but wasn't sure she had the stamina to support William on their uphill journey to recovery.

PALM TREES IN THE STORM

CHAPTER 23

Time to move on

"He's just so bloody needy," Jessica's voice quivered, rising to a high-pitched whine. "I can't breathe or think. It's suffocating!"

"Jessica!" Edith Brown's tone was sharp with disapproval. "This is your husband we're talking about. The father of your child."

Jessica drew a shuddering breath, but her mum soldiered on. "Yes, Jess, the father of your child, and he is hurting, too. I understand you're in pain. Losing a baby is abysmal… for the mother especially, but also for him. Healing takes time, and grief is difficult for men to handle too."

The truth of her mother's words hit hard. Despite not enduring the physical agony of childbirth, William was suffering in equal measure. Sometimes, his empathy was so intense it seemed he shared her pain – a pain so acute it felt like running into the razor edge of a knife every single day. And yet, she rejected his pity. She welcomed the hurt. She deserved to suffer.

After the birth, the midwife had offered to photograph the newborn, even drawing the outline of his hand and his tiny footprints to create memories. Initially too distraught to care, these bits of memorabilia had later become cherished keepsakes, giving both her and Will a focus for their mourning.

Thankfully, her body no longer served as a reminder of the cruel loss it had endured; engorged breasts were now a thing of the past.

She placed the photos back in the baby album, her thoughts momentarily quieting, and returned her attention to her mother.

"*Why me*, Mum?" Her voice was barely a whisper.

Edith sighed before answering. "Sometimes these events are unexplainable. Just life. But I believe if you couldn't cope the good Lord wouldn't have allowed it to happen. You are young and strong. Remember what the doctor told you? The post-mortem confirmed no genetic abnormality and no problem with the placenta or the baby's growth. His verdict was that your body is 'a perfectly healthy vessel, able to carry to full term with no complications.' Isn't that what he said? Take comfort in those words and

CHAPTER 23 — TIME TO MOVE ON

leave the *wahala* behind. It's time to heal, Jessica."

The doctor's words had sounded reassuring months ago, but they did little to ease her ongoing despair or quell the fear that had settled over her like a dark cloud.

"It was *my* fault though, Mum. *I did this.* Everyone warned me against overdoing it – the dancing – and I wouldn't listen. I…"

"Hey! Stop this nonsense, right now. What are you saying? You think you're God? That it was in your power? Young lady, there are some situations *we* cannot control. You hear me?"

"But maybe if…"

"There are no maybes. You weren't over-dancing, or 'over-doing' anything. You *did not kill your baby,* Jessica. *Inate?* I saw you – you appeared fine, so let's quit this, okay? Drop it and move on."

When the doctor had suggested trying for another pregnancy, Jessica had flinched. The very idea filled her with terror. She remained adamantly opposed to it, even after her hopeful spouse expressed his belief that turning their focus on trying for a new baby might help them heal. It wasn't the ideal moment.

And today, hearing her mother's words, her resentment resurfaced – how could they tell her it was "time to move on" when they hadn't endured it themselves? The insensitivity made her angry – furious even. Hot tears welled up in her eyes.

"Mum," she steadied the quiver in her voice, "I've got to rest. Speak to you next week." She hung up abruptly, not waiting for a goodbye.

No one knows how it feels, Jessica grumbled internally. *Nobody understands what I've been through. I had to register my baby's birth AND death on the same day, after carrying him for nearly ten months – that's nearly a whole frickin' year – and they tell me I need to move on after a few weeks?? It makes me furious, J. I literally want to scream all the time!*

It's hard to accept Philip's gone. He looked so perfect, his little face, his hands, his feet. I still don't understand. How could this happen to me? Am I to blame? Will was right. I secretly felt invincible and believed nothing could go wrong. But it did.

﹋

Two months later, William broached the subject again.

"Jess…?" His voice was tentative.

"Hmmm?" She was flicking through a magazine.

"It's been almost four months since we lost him." He paused. "And I expect… it-it's a bit like falling off a stallion… you know… I mean, the sooner you climb back on, the better, right? That's the way to recover. And, who knows, you might actually enjoy getting back on… the horse?" His eyes held the glaze of sheepish uncertainty.

Jessica frowned at her husband. A horse analogy – really??

CHAPTER 23   TIME TO MOVE ON

But the lost look in his eyes reminded her just how much she loved him. She took his hand and they slid to the ground in a blubbering heap. Uncontrollable sobs racked their bodies. When they finally regained their composure, she allowed him to kiss and hold her, knowing she couldn't continue to reject his advances.

She stroked the rough stubble on his cheek. "We'll get through this together, my love. I promise."

William's reddened eyes met her earnest gaze. "Let's do it. The counseling."

"Are you sure? You said…"

"I'm positive. It'll help us and I'm… I'm ready."

Jessica hugged him tighter.

⁓

"So, how are you feeling today?" The counsellor glanced from one to the other, then shook her head. "No," she urged, "don't look at your husband's reaction. This process is individual, and it's okay to be at different stages, even as a couple. Your experience of loss was unique to you. So, I'll ask again, how do *you* feel?"

Jessica sighed. "Not so shitty, I guess. Better than I have in weeks. Exercised this morning."

"That is *very* promising." Jane Wilcox smiled. "And you, William.

How are you?"

Will glanced at his slightly distended gut with a wry grin. "Not bad, all things considered. Plan to pop into the office later, so…" He shrugged.

"Sounds as if you're both making progress. And I'd encourage you to continue. Exercise. Work. Resume normal life." Jane's astute gaze held Jessica's. "Try to get the nourishment you deserve. And soon you'll wake up feeling exactly that – nourished."

Will pulled his wife closer to him on the couch and wrapped a solid arm around her. She rested her forehead against his expansive chest and exhaled deeply.

They were finally reaping the benefits of grief counselling. William returned to work and Jessica resumed dance practice. While the pain of their loss would never completely disappear, perhaps it could become more bearable with each passing day.

CHAPTER 24

Let's Try Again!

The music was on full blast, and Jessica gladly surrendered to its alluring beat. The depressive cloud of sadness that had overshadowed her was evaporating. A new maturity and depth permeated her movements. Though she sensed William enter the home studio, she remained focused on her alignment in the mirror. Gone was the apprehension that had once plagued her early days at RAD.

"You are different," Will observed, his voice reflecting genuine curiosity.

Jessica's gaze met his. "I am more optimistic."

"And it shows. Your form exudes a new kind of confidence."

She shrugged nonchalantly. "Got nothing left to lose. Might as well give it my utmost."

Will's eyes narrowed in concern. "Yes, but surely you need to rest, too?"

She waved a dismissive hand, explaining to a bemused William, "In ballet, flexibility is key. You break yourself to *bend* yourself. But you daren't stop – because the moment you miss a session of training, it becomes a struggle to catch up and regain the progress your body's achieved. It's tough! And even tougher for me because my physique isn't naturally lean and flexible." She saw the disbelief on his face, and continued, "As a sprinter with explosive athletic muscles, I've fought to develop this flexibility. And I intend to maintain it."

Will studied his wife with admiration. "But when I watch you, it looks so easy."

"That's the tricky part; to make it *seem* effortless. Haven't told you this, but my feet literally used to bleed from pointe work in the beginning." Jessica laughed at Will's horrified expression. "It's a fine line between pressing just hard enough and pushing your body over the brink, so it retaliates and tightens anew. Which is why daily practice is essential. You quickly recognize that pain is your constant companion in dance – and you learn to live with it. Channel it into better dancing."

Will was nodding. "Grit and dedication are qualities you have in

CHAPTER 24   LET'S TRY AGAIN!

spades, my darling."

Jessica chortled and executed a graceful pirouette. "Dancing's my only passion. Well, before I met *you*," she teased.

"Yeah, yeah! I realise I can't compete." He lifted his hands in mock defeat. Though he was joking, she glimpsed a shadow of uncertainty flicker across his green eyes. Rather than feed the insecurity, she chose to ignore it.

As she listened for her cue, she could feel her pulse beating to the rhythm of the drums; her breath came in short, quick bursts as she fought for control. At the familiar cadence of violins, she unraveled her coiled form and leapt into the air in a fluid movement, limbs extended gracefully; her frame suspended for an impossible second, before landing nimbly on her toes. Each twist, turn and reach became a conscious effort to release every last shred of inhibition – an attempt to shed all remnants of grief.

Jessica was an intense and fearless performer, willing to exploit her strength and vulnerability in equal measure. She concluded with a rapid twirl, spiraling like a spinning top, until she finally collapsed in a dramatic heap to the eruption of ecstatic applause. The discerning audience rose in ovation, some with tearful expressions.

"That was magnetic, Jess!" Ms Dunn beamed with pride. "Time appears to have reinforced your inner resilience. Absolutely stunning!"

Jessica's large, sorrowful eyes held a steely glint. "I'm determined, Emily. Determined to win. No more silly, self-conscious constraints."

She scanned the crowd for William. He often attended her performances and wept proudly alongside fellow spectators, mesmerised by his wife's incredible talent. Despite their years together, Jessica still experienced butterflies when she knew her husband would be among the onlookers. His praise was the only one she truly valued.

He had meandered his way backstage and enveloped his exhausted spouse in a tight hug. "Wow, that was really something. When you crumbled at the end, I thought it was real for a moment. You were pushing so hard it was both fascinating and frightening to watch."

She simply smiled, knowing he'd be alarmed to discover he wasn't far off the truth. Her obsession with perfection drove her to the very limits of human endurance – until she ached with fatigue and teetered on the verge of collapse, but would not break. If a routine felt difficult, that's when she'd push harder, constantly striving to surpass her own ability. It made her feel alive. It also meant she had found another outlet for her personal loathing and could keep her bulimia at bay.

≈

Jessica's relationship with William had turned a corner. One lazy Saturday morning, she snuggled against him and whispered, "It makes sense, sweetheart. I get it."

CHAPTER 24 🌴 LET'S TRY AGAIN!

He murmured sleepily into her hair, "Get what?"

She rubbed her chin against his rough stubble. "Why… you are you."

"You're speaking in riddles," he mumbled, half-asleep.

"I get how your upbringing affected you and influenced the man you are today." (*And why you possess a ridiculous fear of rejection*, she wanted to add, but didn't.)

"Everyone's childhood affects them, Einstein." His dry tone suggested he was losing patience with this unwelcome interruption to his lazy lie-in.

"I'm serious." Jessica sat up. "Your parents sent you to boarding school at five, correct?"

She ignored his grunt and pressed on. "Which probably made you uncertain of their love…" She'd captured William's attention, and her voice took on an urgency. "It's no surprise this anxiety has infiltrated your intimate relationships, including ours."

William was staring straight ahead. "So, a few sessions with a therapist and you have me all pegged, huh!?"

"Hey, no reason to be offended – only trying to comprehend it. Don't bite my head off!"

"Now look who's sounding annoyed. And *you* raised this bloody subject!"

Jessica flung off the covers and rose. "Ugh! I should've known better than to discuss anything vaguely emotional with you always playing the avoidance game. I have to be honest, Will! I find you…" She paused.

"What? You find me *what*? Spit it out. Go on."

"Claustrophobic! There, I've said it. Sometimes, I can't breathe. You suffocate me. Always so… *needy*. Ever since…" She groaned. "Listen. This is me desperate to understand it. To understand you."

Will was quiet. "What are you saying? That you've stopped loving me? That you don't want this anymore?"

"Bloody hell, that's a massive jump! Of course not. I mean your insecurity and fear of… I dunno… abandonment, or whatever, is getting in the way. You often ask me *why* I love you. And my reply never changes. 'Because I do.' There's my honest answer. I wish you'd believe it and that it would assuage any doubts." She gazed at him earnestly.

He hauled her into his arms, holding her silently for a solid minute. His voice was croaky when he replied, "Sorry, I got defensive. Your analysis isn't wrong. I did crave closeness as a child. And, when we met… I guess I put my hopes in starting a family together. A sort of… safety net to guarantee you'd never leave me."

"What… why would you imagine I'd ever leave you? I adore you, William Armstrong-Bell!"

"I know you do, but fear is irrational. And compounded with grief, hmm! Let's just say the death of our baby flung that assurance out the

CHAPTER 24 — LET'S TRY AGAIN!

window and triggered my worries."

"Yes, I can see that," Jessica agreed, nuzzling his nose with hers. "Thank goodness for therapy, eh?" she mocked.

His light-hearted guffaw reminded her of the charming guy she'd married.

~

2001 had drawn to a close.

Jessica hurriedly fled the Harley Street clinic and hopped into a black cab.

"Hi, darling. I'm home," she called, hanging her winter coat on the hook in the corridor.

William emerged from his study. "How was it? Everything good?"

She avoided her husband's scrutiny by rummaging through her bag. "Oh, fine – usual yearly check-up." After a quick peck on his stubbled cheek, she rushed to the bathroom, locking the door behind her. Retrieving the clinic pamphlet entitled *'Intrauterine Device (IUD) Aftercare'*, she quickly read the instructions, then tucked it away.

William had been waiting outside the locked loo. "So, everything's dandy and we can try again?"

She shook her head decisively. "Uh-uh, I'm on a roll, darling. I've regained my figure and am happy to be dancing again. I'm not ready to repeat the *wahala* of pregnancy – not yet, anyway. You understand, right?"

William's response remained the same. Of course, he understood. He didn't wish to press the issue and was grateful they'd rediscovered their sexual rapport. He jokingly mentioned he hoped she was as fertile as her mother and might *accidentally* fall pregnant.

When alone, Jessica ripped the IUD leaflet into several pieces and threw it into the fireplace. This was the first secret she kept from William.

≈

Jessica stared at the date on the calendar with uneasy restlessness. *25th January 2002*. Mere days before the anniversary of Philip's passing.

"Would you like us to travel to London?"

"No, Daddy. We're marking this birthday as a memorial and final goodbye with no actual service. A simple, private acknowledgement."

"I see. You sound unconvinced."

Jessica sighed, her stomach churning in nervous anticipation of the ominous event. "According to our counselor, there are no rights or wrongs if we both agree. But the very prospect of revisiting the pain makes me quite ill. I haven't discussed my reservations with Will because I think he's actually looking forward to it. He says it'll allow for a bigger step towards recovery."

CHAPTER 24 — LET'S TRY AGAIN!

"Your William is right. It is an opportunity to heal. Difficulties are part of daily existence – but you will overcome this. You're strong enough. Remember, when you search for the teaching in the crisis, the crisis dissipates somehow. Don't waste it by ignoring the lesson."

"But what could I possibly learn from this tragedy?"

"That life doesn't necessarily flow as planned, my dear. We must have the wisdom and resilience of a palm tree and the flexibility to bend through our storms. Once it's over, the palm stands upright afresh, sometimes stronger than before. And you can too."

The day arrived and passed without the drama and crippling sentiment she had feared. A stillness pervaded the atmosphere as they stood side by side in the chilly, damp graveyard. Jessica held a white flower arrangement, tied with blue satin. She knelt to run her fingers along the edge of the smooth stone, catching lingering droplets of rain, then kissed the wreath and laid it down. Rising slowly, her mournful countenance met William's, then drifted back to Philip's tiny grave. Her husband wrapped an arm around her pulling her close; forehead to forehead, nose to nose. Both lowered their gaze for the longest minute, breathing in and out, then refocused on the granite headstone one last time.

It was empowering to acknowledge Philip as a human soul they had lost, and she clasped Will's hand tightly. There were no tears – just extreme tenderness and overwhelming affection for their little angel and for each other. Even so, that loss had created a void inside Jessica; an emptiness she was certain could never be filled.

CHAPTER 25

Out and About with the Media

"Mmnn-Mmmn-Mmmmn!" Annabel's suggestive moans imitated something far naughtier than mere culinary delight. Jessica burst into laughter, her friend's dramatic portrayal of gustatory pleasure drawing amused glances from surrounding tables. Annabel's golden locks shimmered under the restaurant lights, complementing her infectious smile – a charm that had cemented their friendship months ago during the theatre production of 'Knighthood'.

In 'Knighthood', they moved audiences with their modern twist on the classic tale of chivalry and romance. The damsel-in-distress had dual personalities – one, dark and sensuous; the other, light and virtuous – roles played to exquisite perfection by Jessica and Annabel, respectively. Annabel's work ethic mirrored Jessica's fervour for her craft, ensuring their instant bond. Despite its overtones of political incorrectness, 'Knighthood' became a raging success of unprecedented proportions.

"I'm impressed by your characterization of Greselda's virtue. Pretty darned flawless," Jessica had complimented during their early rehearsals.

Annabel's laugh was contagious. "Look who's talking! *You* are frickin sex on legs! Girl, I mean, damn!! Never thought it was possible to express soooo much with one's body."

She flashed another megawatt smile and Jessica was hooked.

Their banter was easy, flowing naturally into shared drinks and deep conversations. In no time, they were inseparable, often chaperoned by Emily, their ever-efficient manager.

Annabel was postulating, "He's afraid if she surpasses him, she'll leave. The poor fellow doesn't understand this chic will love him no matter what." Her delivery was casual as she helped herself to another forkful of watermelon and duck salad. "Hmmm, sooooo good." She directed her nod of approval at Emily, who'd made the menu selection. "The mint truly enhances its flavour!"

CHAPTER 25   OUT AND ABOUT WITH THE MEDIA

Emily wobbled her head in agitation at the oft-discussed topic. "Precisely! I've been saying the same thing for weeks. It's obvious, Jess. He's insecure... maybe you two need some special alone time."

"Mmnn," Annabel agreed, with a naughty grin. "Go to Babington House or somewhere remote, rekindle your passion – remind him how much you fancy him." She flicked her eyebrows up in quick succession, then puckered her lips in a kissing sound.

Jessica suppressed a smile. "Guys, he *knows* I adore him... it's all in his head." She turned to Emily, exasperated. "And when, exactly, would I find the space for this 'special alone time'? We're in the middle of a brilliant production, Ems, swamped with interviews. I don't need any extra stress." (Spurred by her counterpart's easy friendliness with their manager, Jessica, too, had taken to calling her Ems.)

Emily came to William's defence. "Hey, steady on. He supports you, Jess; you know he does. He's simply being a man..."

"A man who needs his woo-man to show him some luurrvve." Annabel interjected with a wink, attempting a Jamaican accent and triggering another round of laughter from Jessica.

Curious eyes of other restaurant goers cast surreptitious glances at the lively trio.

Their visibility had skyrocketed, a sign of rising stardom. In interviews, they referred to each other as "Vanilla and Chocolate", much to the audience's delight. The moniker stuck, and one newspaper likened them to a magnum ice cream – creamy whiteness on the inside with chocolatey smoothness on the outside. Such abysmal, corny descriptions were, of course, spoken in jest, but they did the trick. Beloved by the public, they were fast becoming a household name. Jessica's dark skin contrasted beautifully with Annabel's fair complexion, an irresistible pairing that captivated fans and media alike.

As twenty-one-year-olds in their heyday, they openly reveled in such recognition. And on this sunny day in August 2002, the host had seated the three women at a prime table in Notting Hill's elite eatery, E&O, known for its star-studded sightings and for drawing a slick, well-heeled crowd. E&O had become the new hotspot, frequented by models, movie-stars and musicians, and the ever-present paparazzi showed up in full force to document and disseminate who was lunching with whom and over which bottle of wine. The fickle-mindedness of with-it Londoners (Jessica included herself in this description) meant they were always on the alert for the next best thing, and the glory days of former-favourite 192 Notting Hill were sadly unsalvageable. The launch of E&O, with its enticing cocktails, eclectic Asian food and incredible ambience, cemented the demise of that once adored celebrity-sanctuary in the trendy, bohemian neighbourhood.

Emily was regarding the two girls, her brows furrowed in thought.

"What's brewing in that brain of yours, Ems?" Jessica asked with a cautious smile.

CHAPTER 25 OUT AND ABOUT WITH THE MEDIA

Emily glanced around and lowered her voice. "Not yet certain … said I needed to chat with you first…"

Annabel's impatient gesture egged her on.

"It looks like the network might offer you two a prime-time slot…"

Both girls squealed their delight.

Emily motioned for them to heed onlookers and lower their voices. "Sshhh, it isn't yet confirmed… we're still in discussions, but it looks positive." She beamed. "This will elevate your brand to a whole 'nother level, and…" She left the sentence hanging, her eyes shining with anticipation.

Jessica clasped her hands in unbridled excitement. "You mean they liked the pilot?"

"Absolutely loved it. They did mention switching to 'Chocolate and Vanilla' – said it has a better ring to it – but that's neither here nor there. The key thing is they want you. Your show is unique and it's gonna be *huge*." She smiled. "I'm also scouting networks in LA… maybe taking it global."

She was on a roll. The more she spoke, the more enlivened she got, and it was Jessica's turn to remind her they were out and about with little privacy.

Leaning forward, eyes sparkling, Emily continued in hushed tones, "The nation knows you both – as an actress, and a phenomenal dancer. This show will reveal you're not only attractive and talented, but intelligent, witty, funny…," she was counting these attributes on her fingers. "And dispel the stupid myth that beauty and brains are mutually exclusive – the ridiculous stereotype of the sexy, black temptress and the gorgeous, dumb blonde. Girls, we're changing the narrative." Her enthusiasm was infectious.

Annabel raised a hand to summon their server. "May we have a bottle of Moet and three glasses, please?" She observed her companions' stunned faces with cool indifference. "What?" she asked with a shrug. "We're celebrating, aren't we? Sod it!"

Jessica could only shake her head, adopting Annabel's airy attitude. "Sod it!" became her mantra for life's complexities.

Her mother's wisdom echoed in her mind: "If it doesn't affect your destiny, don't waste your energy on it!" It was this philosophy that guarded Jessica against the pitfalls of sudden fame. Despite Emily's warnings about the media's unscrupulous treacheries, Jessica maintained her unfazed demeanour, navigating both negative and positive publicity with effortless grace and an insouciant indifference. She projected the image of a confident twenty-something-year-old who shunned the need for validation. Attempts by journalists to stir scandal barely ruffled her.

"Even if it gets to you, don't show them that it does. Laugh it off," Jessica advised Annabel, hoping to imbue her with the same empowering beliefs and skillful manipulation of this luminary-game she'd mastered, conscious their effectiveness as a duo depended on their strength as individuals. She daren't risk her partner caving into the pressures of stardom and jeopardizing their success.

"But it's a bloody lie!" Annabel protested, slapping a tabloid on the counter. "I didn't sleep with that footballer... eewww! As if! I'm not so desperate!!!" Her tone was outraged and indignant.

"Of course not," Jessica appeased. "*You* know you didn't, so who cares what they write? They'll say anything to sell papers."

Annabel wasn't easily placated. "But it makes me look like a slut!"

"No," Jessica countered, "It makes you *sound* like a slut... you could never *look* like a slut." She laughed, trying to inject humour into the situation. "Remember who you are, darling. Besides, journalists come and go. But we – you and I – are here to stay... as long as we maintain our focus and don't let them affect us."

William entered, catching the tail end of the conversation. "I must agree with my wife's wise counsel," he remarked, extreme amusement in his voice. "Imagine, Annabel, it could be worse. What if they said he rejected you?" He scrunched his face in mock horror. "This way, you're seen as a woman who can get any man she wants. You know, silver lining and all that."

Annabel rolled her eyes, and Jessica giggled, smiling at her husband. She liked how he could slot in with effortless ease. As a married woman, she faced fewer rumours, most involving minor character assassinations.

"Jessica Brown is over-confident… may be described as entitled."

"There's a thin line between confidence and arrogance, and Ms Brown falls into the latter category."

"Whilst the success of popular chat show 'Chocolate and Vanilla' is undisputed, and its viewership unparalleled, the apparent rivalry between its co-stars might, one day, be its downfall."

This last piece was an entirely unfounded fabrication, based on a brief on-screen altercation, which was just as quickly forgotten. But not by reporters. They'd grabbed a hold of the fiasco as dogs might meaty bones and replayed the scene over and over, even getting body language experts to conclude the ladies hated each other.

"But this couldn't be further from the truth," Annabel defended. "They're painting us as bitches, but we're practically best friends!"

Jessica's confidence shielded her from the media storm. Even though the gossip wasn't always kind, her indifference became a symbol of strength, endearing her even more to the public.

She winked at Annabel. "Let's exploit the interest. Give them conflict to chew on, keep them curious."

And so, they did. Their staged altercations captivated and entertained, solidifying their status. The media frenzy intensified and the duo played their roles to perfection for the paparazzi. They once created a scene by shoving each other in a feigned physical squabble, drawing a stunned

CHAPTER 25   OUT AND ABOUT WITH THE MEDIA

crowd, who stared in disbelief as they watched the drama unfold. As predicted, every newspaper published its salacious version of their volatile relationship.

Finally, it seemed, Jessica's lifelong dream of international stardom was within grasp.

CHAPTER 26

Going Global

Lady Armstrong-Bell wasn't quite sure how to perceive her daughter-in-law's meteoric rise to stardom. Firmly of the opinion that the fairer sex is better suited to cooking and needlework (with the occasional power lunch for the sake of variety), she believed philanthropy to be the only acceptable toil.

While she begrudgingly admired Jessica's breathtaking performance at the Royal Albert Hall in the spring, the dancer's foray into television felt garish and unbecoming to Philippa, who was quick to express her disdain to her son.

"Goodness, Mother, it's just a television chat show – not some ghastly, sordid affair. And Jess is extraordinary at it!" William's patience was wearing thin from his mother's ceaseless critiques.

"Well, I'm not so convinced," Philippa retorted with a haughty tilt of her chin. "We could certainly describe most topics they discuss as 'sordid'!"

"Oh Mother, come on! It's called humour and wit. Interesting. Funny. And immensely successful!" William's exasperation was evident.

Philippa tutted in disdain. "Being disseminated in every tabloid paper could classify as success, I suppose … but it hardly refutes the base nature of the show's premise; pitting fair against dark beauty to get men salivating over them… salivating over your *wife*, William, like some exotic prize."

Suppressing a pang of jealousy, William raised a hand. "You're being ridiculous, Mother. Sex sells. They are stunning, intelligent women, and the public adores that combination."

Lady Armstrong-Bell fell silent momentarily, but soon resumed her tirade. "Her stature as a professional ballerina is one thing. But this gaudy TV stuff, is quite another. I do wish you could see that, darling."

William shook his head in despair.

His mother seemed bent on pursuing her stance. "And now you tell me she's across the Atlantic? With you here *alone*?" She saw his

CHAPTER 26 — GOING GLOBAL

bewildered expression and added, "Naturally, we're thrilled to have you to ourselves, of course we are! Your father and I are delighted you could spend the bank holiday weekend with us, but how on earth do you tolerate your spouse gallivanting in pursuit of… what did you call it again? '… Going global'," she sounded disgusted, "… So the *program* can go global…? Huh! It doesn't make any sense, darling."

"What doesn't make sense, Mum?" Will rubbed the bridge between his nose and forehead. He could feel a headache forming.

"This. LA. Global. All of it, frankly. You. Here. Alone."

"I'm fine, Mum. And, by the way, I support Jess. What they've achieved is incredible. The American TV network discussions about syndication is a major step. It's amazing!" Aware he'd become defensive, he reached for her arm and reassured, "You needn't be so worried. We are ok, and Jessica's happy. We're in a good place. Don't worry."

Seeing her son's protective posture, she spoke more softly. "I hope you're right, darling."

～

Jessica instinctively knew what had transpired even before William detailed the minutiae of his conversation with Lady Armstrong-Bell. His thorough portrayal painted such a vivid picture that it was easy to envision. This was nothing unusual. Her mother-in-law had made no secret of her scorn for the entertainment industry, scrunching her aristocratic nose at anyone "gauche enough to pursue the limelight". To her, Jessica's career was nearly sacrilegious. Women who wed well didn't work – to do so was unheard of and unseemly in her universe. Social decorum dictated that an Armstrong-Bell wife should be a paragon of hosting and homemaking, nothing more. Jessica fathomed she was a disappointment to Philippa, but tried to exude an aura of nonchalance. She scribbled in her journal:

Dear J, that woman despises me. The idea that her son dared venture beyond the confines of Caucasian whiteness is an anathema to her. I'm so tired of her negative comments – she doesn't even pretend anymore. Well, sod her! This is who I am. I enjoy being a household name and I won't hide beneath a bushel. I can't help my looks and I won't apologise for loving the stage or being in front of a camera. I'm here to change the narrative for black excellence. My path is onwards and upwards, and nobody will stop me.

To Will, she said, "I understand she's your mother, and I was raised to respect my elders, but she pisses me off with her judgements and proclamations! You don't believe a word she says, *do you*?" Her question clanged with accusation.

"No, of course not, sweetheart. Mother was raised in a different era – she forgets that this is a new Millennium. I think you're perfect for TV, I really do. How's it going there, anyway?"

Jessica's irritation dissipated as she exclaimed, "Fantastic! SBC have confirmed our licensing deal. They'll commission future content *and* cover production costs," she shared enthusiastically.

CHAPTER 26 — GOING GLOBAL

"Why would they foot the bill for something a British network already produces?"

"Because they want a vested interest. After the first two seasons we're free to license it to others, if we choose."

"Signing with an American network is huge. Widening your reach… I'm so proud of you, sweetheart!"

"Thanks, Will. I'm proud of me too," Jessica piped cheekily. "I love you and miss you terribly," she added.

Will's voice caught in his throat. "How's Los Angeles treating you? Any fun?"

"Oh, yes! Saw Mikey for lunch – which was great! And the girls and I cruised along Sunset Boulevard. Annabel suggested the Mondrian. Sooo cool…"

"The Mondrian? The rooftop is fabulous, isn't it?"

"Yes, with the pool and bar, the ambience and those enormous beds… very nice." Her tone was dreamy, reminiscing.

"I've been there a few times. It's one of my favourite boutique hotels and the food's terrific!"

"The seafood restaurant is glorious. You know how I love my shellfish."

Will chuckled at the sound of her cheery lilt.

"The crowd's young and interesting too. Amazing place to network and meet like-minded individuals."

"And have you?" He kept his tone light.

"Have I what?" She hesitated, knowing he was asking if she'd met anyone interesting, and wondering if she should recount the night's excitement. How the three of them had chosen a table by the beautifully lit poolside and been served a mouth-watering crustacean feast, which they happily washed down with chilled-to-perfection Dom Pérignon. How they'd moved their ultra-relaxed and somewhat inebriated bodies to a more comfortable giant lounge bed and giggled the evening away with carefree abandon.

Before long, a quintessential LA actor-type approached them to strike up banal banter about nothing in particular. Coy skepticism soon dissolved into genuine enthusiasm; this guy was hilarious. Jessica surmised he'd make a suitable companion for Annabel, especially as they were both so darned flawless to look at!

She pressed the phone to her ear and responded to William's question, opting to share details of the dinner and champagne, but not of the sexy stranger TJ, short for Titus Jameson, who might have caused something of a stir had she not been married. Turns out it wasn't his fellow blonde who'd piqued his interest, after all. No harm in mild flirtation and laughter, Jessica had convinced herself. As he'd explained to the captivated three, he lived primarily in New York and was in Los Angeles for a casting. He invited them to join him for drinks at the Chateau Marmont, which they

CHAPTER 26 — GOING GLOBAL

accepted. Effortlessly charming, he complimented each of them in equal measure – this man was clearly skilled at working a crowd, big or small.

When it was time to bid goodbye, Jessica suspected he clasped her wrist for a second longer than necessary. His eyes held the promise of unspoken adventure, and she was intrigued.

CHAPTER 27

No Secrets

A brimming bucketful of guilt drenched Jessica the moment she set sight on William. His puppy dog eyes screamed, "I missed you so much!" and she couldn't shake the unsettling notion she didn't reciprocate that sentiment to quite the same degree.

"Me too," she responded soberly as they embraced.

Will pulled away to survey his wife. "Everything ok, darling? You seem… I don't know… a little…" He left the words hanging, his eyes narrowing.

Jessica again pictured TJ's smouldering countenance and experienced another flash of unsettling shame. She attempted a broad smile. "I'm so happy to see you, my love. Just tired after the flight." Her gaze was sincere.

"And the jetlag, I dare say," he added, stroking her cheek. "Come on, let's get you home."

On the drive from Heathrow, she studied her husband's profile, taking in his firm jawline, chiselled cheekbones and lashes so lengthy they'd easily be the envy of any mascara-wearing girl. She smiled, suddenly glad to be back. William made her feel secure – always had – with his solid-as-a-rock persona and ever-dependable devotion. She needed nobody else. Right here, in this one man, existed everything she desired. And she'd be a fool to think otherwise.

And yet…

… the excitement of LA still coursed through her veins; the memory of her attempts to fend off overwhelming male interest with a stick of prudish morality and her feeble protests, "I'm a married woman!" – to little avail. Truth be told, she'd rather enjoyed the attention, whilst being careful not to flirt or give them much hope. Except for TJ. Titus Jameson. She still hadn't fathomed why they'd exchanged contact details – having convinced herself he and William would someday become friends, but… who was she kidding?! She'd done it because he intrigued her. And yet she felt at fault, though nothing improper had occurred.

Turning towards the sound of William entering the bedroom, she

CHAPTER 27   NO SECRETS

smiled at her husband and proffered him a tender kiss, declaring, "I love you!" Saying it out loud made her feel better.

William folded her into his arms. "Happy to have you back."

"It's good to be home," Jessica acknowledged, "but now I gotta pee." She scurried to the bathroom, conscious she'd been holding it since the baggage hall, and called over her shoulder, "So how was *your* weekend? Your parents?"

"Same old. Fine, I s'pose. Was rather pleasant to see them."

"Without me there to cloud the issue, you mean?" she teased.

"Exactly," he agreed. "Without my piece of African exotica driving me to distraction." He laughed.

She chuckled and flushed the loo. If only they realised how nerdy she was – and naïve, too. The whole sexiness thing was inadvertent and not in the least bit intentional. It was what William claimed he loved most about her.

Dear J, it feels strange to have had such fun in LA. I'd prefer to tell W, but I don't see what good it'll do when nothing actually happened. Maybe I shouldn't have given TJ my number... and not confiding in W makes it worse. I feel kind of guilty. We promised we'd never hide things from each other, so I should tell him. What harm can it do?

"You what??" Will appeared angrier than she'd ever seen.

Jessica swallowed. "It wasn't anything, darling. See? *That's* why I omitted it. I predicted you'd react badly and…"

He turned to exit the room, clearly distressed.

"Will!" she called after him, "You're being ridiculous. We're talking. Don't walk away. I told you because we've always said no secrets. Now, I regret doing so."

He paused at the door, seemingly undecided about whether to stay or leave, opening and closing his fists as one does when agitated, then finally dropping his arms in a gesture of defeat.

Jessica moved to hug his stiff torso. "I'm sorry, darling. Should've mentioned it on the phone, but didn't want to make a big deal."

Will sighed loudly. "Obviously, you're telling me because you *were* attracted to this guy. If it was insignificant, why did you exchange numbers?" He faced her with accusatory eyes.

She winced at his hardened expression. He'd never regarded her in this manner, and she didn't appreciate it. She folded her arms and frowned, bracing herself for a full-blown row. "We *all* exchanged numbers… Annabel and Emily, too. He chatted with *all* of us."

Will's voice was scathing. "Emily and Annabel are *single*, Jess!"

"Which is why I made it clear *I'm* married! Hmm, either you trust me, or you don't. I have nothing to hide. I'm telling you now, aren't

CHAPTER 27 NO SECRETS

I?" Aware she was getting angry, she softened her tone and gazed at him. "Hey, I chose you. There's no one else for me, darling. It's *you* I want... you know that! Ask Ems. I talked non-stop about my amazing husband..." She nudged him and pouted, "... so boring, I was."

With a wry smile, she described TJ's persistence and how she'd fobbed him off with tales of Will's brilliance. TJ had eventually conceded, "I look forward to meeting this wonderful man of yours – sounds like quite a guy! Let's stay in touch and meet up when I next visit London."

Her explanation abated William's anger somewhat, but he was still peeved. She could tell by the set of his jaw and the way he tugged on his running gear and left. When something upset him, Will went for a run, and it usually did the trick. Jessica admitted to herself that TJ's entire approach had been a ruse to obtain her details, but instead of feeling duped she'd felt unduly pleased. She, of course, had no intention of telephoning him but liked the fact he wanted to keep in contact.

She sighed as she gazed out the frosted window on this especially chilly December evening; not the ideal weather for outdoor sport of any kind. But William, being British, didn't regard winter with the same level of caution. She berated herself for hurting him. But then again, she'd done nothing wrong. Not really.

If that were so, how did she explain the tingle of excitement at the prospect of her forthcoming trip to New York? The scheduled end-of-year recital was in forty-eight hours and yes, she typically got a rush of adrenalin before any big show, but that wasn't it. The reason for her tingling was Emily's casual reminder that she'd invited Titus Jameson to Jessica's Lincoln Center performance; first mentioned during their semi-inebriated conversation at the Chateau Marmont, after a few sinfully delectable bespoke cocktails and lots of bonding laughter.

The vivid scene flashed in Jessica's mind, making her long for the seductive allure of that balmy evening in Los Angeles. Sunset Boulevard's Chateau Marmont is legendary for its parties and people-watching. Its mystique and charm, as a French Gothic Hotel, draws a discerning Hollywood crowd and guarantees tons of fascinating if-these-walls-could-talk-tales. Rubbing elbows with beautiful personalities of the movie and modeling worlds thrilled Jessica and Annabel. Emily had been uncharacteristically trusting of the handsome stranger who'd invited them for drinks. She'd become more effusive than usual in the praise of her protégée, and Jessica had been almost embarrassed by the compliments being showered upon her.

Unbeknownst to her, Emily followed up on her drunken promise of an invitation and sent the native New Yorker a complimentary ticket to the concert.

Jessica paused her meticulous folding to survey her handiwork. She'd inherited her prowess for packing from her father, whose skill in

CHAPTER 27 — NO SECRETS

the art of travel meant he could fit any number of items into the tiniest of suitcases. Smiling, she picked up her blackberry and dialed her manager. Not bothering with perfunctory greetings, she plunged straight in.

"I can't believe you did that."

"Hi there. Did what?" Emily appeared genuinely puzzled.

"Invited him… our American friend. What are you trying to do, Ems? Get me into trouble?" There was a smile in her voice.

Emily laughed in response. "Hah! I knew you fancied him. Otherwise, you wouldn't even go there. Hah!"

"It isn't funny, seriously. Will nearly had a fit when I mentioned TJ."

"You what??!... Why on earth would you do that?"

"Errhmm…" Momentarily lost for words, she mumbled, "I dunno. I felt… somehow… guilty." It sounded ludicrous spoken out loud. "I know… don't say it… I'm being silly…"

"Yes, you are, Jess. Unless there's something else going on in that head of yours. Is there?" Her tone became slightly admonishing.

Jessica was silent.

Emily continued, "Young lady, don't – even – think – about – it…"

"I'm not! He was interesting, that's all."

"Yes, and he clearly felt the same, but harmless, mutual admiration is where it should remain. Listen, darling, men like TJ… uh-uh, don't go there, Jess. I wouldn't peg him as 'bad' news; he's certainly charming and all, but everything about him screams *player*!!" She chortled again. "Yep, bad news."

Jessica voiced a thought. "Hey, Ems? What if I persuade Will to join us on the trip? It's so close to Christmas and his work is winding down – it'd be perfect! We could do the Plaza and the lights at Rockefeller. Plus, he could meet the guy and determine for himself there's no threat. They might even take to each other. Problem solved."

Dear J, Will is coming to NYC with me. In fact, we'll stick around for Christmas. Such a pity Freida won't be there as she's in Accra for the hols. But I look forward to doing touristy things. All's well that ends well.

CHAPTER 28

This is Who I Am

The applause was thunderous, reverberating through the grand hall like a storm. Jessica Sokari Brown stood breathless, every muscle in her body still tingling from the performance. The verdict unanimous: she had set a new precedent for excellence.

"A dancer clearly in her prime."

"Rarely have we witnessed such exceptional physical strength and control."

"This girl is a phenomenon."

"It's official. The world loves Miss Brown."

Compliments poured in from spectators and critics alike, their words effusive, gushing and unrestrained. Jessica had wowed everyone, but more importantly, she had wowed even herself. Her pre-performance anxiety, usually masked by adrenalin, had faced a new challenge tonight. Not only was she delivering a headline act at arguably the world's largest performing arts venue, but she was also playing a dangerous game with both her spouse and her admirer in the same auditorium. Despite the nerves twisting in the pit of her belly, the thrill was undeniable.

The buzz of the audience filled the air, echoing backstage. Jessica peeked through the curtain, scanning the crowd for familiar faces. Among them, she saw William seated near the front. His presence was a bittersweet mix of reassurance and anxiety. Then her eyes drifted to TJ, sitting just a few rows behind William, his confident aura unmistakable. She took a breath to steady herself.

The curtain rose, and the music enveloped her. The unfamiliar butterflies in her stomach vanished the moment she stepped onto the platform, leaving her with an indomitable sense of power. Jessica danced with an intensity driven by her inner turmoil, each movement telling the story of her struggle between love, temptation, and loyalty.

When she delivered her concluding bow, her heart was pounding with exhilaration. She did a last pirouette of sheer jubilation and pressed her fingers to her full lips, blowing her audience a flourishing kiss. A fusillade of camera flashbulbs illuminated the concert hall as she stood stage centre, elated and victorious.

Jessica sought William in the third row, his handsome face wreathed in smiles and his pupils alight with pride. She had done it! Had achieved that elusive moment of glory she'd subconsciously awaited her entire life – the point in a performer's career when they recognise they have given their absolute best. *Madame Travers would be proud of me!*

Jessica noticed the striking bouquet of red roses before he entered the dressing room, and flung her arms around him as she always did after every recital. William twirled her in a tight embrace, lifting her feet clear off the ground.

"Magnificent, darling! Absolutely, gloriously executed. You were altogether someone else… incredible!" William's words mirrored her inner knowing, and she welcomed the affirmation.

"Are you up for the after-party?" He asked, watching her step into a shimmery dress.

"Are you kidding?" she replied with a laugh. "I wouldn't miss it for anything!"

The post-performance soiree at the Lincoln Center Kitchen was brimming with congratulatory remarks. Arm-in-arm, the couple breezed in, with Jessica graciously acknowledging the praise that flooded in from all directions. She spotted Emily talking avidly to TJ, who was laughing at something. As if sensing her presence, TJ turned his blue gaze to capture hers. She felt blood rush to her face, grateful her darker hue disguised her discomfort.

As TJ sauntered towards them, her erratic heartbeat quickened, and she gave Will a surreptitious glance. He strode forward confidently, giving Emily a warm peck on the cheek before turning to the other man with his arm outstretched.

"You must be Titus. William. Pleased to meet you."

The two men shook hands firmly.

"Thank you for attending my wife's recital – good of you to come." Will added, sounding disarmingly open and friendly.

TJ responded with a grin of his own. "I bet you're pretty darn proud – not only is she stunning, but talented, too." He threw Jessica his dazzling smile. "You got a sexy fireball in your grip, man."

The New Yorker was dangerously close to crossing a line, but William's expression remained politely amicable, revealing nothing. "Yes, indeed," he agreed, "Very lucky."

Jessica observed the exchange with some trepidation, relieved to note her husband seemed relaxed and unbothered. In fact, they appeared to be getting on relatively well and spent a good deal of time chatting, even after she'd moved apart to mingle.

An hour later, as they were ready to leave, TJ kissed her goodbye,

CHAPTER 28 — THIS IS WHO I AM

igniting a flutter in her belly that warned the young star to keep him at arms-length. This man spelled danger, and she knew she would be wise to avoid any sort of friendship with him.

That night, back in their hotel room, Jessica received a call from a 917- area code. She immediately knew it was from TJ. She slipped out of bed as quietly as she could, went into the bathroom and shut the door, her hands unsteady as she held the blackberry against her ear.

"Hello?" she croaked, her throat feeling foreign and dry.

There was silence at first; she could hear his uneven breathing, almost as though he hadn't expected her to answer.

"Hey you." He finally spoke, and the sound of his voice sent a shiver down her spine.

Jessica lifted a trembling hand to her mouth, tracing its outline. She bit the tip of her index finger, heart racing, and peered at the door, expecting Will to burst in any minute. "You shouldn't be calling me." Her words sounded lame.

"I wanted to hear your voice," TJ confessed simply. His desire was palpable, and she quivered, not knowing what else to say. They stayed silent, listening to each other breathe, the drum of her heartbeat growing louder with each passing second. *This can't be happening,* she thought guiltily, closing her eyes.

"This is wrong," she whispered out loud, then swallowed and

uttered with more conviction, "Don't call me again. Please. It's best you stop." She hung up.

※

Christmas in New York was filled with cliché, touristy experiences they'd typically despise, but their carefree approach left them refreshed and rested for the new year. The next season of the TV program began soon after, and the media were already abuzz, calling it "a show guaranteed to titillate".

Each morning at breakfast, Jessica was amused by William's punctilious plough through the articles, sometimes reading them aloud with an incredulous shake of the head. "These people are completely mad… listen to this one: 'Every male fantasy came alive last night with what has clearly become the show men love to watch.' *Show men love to watch?* What in God's name are they talking about? You two were discussing cosmetics and body lotion – how on earth is that…? *Pfff!* Incredible." He massaged his forehead with the balls of his fingers.

"It's the papers, darling. Publicity. Who cares? Just ignore it," she shrugged.

Will sipped his coffee and picked up his fork and knife, attacking the bacon and eggs as though they might try to make a run for it. He chewed thoughtfully for a bit, then added, "In reality, your viewership demographic is mostly women between the ages of fifteen and forty-five,

CHAPTER 28 — THIS IS WHO I AM

but these damn reporters always need an angle. Quite ridiculous!"

Jessica pursed her twitching lips, and nodded in agreement, deciding not to fan the flame of her husband's irritation. "Erm, I'll have another coffee, please, Chef Lee. Thank you."

The interviewer's tone was skeptical. "So, you're saying you've never changed your name?"

"Changed it to *what?*"

"Well, 'Brown' doesn't sound very African…"

Jessica wrinkled her nose in disbelief. "I shouldn't dignify such ignorance with a response," she snapped. "Do your research, Jim. You'll discover I was born with that name."

The lights of the studio felt harsh as she tried to catch Will's eye.

"Okay, a closing question, Miss Brown. The rumours are rampant – that you resort to excessive measures to stay in shape. Care to comment?"

"Excessive measures?" she repeated, her expression quizzical. "I go to the gym – like anybody else – am careful with my diet and look after my body. Do you call that excessive?"

Jim wasn't put off by her mild hostility. "So, there's no eating disorder?"

"Absolutely not! I'm simply… healthy."

"Ok, let's move on. Choc…"

"Thought you promised that was the final question?" Jessica interjected with no lightness to her tone.

"Aww, come on, give us one more."

Jessica sighed and gestured her assent, irritation seeping through.

Jim dropped his voice conspiratorially. "There's talk that Chocolate and Vanilla may have preferred to be Vanilla and Vanilla. What say you to that?" He smirked.

She didn't smile back but held his gaze for an uncomfortable, few seconds, then addressed the TV audience directly. "Jim's question assumes that 'whiteness' is the aspiration of every black person. But look at him." She pointed to his deeply tanned forearm. "Do you wish you were black, Jim?" Laughter erupted in the studio and Jim grimaced. Jessica continued, "Just as my co-host, Annabel, is content with her 'whiteness', I embrace my 'blackness' and have never desired otherwise. Chocolate and Vanilla is and always will be exactly that. Anyone who insinuates that I'd rather be 'Vanilla' is blatantly racist."

The show presenter lifted a conciliatory hand and parted his lips (probably to deny her accusations), but she carried on in a stronger voice. "And before you inquire, *we* (Annabel and I) coined the phrase as a humorous, tongue-in-cheek allusion to our skin tones. It works because each of us is confident about who we are. That's my response to your question."

CHAPTER 28　THIS IS WHO I AM

Jessica turned her flashing, tiger-eyed gaze on Jim, who was beetroot and shifting uncomfortably in his seat. "I doubt anyone is inferring..." His voice trailed off, but he quickly regrouped. "... No-one's racist here, Jessica. Perhaps I barked up the wrong tree." He gulped, his eyes darting to the producer, who flourished her hands in a gesture of impatience. "I believe the real question in everyone's minds is how an African girl who came to England at age..." he scanned his notes, "age twelve, to a predominantly white boarding school, in a profession dominated by a Caucasian aesthetic of beauty, wouldn't be somewhat... out of her depth?"

Jessica could see William towering in the background behind the cameramen. He had his chin balanced on his thumb and was rubbing his nose with his forefinger. She lowered her gaze and studied Jim through narrowed lids, choosing her words carefully. "Are you implying you *don't* find me beautiful, Jim?" She crossed and uncrossed her long, toned legs, visible under the sheer stockings.

Jim blushed anew, and stammered, "N-n-no, I mean, yes! Of course, I do. That's not what I meant." He looked flustered.

She tilted her slender neck to the side. "I know what you meant. Did I feel out of my depth? Sure, I did. Ballet is gruelling and, at first, I believed I needed to be bone thin to fit in," she admitted honestly. "But I realise now that we don't need to conform to succeed. My current success today is possible because of this strong, athletic form." Her eyes dared him to disagree.

"Yes," the interviewer agreed. "There's no doubt you shine on stage. But as one of the few women of colour to succeed in this arena, do you sometimes feel you're walking a tightrope, which could snap at any juncture?"

"Snap? Why? This is ridi…" She glared at him, took a deep, steadying breath and spoke more calmly. "Contrary to what you obviously believe, not every black person has a chip on their shoulder, Jim, or grows up feeling hard done by. I dance because I love it. Full stop. Whether black or white. And since you insist on mentioning it, let me reiterate to you and to every ignoramus out there: I've *never* wished I was white, and I find the suggestion insulting. This is who I am. My parents instilled lessons of dignity and pride in my heritage, which were rooted and unshakeable by the time I arrived in England. *This is who I am*. Neither England nor ballet has altered that!"

Jessica stared straight ahead, not trusting herself to glance in Jim's direction. He cleared his throat softly, and concluded, "Well, I appreciate your… erm… candour, Jessica. Folks, that's all for today. Thanks for tuning in and to Jessica Brown for gracing us with her presence."

As soon as the cameras stopped rolling, she leapt up, unclipped the lapel mic and yanked the sound pack out of her skirt waistband. She stalked off the set, her pulse racing.

William met her in the Green Room. "What happened up there, baby?"

CHAPTER 28 — THIS IS WHO I AM

"Huh! He was so bloody persistent. Really pissed me off!"

"That much was evident," Will remarked dryly.

Jessica raised an eyebrow. "What's that supposed to imply?"

William crossed his arms in mock self-defence. "Hey, I'm not the enemy. And neither was he. Just a tad ignorant, but he was asking questions he believes the public want answers to."

"So, you think I was too defensive?"

"Well, I figured you'd either slap him, or storm off set." He chuckled.

"Too much?"

"Hmmm, maybe a little."

"He made me sooo angry."

"I saw. But best not to take the bait. Anyway, it's done. At least now everyone knows your position."

Jessica glanced at her husband. "And you. Where do *you* stand?"

He grazed her lips with a tender kiss. "Always on your side, my darling. But I've got to tell you, you were a little rude. Remember, you're in the public eye, and sometimes you just have to suck it up."

Jessica frowned. "Well, I've never liked that guy and I still think he crossed a line."

William's smile was indulgent. "Hey, it's done now. You've got loads to be proud of. You're only twenty-two and see what you've achieved!"

She sighed. "I am so grateful. Couldn't ask for more. Speaking of which, I know it hasn't been easy for you; reading about your wife… me travelling so much…" She looked at him keenly. It was a subject they'd never discussed.

Will proffered another gentle kiss. "So happy for you! I am. But I do wish…" He scratched his head. "… I didn't have to share you with everyone."

Jessica frowned. "Share? Nobody has me, darling. *You* do."

"Do I? Really?" His heavy sigh hinted at unspoken doubt, and she hastened to avert her gaze, lest he glean the secrets that lay within.

CHAPTER 29

Leap Year Superstition

"It's totally beyond my control, Will!" Jessica bristled, alarmed by the sudden and uncharacteristic shift in their dynamic.

William, usually the patient one, had been increasingly out of sorts. The thin line of his lips had sketched itself into a firm downturn, and he was glaring at her reflection in the mirror.

Jessica persisted, "It's irrational to blame me. You're being unfair."

Will rotated his right fist in the palm of his left hand, his agitation obvious. "I accept this isn't your fault, Jess. But I feel distinctly ill-disposed by the regularity of these blasted periods. So… disappointing. *Why* aren't you falling pregnant? It doesn't make sense."

Jessica folded her arms across her naked body and squinted at him with mild hostility. "Disappointing? Hmm. *That's* what happens to women every month, William." She tried to sound annoyed, but her nerves betrayed her resolve.

"I understand that, Jess. No need to be facetious! What's making you so irascible, anyway?"

Jessica leaned against the bathroom door, her lips forming a pout.

Will finished drying himself, then grabbed her by the shoulders, a little too eagerly. "I mean, look at you? You're young, healthy, clearly fertile…" He softened his tone, but his eyes still questioned, *'So what the hell is wrong?'* "… Plus," he peered down at himself with a wry grin, "I don't think we've got any problems here, thank you very much!"

Jessica forced a smile, but his persistence worried her. He'd been reasonable for long enough and was determined to have this out, evidently tired of tiptoeing around the issue. If she got upset, so be it. He seemed beyond caring. Her arm stung from where his fingers had pinched.

"Let's hope this morning's seed was the lucky one to capture that elusive egg of yours," he added awkwardly, chuckling to lighten the tension.

Jessica's face glowed with post-coital endorphins. "Really, Will? Now?" Her expression made it clear she thought his timing was abysmal

CHAPTER 29 — LEAP YEAR SUPERSTITION

and wanted him to drop the subject.

He paused briefly, then pressed on. "Yes, *now*, Jess. We never talk about this." His voice grew stronger, more purposeful. "You said you needed time. Well, it's been three years. I figure that's plenty of time, don't you?"

Her heart almost stopped. This was her moment to tell him. She coughed and murmured evasively, "W… Well, a woman's body needs to be in a state of zero stress and…." Her voice trailed off. She had nothing more to add. William was staring at her expectantly, so she snapped, "I don't want to discuss this any longer! It's upsetting."

His eyes narrowed with concern and something else she couldn't decipher. "Are you claiming you're stressed? You don't appear to be, Jess. Perhaps early on, yes. But now, I'd say you're… in your element!" It sounded like a criticism.

Jessica pursed her lips and replied dolefully, "You make it sound so easy, Will. F… For many people, it isn't. Lots of couples try for months and… and years… before anything happens… and even then… well! Nothing's guaranteed."

He frowned and scratched his head. "I think maybe you should get checked – give Dr Middleton a call tomorrow, see what she says. No harm, right?"

"Mmmmn, yes." Jessica mumbled.

She telephoned the Harley Street clinic as promised the following day, but shared no details of the scheduled appointment with Will.

Dear J, Acts of omission aren't real lies, are they?

"2004 is a leap year!" Jessica announced to her bemused husband.

"O… kay. That's a rather irrelevant piece of information, other than as a reminder to ascribe twenty-nine days to February."

"Tell that to my mother," Jessica challenged. "No-one escapes Edith Brown's household unscathed by her views. According to Mum, it's an auspicious time that invariably brings major events either in the world or in one's personal life."

"Oh. And what major event are you expecting?"

Jessica shrugged, "Nothing. But I've always felt leap years bring both a sense of foreboding and expectancy."

"Hmm," William observed, "Never pegged you as superstitious, darling."

"I'm not. To be honest, I wonder how mum reconciles such beliefs with her Christian faith – the two can't possibly go hand in hand. But then again, the last leap year was 2000, which is when I married you, so maybe this mythical hypothesis carries weight after all."

They shared a smile.

CHAPTER 29 — LEAP YEAR SUPERSTITION

As if to further cement this supposition, on January 28th 2004, an unusual event hit central and southern Britain. It was a wintry evening and Jessica sat alone in the living room, fireplace ablaze, feet tucked comfortably beneath her. This rare, sacred moment allowed her to relax, and get immersed in a good novel.

Without warning, Mother Nature interrupted her solitude with an almighty flash of lightning followed by a heavy clap of thunder. Startled, Jessica dropped her book and rushed to the window, watching in awe as the relentless downpour of rain made a dramatic turn into three inches of snow. News reports dubbed the event "Thundersnow", a rare phenomenon caused by an Arctic squall line. Talk about an act of God!

Jessica was thankful to be snug at home and not out in the gruesome weather. Poor Will wasn't as fortunate and returned soaking wet and freezing cold.

"Nothing a hot bath won't fix," she sympathised, as she helped him out of his drenched clothes.

"It was so strange and unexpected," he recounted with amazement. "Started as heavy rain, then suddenly became dreadfully chilly and turned to snow. Incredible. And of course, it happens the day I decide not to drive into work. Just great!" He shrugged out of his shirt, which clung to the hairs on his chest.

Jessica gave her husband a seductive smile and stroked his manly torso with deliberate intent. "As I said… nothing a hot bath won't fix,

Mr A…" She nibbled his ear.

Will laughed at her suggestive wriggle out of her leggings. "Oh, it's like that, is it?"

"Absolutely!" Jessica shimmied towards the bathroom in an exaggerated wanton walk, wiggling and giggling as he reached out to slap her rounded butt.

Upon reflection, she considered the strange weather a sign the forthcoming year might indeed be unusual. Her sigh was heavy as she contemplated what would have been her baby's birthday. Fingering a baby keepsake, she vowed to be open to new things. So tiny, those hands and feet.

The thought crossed her mind before she could stop it: "Everything happens for a reason." One of her mother's platitudinous sayings, but so true. Had things turned out differently three years ago, she wouldn't be enjoying her current global success. She'd be happily saddled with a young child, who'd take up most of her time and attention, unwittingly preventing her from pursuing her dreams. Besides, they hadn't planned the baby – it had just happened. At nineteen… imagine! It would have changed her life trajectory entirely.

But William's needs were different.

One Sunday morning, Jessica awakened to an empty space beside

CHAPTER 29 — LEAP YEAR SUPERSTITION

her. After first checking the adjoining bathroom, she called out and, hearing no response, threw on her dressing gown to go in search of him. William was in his study, desk devoid of papers, staring into space.

"Will?" she whispered tentatively.

"Head back to bed, Jess, I'll be there in a minute." He sounded despondent, not glancing her way.

"What's wrong? Are you ill?"

His green eyes clouded with emotion. "Everything's wrong. Everything. You, me, us. It seems perfect, but I… sense this lack. Like there's a missing cog in our wheel of life. I can't reconcile why, no matter how hard we try, you don't get pregnant. Maybe the first time was a fluke. Perhaps something's wrong with me, Jess." His voice broke.

Jessica felt like a fraud.

Will regained his composure, speaking again. "I'm not saying a baby is everything, but it is what we agreed. A child would enrich our lives and is definitely something I want. It's been over four years since we got married and high-time we started a family."

Dear J, I'm at the pinnacle of my career and I'll be damned if I allow a baby to end it prematurely. William doesn't know I have zero intention of getting pregnant. Yes, it's selfish, but a necessary evil. I'm still so young. We have forever to start a family.

Jessica later discovered William had taken matters into his own hands by telephoning Dr Jane Middleton, the family gynaecologist recommended by Lady Armstrong-Bell. She overheard him speaking on the telephone, and peeked through the study door gap, holding her breath in trepidation. Initially, Dr Middleton had refused to divulge any information on account of doctor-patient confidentiality. But when William cleverly implied possessing more knowledge than he did, she let it slip that the clinic was expecting Jessica for an appointment to refit her contraceptive coil. Her what?!

Will replaced the handset, looking aghast; eyes filled with the bitter taste of betrayal.

CHAPTER 30

Liar!

William staggered into their bedroom, a ghost of disbelief haunting his eyes. Jessica trailed behind him, her footsteps soft and hesitant. His wide-eyed stare reflected a whirlwind of emotions threatening to burst forth. He could barely contain his outburst the moment he saw her.

"Is it true?" His voice, a snarling accusation, echoed off the walls, eyes ablaze with an emerald fury.

"Is what true?" Jessica's poker face was a mask, her expression betraying nothing, though her heart raced like a caged animal desperate for release.

"You know exactly what I'm talking about." His low growl metamorphosed into a thunderous roar. "You never told me about any contraception!" He was breathing heavily, each breath an expulsion of suppressed rage. With a violent sweep of his palm, he knocked everything off the dresser in a single movement. "Contraception?! You've been *lying* to me all these years!"

Jessica's voice faltered, the ground beneath her seeming to dissolve. "D…Did you…?" she stammered, rooted to the spot in fear. Her world was about to implode and she had no idea how to prevent it.

Will's face contorted. "I trusted you, Jess! Family planning is something we should have discussed. How could you decide alone?" His mouth gaped incredulously.

Jessica fathomed he hadn't once suspected she had taken affirmative action to ensure she remain barren; not in his wildest dreams had he imagined she'd deceive him in such a manner. Tears already forming, she implored, "I tried to tell you, Will. But you wanted a baby so badly; you wouldn't listen…"

"Wouldn't *listen*?? All I ever did was bloody listen – to your excuses and your *lies*!"

"I never lied to you…" Jessica's instinct was to protest against

CHAPTER 30 — LIAR!

being called a liar.

"Yes, you did! By hiding the truth, Jess. It's the same damn thing with the exact same result." His eyes were bright with unshed tears.

"No, it isn't... not quite." Jessica defended, remembering the countless, sleepless nights she'd endured because of this very issue. "Besides, Will, I... I don't think you really understand..."

"You're right, Jess," Will retorted bitterly. "I *don't* understand. How could you look me in the eye, every time we made love... every time we discussed the future, knowing how much I wanted a baby..." His voice cracked, the tears breaking free.

Slumped on the edge of their bed, he cradled his head with trembling hands. Jessica could only watch, transfixed, as he teetered between rage and despair. She flinched when he leapt to his feet, bulging veins throbbing in his temple, pools of saliva foaming at the corners of his twisted lips. The hatred in his eyes soon dissolved into pain, and she knew she had hurt him. Her precious lion was wounded and wouldn't rest until he'd exacted retribution.

"I'm sorry," she simpered, knowing he'd reject her sympathy but offering it nonetheless.

His eyes, blank with pain, met hers. "How? How could you do this to me?" He thwarted her outstretched arm with an angry paw, green eyes flashing once again.

"But this isn't just about you, Will. What about *me*? What about what *I* wanted?" Jessica was weeping now, uncontrollable sobs shaking her frame. "It terrified me to tell you because I guessed how you'd react. But I was even more frightened of getting pregnant. Can't you see?? You have no idea what I've been through. I'm petrified, Will! What… what if it happens again?" She was bawling by this point.

William glared at her, unmoved by her tears. "But you're a liar, Jess. A bloody liar! All these years… you tricked me into believing we had bad luck. Every time we tried for a baby… My God! What a terrible shock to find out your wife has been deceiving you all these years!" He jabbed an accusing finger in her face and her heart recoiled. "You deliberately misled me into thinking your body was dealing with residual grief and stress and hormones and whatever else, but *not this*. Not this, Jess!"

She said nothing, bearing his wrath, hoping the catharsis would calm him into seeing reason. Into seeing her side of things.

"You're right," she finally whispered, looking down at her feet. "I was selfish and dishonest, and it's unforgivable. Can you ever forgive me, W-Will?"

Her voice had tightened to a squeak and broke as she called his name, but Will stormed out of the house without saying another word. Jessica collapsed onto the cold, marble floor, hot tears rolling down her cheeks. She had hurt him – again – and this time…

This time she knew the damage was irreparable.

CHAPTER 30 — LIAR!

Time lost all meaning as she sat there, immersed in a spiral of sorrow and regrets, reliving the anguish of the last few years and the harsh reality of their argument. True, pregnancy scared her, but Will was perfectly justified in his anger. They had prided themselves in their closeness, yet she had kept a monstrous secret.

Her heart ached remembering his look of abject betrayal. Jessica knew he trusted her – had always trusted her – and she'd broken that trust. I must make this right, she resolved, pacing the room anxiously.

Hours passed with no sign of Will. Jessica's concern grew with each glance at her blackberry. He'd charged out of the house without his wallet or phone, so she couldn't even reach him. She felt a mild twinge of annoyance. This wasn't typical of Will; for someone so organized, he was being quite thoughtless.

By midnight, an inner flutter of panic told her something might be wrong, but she was reluctant to call the police and have them accuse her of over-reacting. She gave it another hour, then relented, dialing 999 with some apprehension. After being subjected to what seemed like a million random questions, the officer put her on hold for an eternity, only to return and confirm her worst fears. William was injured. He'd been in an automobile accident and been taken to St Thomas' Hospital.

On this frosty November night, the biting cold cut through her thin jumper as she ran to the car with neither jacket nor coat, then drove like a maniac across the river to St Thomas', her thoughts a chaotic mess. She sped through the deserted streets, heedless of traffic signals, screeching into the nearest parking space, and rushed through the double doors of the A&E Department.

"Is he alright?" Jessica nearly screamed at the receptionist, raw desperation making her oblivious to the fact she was in a public place.

Clearly accustomed to frantic relatives, the nurse remained calm, empathetic even. She said firmly, but gently, "Mrs Armstrong-Bell, your husband is with the trauma team. My colleagues will brief you soon. Please take a seat. It shouldn't be long."

Jessica didn't find this response satisfactory. "But do you have any more information than that? I… we… is he *ok*?" Her voice was a ragged demand for answers.

Just then, another nurse appeared. "Mrs Armstrong-Bell? This way, please."

Jessica followed the kind-looking attendant through the double doors, down the empty corridor, all the while feeling as though she were floating through the scenes of a nightmare. She shivered, a reminder that this was real and not a dream. Oh Will, what have you done, she thought.

When she saw him, a wave of nausea hit her at the sight of his blood. He was unrecognisable – looked like he'd been hit by a bus, literally! In fact, he'd almost collided with a massive truck and had swerved to avoid

CHAPTER 30   LIAR!

it, only to drive head-on into a lamppost. The damage to Flora was irreparable – making her an absolute write-off. Frankly, Will looked like an absolute write-off too! They had him hooked to tubes and bandaged from head to toe, which didn't quite mask the blood seeping through the gauze. The severe injuries to his skull and organs meant they needed to rush him to intensive care, because he required emergency surgery to stop the internal bleeding. Her husband seemed conscious, but not very lucid.

A sense of dread gripped Jessica as she looked at him, lying there completely helpless, unable to string two words together. She held his hand and leaned in close – pressing his fingers to her lips.

"I'm so sorry," she whispered. "So sorry."

Pain had clouded William's gaze. He swallowed with some effort, as though to rid his throat of a sore lump, and muttered quietly, "I… love you, Jess."

"I love you too." Jessica's reply was a whimper, helpless tears flowing freely. "And I'm so, sooo sorry."

Will tried to smile, but failed miserably, the attempt causing him to wince and catch his breath.

Jessica glanced at the medical staff. They nodded.

"It's time. We need to take him through, Mrs Armstrong-Bell."

She released Will's hand with great difficulty, afraid that if she let go, she might never get the chance to hold it again. As the orderlies wheeled him out to the operating theatre, the agony of parting sliced through her heart like a razor.

***

This was torture, this waiting – not knowing what was going on; waiting for the surgery to be over and done with. It had already been two hours, and still no news. How could that be? Jessica shivered again, this time less from the cold and more from the fear of what might be.

And when the news came, she continued to shiver uncontrollably. Her body in shock. Numb.

She had lost her William, her husband – the love of her life. Her everything. And all because she was a liar.

CHAPTER 31

Gone

"Miss, are you alright? Do you need...?"

Jessica stared blankly at the starched, blue uniform. "We argued... before he left. I upset him... it's... it's my fault... I-I ... I lied."

The nurse gently guided her to a nearby seat, her grip firm but comforting. "I don't know the exact circumstances, Miss, but I understand he was in a car accident and *that* wasn't your fault. You cannot blame yourself – it'll drive you mad. Please, Miss, go home. He's gone, there's nothing you can do now. We'll take it from here and you can start making arrangements tomorrow. Ok?"

Arrangements. It sounded so cold. So matter-of-fact. They'd moved Will to the hospital morgue. The *morgue*. Will was dead.

Jessica returned to an empty house that felt haunted by a billion memories. Each step was like wading through a thick swamp. Battered and bruised, bereft and broken, unable to breathe properly; engulfed by pain so great she could feel nothing at all. A void of numbness.

Holland Park was still asleep, the world oblivious to her anguish. As the blackness of night gave way to the pale light of dawn, she crawled into bed, still fully clothed, fiercely clutching his pillow, her tears soaking its fabric as she lay there motionless.

Had it not been for Chef Lee, she would have remained in the same prone position, curled in a foetal ball, willing her heart to stop. He half-knocked on the open door to the master suite, reluctant to disturb their privacy. "Sir, Ma'am…? Sorry to intrude. You didn't come down for coffee or breakfast." His eyes scanned the unruffled bed, noticing one side was empty. "Everything ok, Ma'am? You feeling not so good?"

Jessica didn't stir. Concerned, Chef Lee breached his invisible line of deference and diffidently stepped into the room. One look at her tear-stricken face and empty gaze, fixed on a void only she could see, told him something was dreadfully wrong.

CHAPTER 31 — GONE

He cleared his throat. "S... Sir...? Is he…?" Chef Lee's voice was thick with worry.

Jessica shook her head almost imperceptibly and closed her eyes, and that's when the silent tears began again, big large droplets, falling fast and furious, like a tap with a faulty washer, impossible to turn off. Plop, plop, plop.

"Would you like me to call someone, Ma'am? Lady Armstrong…?"

Jessica moved her lips, forming the words almost soundlessly. "Gone… he's gone… car accident… he's gone." Her voice was barely audible. Her brain, numb. Funny how accidents appear out of nowhere. Unexpected. With neither warning nor special consideration – just wham! No matter who you are. The reality embedded like a cruel thorn.

Chef Lee's professional façade crumbled as he fought to maintain composure. "I- I- I get you cup of coffee and call Lady Armstrong-Bell." He nodded repeatedly, his accent thickening as he backed out of the room, wiping his eyes.

Jessica's phone battery was dead, isolating her from the outside world. She rejected all Chef Lee's offers of coffee, tea, toast, juice and lunch, only sipping water when he insisted.

At 2 pm, the knock on the bedroom door startled her. Expecting Chef Lee, she prepared to unleash her pent-up frustration, but he handed her the phone instead.

"Your mother."

"My mum…?"

"Yes, I called her."

Edith Brown's voice filtered through. "Yes, darling, we swopped numbers years ago when I visited."

"I see," Jessica responded, her voice dull.

"My daughter, is it true… what am I hearing? *Chineke* God!"

"Yes, it's true, mum."

"How? When? What happened?" Edith Brown's voice bordered on hysteria, a stark contrast to Jessica's robotic tone. The tears rolled silently. She felt nothing. She felt dead.

Her parents flew in to be with their despondent daughter. Lady Armstrong-Bell and Sir Michael arrived, devastated by the death of their only son. Freida took a leave of absence from work to support Jessica, with plans for an extended stay if needed. Even Mikey flew in from Los Angeles to be with his sister. Emily and Annabel managed J&A's workload, postponing or rescheduling Jessica's recitals.

William was gone, and Jessica's will to live had departed with him. She allowed his parents to handle all the funeral arrangements. She wanted nothing to do with it. Jessica didn't want to put her husband in the ground. 'Widow' was not a label she could comprehend.

Her perfectly planned, idyllic world was now in orbit, spinning

CHAPTER 31   GONE

abysmally out of control. Perhaps she was going mad? In fact, on the day of the burial, Jessica felt a craziness overtake her as she involuntarily sprung from her father's side and catapulted into the grave, throwing herself on top of Will's coffin. She clawed at it, trying to pry it open.

"Bury me with him!" she howled, her voice raw. "Bury me with him!

Her mother began to cry too, and her father and the pallbearers rushed to rescue Jessica from the muddy pit. Philippa Armstrong-Bell hid her face in her husband's coat sleeve, unable to watch.

Mr Sokari Brown held his daughter tight against his chest. Jessica had never heard her father cry, but he did so now, unashamedly and unreservedly, his deep sobs echoing through the graveyard, like a macabre chorus, in tune with her wailing. He could clearly feel every ounce of his daughter's anguish, and it moved him beyond measure.

Too overwhelmed to attend the wake, Freida took Jessica home, understanding her sister's need for silent companionship. She didn't ask any questions. What had come over Jessica? Why had she flung herself so dramatically into William's grave? Did she really want to die? Freida intuitively knew what Jessica needed, as she always had, and they sat together in the conservatory, enveloped in wordless solace, content in each other's presence – no words necessary.

CHAPTER 32

Family

Jessica stood at the top of the stairs, eavesdropping on the hushed conversation drifting from the living room below. Her mother's voice, taut with annoyance, pierced the silence.

"No, Sokari, I disagree. That girl needs guidance. Look at her! She won't eat, can't sleep and walks around like some... I don't know, what do they call them... zombie! *Eh-eh*, no, she needs help, *O'jare.*"

"Actually, Mum, I can see Dad's point." Freida's voice rang clear and steady. "And if Mikey was still here, he would agree. Jess is grieving and..."

"Grieving, *keh?!*" her mother interrupted, her tone scornful. "*That's not grieving.* The girl looks dead; as if she can no longer feel anything. It's not normal."

Freida's voice remained unwavering in her sisterly defence. "Yes, it is. Some people cry non-stop, some look like they feel nothing. Jess is in mourning and this is *her* way of coping. Denial is one of the stages. It hasn't fully hit her, that's all. She needs to be *ready* for grief counseling or whatever you're suggesting, Mum. It has to happen at the right time otherwise it'd be pointless."

Her father's voice, deep and resolute, carried an air of finality. "So, it's settled, then. No one is to trouble her with talk of therapy. We can't force her into feeling emotions she's not ready to process. She needs time, we'll give her time."

Jessica listened to this exchange, bewildered to hear them at loggerheads. She didn't want to be the cause of a family squabble over what was best for her. Determined to resolve this once and for all, she walked into the room and the conversation abruptly halted.

"Mum, Dad… Fif…" She cleared her throat and took a deep breath. "You're right. I do need help, but not the kind you imagine. I don't need a therapist to tell me what I'm feeling, and I certainly don't want to be alone."

They looked at her with a mix of expectation and concern.

"I appreciate your care, but I know what I must do…" Alarm

flashed across her mother's face and Jessica quickly reassured her, "Don't worry, Mum, I won't try to harm myself. What I need is to get away – far away – like I did, we did, before the wedding. That's what I need."

Freida moved to wrap an arm around her sister's waist. "Any idea where you'd like to go?" she asked softly.

Jessica responded, "Not Bali – that would be too much for me." Both parents nodded in agreement. "But maybe somewhere like Thailand. Koh Samui has some great retreats. Annabel told me about one that sounds perfect."

Fifi gave her sister a light kiss on the cheek. "Whatever you choose, we support you a hundred percent."

Edith Brown looked at her younger daughter. "Yes, we're your family and we support you, Jess. But what of his parents? Have you called them since the funeral?"

Jessica's face hardened. She shook her head. "No, I haven't."

"Don't you think you should?" Sokari Brown laid a gentle hand on Jessica's hunched shoulders. "My dear, they'd appreciate that."

"I'm not ready, Dad," Jessica mumbled and her father nodded.

Jessica's mother stepped closer; her voice insistent. "But, remember, they've just lost their son, eh – their *only* son. It's tragic! Besides, they consider you a part of their family. You must call them."

Sokari silenced his wife with a gentle nudge, then empathised,

"We understand, my dear. You'll call them when you're ready."

Jessica exhaled, feeling cornered. "Thanks, Dad. I really can't think about them, right now."

"Jessica!" Her mother's voice prickled with reproach. "This is not the time to act spoilt! No, stay out of this, Freida. It's about time your sister grows up and starts considering others. Yes, yes, you lost your husband, but *they* lost their son. So please… please stop being selfish and call them. They're hurting too." Edith Brown moved over to the nearest chair and sat down with a hefty huff of disapproval.

Jessica peered beseechingly at her father, hoping *he* might jump to her defence. Instead, he nodded at his wife with a thoughtful expression. Her mother had pursed her lips in a thick fold of displeasure, heavy lines of disappointment etched into her otherwise youthful face. Evidently, she could sympathise with William's parents. She looked like she was about to cry.

Freida's silence implied she agreed with their mother, and the realisation of their waning patience hit Jessica hard. She wanted to shake herself out of her pathetic pity-party, but couldn't. It was easier to stay feeling sorry for herself – easier to curl up into a ball and not have to deal with anyone else's grief. But her mum was right. It seemed selfish, and she needed to telephone her in-laws. She swallowed painfully, wanting to say something.

Her father's voice filled the silence. "Jessica, the ability to commiserate

CHAPTER 32 — FAMILY

with others shows love and consideration. Such compassion will take you out of your own grief and, I dare say, it'll help you feel stronger. You *should* call them, my dear."

Feeling small and ashamed, Jessica retrieved her phone from her pocket. This was the one conversation she'd been avoiding, but it needed to happen. Now.

Taking affirmative action empowered Jessica, making her feel human again. Three weeks had passed since Will's death and she had lost a considerable amount of weight.

"Look at you," Edith Brown chided gently, "You're all skin and bones. Come. Let me cook you some Fish Pepper Soup or *Egusi*. You love *Egusi*, eh?"

Jessica winced, "I'm fine, Mum. If I eat anything like that now, I'd probably throw up."

Her mother looked offended, ready to argue, but thought better of it. "Oh! Ok then. Hmmm." She left the kitchen, shrugging in a forced show of nonchalance.

For the first time in almost a month, Jessica sat down to write. Her family's concern meant someone was always lurking around, offering little privacy. Now, with assurances that she wouldn't harm herself, maybe they'd trust her to be alone.

"My daughter, Winter always gives way to Spring – your grieving shall pass. You will get through this, you hear? *Inate*?" Her father's voice was gruff, and he cleared his throat before continuing, "I wish we didn't have to leave, but this journey is a solitary one – for *you*. It won't be easy, but I know you'll pull through. Remember, my dear, trust your feelings, and allow a stronger Jessica Sokari Brown to emerge."

Jessica gave her beloved father a hug, appreciating his wisdom.

The gist of Edith Brown's parting advice was, "Weep, my daughter. Weep until there's nothing left to cry about. Do that and you'll surely laugh again."

Jessica loved her parents. They were well-intentioned and wise, but couldn't fully understand her pain. She had lost her soulmate. They still had each other.

Once they'd departed for the airport, Jessica's shoulders dropped as she breathed a sigh of relief. For the past few weeks, she'd been forcibly holding her breath whilst simultaneously drowning. And now, she exhaled all the repressed emotions that had been smothering her and swamping her desire to live. Yes, she wanted to die. It was a strange feeling; one that was difficult to comprehend. The only person who'd ever understood her was Freida. Fifi was her rock, her best friend, her confidante. Yet, even she was showing signs of losing patience with Jessica.

CHAPTER 32 — FAMILY

It was time to stop wallowing in grief.

PALM TREES IN THE STORM

CHAPTER 33

A Small World

Annabel and Emily meticulously orchestrated Jessica's trip to Thailand. Anticipating her potential reluctance to embrace the journey, every detail was prearranged, ensuring the airline and health spa would cocoon her in luxury and care.

"Oh, Annabel, you shouldn't have!" Jessica's voice trembled with emotion. "I could've paid for this! It's…"

"It's what you deserve after all you've been through," Annabel interjected, her tone solemn. "We wanted to spoil you."

Emily chimed in with a nod, "Plus, with any luck, you'll come back refreshed and I'll be able to make a ton of money from my star duo once again." She winked, lightening the mood.

Jessica hugged them both, a silent testament to her deep gratitude.

At 16:30 on Friday, December 3rd, 2004, she embarked on a first-class British Airways flight from London to Bangkok, arriving in the Thai capital the following morning at 10:10. The eleven-hour-forty-minute journey left her wide-eyed and weary, having foolishly spent it in a sleepless state, watching movie after movie to stave off thoughts of William and the brutal reality of her solitude. For the past five years, they had done almost everything together. Now here she was, alone. A widow at twenty-three.

The domestic flight to Koh Samui, a brief hour and six minutes, felt interminable. Stepping off the plane into the open terminal, the humid, fragrant air clung to her skin, invoking memories of Accra. The familiar scent stirred a longing to return to her childhood home as soon as she could. She vaguely regretted not accepting her dad's suggestion that she return to spend Christmas with her family.

Well, here she was in Thailand. Though skeptical of the lengthy yoga and detox holiday, Jessica sensed deep down that this '28-Day Ultimate Transformation Wellness Retreat' was exactly what she needed. Annabel's persuasion had quelled her reservations, and the less appealing alternatives of spending Christmas and New Year alone or with Will's parents had made her decision easier.

CHAPTER 33 🌴 A SMALL WORLD

The colourful flowers and bamboo motifs surrounding her created a tropical paradise, a stark contrast to the memories haunting her. "Will would've loved this," she murmured, a bittersweet smile tugging at her lips as she imagined her husband's ease with the locals.

"Excuse me, Ma'am," a gentle voice interrupted her thoughts. A man held a make-shift cardboard sign reading "Jessica Brown". He was her driver, punctual and polite, ready to whisk her away to the resort.

Overcome by a tidal wave of exhaustion, she was relieved to find the printed schedule he handed her focused on "informal rest" for the remainder of the weekend, with the real program starting on Monday. She intuitively knew this space – away from Holland Park and the life she had known – would be invaluable.

～

Perhaps it was the gentle breeze filtering through the thatched windows of her private bungalow or the serene stillness highlighting the absence of discordant city sounds, but Jessica succumbed to a deep, uninterrupted sleep that had evaded her for the past month. She briefly woke to a warm broth of julienned vegetables and butterflied prawns, seasoned with ginger, garlic, chilli and coriander, then slipped back into a blissful slumber.

Monday marked the beginning of her "Mental, Emotional and Physical Detox journey" *(what a mouthful!)*, an endeavour she approached with a sense of hopeful expectation. Will wouldn't want her to mourn forever. She owed it to him to give this her best shot. She was doing this for him.

Jessica said as much in the first welcome session, which was an open forum (the kind she dreaded), with a group of twenty participants sitting in a circle; a setup designed for sharing personal stories. Berice, the Belgian moderator, paused Jessica mid-speech to mirror what she'd just said.

"You are doing this for *him*? For your husband who is gone?"

Jessica bristled at the question. "Yes! *Yes*, I'm doing this for him. He wouldn't want me to be sad for too long." She sounded defensive.

"Oh!" Berice's tone was curious, not flippant. "And *you*. You want to stay sad, yes?"

Jessica hesitated, searching for a hint of trickery in those blue eyes but finding only genuine concern. The woman wasn't trying to be facetious. Swallowing self-consciously, she nodded, knowing there was nowhere to hide. She might as well be honest. "Yes. I want to be miserable. I deserve this pain." Her face flooded with tears of self-pity. It appeared counter-intuitive to admit she wanted to feel wretched.

Berice probed, "May I ask why?"

Jessica sneaked a furtive glance at the others, but their supportive silence encouraged her to continue. "I-I…" She blinked. "We argued. I

CHAPTER 33 — A SMALL WORLD

lied… he drove off, and that's when it happened."

"I understand," Berice empathised in her soft French accent. "Have you considered the possibility you had nothing to do with the accident? Jessica, each of us has a specific time on earth and when that time is up, it's up. This might not be what you want to hear, but I can see it means something to you, yes?"

She nodded, the simplicity of her mother's old belief, resonating in the open environment of the Koh Samui resort, no longer sounding like mumbo-jumbo to Jessica. Still, it made her angry that William's death could be explained in such simple terms. Her fists clenched at her sides, her nails digging into her palms as if the physical pain could somehow ground her swirling emotions. Her voice rose, raw and jagged, slicing through the heavy silence of the room. "You will never understand what I've lost!" she cried, each word laced with a bitterness that left a sour taste in her mouth.

Berice remained calm, her eyes filled with a mix of empathy and quiet determination. "I may not know your exact pain, Jessica, but grief is a language we all understand in our own way," she replied softly, her tone a soothing balm against Jessica's fury.

The room's atmosphere was thick with the scent of burning sage, a faint haze curling around them, but Jessica barely noticed it over the pounding in her ears. Her vision blurred with unshed tears, and she rose and stepped away from the circle, desperate to hide the vulnerable cracks in her façade. "I can't do this," she whispered, her voice trembling like a fragile leaf on an autumn breeze.

"You can, and you will," Berice countered gently, stepping closer with a soft rustle of her skirt. "Because you owe it to yourself to heal, no matter how impossible it seems right now."

Jessica's breath hitched, a sob catching in her throat, as her walls began to crumble. Memories of her late husband flooded her mind – his laughter echoing in the halls of their home, the warmth of his embrace, the quiet strength in his emerald eyes. Each recollection was a knife twist of agony.

"I don't know how to live without him," she admitted, her voice barely more than a broken whisper. She sank onto a nearby chair, her body folding in on itself as though she could make herself disappear.

"I know," Berice said, kneeling beside her, offering a solid presence without crowding her space. "But piece by piece, breath by breath, you will find a way. And we'll be here to help you every step of the journey."

Jessica looked into Berice's eyes, seeing not just a counselor, but a beacon of hope in her darkest hour. A tiny spark flickered within her – fragile, but there. She nodded, wiping away her tears with trembling fingers. "Alright, I'll try."

Berice gave a small, encouraging smile. "That's all you need to do for now, Jessica. Just try."

The atmosphere in the room lightened, just a fraction, as if the

CHAPTER 33 — A SMALL WORLD

sage smoke that had encircled them was beginning to lift, taking with it some of the weight of her burden. Jessica took a deep breath, the first one in a while that didn't feel like it was shared with ghosts, and felt the smallest hint of resolve fortify her heart.

Berice was addressing the group. "During these 28 days, we will press the 'reset' button on our lives, shedding preconceptions and limiting beliefs; anything blocking us from living our best lives." She emphasised the last part while looking at Jessica.

Jessica cringed. Living-our-best-lives…?? Ok, this is where you've lost me, she thought. What on earth does that mean? I *was* living my best life before it was cruelly snatched away! The others were nodding their brain-washed heads in agreement, their enthusiastic applause only deepening her frustration.

Berice concluded her welcome speech with the words, "… so I encourage each of you to tap into that vulnerability; take a chance and share parts of yourselves you're normally frightened to share with others. In your vulnerability lies your strength. So, let's try something new and take a chance together."

Jessica had tuned out and registered this speech as complete codswallop. With a sigh of exasperation, she rolled her eyes in disbelief. "Oh Annabel!" she murmured, scratching her head in dismay, "What in the world have you signed me up for?"

On the second day, a one-on-one session with Berice left Jessica feeling scrutinized.

She confronted Berice. "Is there something you're not telling me? I feel I'm being treated differently from everybody else!"

Berice's stare was unwavering. "That is correct, yes."

"But, why?" Jessica was alarmed by the direct admission. "Why am I different?

The counselor's expression revealed nothing. "Why not? Everyone is unique – it's never one size fits all."

Suspicion flared in Jessica. "What did they tell you, the people who arranged this?"

With a rare smile, Berice replied, "What do you suppose they told me?"

That she'd smiled infuriated Jessica even more. Her irritation boiled over. "Stop answering my questions with your own!" Jessica knew she was being rude, but couldn't help herself. She squeezed her right hand into a tight fist, painfully pinching already tense thigh muscles into a greater knot of fury. The urge to scream was overwhelming. "Why do all you people speak in the same ridiculous way? '*What do you suppose they told me?*' Gosh! Say *something*... I don't know... anything original! Instead

CHAPTER 33 🌴 A SMALL WORLD

of spewing the same meaningless bullshit over and over. Aargh!" She slapped an open palm across her forehead, holding it there for a dramatic second.

There was silence.

Jessica peeked at her Belgian agitator through her fingers, noting her outburst had sparked no reaction. The woman scribbled calmly on her notepad, unfazed, reading glasses stylishly perched on the tip of her pointy nose.

Jessica felt so foolish – like someone in an amateur school play or a spoilt child summoned to the head teacher's office. She dropped her hand back in her lap and waited.

The retreat manager finally laid down the bamboo pen and removed her blue rimmed spectacles. Folding her arms in a gesture of finality, she leaned against the high-backed cane chair and surveyed Jessica, her gaze unflinching.

Jessica swallowed self-consciously; it was impossible to read this woman.

"What do you imagine they told me?" Berice repeated her question, her tone so gentle it diffused Jessica's anger.

Jessica bowed her head, defeated. "That... I'm... in danger of trying to kill myself?"

Berice raised an eyebrow. "And are you?"

"No!" Jessica exclaimed. "No, I'm not."

Berice's smile was reassuring. "Then you have nothing to worry about and neither do we." She glanced at the clock on the wall. "*Bon*. It's time for your first yoga session. Just head to the large hut by the beach. You don't want to be late."

Jessica's heart skipped a beat during the yoga class introduction. No way! She exclaimed to herself. It couldn't be! But the Spanish accent was unmistakable.

"Hi, I'm Magdalena. Pleasure to meet you all…."

Jessica stared in wonder and disbelief. This was the same woman she and Will had met in Bali all those years ago. "Goodness! It *is* her. What a small world," she blurted, drawing odd glances and uncertain smiles. With a dismissive wave, she settled into a cross-legged position on her yoga mat; feeling calmer and curiously uplifted.

After an intense hour-and-a-half of manipulating her body into unnatural positions that promised release, Jessica approached the front of the hut and waited. Once the other participants had relayed their obligatory thanks and comments, Magdalena turned to Jessica with a smile, and the two women embraced like old friends.

"I was amazed when I spotted you," Magdalena beamed. "Hard to forget your pretty face. Alone this time?"

A shadow of sorrow flickered as Jessica nodded. "Yes, I'm here alone."

CHAPTER 33   A SMALL WORLD

Magdalena, unaware of Jessica's circumstances, suggested, "How about a walk on the beach?"

It occurred to Jessica that Berice, or whoever was in charge, hadn't bothered to brief all the retreat leaders about her "unique" situation. It might have been easier if they had, Jessica considered with a flash of annoyance.

She surveyed Magdalena whose expression was open and warm, making Jessica feel unexpectedly understood, like she could trust this relative stranger. As they walked, she shared her pain over losing both her child and husband in a four-year period!

"I wanted to die. It's been unbelievably painful and unfair," Jessica admitted.

Magdalena's empathy was palpable as she commiserated, "First, your child, then your husband… that's really tough."

They walked in reflective silence for a moment.

Jessica mused, "After the initial shock, I felt nothing. Just wanted to give up on life. Shutting the door to my heart felt like protection. Thought if I shut the door, it won't hurt."

"Did that help? Does it no longer hurt?"

Jessica shrugged. "No pain, but no pleasure either. I feel empty."

"Feeling nothing is part of grieving, too…but that's no way to live. We're meant to suffer and enjoy – experience ugliness *and* beauty. That's life. It's what makes us human."

They stopped walking and Magdalena's sincerity touched Jessica deeply. "For some people it starts with anger. Others just get depressed, Jessica. Everyone grieves differently. Trust that what you're experiencing is natural and will pass."

Jessica smiled ruefully. "D'you know, I couldn't even cry for a while? It was so strange. Now, I'm probably at the anger stage," she admitted, remembering how she'd felt towards Berice that morning.

Both women were quiet, each wrapped in their own thoughts.

"Let's do this again," Magdalena offered as they returned to the resort compound.

Jessica nodded, gratitude swelling within her. These walks with Magdalena became the highlight of the retreat, transforming her skepticism into a renewed sense of purpose – like Magdalena was an intrinsic part of Jessica's journey through life.

By the end of the 28 days, it became clear it wasn't mere coincidence but destiny that had brought Jessica to Koh Samui and reunited her with Magdalena. She was ready to face life anew, with the strength she'd rediscovered in the tranquil beauty of Thailand.

CHAPTER 34

What the hell happens next?

Jessica was thrilled to find Emily waiting for her at the airport. Despite the clamouring paparazzi eager to capture a glimpse of the "grieving widow", it was the sight of her friend that brought her a semblance of peace. A pre-arranged protocol officer escorted her from the plane and, at first glance at her protégée, Emily surmised the trip to Thailand had done wonders. Jessica's skin glowed again, having shed that dull, tired pallor that had made her look far older than her years. She wasn't quite back to her old self, but she was close.

Emily beamed and squeezed her friend tight as she whispered in her ear, "Good to have you back, Jessica Brown."

Sleeping alone in her Holland Park home conjured too many distressing memories. The following morning, Jessica awoke groggy-eyed and irritable.

"So, what are you going to do about it?" Annabel wasn't one for subtlety. She bit into a croissant from Patisserie Valerie, crumbs scattering.

Jessica's eyes widened in feigned ignorance. "What d'you mean?"

"Well, look at you, Jess. One day back and you look like shit again. It's this house! You can't stay here. Not without him." Annabel was incapable of mincing her words.

It was what made their on-screen rapport so riveting; her unexpected bluntness juxtaposed against Jessica's deliberate diplomacy. Annabel's prissy, angelic television persona belied her sharp tongue and often brazen attitude, while Jessica's sultry, sexy allure masked her tomboyish naiveté. Together, they were a magnet for viewership.

She looked affectionately at her friend, who was munching away without a care. And it struck her: Life goes on. That's the simple truth. The tragedy was devastating, but wallowing in it would do no good. *Disappointments are inevitable, but misery is a choice.* She needed to figure out how to live the rest of her life without the ever-present shadow of recent misfortunes.

CHAPTER 34   WHAT THE HELL HAPPENS NEXT?

The question was, what the hell happens next? What changes would smoothen her transition from "Jessica with William", to "Jessica alone"?

The answer hit her. She should sell the house. That was it. She couldn't stay surrounded by the ghosts of the past and expect to 'live her best life'. A couple of years into their marriage, William had placed the property in both their names, so it now belonged to Jessica. Whilst she was well within her rights to do with it as she pleased, she felt duty-bound to inform her in-laws of her intentions.

"You're planning to *what?*" Lady Armstrong-Bell's voice crackled with displeasure over the speakerphone; displeasure, tinged with a mixture of disbelief, grief and anger.

Jessica's words tumbled out awkwardly. "To sell the house… erm… you know… Actually, forget it. Why don't I just hand it back to you? It'll be easiest. I-I just know I can't carry on living here, and it was yours before all this, anyway." She suddenly felt dreadful.

"Hmmm, I see…" Philippa's voice quivered with restrained emotion.

Jessica continued backtracking. "I should move out and… you take over. I could transfer it into your name. It's been in your family for years and…" She was at a loss for words. "I'm so sorry. I don't mean to upset you."

Sir Michael's tone was decisive and unyielding. "Jessica, my dear, please don't worry about how it makes us feel. We're just a bit sentimental,

I suppose."

"Um…" Jessica tried to interject, but Sir Michael stopped her mid-flow.

"No need to apologise or feel bad. The house is yours to do with it as you please. But, if it's all the same to you, Dear, do allow us to purchase it at a fair price. That way, it stays in the family."

"*Purchase?*" The suggestion startled Jessica. "Oh no! I wouldn't dream of selling it back to you! That would be…"

"That would be fair," Sir Michael stated firmly. "Don't you understand, my dear girl? It's what our William would have wanted. He gave it to you and would expect you to get some compensation."

"Well, okay, I suppose so." Jessica hesitated, biting the edge of her index finger, and exhaled. "I accept your offer. Thank you."

"Jolly good. My lawyer will handle the paperwork, we'll agree a fair price and it'll be off your hands."

"Thank you, Jessica." Philippa said, her quiet sobbing subsiding. "Thank you for understanding."

"You're welcome," Jessica replied, feeling awkward about the shift in power dynamic.

Barely a week later, the sale documents confirmed the market price for the house at £12.8 million, but Sir Michael insisted on rounding it up

CHAPTER 34 — WHAT THE HELL HAPPENS NEXT?

to fifteen, given Jessica was their daughter-in-law and the like. Their generosity astounded Jessica, but she resolutely declined, suggesting the fairer proposition of £10 million. Despite her vehement protests, Sir Michael and Lady Armstrong-Bell would entertain no negotiations. They deemed it a matter of principle.

And so it was that Jessica Sokari Brown became £15 million richer, but would have given anything to be without a penny to her name if it meant having William by her side. She had lost her inamorato, the love of her life, and no amount of money could fill that void.

～

"A first-floor flat in Knightsbridge. Could be worse!" Emily Dunn glanced around the impressive space, nodding appreciatively. "Smaller; more manageable than Holland Park – I like it!"

"So do I," Jessica agreed, her expression somber.

"Hey!" Emily nudged her, "More enthusiasm, please! What's not to like?! It's a Victorian conversion boasting high ceilings, tons of light, two bedrooms and bathrooms, an enormous reception room – plus it gives you the fresh start you crave."

Jessica shrugged. "I suppose so."

She purposely chose a new area of London to minimize her pain. Familiar places only kept her wounds fresh. *Dear J, there's nothing worse than losing someone and then being daily confronted by sights and places you used to frequent with them.*

"But I feel frightfully alone… I bought it with money from the house sale, which just reminds me William's gone." Jessica sniffed, her eyes glossing over. "I'd like to put some of it to good use… you know."

"Then do that, darling. Whatever makes you feel better!"

And so, Jessica partnered with a charitable organisation that supported victims of road accidents and bereaved families, pledging regular financial aid. It was a small way to cope with her guilt and sorrow.

The Armstrong-Bells' fifteen million had been pocket change to them, but to Jessica it symbolised a lifeline she hadn't asked for and didn't want. She wondered if their extravagant offer was an attempt to assuage their guilt. They hadn't caused their son's death, true, but perhaps they felt they hadn't loved him enough. Perhaps, if they had, he wouldn't have been so dependent on Jessica. Truth be told, she'd been flattered by the extent of his love for her; that he'd wrapped his entire existence around her; that he referred to her as his "most prized possession". But after a while it had felt constricting and cloyingly claustrophobic. His possessiveness had become stifling, and their co-dependence borderline unhealthy. She had become Will's lifeline, and *that* was what ultimately killed him.

Jessica laid down her pen and sipped her coffee. She rubbed her stiff neck with a weary sigh. The blasted bed was still to arrive, so she'd slept on a mat on the floor – pretty uncomfortable when you've been spoilt by luxury. She smiled sadly, recalling William's obsession with perfect mattresses and duvets and thread counts and pillows. "A good sleep

CHAPTER 34 — WHAT THE HELL HAPPENS NEXT?

begets a good life," he'd often say, before scooping her up in his powerful arms, spinning her around as though she were a child, and then unceremoniously dumping her on the plush bedding.

I miss him, Jessica pondered, her tearful gaze scanning the 20-foot ceilings, the original Victorian fireplace, and the beautifully carved wooden doors leading to her dining room. "This is a far cry from Kilburn", she whispered bitterly, "but look what I've lost to get here".

Here she was... standing on her own two feet. Alone. Single. No husband. No child, even. Imagine that!! Imagine if Philip had survived... he'd have no father, and she'd have been a single mother grappling with even more loss.

Ok, J, enough I'm going crazy with these thoughts. Heavens, all I do is sit by this bay window and drink coffee (far too much, if you ask me). I spend all day writing. I need to stop over-thinking, go out there and get my life moving again. Sitting here alone is driving me insane.

CHAPTER 35

No holds Barred

"I love it!" Jessica exclaimed, eyes sparkling. "Gosh, I was just contemplating how I need to work again… you know, perform. Then you call me with this. Incredible!"

"So glad you're up for it. It's at the Radio City Music Hall – what you've always dreamed of – and promises to be a spectacular event all round."

"You're coming along, right Ems?" The prospect of doing a show without the stalwart presence of William by her side made her feel jittery. It'd been months since her last production and, given all the life-changing events, she knew her headspace might not be so conducive to "giving the performance of her career", as the organizers apparently expected.

Emily's response was unequivocal. "Of course! This is the 'World Cup of Dance' and I wouldn't miss it for anything. They're dubbing it your 'comeback', you know." She reacted to Jessica's quick intake of breath by adding reassuringly, "And you have *nothing* to worry about. Dancing is in your veins, Jess. You hit that stage, the music starts and *bam*! Every time. You never disappoint. I know you'll be amazing."

Jessica sniggered, "Yeah, right! Remember that time I froze on stage? Sooo embarrassing!"

"That happened *yonks* ago, silly! You shouldn't even be thinking about that."

"But… I'm so… out of shape," Jessica complained, revealing her self-doubt.

"Huh!" Emily scoffed, "*You??* Have you looked at yourself in the mirror lately? Darling, you're in better condition than ever. Ok, you initially lost a little too much weight, but then after Thailand you got better and now… nah, don't fret. You're ready."

Jessica sighed. Emily always had a way of inspiring confidence. "Thanks, Ems. I know you'd never bullshit me… but I…"

"Need to get stronger. I agree." Emily pre-empted Jessica's concerns. "Don't worry, it's handled. I'm still your manager, after all!"

"You're the best! But how…?"

"Tomorrow at 9am, you begin a strict workout regime with the

CHAPTER 35 — NO HOLDS BARRED

one-and-only… Rodney…!" Emily's voice mimicked that of an American sports commentator.

Jessica stifled a giggle. "The one-and-only *who?*"

Emily Dunn chuckled in response, reverting to her clipped English accent. "Rodney, darling. Rodney Pascale – probably the best Personal Trainer this side of the Atlantic."

"Oh!" Jessica had nothing to add. She studied her manager and friend with gratitude.

Emily had taken care of everything.

Rodney Pascale resembled a comic-book caricature of a fitness guru. With muscles in unexpected places, he was the epitome of six-pack perfection and lean, flexible strength all coiled up in a flawless mass of masculinity. And, of course, he sported a shaved head and practised martial arts with extreme discipline. He was ridiculously perfect and precisely what Jessica needed to help regain her power, both physical and mental.

Their scheduled daily workouts were grueling, so it was helpful that he was upbeat and positive, though not in a sickeningly annoying manner. Excellent choice, Ems!

"Come on, you can do this J – I have every faith in you!" Prone to over-familiarity, Rodney began calling her "J" during their second week together, when she hit rock bottom and insisted there was no way she could carry on. He proved he wasn't all meathead, but also sensitive and intuitive, with an uncanny understanding of the human psyche. Amazingly, he'd bullied and cajoled, and finally persuaded her she could achieve the impossible. Here they were, 10 weeks after that momentary lapse in self-belief, and she felt re-energized and raring to go.

On her 25th burpee, Rodney started to count her down – five… four… three… two… – all the while executing each squat-thrust alongside her with athletic precision. The man hardly broke a sweat, and never seemed to run out of breath. He was a damn machine!

Jessica performed her final concluding leap in the air, gentle land and drop, perfect plank and press down, graceful hop of feet to hands, up and repeat.

"… And one! Superb!" Rodney applauded her efforts with glee and declared her fit and ready to tackle the world once again.

"I should bloody hope so!" she retorted, panting and wiping her dripping brow. "It's taken me long enough. 12 weeks, huh!" She rolled her eyes in self-disgust.

"It's bizarre, this feeling in the pit of my stomach," Jessica admitted, rubbing her sweaty palms against the sides of her shimmery Lycra-clad legs.

CHAPTER 35 — NO HOLDS BARRED

"You'll shine, darling… as always. Just trust your body to deliver," Emily reassured her.

"Mmm…" Jessica agreed absentmindedly, her brain already picturing each move and twirl to "get in the zone".

A reporter had sneaked backstage and shoved a microphone in Ms Dunn's face. "So, tell us, how did you secure this rare headline act with The Rockettes? How does Jessica feel about tonight?"

Jessica turned away so they wouldn't see her discomfort. Emily was speaking, "Well, it's a real honour for her. And she's worked hard to get here. The audience is in for a treat tonight!"

Jessica tried to tune out their voices and focus on her pre-show routine. Moments later, her cue sounded, and she made her entrance on stage, delivering one high kick after another to the utter delight of her audience.

For a brief second mid-performance, she felt that old familiar flutter of panic, threatening to sabotage this moment of glory. But sheer will and determination made her battle through her irrational childhood fear of failure, and Radio City Music Hall exploded into rapturous applause.

Joyful tears of gratitude overcame Jessica as she hugged a bewildered Emily backstage. "Thank you! For giving me my life back!" Her smile was ecstatic.

"This was all *you*. I only arranged it, nothing more. It's all you. Well done!" Emily, too, had damp eyes.

They spent forty-five minutes to an hour schmoozing the press and signing autographs, but just as Jessica was preparing to leave the Rockefeller Center, a couple approached her.

"Miss Brown, we've been waiting to catch you alone. Congratulations on a stunning performance!"

"Thank you," was Jessica's felicitous response. She glanced at Emily, who was standing about ten metres away and on the phone.

"Wonder if we might have a quick word to discuss a profitable proposition…" The man, too, glanced at Emily before continuing, "which we would prefer to share in private." He handed her a business card. "Call us at your earliest opportunity?"

Jessica hesitated, then slipped the card into her purse. "Sure, once I'm back in London," she promised, just as Emily approached.

"Car's here," her manager confirmed.

The journey from midtown Manhattan to their downtown Soho hotel didn't take too long. Completely zonked after her impassioned performance, she craved nothing more than a good night's sleep.

Eight-and-a-half hours later, the familiar, but annoying, ringtone of her blackberry shattered her contented state of sweet slumber.

"How did it go? Tell me everything!"

Jessica smiled sleepily, pleased to hear her sister's voice. Although well-rested, her mind was still tingling from the excitement of the night

CHAPTER 35 — NO HOLDS BARRED

before. "Oh, Fifi, I wish you'd been there to see their faces!"

"I know. Couldn't get out of being on call." Freida sounded genuinely miffed. "This performance is something you've dreamed about since you were five, when you used to obsess over that woman on TV, Diana, remember? I'm bummed I missed it! Go on. Describe it to me."

Jessica giggled. "It was magical. The press said I was like... a leopard, hahaha. Don't know how PC it is to liken me to a wild cat, but hey! They loved it. I received so many compliments, and even got approached by a Hollywood producer."

"That's fantastic! This could open serious doors for you."

"Yeah, and I'm grateful to Ems for arranging everything – for pushing me. I wouldn't be here without her." Jessica glanced at her watch. "Oh, shucks! I'm already ten minutes late." She threw off the bedcovers. "I promised we'd meet for breakfast. Sorry, Fif, gotta go – she's heading back to London in a few hours, and..."

"Don't worry, off you go, then. Glad I caught you. Congratulations again, darling!"

Later that morning, Jessica headed out for a spot of shopping, skipping along the gridded streets of Manhattan, and waltzing back to The Mercer heavy laden with bags and happily humming to herself. She was so wrapped up in her thoughts she literally stumbled into him and had to steady herself.

"Jessica!" That deep, sultry American drawl was unmistakable. Titus Jameson.

"Oh! Ti… TJ… hello… fancy seeing *you* here…" Jessica felt a surge of embarrassment. It had been, what… two… three years? She'd totally ghosted him; ignored all his calls and had even been downright rude on one occasion, telling him to please leave her alone. After their last encounter at the Lincoln Center, she'd clocked her attraction to him as dangerous.

But that was then, and this was now.

Her heart thumped when he smiled. She melted. They sat in the Mercer Kitchen Bar and played catch-up. TJ offered sincere condolences and expressed genuine horror at the news of William's car accident. She saw another side to him. Gentle. Kind. And *seriously* funny. They talked about everything and, by the end of the evening, Jessica concluded she hadn't laughed quite that hard in a long while. He made her smile, this TJ.

And something else, too.

At one point, his gaze was so intense she glanced away, lest he glean her obvious desire. She fancied him, plain and simple. He was the sexiest guy she'd ever met.

"Hey, you." He said it with his growingly familiar lopsided grin, lifting a hand to tuck an imaginary misplaced hair behind her ear. He looked at her as if he knew more than he was letting on and her cheeks grew hot. She bit her lip. It was an excuse to touch her, but she didn't mind. She squeezed her knees together. She wanted to touch him, too.

CHAPTER 35 NO HOLDS BARRED

Giving him a sideways glance through the fan of her lashes, she rose gracefully, and breathed, "I'd better get myself to bed." *Before I do something crazy like invite you up,* she thought.

He stood too, clearing his throat. "I'll pick you up tomorrow at noon." It wasn't a request, but a statement, followed by a lingering kiss to her temple; absorbing her scent before he strode out of the bar.

At 2am, Jessica let herself into her Loft Suite and suddenly felt alone. She looked around the pent-house style room, with its gorgeous exposed-brick arched windows and wall-sized giant mirrors, and wished she'd heeded the call of her inner siren; this impulse to let go of every Brown-instilled inhibition – to spread her sexual wings and sail into a storm of wanton, unadulterated pleasure. No holds barred.

PALM TREES IN THE STORM

CHAPTER 36

A different Kind of Love

At the sound of the unexpected knock, Jessica glanced at her watch. *9:45am.* Damn. If she hadn't already been awake, she'd have given whoever dared ignore her Do Not Disturb sign a real bollocking.

"Room service," the voice announced.

Room service! I didn't order bloody room service, Jessica almost blurted in response, but held her tongue, her manners getting the better of her. With jerky movements, she pulled on her Japanese silk robe and flounced to the door.

"Just a minute…" she muttered as she unlocked and opened it with an exasperated sigh, which turned into a gasp of disbelief when she saw who and what awaited her. Obscured by a huge, over-the-top display of red roses was a diminutive member of the hotel housekeeping staff, who stumbled under the weight of the vase she was carrying, and hobbled across the room to place it on the round glass table by the window.

"Thank you, Ma'am." The chambermaid pocketed the generous tip and scurried out, disappearing as quickly as she'd appeared.

Like a scene from a romance, Jessica trotted over to the eye-catching display, eager to confirm her suspicions. Red roses wouldn't be a belated congratulation for her performance – no, the bouquet was far too grand for that. It was him. Of course, it was. The note read: "JB, I insisted they deliver these to you immediately. Sorry if I woke you. I couldn't sleep. You have me spellbound. TJ."

Jessica read and reread it, smiling to herself at the satisfying sensation of requited desire his message evoked. He wanted her as much as she yearned for him, and it made her feel incredible.

Noon couldn't arrive soon enough, and by 11:45 am she was twiddling her fingers in anticipation of their first date. She'd chosen to wear something simple and light, especially given how oppressive summer can get in the concrete jungle of Manhattan. Her strappy yellow sundress paired with crimson lipstick was the perfect ensemble. Red rose in hair? No, she concluded. Too tacky.

CHAPTER 36 — A DIFFERENT KIND OF LOVE

She nearly jumped out of her skin when the shrill ring of the telephone interrupted her reverie.

"Yes?"

"Ms Brown, there's a Titus Jameson here for you. May we send him up?"

Send him up? Jessica had been expecting to go down to Reception, not have him in her room. She hesitated before responding, "Erm… sure, thank you."

The second she laid down the receiver, she clutched her head and spun around. What to do… what to do? Calm down, Jess, you're a grown woman… you *like* this man… so what's the problem? Oh, goodness!

Knock, knock, knock.

He must have sprinted up the stairs or something because the sound came much sooner than she expected. Her heart began to thud.

With a deep inhale, she unlocked her suite. And there he was, looking even more glorious and sexy than she remembered, evoking that now familiar flutter in her groin.

Their eyes locked for the longest moment, and Jessica could tell from his heaving chest he was out of breath. He stepped in and shut the door behind him.

She needed to say something, so gestured to the flowers and cleared her throat. "They're gorgeous, thank you… I…"

TJ had moved closer and lowered his head with deliberate intent, smothering her words with his lips. Her body melted against his firm, muscular form. He felt incredible. She fancied him. Full stop.

His voice was unsteady when he finally pulled away. "I've wanted to do that for the longest time. You drive me crazy, girl!"

Jessica gazed into his sincere, almost boyish eyes. With a coy grin, she pulled him back towards her. "Crazy, huh?" she mumbled against his mouth, whilst teasing and nibbling his bottom lip.

TJ stepped backwards and turned away slightly, visibly trying to recover a modicum of self-control.

Jessica gave a knowing smile then laid a hand on her rumbling stomach. "I'm starving, actually… maybe we should eat first?" She'd been too nervous for breakfast that morning, and his kiss had oddly made her ravenous.

TJ almost sighed with relief, grateful for her rescue attempt. "Let's do that. And afterwards…," his gaze was smouldering. "… Afterwards you can choose what we do."

His inference was abundantly clear and Jessica simply nodded. TJ was a man who didn't play games.

⁓

He took her to Les Deux Gamins, a French Bistro in the West Village, close to his home on the corner of West 4th and West 10th Street, a calculated

CHAPTER 36 — A DIFFERENT KIND OF LOVE

move, but Jessica didn't mind. In truth, she pretty much didn't mind anything he did and, after their hasty brunch, gladly followed him up to his loft-style apartment.

The décor in his home was reminiscent of a Moroccan teahouse – not that she had the foggiest idea what *that* might look like. The room smelled of cinnamon. She drank in the combination of sultry colours, bold patterns, and intricate details; the red cushions and beaded rugs, the lampshades of different sizes and the huge, draped four-poster bed, dressed in satin-silk. Eclectic.

TJ started to undress her the second he shut his apartment door. "I want you!" he growled, and Jessica could feel the corresponding bulge in his trousers as she succumbed with a meow, pulling him closer. Hot lips fused in unrestrained passion, and he unzipped her in one expert movement. She kicked off her sandals to accompany the yellow heap of sundress, gasping as TJ's hands kneaded her pert breasts. His lips teased her nipples before sliding down her body. Still fully clothed, he dropped to his knees and pressed his mouth to her pelvis, causing her to moan out loud. Jessica twisted her fingers into his blonde hair, urging him closer still. As she glanced down, she was suddenly glad William's had been darker. She groaned with pleasure as his flickering tongue found her sweet spot. "I'm going to burst," her mind screamed, just as he pulled away to stand upright – unbuttoning his shirt with an urgency, his breath coming in short, quick gasps.

As the image of William again flashed across her consciousness, Jessica imagined what he would think. *He'd want me to be happy*, she reasoned, grabbing onto the edge of the dining table to steady herself. TJ leaned in to kiss her slowly, while still undressing. As though with a mind of their own, Jessica's hands reached out to hasten his progress, and when he hoisted her atop the table, she wrapped her legs around his waist and thrust her hips forward, so he entered her with ease. TJ let out a cry of pure animal pleasure and grabbed the soft flesh of her ample bottom. After a few thrusts, he pressed his lips against hers and carried her to the four-poster, where Jessica used her strong dancer's thighs to flip him under so she could be on top. What had begun as ardent and passionate, became sensuous and mind-blowing.

"Oh-oh-oh…" TJ sounded like he'd lost control, and she felt oddly powerful, riding him slowly and deliberately, her writhing hips undulating back and forth. Back and forth. Then she changed the rhythm, gradually moving faster and faster, until he could contain himself no longer. Their bodies exploded in tandem, and Jessica collapsed on him, surprised by how quickly she recovered and wanted to do it all over again. She was hooked.

"Yes… absolutely! Thank you! I'll expect to receive the contract." Jessica replaced the handset and shook her wrists in excitement. She put both hands to her cheeks and tried to catch her breath, her head spinning

CHAPTER 36 A DIFFERENT KIND OF LOVE

with the news.

The phone rang again, and she jumped.

"Hello, who's this?" she couldn't recognise the number.

"Hey slag!" It was Debbie's dulcet tones, and Jessica laughed in delighted surprise.

"Slag yourself!" she retorted good naturedly. "How are you? It's been ages! By the way, thanks for reaching out after the funeral."

"Of course." Debbie's drawl sounded more American. "I hear you're a regular visitor to my city these days."

Jessica chortled, "Wow! News travels fast. Yes. I'm dating a guy who lives in New York."

"Ooooh, tell me more."

Jessica giggled. "Not now. It's late here. But I'm back next week. Hey, why don't you join us for dinner? Then you could meet him."

"Sure. So, why are *you* still up?"

"Business. Actually, it's good you rang. I'm in a bit of a predicament."

"Oh? Tell me."

Jessica paused before sharing the bare-bone details of her new deal; "*A major blockbuster and my very own dance program.*"

Debbie's reaction was unequivocal. "Jess, that's a no-brainer. This is Hollywood we're talking about!"

"The offer is unbelievable, but I dunno. It would mean ditching Emily and Annabel and moving to LA. They've been such amazing friends to me, Debs."

"So?" Debbie remained unfazed. "It's an enormous opportunity. You'd be a complete fool to let it go."

Jessica closed her eyes, palm against forehead. "You know, they're the ones who sent me to that healing retreat in Thailand after Will's death. And then they waited almost eight months until I was ready to work again. I owe them."

"You owe them nothing. Please! Do you think they're doing anything from the goodness of their hearts? These smart *Obroni* girls are only out to exploit you. 'Chocolate and Vanilla' wouldn't exist if not for you."

"No, that's not true. Not at all," Jessica rebutted. "We need each other." She knew her protestations could have been more fervent; but, with Debbie so adamant, she didn't see the point of arguing.

༄

"So, what's this about? Why the generous spread?" Annabel surveyed the mini strawberry tarts and chocolate beignets with suspicion, even as she grabbed a chouquette and popped it into her mouth.

Jessica smiled and offered, "Tea, coffee, juice for either of you?"

Emily was perched on the edge of the sofa and observing her with

CHAPTER 36 🌴 A DIFFERENT KIND OF LOVE

narrowed eyes. "You seem nervous, Jess. What's going on? You ok?"

Jessica stopped twiddling her thumbs. "Yeah, fine," she said breezily.

Annabel licked her fingers before picking up a paper napkin. "Since you asked (rather formally, I might add), I'll have some tea, please. Uh-uh...!" She waggled a finger, before shooing Jessica to the kitchen with both hands. "Not another awkward word from you. You're making *me* nervous."

In the privacy of her kitchen, Jessica paced while the kettle boiled. As she lay the tray on the low, wooden coffee table, her fingers trembled slightly. She wiped them against her thighs and took a stilling breath.

"Right. There's something I need to talk to you about."

"Ahhh, so I was correct. This isn't just a tea-party between friends." Annabel grinned and winked.

Jessica looked at Emily, who'd poured herself a cup of Earl Grey and was stirring it delicately. She swallowed and spoke. "After the concert with The Rockettes, a chap and a lady approached me, remember?"

"Vaguely." Emily shrugged.

"Well, they weren't just fans." Jessica hesitated, then blurted, "They offered me a role in a Hollywood film, and the chance to produce and host my own television dance show."

She glanced from one silent woman to the other. "Ok... say something!"

Annabel wore a puzzled frown. "So, what happens to *us*? Does 'Chocolate and Vanilla' just go up in smoke?"

Jessica bit her lip. "I don't know. Haven't really thought it through."

"But that's just it." Emily's tone was frosty. "You *have* thought it through, Jess. And you called us here to what? Say you're taking the job? That you're moving to LA and abandoning everything we've built?"

Wincing, Jessica responded, "I asked you both here to talk to you about it… I dunno… get your opinion."

"You don't need our opinion, Jess. You've decided."

"No, I haven't! What are you so up in arms about, anyway? This is the opportunity of a lifetime for me – you're my manager – you'd get a *massive* cut. You should tell me to take it, Ems!"

The initial shock had worn off and Emily said more calmly, "Actually, as your manager *I* only take a percentage on deals *I* bring to the table. But that's not the point." She waved a dismissive hand. "Accepting this offer would mean letting go of everything we've worked so hard to achieve, ever since you were fourteen years old. Plus, what happens to Annabel? I can't believe you mentioned nothing to us before."

"Well, I'm telling you now, aren't I?" Jessica countered.

"Yes, now they've handed you a contract!" She pointed at the papers on the mantelpiece. "Really, Jess?"

Annabel gave Jessica an assessing stare. "So, you've outgrown us.

CHAPTER 36 A DIFFERENT KIND OF LOVE

Your friends. The show." She was shaking her head and scrunching her pretty nose as though there were a foul odour in the room.

Her disgusted expression angered Jessica. "Look at you both!" she exploded. "Acting like you really care about what's best for me." Emily started to interject, but Jessica blazed on. "I'm telling you as *friends*," she glared at Annabel, "because it's a dilemma for me. Huh! Maybe Debbie was right and you're only out for what you can get from me!"

With that, Annabel rose, hands on hips, blue eyes flashing. "Oh. I see you're back with your flaky friend Debbie?! Huh! She's the one advising you now, is she? Well, I don't need *anything* from you, Jessica Brown. Go on then. Off to LA. And good luck!"

Jessica gaped as the flaming, flurry of blonde hair stormed out and the front door slammed shut. She turned to Emily, whose reddened features reflected conflicting emotions. The older woman gathered her printed itinerary for 'Chocolate and Vanilla', and placed the redundant sheets back in their folder, snapping it closed with a decisive click. Then she nodded a silent, icy goodbye, and departed.

Jessica paced her living room for a good half-hour, lips folded in and pressed together. "What shall I do?" she mumbled miserably.

"Hello? It's me."

"Hi." Freida's greeting was monosyllabic.

Jessica raised an eyebrow, then cleared her throat and plunged straight in, sharing her conundrum.

Her sister responded in an incredulous tone. "What's the dilemma, exactly? Seems pretty obvious, Jess. These women have stood by you through thick and thin. Emily especially. She pushed you to grow; to believe in yourself and now you want to ditch her?"

"No, I never said I wanted to ditch her."

"C'mon, be real. The moment you get to LA, that's it."

Jessica scratched her head and closed her eyes.

Freida sounded impatient. "Plus, there are no guarantees in Hollywood. You know that. Friendship and love are more important than your career." Jessica noticed an uncharacteristic tremor in her sister's voice before she continued, "You'd be stepping into the unknown, Jess. Think with your heart, not your head. The answer will come. I'll call you tomorrow."

She hung up quickly and Jessica frowned at the telephone, wondering whether to press the redial button. After a while, she stood and rubbed the back of her neck, her mind filled with regret. I should have asked Fifi if she was ok, she thought, pouring herself a glass of water. She placed it on her nightstand and crawled under the duvet.

The following morning, she awoke with a clearer head, and when Fifi telephoned that afternoon, her reply to the question, "Did you decide?" was, "It's a no. I'm going to stay."

CHAPTER 36 — A Different Kind of Love

"Good call."

Both women fell silent.

"Fif?"

"Hmm?"

"Are you ok? You sounded off last night."

Freida's sigh was heavy. "No. I'm not ok."

Although Jessica had enquired, the response took her by surprise. "Oh, what's wrong?"

"Everything." Her voice broke. "It's over, Jess. He's gone."

Jessica pressed the phone closer. "Yinka? What d'you mean, 'he's gone'? Gone where?"

Her usually stalwart sister sniffed and replied, "Said, he'd had enough. That he wants to be with someone who isn't always 'on call' and who can meet his needs."

"*Meet his needs*? You guys have been together for ten years! Oh, Fif, I'm so sorry. I was wrapped up in my silly problems and didn't even ask about *you*." Jessica felt a wave of shame as she recalled the countless times her sister had supported her. "I wish I was there to give you a hug. What can I do to help? Anything."

"No, I'll be fine. It's been brewing for a while, so…" Her voice was tinged with sadness.

"But I was just there in New York – and you said nothing."

"You were busy… with your show and your new boyfriend and…"

"The world of Jessica Brown," Jessica interjected in a dry tone.

There was silence again.

Jessica swallowed. "I'm back next week. Could stay with you, if you like. Keep you company?"

"That'd be nice. But I can't ask you to do that. You're coming for him."

"He can wait. Family comes first. What shall I bring that's quintessentially British?"

"Umm, Mar…" Freida began, but Jessica pre-empted her words.

"Nooo, not Marmite. Ugggh! No idea how you can stand that stuff!"

Freida had a smile in her voice. "It's delicious, and only for those with discerning taste."

Both sisters laughed and Jessica felt the mood lighten.

"Ok, I'll see you next week. Can't wait."

"Me too. Thanks, Jess."

"No, thank *you*, for helping me figure out what to do."

CHAPTER 37

Deborah

"He's called every day since you arrived, Jess," Freida laughingly pointed out. "Go join him. I love having you here, but the whole Yinka fiasco was months ago. I'm fine now."

"Are you kicking me out?" Jessica quipped.

"Yes! Go. The man obviously needs you."

"You mean he needs my body," Jessica countered cheekily.

"Hey!" Freida reprimanded with a giggle of her own. "Miss Jessica Brown, what are you saying?"

Jessica's eyes twinkled as she grabbed her sister's hands. "Oh, Fifi, our connection is phenomenal. Whenever I picture him, I feel this wave of… primitive desire."

"Wow, you're hooked, huh?"

"Addicted. The man is a drug, I swear! The more I have him, the more I want him."

"So that's why you visit practically every two weeks!"

"Precisely. Now, when people ask where I live, I say London *and* New York. The West Village has become my second home." Her eyes looked dreamy.

Freida gazed thoughtfully at her sister. "You love him."

Jessica sighed. "It's not quite what I envisaged when we first started dating. I thought I'd be in absolute control – calling the shots and keeping a tight rein on my heartstrings. Instead…"

"You never imagined you'd fall for another man after Will?" Freida postulated.

Jessica nodded. "It's a different kind of love. Will was my soul mate, but TJ… he's my sex-mate or some other crude categorisation. The thing is he never gets jealous and he really supports my career."

"Hey, don't overthink it. You're having fun; which is what you

CHAPTER 37 — DEBORAH

need right now. No need to compare what you shared with your husband."

Jessica had a faraway look on her face. "I loved Will with my entire being. He was flesh of my flesh; a part of me that can never be erased."

Freida nodded.

"TJ is my lover, nothing more. I love him not with my mind or soul, but with my body. Yes. I worship him with my body, Fif. It's crazy. Mum definitely wouldn't approve."

∼

Jessica hopped out of the cab at 51st and 8th, and gestured to the sullen New York driver, "Keep the change!" whilst muttering under her breath, "Let's hope that cheers you up, you grumpy sod!"

She looked up at the boutique sign EROS and grinned as she pushed the door open.

"Hiya!"

Debbie was handing over a pretty, pink-ribboned package to a customer and looked delighted to see her former housemate. "Hey, stranger! What are you doing here? (Thank you, Ma'am. Hope to see you again soon...) When I didn't hear from you, I figured you'd moved to LA."

"Nope! Didn't go." Jessica held the door ajar for the lady and her numerous bags of shopping.

"Thanks. You have a nice day!" the woman drawled and exited.

Debbie moved from the service counter to stand in front of her friend. "Where's my hug then, Bitch?" She squeezed Jessica affectionately. "I've missed you!"

"Me too," Jessica acknowledged.

Debbie shook her head. "Yeah, right! You're too busy to have missed me! And saying no to LA was the wrong decision, by the way."

Jessica asserted, "Nope. The right one! Emily and Annabel are such loyal friends – I didn't want to lose them. It was the proper thing to do."

Debbie shrugged. "If you say so!" She moved away to rearrange a shelf of merchandise. "So, you've been visiting Manhattan for over a year and haven't looked me up?" Her tone was admonishing.

Jessica grinned guiltily. "They're always whirlwind trips... you know."

Debbie pursed her lips and nodded her chin towards her friend in a gesture of disbelief. "Yeah, whatever!"

Jessica fingered a lace camisole with appreciation. "Nice place you've got here."

Debbie's eyes lit up. "My pride and joy!"

"It's beautiful. And sexy… some of these garments are quite risqué, *chale*. Look at *this* one!" Jessica held up a black and red one-piece with a thong back and crotchless front.

"I know. 'Lingerie that brings out the grrrrr in you!'" Debbie let out a mini roar and Jessica laughed.

CHAPTER 37   DEBORAH

"You're so silly. New York won't realize what hit it."

"*Eiish*, they already do. I'm being dubbed the 'Sex Queen of Manhattan', at age twenty-five." She chortled triumphantly.

Jessica offered, "Would you like to join TJ and I for dinner tomorrow night?"

"Wow. Finally. I get to meet this TJ." Debbie said sarcastically.

"Oh, *commot!*" Jessica teased with a radiant smile. "I'm following through now, aren't I?"

～

"Wow, Jess, he's seriously hot!" Debbie whispered under her breath as an effusive actor-turned-waiter led the threesome to their table. TJ had paused to say hello to yet another person he knew – this man seemed to know *everyone* – and Jessica and Debbie had a moment to themselves.

Jessica smiled jubilantly. "He's gorgeous, right?! And in bed... *OMG*... he's unstoppable." She chuckled self-consciously, glancing back at him. "I mean... I thought the novelty would wear off, but... uh-uh... all I want to do is shag him... all the time... and it's been like a year and a half already!"

The two girls giggled and sat down. Debbie prodded and pushed for every scintillating piece of dirty information and was laughing with delight when TJ eventually joined them at the table.

He looked from one to the other in amusement. "And what's so funny? What am I missing out on?"

"Oh nothing, darling, only frivolous girl-talk." Jessica glanced at Debbie, who was grinning naughtily.

Debbie couldn't resist adding a bit of spice. "Ah, Jess was just describing your insatiable sexual appetite and how…"

"Insatiable, huh?" TJ interjected, turning to meet Jessica's gaze with those come-to-bed eyes of his.

It was an impenetrable moment of privacy, a look so secret and sensual Debbie cleared her throat loudly, hating the feeling of being ignored and realising her attempt at flirtation had backfired. "Ok, lovebirds, shall we order?" She sounded a tad put out, but masked it with a pretty smile.

"Ooh!" TJ suddenly exclaimed with a wriggle of his hips, and Jessica looked at him enquiringly. He smiled and teased, "Can't get enough of me, huh, baby?"

Jessica raised a brow, unsure of what he meant. She glanced at Debbie and from her friend's guilty expression grasped what was happening.

"Are you playing footsie with my boyfriend?" she asked with an incredulous frown.

TJ made an awkward sound in his throat. "Boy, you got me there! I thought that was Jess for a second."

Jessica wasn't sure how to react. "I can't believe… pfff! What?!"

CHAPTER 37 — DEBORAH

She glared at them both.

Debbie quickly offered, "Hey, I was just kidding. Wanted to see for myself what all the fuss is about." She laughed.

Jessica gave her friend a playful slap on the wrist. "Geez, you're crazy!"

TJ took Jessica's hand, then turned to study the menu, ostensibly dismissing the matter as insignificant, so Jessica deemed it best not to cause a ruckus. She excused herself and headed to the Ladies' Room. Upon her return, she noticed that TJ looked a little flushed, and Debbie seemed self-satisfied. Yet, they both acted like nothing untoward had transpired, so Jessica assumed it was her imagination and slipped back into their easy dinner banter.

One thing was true. Edith Brown certainly did not approve of any daughter of hers conducting herself like a sex-crazed (blip the word!) who travelled across the Atlantic just to see a man.

"How did Mum find out?" Freida took a sip of her coffee.

"Take a wild guess…" Jessica rolled her eyes.

"Nooo. Not again! You can't trust that girl with anything."

"Yep. Well, I never told her it was a secret, so…"

"Jess, stop making excuses for her, please!"

Jessica changed the subject. "She's been living in New York for several years. Owns a business which is quite successful. A lingerie boutique."

"Yes, I've heard of it. It's got that ubiquitous and somewhat reductive name…"

"Eros," Jessica said.

"Yeah. Such a Debbie-name. I think she revels in the notoriety her shop brings."

"Hey! Be nice." Jessica smiled at her sister's loyalty.

Freida's gaze narrowed. "Looks like you two have resumed your weird friendship?"

"Which you frown upon. Don't worry, Fifi. She's older now, and easier to talk to. And quite the quintessential New Yorker. Totally unshockable. I admire her open-mindedness."

"Suits your current craziness, I'm sure." Freida stuck out her bottom lip the way their mother always did when she disapproved of something.

"I'm not crazy," Jessica chuckled, "Just pushing the boundaries a little."

"Hmmm. Be careful not to push too hard."

"Oh, Fifi, always the voice of reason. Right now, I don't want to be reasonable. I crave a carefree life with no inhibitions, and TJ and Debbie are two perfect pieces in that jigsaw. Honestly, I envy their ability to do whatever they choose, whenever, with no regrets."

"That doesn't sound like a healthy approach."

CHAPTER 37 — DEBORAH

"But it's what I need, right now. All my life I've struggled with this very thing. With my Edith Brown instilled principles and values…"

"Which are not bad qualities to have," Freida defended.

"No, but they've made me kinda old-fashioned in my behaviour. And now I want to step out of my comfort zone."

"Ok. You do as you like, but be careful, Jess. That Debbie-girl… I've never liked her. She covets everything you have and would give anything to be in your shoes. Her envy has always simmered beneath the surface, and will rear its ugly head soon enough. Be careful!" she repeated.

When their mother called that afternoon, Jessica was still feeling over-sensitive. "I'm a 25-year-old woman, mum, I can see whomever I want! Yes. Ok, yes. I'm having sex with him. So? I'm not married. He's literally the second man I've *ever* slept with in my entire life. Hardly makes me a slut! And frankly, this is what I need after everything. I'm enjoying myself and…"

"*Jess*!" Her mum's stern tone stopped her defensive tirade. "*Enough*. I think you've said enough. I just wanted to tell you to watch out, that's all."

~

It was a delightful, sunny afternoon, and the two girls were gallivanting through the streets of 7th Avenue. Jessica noted how Deborah flaunted her knowledge of the fashion district of Manhattan. Who could blame her? This was her city now. She sauntered along the pavement like she had in their childhood playground, moving and acting as though the entire world was watching her. At one point, she gazed up at the New York City skyline with her lips agape, apparently revelling in her own splendour. In an instant, a pigeon flew overhead and poop! Right in her eye! Jessica almost burst out laughing. The scene was hilarious. Debbie screamed in horror as she grasped what had happened. She was lucky it had missed her mouth… How disgusting! As horrific as it was, Jessica struggled to stifle a giggle and dutifully rushed to her friend's aid. Although moderately empathetic, she couldn't shake the feeling this was some weird karmic justice.

Chuckling under her breath, she ushered a distressed Debbie into the nearest shop. The sales assistant regarded them with suspicion until Jessica explained what had happened as best she could. They led Deborah to the bathroom, where she washed out her eye with warm water. She returned in a calmer state, albeit not quite as beautiful or confident, with one bloodshot eye.

"Are you ok?" Jessica felt duty-bound to enquire.

To her surprise, Debbie didn't kick an undue fuss, but shrugged and replied, "I hope it doesn't get infected."

It was as though she knew, deep down, she deserved what had just happened to her.

CHAPTER 38

Long-Distance

"You promised you'd call!"

"Yeah, sorry sweetie. My meeting ran late. You get how it can be, baby."

"What meeting? Weren't you in the Hamptons this weekend?"

"My agent, Bob, called me last minute. Wanted us to meet this director and… it's all good. We're talking now, aren't we?"

Jessica sighed, her frustration rising. "Yes, we are." She hung up abruptly, tossing the phone onto the plush sofa. An unshakeable feeling of unease began to seep into her thoughts. It was hard to believe that nearly two years had passed since she and TJ had started their whirlwind romance. The calendar had turned to March 2007, yet the mounting doubts weighed heavily on her soul. Handling this long-distance relationship – tricky at the best of times – left her constantly wondering about his whereabouts, his actions, and the company he kept. Normally confident, Jessica found herself grappling with insecurities she never knew she had, spurring her frequent, impromptu visits to New York.

Her mind wandered to a recent trip, the vivid memory of which sparked a deep blush of embarrassment. TJ hadn't been home when she'd arrived, leaving only a note that mentioned drinks with "friends" and inviting her to join after freshening up. His younger sister Beth, whom Jessica liked, was also in town, staying at the family residence on the Upper East Side. The fact that she would also be present made it appear innocuous. Still, Jessica couldn't shake the insidious suspicion that TJ might be leading a double life.

Determined to catch him unawares, she hastily applied makeup, transforming a tube of lipstick into a makeshift blush. In her haste, she failed to blend it, arriving at the bar with conspicuous red blotches on her cheeks. And there he was deeply engaged in conversation with a "friend" named Heather, whose gaze lingered on TJ with unsettling familiarity. Jessica's blood boiled at Heather's brazen flirtation, her eyes narrowing into daggers, wondering why the arrogant cow kept glancing her way and sniggering under her breath. Jessica's internal rage was

CHAPTER 38 — LONG-DISTANCE

interrupted only by Beth, who sweetly pointed out her makeup mishap. Mortified, Jessica scrubbed her cheeks, her flaming embarrassment a cruel reminder of her unravelling sanity. The nagging uncertainty was gnawing at her mind.

Back at TJ's apartment, his sudden urgency to take a shower only fed her growing paranoia. Though he later prepared a romantic candlelit dinner, the evening was stripped of sexual intimacy. Had theirs been a typical romance, these lapses might have gone unnoticed, but the vast ocean separating their lives demanded a deeper connection. She lay beside him, eyes wide open, her mind churning with torturous thoughts. A grim article she'd read about men's post-coital struggles loomed large in her memory – was this why TJ couldn't be aroused?

Hmmm. The explicit and rather detailed magazine article now made sense. But after a couple of hours of this mental and emotional torture, Jessica realised she'd become fixated on the idea of him cheating. The only solution was to do some investigating and ascertain the truth, once and for all.

Upon her return to London, she confided in her friend. "I think he's being unfaithful," she blurted out to Annabel.

Annabel's response was immediate and unsympathetic. "Who? You mean your blonde Adonis? Duh!"

"No, I'm serious."

"Why? Not shagging enough?"

"I dunno. He's... just… he's so darn secretive and I often can't get hold of him."

Annabel's expression said I-told-you-so.

Jessica continued, her frustration needing an outlet. "It's ridiculous the countless times he's gone M-I-A. I leave messages, and his excuses about why I can't reach him are sometimes the same exact excuse he used before, almost word for word. So ridiculous!"

"What's ridiculous is why you haven't called him out on it."

Jessica sighed. "I can't. I… it's just a feeling. Plus, he's so supportive. Never jealous. I have no proof."

"A woman always knows, Jess. Always."

Deep down, Jessica knew Annabel was right. TJ was lying to her. She knew it. Could feel it in her bones. Pretending to trust him was exhausting, and the effort was taking a toll on her. Was she so desperate to remain in this relationship that she was willing to ignore the obvious signs of perfidy?

Just thinking about it put her in a foul mood and she dumped her groceries in the boot of her car, throwing them in as though they were the enemy. Slamming the door, she was greeted by a radio tune aptly entitled "Call me," about a woman lamenting the fact her boyfriend never answered his phone. The lyrics mirrored her own plight, pushing her into a deeper pit of despair. She switched it off, kissing her teeth in pure vexation. Enough was enough. The long-distance arrangement was

CHAPTER 38 LONG-DISTANCE

failing miserably.

About a month had passed since the Debbie-bird-poo-incident and Jessica was again in Manhattan, basking in post-coitus contentment in TJ's West Village apartment. A pigeon landed on the windowsill, it's oafish antics causing Jessica to burst out laughing. The memory of Debbie's unfortunate encounter surged back, and she recounted the tale to a baffled TJ.

"Hey, girl, that's your *friend* you're mocking," TJ said, bemused.

Jessica nodded, "Yes, but… her face! It was soooo funny. She seemed more appalled by the fact that something so awful had happened to *her*, the beautiful Deborah Pariwa."

TJ's response was unusually dismissive. "Beautiful? I've never deemed her beautiful."

Jessica's curiosity was piqued. It was something in his tone that made her pause. Why would he say that? She pressed further, "Well, she is clearly stunning… but I suspect… she might envy me a little." She watched him closely, awaiting his reaction. When he offered none, she continued, "… Even the way she looks at *you* sometimes. Remember when we dined together? I can't believe she played footsie with you, and I swear I saw something more when I returned from the loo."

TJ hesitated before finally speaking. "Deborah not only flirted with me, but also offered sexual favours by virtue of her wandering foot, which I, of course, declined.

Jessica's eyes widened in shock. "What?! And why didn't you tell me? Why tell me now?"

He shrugged. "You asked. I didn't want to cause a rift between you two. You'd have gotten mad over nothing. I don't think she meant anything by it." He pulled her close, seeing the distress in her eyes. "You know I'm right, baby. Plus, your friend Debbie's a little crazy. It's no biggie."

Jessica tried to laugh it off, though she remained unnerved. "Debbie *is* crazy. She's always been naughty like that. I mean, she's very attractive and likes to imagine every man fancies her." She frowned, still perturbed.

TJ's smouldering smile softened her. "Attractive, but not half as gorgeous as you, Jessica Brown." He nuzzled her ear and continued carefully, "But why do I get the impression you're a little pleased she got dumped on by a pigeon?"

Jessica chuckled, "You're not wrong. Guess I felt she deserved it somehow… now I *know* she did. Hmmm! Plus, did I mention she once called my mother in Ghana to tell her about my 'illicit' relationship with you? Why would she do that?"

TJ stepped away to pull on his running shoes. "Have you asked her why?"

"No," Jessica replied, shaking her head. "Didn't bother. This

CHAPTER 38   LONG-DISTANCE

isn't the first time she's done something like that."

"It's probably nothing." TJ shrugged nonchalantly. "I never understand you girls and your friendships. We dudes are much simpler." He leaned in to kiss her. "I'm off to the gym. See ya later, baby! Back in a couple."

Yet, as the door shut, Jessica couldn't shake the overwhelming feeling there was more to the story. His dismissive tone, his hurried change of subject – something didn't sit right with her.

That was it. His lack of surprise about the poop story – almost as though he'd heard it before, but she was certain *she* hadn't told him anything. Was it possible he'd bumped into Debbie while she was in London? That would explain how he knew, but if so, why would he hide it?

As she sat there, alone in her lover's apartment, her thoughts churned. She suddenly got the urge to snoop around. But just as she stood up, the sound of a key turning in the lock froze her in place. TJ was back, and her chance had slipped away.

Jessica knew she couldn't continue like this. But what should she do next?

PALM TREES IN THE STORM

CHAPTER 39

Play with Fire and You Get Burned

Once again, Jessica questioned her judgement, still grappling with the sting of Debbie's betrayal weeks earlier. Even though she tried to brush it off as minor, it gnawed at her

that Debbie had easily propositioned TJ. Such deceitful behaviour made her more appreciative of friends like Annabel, who was always candid, and rarely took offence.

Annabel's matter-of-fact tone cut through Jessica's thoughts. "For something that began as a fling, you're pretty obsessed with this bloke." She took a long sip of her iced coffee, batting her long lashes meaningfully.

Jessica leaned back with a rueful expression. "I'm hooked," she admitted. "He makes me feel… I dunno… desirable, sexy… like a real woman."

Annabel rolled her eyes theatrically and pretended to puke. "Eewww, Jess! Hellooooo?! You *are* desirable and sexy *and* a woman, for sure. You don't need anyone to validate you in that way, do you?"

Seeing the uncertainty flit across Jessica's face, Annabel softened her tone. "Hey, listen. You're beautiful, that's all I'm saying. Seeing you like this… I don't know. This long-distance thing isn't…."

"Isn't what? Go on… say it, Annabel."

"Well, it's making you doubt yourself. Not an attractive quality! You used to be so incredibly self-assured… no, don't shake your head, it's true. It's the first thing I noticed about you… that supreme inner confidence – damned impressive!"

"Yes, but TJ… being with him makes me feel… amazing. He brings out a passion I didn't even know existed…"

Annabel shook her head. "No, Jess… *You* are amazing, and it's nothing to do with him. You shouldn't lose that, darling… Don't become so reliant on his compliments that you forget who you were before you met him." She continued earnestly, "I know you claim he's supportive of your career, but you're not even that passionate about dancing, anymore. It's kind of pathetic, Jess. Honestly, at only twenty-six you behave as though you're more dead than alive."

Jessica raised both hands defensively. "Hey, steady on. I *am* sexually on fire with a man I fancy…"

CHAPTER 39 PLAY WITH FIRE AND YOU GET BURNED

"Yes, but in danger of losing your sense of self. You rely too much on the approval of others, Jess!"

"You're right," Jessica conceded. "These days, I spend more time worrying about where he is." She pouted thoughtfully. "It's not the life I want. But I'm addicted. It's ridiculous! He says, 'Girl, you got booty for days!' and I melt. How silly!"

Annabel snorted, "Yeah. But deep down you know you deserve more than pure lust. It's superficial, Jess. It isn't you."

"Hmmm. Plus, I'm pretty convinced he's living a double life. But I have no proof and just need to be sure."

Her next trip to New York presented the opportunity she'd been waiting for. As Jessica turned the key and pushed open his door, TJ nearly jumped out of his skin.

"Sorry, sweetheart, it's only me. I startled you." She stated the obvious.

TJ took a moment to gather his wits before unwinding from the sofa to move toward her. "I thought you were arriving tomorrow?" He looked unsettled.

Jessica nodded. "Supposed to. Tried calling from JFK, but your phone didn't even ring – like it was switched off or something? Strange." She gave him a piercing look.

His face revealed nothing. He kissed her lingeringly. "Welcome, baby."

Jessica returned his kiss, though her mind was racing.

TJ nuzzled her ear. "Listen, I'm afraid I've made other plans for tonight. Will be difficult to cancel."

She stiffened and pulled back. "Oh?"

"Won't be long," he promised.

"Ok." Stepping away, she hid her miffed expression, feigning nonchalance as she started to undress.

His eyes glinted with desire. "What are you doing, baby?"

Stripping down to her lace underwear, she kept her heels on and turned away, then bent over, knowing it would drive him insane with lust. *He's so basic and predictable,* Jessica thought. *I'm in control.*

After their impassioned lovemaking, he rushed to the shower. That's when divine serendipity intervened. He'd left his precious blackberry on the bedside table, although it usually never left his sight. The ping of a new message caught Jessica's attention, and the notification read, "Waiting for you, my love."

With a thudding heart, she quickly scribbled down the number, intending to dial it once alone in the apartment. It seemed strange his phone *was* on and not switched off nor dead. So why hadn't she been able to reach him earlier?

Lying there in bed, Jessica noticed a medium-sized chest, partly

CHAPTER 39 PLAY WITH FIRE AND YOU GET BURNED

hidden underneath a pile of clothing and blankets. She felt like a little spy, plotting and planning and snooping and searching. Though her actions felt wrong, she knew she had to do this to keep her sanity in the relationship.

No sooner had TJ departed than she leapt out of bed, clearing the top of the chest with one sweep of her hand. Thankfully, it had a latch, but no lock. She opened it cautiously and peered inside, spotting several items of clothing, some books, and magazines. Oh, wait. One of those garments belonged to *her*… a silk nightie from a previous visit… funny, he'd forgotten to give it back. And there were a pair of lace panties… which were definitely *not* hers. Jessica gingerly pushed them to the side. This was not looking good.

Oh, and look! There's a phone, another Blackberry. Odd. She picked it up – it looked remarkably like TJ's. Maybe a spare... or perhaps...? Could it be he had two phones? Is that why he'd been unreachable earlier?

Frowning, she grabbed her phone and dialled his number. Same result as before. Dead. No ringing. Goodness! That was it! She had a *different* number for him, and the phone he was holding obviously wasn't the one he used for *her*.

Jessica's guts surged in her throat as the truth shattered any thread of hope in her already suspicious mind. This mobile handset in the trunk was switched off because he hadn't been expecting her. No wonder it didn't ring.

The lying, cheating bastard!

Jessica continued rummaging. Under the pile of magazines lay a black diary. Opening it, she anticipated the worst. She flicked through looking for clues, and it became apparent it belonged to a woman. Entries about weekends spent together and meals cooked detailed someone who "lived" with TJ sometimes. Jessica felt sick to her stomach.

Then she saw it. On the inside cover was a telephone number. Trembling, she punched the digits into her phone, her rage, hurt, and disgust intertwined.

"Hello?" The voice sounded unmistakeably familiar. Jessica blinked in disbelief, confused for just a moment. This wasn't Debbie's usual number, but it was her voice. Flabbergasted, Jessica hung up without a word. There was nothing to say. The ultimate betrayal.

Still shaking, she sat on the edge of the bed, her mind in turmoil. So, who is he with right now? Clearly not Debbie.

Oh, my Goodness! He's a serial cheat!

Mouth ajar, she dialled the number she'd scribbled down from his phone earlier. Another woman's voice answered, although unfamiliar, the greeting was a dead giveaway.

"Hi. Heather speaking…"

It was that woman he claimed to "work" with. The person introduced as "just a friend".

CHAPTER 39   PLAY WITH FIRE AND YOU GET BURNED

Jessica took a deep, calming breath. "Heather, is my boyfriend with you?"

"W-what...? Who is this?"

The cheek of the woman! Jessica's tone sharpened. "The man you're with. TJ. Titus Jameson. *My* boyfriend!" Her voice grew louder with each word. *"Is he with you?"*

"Errhmm, yes... would you... like... to..."

"No! Just tell him this. Tell that dog the woman he claims to love, who's been his girlfriend for the past *three years*, who trusted he was being faithful, has discovered he's a lying, cheating bastard. He will never lay eyes on me or touch me *ever* again. Oh, and you know what? He's cheating on *you* too – with someone I believed was my best friend." She spat out the words. "Tell him I know about *Debbie*, Heather. He's a dog and you're a bitch. You two deserve each other."

Click!

Jessica's entire being trembled. Though the vitriol spewed was out of character, she felt no regret. "Dog" and "Bitch" were the only two words she could think of. He deserved this life-upending explosion after what he'd done to hers. She never should have become involved with him. Her grief, loneliness and the raw attraction she'd felt had blinded her, causing her to ignore all the early warning signs. Everyone had warned her about playing with fire. You get burned!

By the time TJ returned to his apartment, Jessica was gone. On the flight back to London she felt devoid of emotion. Cold and heartless, but strong. This was the last time she would ever speak to him. After that day, Jessica never again laid eyes on Titus Jameson.

And as for Debbie…

Not one for ugly confrontations, she ignored all of Debbie's subsequent calls and frantic messages. Curiosity about the hows, whys, and whens of Debbie's affair with TJ didn't matter. Debbie wouldn't get the satisfaction of hashing out the details.

That day marked the end of the peculiar friendship between Jessica Sokari Brown and Deborah Pariwa.

CHAPTER 40

Go with the flow

Jessica wanted to kick herself.

Stupid, stupid, stupid girl! She wrote in her journal. *I saw Debbie's betrayal coming. For 17 years, since the beginning of our friendship, she's shown signs she was jealous of me. Signs I couldn't trust her. Even when we were kids. Of course, she'd want what I have. She always did. What a complete bitch. Goodness, how she must hate me! Mum, Fifi, Emily, and even Will warned me about her – but I wouldn't listen. Kept making excuses. Silly, silly me!*

But TJ… him, she didn't see coming either. The signs were there from the start. *I'm sooo STUPID. How could I have trusted him? Annabel warned me against the seriousness of something that began as purely physical. What was I expecting? Why am I so reluctant to confront issues and negative people in my life? What am I frightened of? Am I such a poor judge of character?*

~

"It's been ages, but you're finally back!" Freida exclaimed, her eyes lighting up at the sight of her sister.

"Yep, choreographing a music video. Haven't been here since that whole nasty TJ/Debbie affair. Ccheeeww!" Jessica kissed her teeth at the memory.

"You're alright now, though?" Freida enquired, her tone laced with concern.

"Yeah. They're not worth my energy. It was difficult at first, and my attempts at daily meditation soon became whenever-I-remember. Poof!"

Freida laughed. "Hah. I'd be the same!"

"It's easier to immerse myself in work," Jessica admitted.

"Well, dance has always been your go-to," Freida agreed.

"Uh-huh. The one aspect of my tattered life that remains within my control." Jessica sighed, and pronounced, "I'm off men for the moment."

"Oh? Thought you were 'inundated with suitors'?" Freida smiled mischievously.

CHAPTER 40 — GO WITH THE FLOW

Jessica wrinkled her nose with disdain. "Nah. Not interested."

"Then where, pray tell, are you off to tonight? And with whom?"

Jessica giggled. "It's nothing, trust me. Just that Brazilian guy, Marcel, and only because he flies me all over the world."

Freida shook her head in mock disapproval. "Shameless girl! You and your billionaire boyfriend! Is he the older guy?"

"Well, he's forty-one." Jessica winced.

"That's hardly old. Anyway, sounds like a welcome distraction from the craziness of TJ."

"It's a good rebound. And I find him rather amusing, his accent especially and the intensity with which he tackles life." Jessica chuckled at the image. "Even ordering a cup of coffee is an experience; from the way he describes the desired number of shots, to his painstaking breakdown of how much milk is needed to create the correct amount of foam – Fifi, every word is uttered with such passion. It's hilarious!" she giggled.

That evening, she gleefully observed the bemused expressions of whichever unfortunate server had been given the near-impossible task of pleasing an obsessive-compulsive.

As she took in Marcel's tanned good looks, his crisp white linen suit and coifed hair, she conceded she liked him well enough. He was thoughtful and attractive, wealthy and super-attentive, all of which didn't hurt. Jessica willed herself to be more captivated by his Latin charms, but the truth was she was just not that into him. Although intelligent and evidently successful, Marcel Di Santiago was a bit of a simple man, who talked a lot about nothing in particular, and Jessica found him boring beyond belief. He wasn't interested in entertaining or going to the theatre or dancing the night away, as Jessica enjoyed doing. Marcel wanted to spend time alone with her, and she didn't feel the same way about him. But he was a good man – the opposite of all TJ represented – and exactly what she needed right now. Solid, dependable, and incapable of breaking her heart.

As these thoughts swirled round her head, she found herself mesmerised by the full lips of said Latin lover speaking words she could not hear, and she pinched a thigh to drag her fickle attention back to whatever he was prattling on about.

On this balmy Saturday evening in New York, they were seated at their favourite table at Indochine on Lafayette Street. Jessica half-listened to the infinitely more interesting conversations around her, idle fingers twiddling a stray afro-strand by her temple. She cringed inwardly as she watched Marcel eat. Table manners, or the lack thereof, speak volumes about upbringing, she reflected, and Marcel's vice-like grip far too close to the neck of his fork was a dead-giveaway. His had been humble beginnings – dirt poor, in fact – and it was a marvel he'd risen to such heights.

Marcel's strong Brazilian-Portuguese accent had an almost lyrical

CHAPTER 40 — GO WITH THE FLOW

flow, revealing the occasional discordant note where he struggled with proper pronunciation. It was quite endearing, actually, and Jessica desperately tried to keep her eyes on him, but could sense the heat of another gaze.

She glanced around the room and smiled tentatively at the handsome stranger seated at a corner table. He didn't smile back, but the soft caress of his sensuous stare implied otherwise, making her blush and shift uncomfortably in her seat. The tremor of excitement spiralled up her groin and shivered down her spine. Her smile turned coy and uncertain. The man exuded such power and self-assurance.

Disconcerted and a little embarrassed by the surprise betrayal of her body, she made a last-ditch attempt to focus on Marcel as she picked half-heartedly at her plate of Steamed Vietnamese Ravioli. The only other time she'd felt this was… yes, with her beloved William, when she'd first met him in an elevator almost a decade earlier.

As though enacting lines from a script, their server brought two glasses to the table. "Champagne. A gift from that gentleman over there," he said.

Jessica beamed, enticed by the thrill of being chased anew. Marcel, being hot-blooded and Latino, waved a hand to reject the gift, but Jessica reasoned gently, "It's only a drink, darling, let it go."

Apparently threatened by this unknown alpha male competitor, Marcel placed a proprietorial hand on Jessica's lower back and leaned in to give her a wet kiss.

Jessica felt sexy in her red backless jumpsuit and was aware the dark stranger still wouldn't take his eyes off her. She raised her glass and nodded a gesture of thanks, perhaps an inadvertent invitation for him to follow her, as she excused herself from the table and headed to the Ladies'.

"I'm Joseph Kwame Ofosu," he introduced rather formally, still with no hint of a smile, just the same intense brown gaze.

"I'm Jessica," she offered, smoothing an eyebrow with nervous fingers.

"Hello, Jessica. I can see your companion is all but boring you to death." That's when he smiled, and his eyes sparkled as though they were laughing out loud, causing Jessica to do the same.

"Oh! Goodness, is it *that* obvious?" She scrunched her nose in embarrassment at having been caught out. "Ouch! And there I was, desperately trying to listen to his incessant chatter. What an effort it is to put on a kind face. I'd never realised how much scaffolding a smile requires."

This time Joseph laughed, and he looked like a boy when he did. Jessica, suddenly feeling more relaxed, leaned against the wall, grinning stupidly at this confident, Ghanaian stranger.

"So, do you live in the city?" she asked to break the silence.

"Not in *this* city." His eyes were still amused. "In London."

"Oh, so do I!" Jessica exclaimed, oddly pleased.

"I figured you did." Joseph didn't appear surprised. "You don't

CHAPTER 40 — GO WITH THE FLOW

dress like a New Yorker; much too stylish to be one," he explained.

"Hmmm," Jessica mused doubtfully. "I might still *live* here, though..." she countered.

"Sure, but everyone who does adopts an inherently casual vibe eventually – just to fit in. You, my dear, are *not* trying to fit in. It's obvious you don't live here." He sounded a tad self-satisfied.

Jessica's smile turned playful. "Ok, but why *London* and not somewhere else? Or does my style specifically scream London, Mr Know-it-all?"

Joseph chuckled. "As a matter of fact, it does, Miss Skeptical." His brown eyes scanned her frame. "It doesn't shout Paris, or Milan, or any European city... it's London, for sure!"

Jessica cocked her head. "What are you, a fashion guru, or something?"

"Designer, now business executive – still in fashion." His voice was deep. "Born to Ghanaian parents – standing outside the loos of Indochine with the most beautiful woman I've ever laid eyes on. A woman I'm convinced is my future wife." He blinked. "Is there anything else you'd like to know?"

Temporarily tongue-tied, Jessica stared at him in stunned silence. He wasn't smiling anymore. He was serious. What an oddly assertive man!

She quickly gathered her wits and said with a laugh, "That's ridiculous! These things don't quite happen that way."

Moving closer, Joseph simply murmured, "No, this is it. I feel it. You're the one." He tilted her chin and stroked it with his thumb. "Let's just go with the flow, shall we?"

Her hammering heart skipped a beat. His gentle touch was enough to persuade her.

This was it. Somehow, it didn't feel reckless, but right. Jessica decided she would follow her gut and allow this mystery man to sweep her off her feet.

CHAPTER 41

Second time Around

"*I have met my wife.*"

His words reverberated through her mind, dancing around her thoughts with a confidence that left no room for doubt. He'd said it with such certainty, as if he possessed an oracle's insight into their future – her future. She didn't even know the man, yet here she was, willing to "just go with the flow" as he'd so nonchalantly advised.

Joseph Kwame Ofosu. Fashion designer extraordinaire. His self-assured demeanour and straightforward approach were like a breath of fresh air to Jessica. There was no hiding behind a façade, no manipulative undertones. It felt safe to be around him, a sentiment reinforced by two glasses of champagne and one impactful conversation that had led her to sever ties with Marcel.

Dear J, being with him feels refreshing and non-threatening. Safe. Joseph has pulling power, that's for sure. He lives in London too, which makes things a lot easier. This is moving so fast, but doesn't feel like it is. Feels natural. Normal. Plus, he's West African, too. Maybe this is meant to be.

<hr />

Despite the speed with which he formally proposed – exactly five weeks after their first meeting – Jessica felt it was anything but a whirlwind romance. Their wedding, six months later, was a modest affair attended only by immediate family, reflecting the pragmatic nature of their relationship. Deeply loving and undeniably attracted to each other, there was a mature quality to their union that made Jessica feel equally grown-up. Joseph's practical nature was evident in his reasoning: "I know I love you. I'm sure I want to spend the rest of my life with you, so what's the point of waiting? Let's get married immediately."

He never considered that she might not be as ready for marriage as he was.

"Sweetheart, you've been there and done that, so you're an expert at this marriage thing. You know what to expect. I think you'll make the perfect wife."

Joseph's matter-of-fact approach to life included planning every minute detail, even down to the dress she wore for their wedding.

Dear J, he insisted on choosing my gown for the wedding – and even though

CHAPTER 41 — SECOND TIME AROUND

it wasn't what I'd have gone for, he was right. It looked stunning on me. Well, what did I expect? He is a fashion designer, after all.

Dependable and strong, Joseph organised their lives with precision and unwavering certitude. A simple wedding led to an exquisite honeymoon. Mr Ofosu was definitely the captain of their ship, assuming total responsibility for their future. Jessica, now twenty-eight, only six years younger than Joseph, accepted with a mix of amusement and warmth his plans for a life filled with children.

"Children…?" Jessica asked, noting his use of the plural.

Shiny white teeth had flashed in the dark as Joseph pulled her naked flesh against his. "Yes, sweetheart, especially if we keep up *this* level of activity."

Their giggles morphed into soft murmurs of contentment, and she nuzzled closer to his warm body. Life with Joseph felt effortless, as though they'd always been together.

Charming and educated, handsome and African, he was the ideal partner her mother desired in a son-in-law.

"Finally," Edith Brown had said with all the subtlety of a bulldozer. "You've found someone we can receive into our family."

Jessica could only smile and hug her mother. "I'm glad you approve, Mum."

Once the honeymoon ended, Jessica began to see a different side to her husband. The light-hearted Joseph faded, as did any blatant disregard for the pressures of time; replaced by a more serious version of himself, the pragmatic planner who orchestrated every detail of their lives.

Week 1: move into new house. Week 2: finalise furniture. Week 3: Jessica ovulating/try for a baby. Week 4: trip to Milan… and so on.

When Joseph handed her a printed schedule of their lives, Jessica couldn't help but laugh. At first, it felt like a joke, but then she realised he was deadly serious, handling their marriage like a business arrangement. She shot him a beleaguered look, feeling rather insulted, then brushed it aside as mere over-zealous planning on his part and nothing to be unduly concerned with.

Week 3… try for a baby. Jessica shook her head as she re-read the planner. Such a ridiculous thing to write. I mean, who plans for these things?

But, Week 3 came and passed seamlessly, with Joseph performing his role diligently. Not that Jessica had any complaints – she adored their lovemaking and marvelled that two bodies could fit together like they'd been carved from the same clay. This week in particular, her husband was a very ardent and thorough lover, leaving nothing to chance, emptying his seed into her willing vessel as though a misdirected drop might be the

CHAPTER 41 — SECOND TIME AROUND

very one containing his lucky sperm.

But week 5 came and Jessica's period was right on time – her 28-day cycle had always been spot-on. Although immensely disappointed, Joseph took a pragmatic approach to the setback.

"Well, this was only our first attempt. Maybe we'll have better luck second time around."

⁓

But a whole seven months passed and Jessica still wasn't pregnant. She marked yet another X in the Ofosu Year Planner and sighed. Her period was two days late, and Joseph insisted on a test. When she'd sceptically pointed to the usual pre-menstrual signs, he'd snapped at her

"Oh! Just do the bloody test and stop pondering it. What's the big deal?"

It wasn't a big deal, sure, but anyone who's ever been around a hormonal woman knows everything can become a big deal – scratch that, a *huge* deal. Jessica spun like a lioness and lunged at her adversary.

"If it isn't such a big deal, why don't *you* get bloody tested? Maybe the problem is with you!"

Joseph stared at her aghast, but she was on a roll. "I'm fed up of your schedules and plans and bloody lists! Instead of relaxing and enjoying our life together, these first few months of marriage have been..." She lifted inept hands in frustration. "It makes me feel I'm just a baby-making-machine in your master plan of life, Joseph. What about what *I* want – have you even considered that? Or doesn't it matter to you?"

Rather than succumbing to the shot gun retort of explosive, hurtful words on the tip of his tongue, Joseph's features mirrored his visible attempt to remain calm, and not exacerbate his wife's frustration. He took a deep breath and responded, "Of course, what you want matters. I was under the assumption we wanted the same thing. Don't we?"

Jessica sighed. "Yes, I *do* want a baby, but... not like this, Joseph. I find it pressurising and... unsexy." She squeezed her lips together in a pout.

He took his wife's hand and pulled her mildly resistant form into his arms, pressing her closer until she yielded to the hug. They were silent for a moment, neither wanting to be cross with the other.

"Ok Jess, let's give it another day and if there's still nothing, we'll do a pregnancy test, agreed?"

She nodded.

※

Being only slightly imprecise in its timing, her period dutifully arrived that afternoon. Joseph tried not to look disappointed, but Jessica could tell he was. She suspected he was under the weight of some weird self-imposed timeline because of his mother's expectations. Having lost

CHAPTER 41 — SECOND TIME AROUND

her husband to prostate cancer when the boys were little, Josephina Ofosu now placed all her hopes in her two sons, and on her eldest in particular. Much to Jessica's chagrin, the spotlight was on her suitability as a wife to Joseph; a determination based almost solely on her ability to bear him a multitude of children.

Josephina believed in the teachings of the Bible and, at a luncheon in the Ofosu family home in Colindale, was quick to point out to her irreverent daughter-in-law that if a woman didn't give her husband children she was frowned upon.

"By whom?" Jessica had asked, somewhat incredulously.

"Oh, by *everyone*, my dear. If you can't have children, you're not a real woman!" Josephina then pursed her lips as though to say, "Matter closed", and turned to talk to someone else, giving Jessica the impression her mother-in-law's categoric view of life wasn't often challenged.

Jessica could tell her dig at Joseph about a potential fertility problem had left a seed of malcontent in their otherwise smooth-sailing marriage, because he'd never considered his sexuality an issue. He regarded himself as the skipper of this boat and took his husbandly duties to heart. Having tried his utmost to please his mother since boyhood, his primary concern was to meet her aspirations for a grandchild and heir.

The ninth month in their calendar promised to be an answer to prayer, for Jessica's normally punctual period was tardy once again. This time five days had passed and still nothing. On her way home from dance rehearsals, Jessica bought one of those easy over-the-counter pregnancy tests, which profess 99% accuracy, especially with morning urine.

So, the following day, she unfurled her sleep-cramped body, while mentally bracing herself for a possible negative result. Sitting on the loo, holding the pee-soaked stick in nervous fingers, she tried to imagine what she'd say to appease Joseph's inevitable despondency once she shared the likely unwelcome news.

"Oh, my Goodness!" Jessica's subsequent squeals of glee awakened her slumbering husband, who rushed into the bathroom to see his jubilant wife seated on the toilet, mouth agape.

She thrust the offending embodiment of proof towards him, transforming his sleep-induced expression of confusion into sheer delight. He pulled her into a heartfelt embrace with tears in his eyes and said, "Thank you, my darling, thank you."

But she was quick to dismiss his gratitude. "Oh, don't thank me, it's just luck of the sperm draw. And this is only the beginning of a looong journey."

Joseph gave her a reassuring look. "I know what you're thinking, sweetheart, but this is a new pregnancy and everything will work out fine." He tickled her nose with his and kissed her tenderly. "I must crack on with getting ready for work, but let's celebrate tonight, eh?"

Jessica nodded, "I need to get ready too, otherwise I'll definitely be late for my rehearsal." She turned to flush the loo and throw the

CHAPTER 41 SECOND TIME AROUND

plastic test in the bin, adding, "We're still making tweaks to the upcoming performance, so today is busy!"

Joseph was already removing his boxers. "Pity you can't ask someone to cover for you. You should take the day off," he suggested, as he stepped into the cascading shower. Rivulets of scalding water rolled down his shaven head and broad shoulders, and he closed his eyes to embrace its welcome assault. This rainfall effect shower had a head so large it took up more than half the square footage of the unit.

Jessica discarded her robe and watched him as he twisted and turned, suddenly feeling a burst of desire at the sight of his muscly buttocks and impressive manhood. She opened the steaming glass door and joined him, wrapping her arms around his firm body.

He swivelled to kiss her long and hard and murmured against her temple, "So why can't someone else take your place, hmmm?"

"Because," Jessica said, sliding one foot up his torso and rested it on his shoulder. "They need me to show them how to do this," she smiled seductively as she massaged him, "and *this.*"

"Awww, baby, I've no idea *how* you do that, but damn! It feels good." Joseph kissed her inner thigh, and she moaned appreciatively as he slowly entered her. "So," he continued to speak while thrusting, "you were saying?"

"I-*uh*-was-*uhh*-saying," Jessica was speaking in staccato bursts as her body moved in time to his. "*Uhh*-that-*uh*-they need-*uh*-meeee. Uh, yesss! No, don't stop! Yes, yes, yessss! Uhhhhhhh." She clung to him, savouring their moment of climax. "That was… amazing." She began to soap her body. "The dance ensemble really depends on me, both as a performer and as their choreographer. A day off is out of the question, sadly." She kissed him sensuously. "Ok, Lover Boy, you may continue, but I have to go." Jessica giggled as he playfully pinched her butt.

She got dressed and rushed to the rehearsal studio. After so many years, she'd become a well-renowned expert in her field. They'd be awaiting her arrival with excitement. Most still regarded her as something of a celebrity and, although the television show had long since aired its last season, "Chocolate and Vanilla" remained dear in the minds of those who watched TV.

〜

Jessica's thirtieth birthday was a month away, on 10th July 2011. Given all the highs and lows of the past decade, she hoped to mark the occasion with a proper celebration, maybe even a party, like the one she'd thrown for her eighteenth so many moons ago.

Initially, she'd planned something at Nobu, the chic Japanese-Peruvian fusion restaurant on Old Park Lane in Mayfair. Now she was pregnant, sushi no longer held appeal.

Annabel suggested the cool vibe of Hakkasan was a much safer bet, with its contemporary Chinese cuisine and zero chance of any

CHAPTER 41 — SECOND TIME AROUND

problems from ingesting raw fish. Yes, Hakkasan it was, especially because the DJ had promised to tailor the evening's playlist to suit Jessica's eclectic taste.

As she surveyed her appearance in the mirror, she smiled contentedly, knowing she looked attractive in the colour red, which had been her staunch favourite since childhood. It always put her in a great mood. She felt invincible – well, almost; if only she wasn't still smarting from Joseph's earlier remark about her choice of attire: "Oh, Jess, honestly. Red again? It's so… *obvious*. Why not choose something less tacky like green or blue, or even that black and white dress I bought you?"

Oh! So that's what it was about. He wanted me to wear the bloody dress he bought me.

Jessica knew her selection wasn't at all tacky. Determined that nothing would ruin her evening, she deliberately twirled in front of her fashion-snob-of-a-husband and said, "Red isn't your preferred choice, but even you can't deny it suits me, darling, hmmm? Besides, it's *my* party, right?"

Joseph had grunted a quick apology, acknowledging his comment as a tad untimely and perhaps a little thoughtless. To make up for his lack of consideration, he whipped out his birthday gift to her, a stunning set of diamond studs, which he'd secretly hoped she'd pair with the dress he'd given her. Jessica remained a woman in red.

Hakkasan didn't disappoint, and it thrilled Jessica's thirty handpicked friends to celebrate this milestone with her.

"I feel a little queasy," Jessica complained on the drive back.

"You think it's something you ate?" Joseph asked, his tone laced with concern.

"Don't know… ahh!" She doubled over, crippled by the sudden sharp pain of a cramp.

She rushed to the bathroom in the hallway as soon as they got home, aware Joseph was hovering and could hear her moaning.

He gingerly pushed open the door to the loo and gasped, startled to see his wife sitting there with tears streaming down her cheeks, holding a blood-stained tissue in her hand.

CHAPTER 42

It's not you, it's me

Joseph stood still. Absorbing the enormity of what confronted him. Jessica was having a miscarriage.

She sat speechless, sobbing silently, eyes fixed despairingly on the blood-stained tissue in her trembling hand.

This wasn't just the loss of a much-anticipated pregnancy, a reality evidenced by the spontaneous discharge of blood clots. It was the crushing weight of seeing her husband's sorrow, knowing he was already grappling with how to present their union as yet another failure to his mother.

The year that followed was marked by a series of heart-wrenching miscarriages, each one deepening the divide between Jessica and Joseph. Typically reserved, her husband grew even more distant, opting to place blame rather than support his wife through these dark times. His thinly veiled accusations alluded that the problem lay with Jessica. His mother, Josephina, also fanned the flames by suggesting Jessica's dance training had left her with a physiological defect. She openly lamented that Joseph hadn't crowned a less accomplished woman as her daughter-in-law, often remarking, sometimes within earshot of Jessica, "That girl is just too ambitious!" Josephina was relentless, often undermining Jessica in front of her son with barbed comments. Her disdain was palpable, and she viewed Jessica's previous stillbirth as an ill omen.

Joseph openly tried to defend his wife, but his mother's persistence seemed to wear him down. He made a last-ditch attempt to rebut Josephina's cardinal argument that Jessica was already over thirty and therefore not at the ideal child-bearing age, according to her traditional African sensibilities.

"Ma, things have changed. Women rarely have babies before they're well into their thirties… and sometimes far beyond. There's no need to worry. Jess is…"

"Jess is too busy trying to maintain her figure for this nonsense career of hers. Having a child is obviously not her priority. Look at her! Hmmm! It wouldn't surprise me to find her body is rejecting these poor

CHAPTER 42 🌴 IT'S NOT YOU, IT'S ME

babies. *Kai!* These modern women, honestly! You should have married one simple girl from our village. By now, you'd have plenty, plenty children, but instead… *cchhheewwwww!*" Josephina Ofosu kissed her teeth in loud disgust at the disappointing image of her son's poor choices.

Joseph hung his head in shame, unable to counter his mother's harsh words. Neither he nor his mother noticed Jessica standing in the doorway, silently witnessing their entire conversation.

Jessica knew Joseph loved her, but was torn by his desire to appease his mother; a woman completely lacking in diplomacy and very vocal about Jessica's supposed shortcomings. After Jessica's third miscarriage, Josephina publicly humiliated her already distraught daughter-in-law, reducing her to tears in front of Joseph's fashion colleagues. Joseph's failure to shield her from his mother's vicious onslaught, or come to her defence, resurrected feelings of childhood betrayal in Jessica. She stuttered, wanting to remind her mother-in-law the problem couldn't be with her because she'd already had a son. Yet, she stayed silent, the renewed pain of loss rendering her mute, as she stumbled her way out of the room. Her mother-in-law had won that battle.

At home, Joseph's half-baked attempt to apologise with a lukewarm cuddle fell on deaf ears. Jessica pushed him away and sought refuge in a bath filled with Epsom salts, hoping to soothe the visceral pain that wracked her body.

Joseph followed her, his eyes welling with tears as he watched his wife ease her bruised form into the steaming water. "I agree we should get checked by a doctor," he whispered gently.

Jessica, saying nothing, closed her eyes and nodded, letting the soothing bubbles envelop her.

༄

The tests confirmed it: the problem lay with Joseph. His sperm count and quality were well below average.

"A man whose sperm concentration is below fifteen million per ml can be considered sub-fertile and is more likely to encounter problems conceiving, regardless of the fecundity of his partner," explained the reputable fertility consultant. "Mr Ofosu, your wife is extremely fertile and her body wants to get pregnant. However, it ultimately rejects the embryo because the quality of the sperm is too low to promote a viable pregnancy."

Joseph was utterly speechless; dumbstruck by the doctor's words. *Subfertile??* He repeated the words to himself, then turned to Jessica, his wide gaze reflecting a mixture of apology and shock. "It's not you, it's me," he mumbled.

Jessica reached for his hand. The doctor's words vindicated her, proving the miscarriages were not her fault. Yet, she still yearned for Joseph's child, making the news both a relief and a sorrow. Knowing her husband felt his manhood was being questioned, she fervently wished to

CHAPTER 42   IT'S NOT YOU, IT'S ME

somehow ease his pain. A part of her was glad his mother could no longer point the accusatory finger at her but, even more, Jessica wanted a win. She *needed* a win in this area of childbirth.

Edith Brown had always been Jessica's rock. And this occasion was no different. When informed of the situation, she immediately responded, "Let us pray! Children are a blessing and there is nothing our God cannot do."

"Oh Mum, not this again." Jessica sighed, feeling somewhat jaded and unable to muster enthusiasm for prayer.

"Eh, eh, eh, Jess! What are you saying? If there ever was a time for faith, then it's now. I understand you young people like to dismiss these things, but what harm can it do? Look at your brother Mikey and Damilola. I prayed for every single one of their pregnancies and have been blessed with three grandchildren."

Jessica winced at this unwitting reminder of her failures.

Edith continued, "As your mother, as a woman who bore eight, I am standing in the gap for you and am asking my God to bless you, my *pikin*. Do you hear me?"

"Yes Mum, I hear you."

Jessica contemplated the doctor's advice, her belief in a natural conception bolstered by Edith's unwavering faith. Adoption felt like a last resort, inappropriate within their cultural context. The suggested fertility treatment, ICSI, seemed their best hope. The doctor explained that intracytoplasmic sperm injection is like the male version of the more common IVF procedure. It involved injecting a single specially selected sperm cell directly into the cytoplasm of an egg, with the resulting embryo transferred to the womb.

Desperate for a sounding board, Jessica called her sister. "The real bummer is that, although it's an issue with him, all the *wahala* falls on me! All he has to do is masturbate into a cup or whatever."

Freida barely got a word in. "You sound resentful."

"I am! I've got the crappy end of the stick, Fifi. So unfair. I've endured so much pain and now I'm supposed to endure hormone injections? What irks is Joseph doesn't appreciate how disruptive this will be for my life, and his horrid mother dares to imply if he'd married someone younger, his sperm quality wouldn't matter. Helloooo, what?! Did she not read the results? The problem is with *your son*, not me! *Oooof*, that woman makes me so angry. Why should I suffer for something that isn't my fault? And what if… what if it doesn't work?"

Freida's speciality wasn't fertility or obstetrics, but she understood the situation. She reminded Jessica, "You've had a child before, so you know you can have another. Where is your faith, Jess?" (Oh Goodness, she sounded like their mother!) "Yes, you're scared and it seems unlikely, but I already visualise this happening. And you need to trust that it can,

CHAPTER 42 🌴 IT'S NOT YOU, IT'S ME

because if you don't, it won't. Remember, darling, shift your mindset and even the physical manifestations within your body will change. Just be positive and believe in your heart of hearts there's a baby coming."

Freida laughed self-consciously; aware she'd given quite an impassioned speech. "And yes, before you ask, Mum spoke to me. And I agree with her. Look at how many people struggle with IVF treatments and similar procedures for years on end with no results! But I feel things will be different for you, Jess."

Freida's conviction emboldened Jessica. She proceeded with preparing for ICSI, feeling more determined. Part of the preparations involved the sweeping of her fallopian tubes, but during the ultrasound, the physician gave an exclamation of genuine surprise, "Oh my Goodness! I can't believe this."

Jessica feared the worst. These days seemed to bring nothing but bad news and she held her breath as the doctor confirmed, "Young Lady, you're pregnant!"

Astounded by this unexpected proclamation, tears of gratitude rolled down her cheeks, and she gasped, "This is my miracle baby." She'd been so nervous about the blasted ICSI treatment that, the night before, she'd uncharacteristically gone down on her knees and prayed to the God her mother and sister so fervently believed in.

And God had answered her prayer.

PALM TREES IN THE STORM

CHAPTER 43

Sophie Abena Ofosu

Each fibre of her being felt connected to every growing cell of the baby in her womb. Jessica hoped this foretold a special relationship.

The doctor's advice rang clear. "So, try to minimise the dancing and, apart from swimming and gentle exercise, rest as much as you can."

"Thank you. She will," Joseph affirmed on Jessica's behalf, before promptly guiding his pregnant wife from the examination room.

He looked at her expectantly. "Coming along to Mum's today?"

Jessica envisioned her mother-in-law's negative aura and fumbled for an excuse. "No thanks. Better I relax this afternoon. Doctor's orders." She shrugged.

"Sure? I can stay if you prefer."

"No, no. You go. It'll be good for you to spend time with your mum and brother. In fact, I'll use the opportunity to call my siblings; it's been a while." She smiled encouragingly.

"Ah, yes. Mikey's about to become a dad again, right?"

"Yep. Baby number four!"

"Wow! Lucky man!"

Joseph's comment held no malice, but Jessica felt a jab of inadequacy and glanced at her tiny bump. He immediately wrapped his arms around her and clarified, "No comparison, darling. We're fortunate to have this one gift." He caressed her belly and kissed her gently.

She swallowed. "Maybe my mother's right. It's a blessing from God – an answer to prayer."

"It would appear that it is," was Joseph's uncharacteristic reply; evidence that this apparent act of supernatural intervention had astonished even he, who prided himself a devout atheist. As he'd admitted to Jessica, he couldn't shake the impression that its unexpected timing was beyond the realm of human reasoning, and so welcomed his daughter into the world with a reverence that felt more than just fatherly. To him, this child was an angel sent to bless them.

CHAPTER 43 — SOPHIE ABENA OFOSU

On her due date, stirrings of doubt and fear threatened to resurface, but Jessica instinctually knew this occasion would be different. She was older, her body more mature, and everything about this pregnancy spoke of divine intervention. She *wanted* this baby.

Her waters broke at 03:05 hours, and less than sixty minutes later she was being coached through labour at the Portland Hospital. She felt remarkably calm, finding strength in Joseph's quiet presence. He clasped her hand, squeezing it tightly whenever she gasped at the onset of a contraction. Pushing the baby through the birth canal felt almost easy, a far cry from her first childbirth experience.

Sophie Abena Ofosu graced the world with her presence on 4th December 2012 at 06:10 hours. In line with the naming culture of the Akan people of Ghana, her middle name denoted she was born on a Tuesday.

Jessica remained in the private ward for two days, falling in love repeatedly with her little bundle of blessings. As she kissed the tiny fingers and gazed into those beautiful, luminous brown eyes, she whispered with grateful tears, "You are my miracle!"

With another mouth to feed, Joseph threw himself into work. When home, his daughter became the focal point of his affections, her existence proof of his virility; that he was a man capable of siring a child unaided, despite troubling medical reports to the contrary. It amused

Jessica to note how quickly he dismissed talk of low sperm counts and discarded the notion of luck or divine intervention. What then explained the odd coincidence of falling pregnant just before the start of the invasive fertility treatment?

Some things simply cannot be rationalised, she mused, watching Joseph. She had come to recognise her husband as someone who didn't believe in anything he couldn't justify. In his view, most positive results boiled down to hard work and planning; faith had little to do with actual life.

"But darling, your theory doesn't make sense. We were unsuccessful for so long, then bam! This angel arrives – just like that." She gazed lovingly at their chubby-cheeked daughter, asleep in her arms.

Joseph tutted dismissively and lifted his newspaper higher, making Jessica stifle a sudden wave of loneliness. After laying Sophie in her day cot, she shuffled her tired, breastfeeding frame to their home gym for her daily workout.

Why she was still nursing a twenty-one-month-old was anybody's guess. How ridiculous to be doing so at this stage (her mother's exact words)! She pinched her flabby, fleshy flanks and sighed. Getting back into shape was proving more difficult than expected. This so-called "Nature's Liposuction" wasn't working! Her body downright refused to play ball – and Sophie's toothy attacks on her nipples had done nothing for her bulging belly. To give birth at nineteen is a different endeavour

CHAPTER 43 — SOPHIE ABENA OFOSU

than at age thirty-one, she mused with a grimace. She didn't feel as confident and the prospect of life as a stay-at-home parent held no appeal. Since she'd quit dancing, Emily had joined Annabel in LA and was now managing the other girl's acting career. Jessica was left to handle motherhood on her own. What did she have to look forward to? School runs, lunchboxes, after-school clubs, home dinners and very little time for herself. The terrifying thought of becoming a frazzled housewife left her more determined to regain her shape and get her career back on track.

First on the list was weaning the baby. It didn't help that her husband appeared distinctly disenchanted with her… or maybe he felt unhappy at work, and his discontent was spilling over into their family life?

"Joseph hates his job, you know," she confided to her sister Fifi.

"Yes, you said so. Must've been tough when the recession hit in 2008."

"Yeah. Forced him to sell the business to a bigger brand. A company he built from scratch."

"That couldn't have been easy."

"I know. Can you imagine? Ugh! I think he's bitter… maybe subconsciously wants to bring me to his level by ridiculing my aspirations."

"Hmm, what makes you say that? He used to attend your

performances, didn't he?"

"Sometimes. But he mostly travelled or worked late. He doesn't appreciate what I do, Fifi. Whenever I hint at resuming dancing, he tries to dissuade me."

"Why?"

"He insists Sophie needs hands-on care in these early years. A nanny is out of the question for Joseph, and things get ugly when I press the issue. Nowadays, all he does is criticise and find fault, with no energy for anything else. But I want more, Fifi."

~

It had become apparent to Jessica the man she married lacked ambition. Yes, he was a CEO and provider, but he truly longed for a simpler life. Jessica, needing an outlet, voiced some of her thoughts to Emily, who was cradling Sophie in her arms.

"He's such a mama's boy, Ems. Does everything to fit into her traditional idea of a 'real man' – gets married, has children, provides for his family, yadayadaya. Yet, I bet he'd still be living at home with her if he could!"

Emily continued cooing and tickling the babbling baby, paying little heed. Jessica sighed, inwardly berating herself. She should be grateful, she supposed. But oh, how she resented her mother-in-law's hold on Joseph and the fact that he seemed unaware of her manipulation. That woman

CHAPTER 43 — SOPHIE ABENA OFOSU

was… uurrgghhh! Jessica felt infuriated and lost for words, even in her thoughts. She remained silent for a moment, then added sadly, "He actually lives under the illusion he's capable of making his own decisions. But he can't even keep his wife happy!"

That caught Emily's attention and she glanced up. "And what makes you say that?"

"For years, all Josephina talked about was whether I would give her son a child. And now I have, I've become irrelevant – completely ignored by this husband of mine. So bloody unfair!"

"Maybe, you need to busy yourself with other things, Jess. Like dancing. You shouldn't have quit."

Jessica looked at her mentor-friend, who'd come all the way from LA to visit her. "You're right, Ems," she sighed. "Having a baby is no excuse. And neither is Joseph's attitude. I mustn't let that stop me from achieving my dreams. I refuse to be relegated to a life of mediocrity."

What she didn't add was that she increasingly pictured a different life; possibly using the money she'd stashed away ten years earlier. Cash that might prove handy for a rainy day.

CHAPTER 44

How did we get here?

J essica threw down the tape measure and scrutinized her naked form in the full-length mirror, frowning as she pinched the jiggling flesh of her inner thighs. Despite years of self-work, the image in front of her failed to reconcile with her deeper insecurities. Nature's generous gift of a curvaceous lower body, exaggerated post-childbirth, seemed almost comical, a far cry from her ideals of lean, toned dancer's legs.

Thighs – 27 inches, Hips – 40 inches! She sighed. *I look more like Jessica Rabbit than Jessica Brown.* The irony stung, considering the current world obsession with being "bootilicious" and the surge of butt enhancement surgeries. *My natural curves need no enhancing, for sure! I so want to cry right now.*

Jessica's inner turmoil bubbled over. She'd always been plagued by self-doubt, seeking validation from those around her while struggling to accept her own worth. She'd toiled with her image since childhood, spurning the veracity of her own beauty with a self-deprecation that cut more than skin deep. Despite all her success and worldly accolades, she could not shake the belief that she was not enough. Being easily affected by the opinions of those closest to her had left her vulnerable and prone to insecurity. And insecurity drove her to bad habits.

She spluttered as she choked on her own vomit, quickly rinsing her mouth and wiping away all traces of distress.

Dear J, there are few things worse than being under constant judgement, condemned even before you act; doomed to failure before you've made a mistake; dismissed before you've spoken; ridiculed no matter how you look. Such is my daily existence.

"Are you certain you want to wear that, darling?" Joseph would ask, his expression deadpan.

"Uhm, yeah, I like this dress. I think it looks o… kay, doesn't it?" Jessica would respond, suddenly unsure.

"Well, you'd need to be model thin to get away with that," Joseph would say with a slight snigger and a look of disdain.

Wham! Every time.

CHAPTER 44   HOW DID WE GET HERE?

No matter how she dressed, there was usually a comeback; and it wasn't pretty.

Jessica loved clothes, but her husband's criticism fueled her self-doubt.

When did we get like this? She wondered, pondering how hypercritical he was of everything she did and, worse, likely didn't realise it. It had become their state of being.

This was absolutely no way to live.

Joseph wasn't always outwardly combative, but his silent, insidious negativity – an unkind gesture, an indifferent look – spoke volumes. His attachment to the screen of his bloody phone and his frequent unwillingness to meet her gaze, or even glance up in acknowledgment when she entered the room, hurt the most.

What happened to my fairy tale? It died with William, that's what. William. So many years had passed since he'd gone; since she'd visited his grave. Her life was different now. But the pain never fully left, ebbing and flowing like the tide. Some days are better than others.

Jessica sighed, and wrote:

I must make peace with that memory, and my residual feelings of guilt at having benefitted financially from his death. This is why I stashed away the millions from the house sale – hid it in a trust which I've adamantly refused to touch. Except for a rainy day...

Maybe, soon... it could be my means of escape.

Dragging her thoughts back to the present, Jessica knew something had to change. The real issue wasn't losing weight. It was how motherhood had swallowed her identity, making every decision revolve around Sophie. They, the couple – husband and wife – no longer mattered. Their marriage had taken a backseat. Most conversations were about Sophie's growth or progress at school and were usually sandwiched by one proviso or another.

"I don't think Sophia eats enough fruit," he'd comment.

The pretentious way he called her Sophia irked Jessica, who retorted, "Well, given you're not here all day, how would you know what *Sophie* eats?" She'd find herself on the defensive detailing the healthy contents of their child's lunchbox. But his eyes would betray his disbelief, leaving her abundantly aware of his disapproval. He disapproved of *everything*.

Joseph's fury over rare treats or his dismissal of cereal as "dog food" sparked frequent arguments. It didn't matter that such treats were extremely rare, and seldom on any day other than sweet-treat-Saturday. Yet, Joseph would buy Sophie toffee waffles to get on her good side and allow her to eat chocolate spread, both of which Jessica pinpointed were brimming with sugar and no better than the "dog food" he despised. In her opinion, they were doubly detrimental for Sophie's health – not to mention her teeth, too. However, as long as it was *his* decision, it was the right one. For Joseph, it was his way or the highway. His hypocrisy was maddening.

CHAPTER 44 — HOW DID WE GET HERE?

Dear J, if I'd known how controlling he can be, I'd never have married him. It's incredible how he says one thing and does another. Why do I tolerate this nonsense?

It was only a matter of time before Sophie picked up on her parents' malcontent, and by age five she'd become a sulky, critical and dissatisfied child. She would whine and whine and whine – it seemed that Jessica could do nothing right in her daughter's eyes, and even meals Sophie usually loved became fodder for remonstration. On one particular morning, a simple enquiry about an egg sandwich triggered an uncontrollable crying fit.

"But darling, it's only a lunchbox," Jessica reasoned, as she gave her daughter a cuddle and stroked her hair.

To which Sophie had whispered, "Yes Mummy, but you promised I could have more of those sausagey things."

"Sausagey things?" Jessica had to crack her brain to remember which elusive delicacy she'd included in the packed lunch the week before. "Oh, you mean the chicken and lamb Koftas from M&S... yes, of course you can have them, darling, but not today. I'll stop by and get them for tomorrow, promise."

This seemed to calm little Sophie and, in that moment, Jessica deduced the problem in their home was a great deal bigger than *sausagey things*. Sophie had become infected by their toxic environment and the state of her parents' marriage, and even the slightest matter would set her off.

Jessica knew it was time for an intervention.

~

"I need peace and calm and serenity in my life," she mused, panting, pushing pause on the treadmill to catch her breath. She remembered the solace she'd found at the retreat in Thailand and felt an urge to reconnect with her Venezuelan yoga friend, Magdalena. The past few years had flown by and she'd lost touch with many people. She grabbed the towel hanging on the machine and held it against her sweaty face, exhaling in sharp bursts. Another fifteen minutes and I'm done, she timed, pressing the plus button for speed. Determination coursed through her veins as she gritted her teeth and persevered. Her legs were on fire, but it felt good.

Her thoughts returned to Magdalena, who'd been a lifeline in her time of grief. She'd selflessly devoted so much energy to Jessica, and her non-judgmental, non-preachy manner had made her long speeches about life more tolerable, with each morsel of truth more easily digestible. Jessica smiled as Magdalena's words echoed in her memory:

"Each of us has been perfectly formed. *You* are perfectly formed, Jess. **You just** have to believe it. Your Creator didn't make a mistake when he made you in your mother's womb. All that you are, the way you look, the way you're feeling right now – none of that's a mistake. So, trust, believe, and surrender to that truth. You are beautiful, Jessica."

CHAPTER 44 — HOW DID WE GET HERE?

Revived after her post-workout shower, Jessica sat down and stared at her phone. Right now, what she needed was a good dose of Magdalena's positivity.

Not knowing where to begin, she searched for her on Facebook and to her utmost surprise found the correct person. Excited, she sent a quick message, smiling when she got an almost immediate response. It transpired that Magdalena had been planning to reach out to Jessica too, because she was on the verge of a move from Barcelona to London the following month.

Strange how these things turn out.

"When exactly are you coming? Do you need my help? Oooh, I'm so excited – it'll be great to have you here! Where are you going to live? Such a pity I've rented out my flat in Knightsbridge, otherwise you could've stayed there…" Jessica's words tumbled out fast and thick, with hardly a pause for breath. The phone was wedged between her shoulder and the side of her delighted face, freeing both hands to prepare Sophie's supper.

Magdalena gave her customary light-hearted chortle, music to Jessica's laughter-starved ears. "I'm fine, darling. I have everything sorted out."

"Of course, you do," Jessica concurred. "But I thought you were in Venezuela. When did you move to Spain?"

"About four years ago." Magdalena's voice sounded guarded.

Jessica knew better than to press. "And now to London!" she declared cheerfully.

Magda's tone relaxed. "Yes. A big change, but change is good." She paused for a moment, "How about you, Jess? How's life treating you these days?"

Jessica's sigh spoke volumes.

"Actually, scratch that. Don't tell me… just describe what the ideal existence would look like for you?"

Jessica released the cork she'd plugged on her hurt and rage, her frustration and self-doubt, and her words came spilling out to Magda's willing, sympathetic ears: being seen, heard, appreciated, loved, accepted, valued, respected, happy – finding herself again.

"So, what's stopping you, Jess? Why don't you simply take what you want from life? Dance, if you want to. If it's love you desire, then show yourself love. What you focus on magnifies."

"It's not that easy, Magda. It's like… ever since I had Sophie, I've ceased being me."

"No, you're still you. But do *you* accept yourself, Jess?"

It was an odd question. Yet, it struck a nerve. Jessica stayed silent. Maybe that was it. She was her harshest critic. Her self-criticism gave others, especially Joseph, permission to be critical of her too.

CHAPTER 44 — HOW DID WE GET HERE?

"People treat you the way you treat yourself. Accept yourself and others will accept you."

Simple, perhaps, but true.

"You're right, Magda. It begins with me."

PALM TREES IN THE STORM

CHAPTER 45

Iron Out the Creases

Jessica walked through the ostensibly empty house with her mind racing. This was her precious moment for reflection, stolen in the early morning hours while both Joseph and Sophie still lay asleep. She leaned against the windowsill in the kitchen, pen in hand, the bleak reality of her less-than-satisfactory existence scrawled out on the page before her.

Here she was, thirty-seven-year-old Jessica Sokari Brown, once destined for greatness, yet now seemingly relegated to a life of mediocrity. Such a sobering thought; dismal even. And decidedly dissatisfactory.

This is my own doing, she mused. Somewhere in her belief-system, she'd equated having a family with the death of a successful career. But that needn't be.

Magdalena's encouraging counsel was playing on repeat in her mind: "What you focus on magnifies." Everyone around her seemed to be offering advice these days. Perhaps it was time to take heed?

She sighed at the sound of the creaking floorboards overhead. There we go... me-time over! I have to prepare Sophie's breakfast and get her ready for camp.

Sophie – her adorable six-year-old teenager. What a character. Jessica smiled as she thought of her daughter. Sophie wasn't your regular child. Her aura of self-assurance and astonishing intuition belied her age, making her appear older than her years.

She was clever, manipulative and disconcertingly aware of how to turn situations to her advantage. *Six-going-on-sixteen* was an accurate description.

Poor little Sophie. The ridiculous and constant food arguments between her parents were doing her a disservice, leaving her confused about treats she was supposed to enjoy. The subterfuge acted as a corrosive agent, needling its way into the child's mind, nudging her to pit one parent against the other. She clearly viewed her mother and father as two separate individuals on opposing sides of the trench, not as the unified entity they should exemplify.

CHAPTER 45 — IRON OUT THE CREASES

Children have the ability to discern hypocrisy and call out B-S. "Why does Daddy get angry when *you* give me chocolate?" "Why do you say I must use my words and not my emotions, but you and daddy shout and throw tantrums all the time?"

Why? Why? Why, indeed.

～

Jessica pulled into the narrow drive of their semi-detached house in Barnes and switched off the ignition.

Home meant household chores, which had been piling up since her unreliable cleaner had let her down yet again.

The systematic pressing and folding of the heap of clean laundry afforded her some respite, and she felt order and clarity return. She hated ironing, but this was somehow therapeutic; the heavy weight of metal in her hand, the puff of steam as it glided through the creases – it was a metaphor for her rumpled life, with her constantly furrowed brow and the deepening lines of sadness almost permanently etched into her once-beautiful face.

Jessica released a deep breath. *It's up to me to sort out the 'dirty laundry' of my life, to come to terms with the ugly truth of my current status quo. Change begins with me.* She needed to feed her mind with positive materials, let go of limiting beliefs and learn to relax. A critic might argue that, with a husband at work all day and a child at camp, she shouldn't complain.

But any housewife or stay-at-home mum will appreciate that, even with lots of time on one's hands, there's always something to do to ensure the smooth running of the household. And *that* doesn't classify as 'me-time', which is the mental break *everyone* requires. Even home-makers. Yes, she liked her little analogy. Iron out the creases. That's what she needed to do.

I want to return to work, but Joseph's so against it. I shouldn't let that stop me… Like begets like and unwavering conviction will bring out the same feeling in others. It's the power of projection – people see what we project of ourselves.

Yeah, yeah, Jess – motivational clichés and self-help blurb she used to scoff at, yet here she was guzzling it up out of sheer desperation. *Confronting problems head-on is a crucial aspect of my quest for change – the creases run deep and I need to tackle them with impunity. No more pretence!*

≈

She wasn't hungry, but knew she must eat. Staring at the leftover tuna in the fridge, Jessica debated between making a salad or piling it on a piece of toast with butter, yum! No, she decided as she caught her reflection in the glass of the sliding door, startled by the image of a belly where a washboard stomach had once been. She pinched her squishy flesh. Not exactly a muffin-top, but definitely a spare tyre. She grimaced. Hard to imagine Jessica Sokari Brown with a mummy-tummy. And not a soft, flabby undercarriage, but a firm rounded pouch, which wouldn't flatten no matter how hard she sucked it in. It was just… there; impossible to hide, and she hated it. Could this be middle-age? Decision made. Salad it was.

CHAPTER 45   IRON OUT THE CREASES

She threw a remaining quarter bag of watercress into a bowl, added the tuna, half an avocado and a sprinkling of seeds. She loved seeds. Having read somewhere they're supremely healthy, she tried to have a tablespoon every day. A drizzle of olive oil, a squeeze of lemon juice; salt and pepper, then a quick toss! Basic, but exactly what her body needed. After all, you are what you eat and she needed her skin to reflect the suppleness of youth once again.

A short while later, she found herself kneeling by the toilet bowl, habit reasserting itself. She stared into the water, her reflection rippling back. Not today, she decided, standing up resolutely.

It felt like a win.

Her watch caught her eye. Oh shucks! Time to collect Sophie from tennis. Ugh! She hadn't accomplished anything on her to-do-list. A stab of guilt pierced her as she pictured her daughter's vulnerable expressions. Guilt for not showing more affection toward her child, for being emotionally constipated. She was doing to her daughter what had inadvertently been done to her as a child. Shaking her head in self-reprieve, she vowed to make amends by spending quality time with Sophie that afternoon.

Driving to the camp, she gazed at the impressive swirl of orange and gold leaves conjured by the strong Autumn breeze; leaves moving hither and tither in all directions. Some skittered across the damp drizzle, while others remained plastered to the ground, squashed and stuck there by the indifferent wheels of speeding vehicles. Jessica felt like one of those fallen leaves. Crushed. Stuck. Glued to the repetitive nature of her circumstances.

She watched, captivated by a perfectly shaped solitary leaf, which stayed suspended in the air for an impossible moment before floating gracefully to the ground. She envied its delicate dance.

"I understand you feel you have the problem under control. That's good." Magda's piercing gaze was as direct as her words. "But what I don't get is how you can say you love your heritage, but hate the way you look?"

Jessica frowned thoughtfully, "I don't hate the way I look."

"Uh huh. If you say so."

"You don't believe me?"

Magda shook her head. "No, I don't, Jess. You make yourself throw up, for God's sake! That's an eating disorder."

"Not *all* the time. Only when I feel… sad, or stressed," Jessica argued.

"Like I said – an eating disorder."

Jessica folded her arms. "What does this have to do with my heritage, anyway?"

Magda mimicked her gesture and folded her arms, too. "Your

CHAPTER 45 — IRON OUT THE CREASES

heritage," Magda spoke with slow deliberation, "is why you have a propensity to be more 'curvaceous'."

"Curvaceous," Jessica scoffed. "I'm just fat. You're underplaying it to make me feel better."

"*Fat?* Woman, do you even see yourself in the mirror? It's time you accept that you are African, you have a bigger bottom than most Europeans, and your self-deprecation is racial self-hate."

Jessica gasped, but Magda bravely carried on, "Yes, in the white-washed world of ballet, you're seen as unusual, different, exotic…"

Jessica rolled her eyes and lifted a palm. "Hold up, Magda. Why is it that if a white woman complains about her body, it's a complaint about her body. Full stop. But when it's a black woman it becomes *'racial self-hate'*? I'm just a woman hating on herself, nothing to do with colour."

"Perhaps. But it's still self-hate. And why? Because you look different from other dancers? Embrace it. It's your super-power. The thing that sets you apart. You're beautiful, Jess. Own it!"

PALM TREES IN THE STORM

CHAPTER 46

20 May 2020

Meticulous. Compulsive. OCD, perhaps? Anal, even!

But Jessica couldn't help it. Here she was (again) on her hands and knees, scrubbing the floor with an anti-bacterial cloth from M&S, her go-to store these days. She was forever in bloody M&S – always buying something essential, usually milk! And she didn't, in fact, drink milk. But everyone else did. Oh, how she wished she hadn't just reminded him of their silly arrangement. Now, her thoughts couldn't drown out the incessant hammer of his voice, getting louder and louder as his inner frustration bubbled over and left him bereft of control. He felt entitled to shout at her. She felt her brain might explode.

"No effing way! It's my day off and I'll do whatever the hell I please. No way am I spending my Saturday cleaning the damn house."

Jessica glanced at Joseph, sprawled arrogantly in his self-appointed, antique armchair, an indignant king of nothing. Sunlight poured through the bay windows, casting shimmering patterns on the wall and exposing dust motes on the marble coffee table. Even after all these years, his ability to avoid outright profanity amazed her. Yet, his raised voice more than compensated.

"I'm not asking you to spend your entire Saturday, Joseph, just a couple of hours. It'll fly by if we do it together like we agreed." Her tone exuded patience as she reasoned with him. "I don't enjoy it either, but with all that's happening these days there's no alternative."

Her voice was a soothing balm in the volatile atmosphere.

His chair scraped the floor with grating emphasis as he stood. "Always nagging me!" he spat through gritted teeth, his words slicing through the air.

Foreseeing an onslaught of abuse, she turned away, shaking her head in annoyance. This show of defiance seemed to exacerbate his anger, and he moved towards her with bared fangs. "Such a cow!" It escalated in volume. "What d'you want from me? Nothing I do is ever enough. Why the hell couldn't *you* take her to the park yesterday if you're such a… an amazing mother? Huh?"

She raised a brow at his reference to their earlier quarrel.

CHAPTER 46 20 MAY 2020

"But I…," she interjected in defence.

He steamrolled on. "You sit on your arse all day doing *nothing*." He was shouting now.

"No, that's not…"

It was as though she hadn't spoken.

"I work all week, month after month in a job I despise so you can enjoy this lifestyle, and you have the nerve to talk to me about cleaning."

"Me! What lifestyle?" she roared back. The dam which curbed her swelling vexation and resentment finally broke. "I only mentioned it because it's what we discussed."

Had he been more in tune with reading her signals, he'd have seen the flood advancing. But bent on his mission to annihilate, Joseph pressed on, guns ablaze.

"I've repeatedly had to strive for my lot in life, but *you*…" The word 'you' sounded like a curse. "Your wealthy upbringing means you expect everything to be easy."

Jessica braced herself against the war-tactic-killer-move she saw coming – the obvious taunt about her supposed dearth of education (she never attended university); his way of keeping her in her place and possibly masking his own sense of inadequacy.

"What have you ever achieved? You don't even have a degree!"

There it was, right on cue. But she had amassed enough emotional armour to cultivate a satisfactory comeback and was ready. She scowled her indignation, hackles rising, the torrent finally bursting forth. "What did *your* damn degree get you?" Her voice was stronger, fueled by years of pent-up frustration. "*I* signed with two major dance companies and starred in countless shows. Yes, Joseph! Stop shaking your head. I was a star – whether or not you believe it. What have *you* accomplished?" She ignored his warning gaze and pressed on. "I s'pose you had *some* success as a fashion designer once upon a time, but you gave it up – *you* chose to give it all up and somehow you blame *me*?" Her lips twisted in disgust. "It isn't my fault you work in a position you loathe. That's *your* choice! At least I excelled at doing something I loved! Huh! I'll never let you demean my achievements!"

No doubt, their nosey neighbours could hear the deafening din of voices through the open windows. Her daughter stomped and covered her ears in distress. But Jessica, immersed in her rage, was oblivious.

Her chest heaved as she continued to defend her status. "I wasn't a nobody when you met me, Joseph! You didn't rescue me. What bloody lifestyle? You are so…" She glared at him, her fingers curling into a ball of exasperation, "… aarrgghh!" Rage had rendered her incoherent.

Joseph took a step toward her in a seeming act of concession, then said quietly, "No, I never said I rescued you." His dark eyes held hers as he whispered through snarled lips, "Despite how quickly we got married, I predicted you'd be an asset. You are nothing but a liability to

CHAPTER 46 — 20 MAY 2020

me, Jess. This isn't the deal I signed up for."

The venom in his voice stung her into silence, and in that moment, she knew. He didn't love her anymore. Perhaps he never had. He had been enamoured with the idea of who she might be. But that wasn't love.

Sophie's hunched shoulders trailed behind her father as he stormed up the stairs. Jessica heard his forced, falsely gentle tone addressing their little girl, attempting to erase any residue of the hatred she'd just witnessed.

Jessica continued her scrubbing through tear-glazed eyes.

They hadn't always been like this. It hadn't always been like this. Or maybe it had. There had been an undercurrent of disharmony, but the pandemic lockdown intensified it. Small disagreements now sparked arguments, leading to explosions. Jessica stifled an involuntary sob.

Seeking solace in the kitchen, she flinched when he slammed the front door. Phew. Alone at last, she breathed a sigh of relief, cheeks burning, emotions swirling. *Who have I become? Why is everything so difficult? Me, a liability?! Wow!* The words still prickled.

She dragged dejected feet upstairs, retrieved her journal from the nightstand drawer, and poured her heart out on its crisp blank pages. Almost cramped to capacity with her scribbles and rants, she'd soon need a new, thicker one, given the frequency of her outpourings.

With each upward stroke of the moist cotton pad, Jessica wiped away all traces of her distress, even while the words whirled around her mind like a spinning wheel out of its axis. Mean, rude, unkind, controlling, angry. He was hateful! "I don't care," she screamed in her being as she scrubbed her body clean. "I don't bloody care!"

She'd reached the end of her tether. Their toxic parenting set a poor example for their seven-year-old. Why was she with him? What did it say about her?

She found herself contemplating the money she'd stashed away and the freedom it symbolised.

CHAPTER 47

Don't just Bitch about it, Do Something

Magda and Jessica's long walks were reminiscent of their time in Thailand, digging into the debris of emotional baggage, while seeking clarity and progress. Yet, life felt stagnant.

"I'm reading all the books you recommended and listening to motivational podcasts, but…! Look at me, Magda," Jessica stated with exasperation, "Feels like… I'm getting nowhere! I mean, I understand the stuff on a cerebral level – I get it – but putting it into practice? Nearly impossible."

"Do you really believe what you just said? Have you made *zero* progress?"

Jessica sighed. "Well, I suppose there's been *some* improvement, but my life's pretty much the same."

"Which is…?" Magda sounded less indulgent.

"Which is decidedly ordinary! There, I've said it. I lead a boring life, Magda… I'm bored out of my mind."

Jessica wasn't prepared for the explosion of laughter that ensued. Magda doubled over, shoulders heaving, letting out a loud and unabashed chortle.

"What's so funny?" Jessica demanded, unamused by her friend's unsympathetic reaction.

"You are, darling! You take yourself far too seriously. Admitting you're bored, really??" She giggled again. "And if life bores you, who's to blame? Sort yourself out, Silly! Get busy!"

Jessica was in the mood to feel sorry for herself, and countered, "That's easy for *you* to say. You don't have someone breathing down your neck all the time, criticizing everything you do…" The tears welled up.

"Hey, hey… don't get upset. Tell me what happened. What's wrong?" Magdalena put a comforting arm around her friend.

Jessica sniffled. "This weekend, we had the most God-awful row. Over nothing! I mean, the bloody cleaning… *nothing*. That's what sparked

CHAPTER 47   DON'T JUST BITCH ABOUT IT, DO SOMETHING

it off and I have no idea what came over Joseph, but he got so angry and was so rude... said some horrible things... and poor Sophie was right there. Even our neighbours must've heard, for sure. Extremely embarrassing. I-I don't see how I can take much more of this."

Magdalena remained silent, giving Jessica space to continue.

"He literally said I sit on my arse doing nothing all day and have become a liability to him. Can you imagine? *A liability!*" Her tears turned to anger, eyes glinting with steely determination. "And yesterday, he went off on one of his morning escapades, leaving Sophie and I to enjoy some peace ... until his dark cloud returned... raining down insults because I'd moved his bike to the basement. Such a whirlwind of negativity! He's always so bloody angry, Magda. *I* make him angry."

"Perhaps there's something you can do to prevent his anger...?"

"*What? Me??* No," Jessica huffed with infuriation. "I'm done trying. I'm out!"

Magda gave Jessica a surprised look. "What do you mean, you're out?"

"I'm gonna leave. Take Sophie. Run away."

"Run away from *what?*" Magda sounded unimpressed.

"From him, from our constant bickering, from the struggle that's become my existence."

Magda's sigh was heavy. "But is that the solution? It sounds like you're running away from yourself, Jess."

Jessica's eyes narrowed. "What do you mean? That *I* cause my problems?"

Magda's gaze was unwavering. "What *problems*? Besides, you get angry too, just like him. Huh! I could tell you about *real* problems!" The shadow that flickered across her friend's face vanished as quickly as it appeared. Magda continued, "You call them problems, but it's just life. And in life, shit happens, people argue, they fall out of sync with one another, but eventually reconnect. It happens every day – your situation's not unique. It's how you respond that matters."

"Hmm! Well, I expected a little more support from you of all people."

"Excuse me?" Magda squinted and stopped walking. "I've done nothing but support you, Jessica Brown. What I won't do is watch you throw your life down the drain because it isn't going the way you expect, 100 percent of the time."

Jessica took in Magda's flushed face, and could tell she'd left a lot unsaid. She swallowed and focused on her shuffling feet. "You're right. How ungrateful I must sound. I'm such a silly goose. You've been so instrumental in helping me debunk my issues. Yet, here I am, ready to throw in the towel because I hate the monotony of my life." Spoken out loud, it sounded pathetic and Jessica felt a deep shame. "I'm sorry."

Magda was still frowning. "Running away will achieve *nada*, trust me. You've got to stop blaming others for your unmet expectations. Let go of your past, Jess. *That's* what's holding you back." She sighed and

CHAPTER 47 — DON'T JUST BITCH ABOUT IT, DO SOMETHING

reached for Jessica's hand. "We always feel if we run away things will get better but, the point is, circumstances can change at the drop of a hat… and your 'problems' follow you wherever you go."

Jessica shot her friend a curious glance. "Sounds like you're speaking from experience."

Magdalena let go of her hand and turned away slightly. "I am," she admitted, "but that's a conversation for another day."

Upon returning home, Jessica headed to her walk-in wardrobe and unpacked the suitcases she'd prepared for her get-away. Magda was right; fleeing wasn't the solution. Separating Sophie from her father would be unfair.

But her resolve dissolved when she saw Joseph's stony expression a short while later. Still angry from the previous day, he didn't say hello; he just looked through her and walked away.

It incensed Jessica. Her body trembled with gallons of bottled-up rage – rage that had built over years of being belittled by a thankless husband. He couldn't be bothered to have a conversation and, when he did, it was usually one-sided. She resented him. With his entitled attitude and beady, brown eyes constantly spewing judgement. Nothing she did was right. She wished he would leave and stay gone.

She glanced with frustration at her now empty suitcases. Maybe she *should* leave, after all!

The irrational feeling that welled up within her was like a grenade on the verge of explosion. She choked on her very breath as indignant hurt threatened to consume her. Everything she did for this family, all her attempts to follow in her mother's footsteps, to be the perfect wife and home-maker, her very self-worth and contribution, once again, dismissed out of hand. Being unappreciated is the worst kind of put-down because it's a form of withholding love, and the repetitive nature of such abuse is more than most can endure.

Yet, Jessica conceded she was unlike most. She'd been conditioned to accept crumbs of affection, hoping the elusive loaf might someday be hers. As such, she often embraced anything that vaguely resembled a gesture of kindness with misplaced enthusiasm, which invariably weakened her stance in most relationships. Her lifelong search for acceptance meant she constantly sought attention and approval, firstly from her parents, and now from Joseph.

This was the story Jessica told herself, but was it true? Based on what Magda had said that morning, it would appear Jessica had invented this narrative to justify playing the victim, and running away from her 'problems.' Was it true her parents had begrudged her love? Jessica's eyes misted over as she thought of how they'd supported her throughout the years. The truth hit her with glaring clarity. For most of her life, Jessica had been so wrapped up in the insecurity within her own mind she'd failed to recognise her parents' love for each another was not discriminatory against their children, but rather corroborated her existence and that of

CHAPTER 47   DON'T JUST BITCH ABOUT IT, DO SOMETHING

her siblings. Shame on her for imagining otherwise.

And Joseph?

Elusive and miserly though it might be, he did show affection sometimes.

"But what of Sophie? Where does *she* fit into all this?" Magda had poignantly asked at the end of their morning walk, before rushing off to teach a yoga class. Jessica's eyes smarted at the mention of her daughter. She regretted scolding Sophie on the way to school that morning. It felt so frustrating, constantly repeating herself to get Sophie ready on time.

Sophie reflected the toxic dynamic between her parents, and had imbibed some of its characteristics. It dismayed Jessica to witness her daughter's beautiful spirit waning. *She's only mimicking our behaviour – my behaviour. I need to tap into my calmer self and be a better example.*

But I feel so angry, Jessica grumbled to her diary. *I hate it!* The tears welled again, blurring her vision. *I think of her as difficult, but that's unfair. She's just being a seven-year-old. It's not her fault I'm frustrated. I need to take it out on someone. It should be him, but... aarrgghh! This is definitely not where I want to be.*

Her inner voice reprimanded her, "Do something about it. You're not powerless. *You* have control over your responses, feelings, words, thoughts, who you are. *Do something.*" Jessica nodded at her reflection, smoothing the parting of her weave-on, conscious it was growing out and needed urgent professional intervention. Inspecting her chipped nail polish, she said self-admonishingly, "C'mon, Jess, sort yourself out!"

Joseph's unkind, but truthful, words still taunted her: "All you do is wake up, take Sophia to school, go to the gym, and sit on your arse all day. Do something with your life!"

He was right.

CHAPTER 48

Little Things

"**I**'m exhausted!"

Jessica's first thought as she awoke on that mid-July morning in 2020 echoed through her aching body. Her puffy eyes fought to stay open. Gently twisting into a backstretch, she winced as her vertebrae squeaked and clicked in mild resistance. She felt old. And she wasn't even forty yet. Having just celebrated her 39th birthday, she felt as if she'd crossed an invisible line into true adulthood. It was now or never.

Life resembled a struggle of one form or another. No wonder her back had given way, with her body rebelling against the lack of attention and abuse.

Dear J, you must be bored of my complaining. I'm tired of it, too. It's only reinforcing my unimaginative echo-chamber of negativity – a damaging cycle I must break. But I fear I've ceased to exist. My eyes have no sparkle. Dull. No zest for life. Frustrated because there's plenty I'd love to do in the world, but where do I start? Things won't improve by themselves. Need to do something, but what?

Once dressed, she headed downstairs to study the wall calendar. Their summer holiday wasn't due for another three weeks and Jessica longed to escape London, after being cooped up for almost six months!

The shrill sound of Joseph's specially selected ring-tone interrupted her thoughts. There it was – another subliminal form of control. He'd programmed her phone to ensure she never missed his calls. Well, she would damn well miss this one, she thought spitefully, pressing the ignore button and grabbing the car keys. "I'm not your beck and call girl," she grumbled to herself. "This is my alone time."

She hurried to Hyde Park for her customary walk with Magdalena and plunged into her usual diatribe of complaints, ranting for a good ten minutes before even glancing at her friend. Magdalena was staring straight ahead.

Jessica frowned and reached for her arm. "Hey, are you ok? I don't think you heard a word I said."

CHAPTER 48 LITTLE THINGS

Magda turned, tears brimming in her eyes. "Sorry. I've got some things on my mind. I'm usually ok, but today…"

"No, don't apologise. I'm blathering on about the same old nonsense and here you are clearly upset. What's wrong, darling?"

Magda paused, then spoke under her breath, "My son…"

Jessica cocked her head to one side, certain she'd misheard. "Your *what*? You – have – a – son?"

"Yes," came the quiet reply. "Hector. He'll be nine next week." She sniffed.

Jessica realised with stunned embarrassment that this meant she knew very little about her friend. "Oh." She stared at Magdalena's pained features. "And where is Hector now?"

"He's… he's with his father. In Venezuela."

Jessica tried to piece everything together. "Your husband? Ex?"

"We never got married. When I became pregnant, things changed with Esteban."

"Esteban… Esteban who?"

"Delgado. He's running for governor of Estado Miranda." Magdalena's voice was flat. She sighed heavily and sat on a log from a felled tree. Her hands trembled as she ran them through her dark, wavy hair. "I was young and stupid. We were in love – I should've known better."

"So, he's a politician. How did you meet?" Jessica perched next to Magda.

"At the university in Madrid. I was studying International Relations, and he was a guest lecturer for one of my modules. He was fascinating. So smart and ambitious. He had a genuine passion for the liberation of the people, you know? I was so impressed. Fell for him, completely." She exhaled with a faraway look on her face, then glanced at Jessica's bemused expression and continued, "I joined him in Caracas immediately after my masters. Then I got pregnant and had Hector. That's when everything changed." An aura of sadness overcame her as she gazed wistfully at children frolicking with a golden Labrador by the small lake.

Jessica cleared her throat, a thick blanket of shame enveloping her. She took Magda's limp hand. "Wow, I really had no idea you had a son."

"I'm supposed to meet Hector for his birthday. Esteban visits London once a year for business, and that's when I get to see my baby. But now he says they're not coming." Magda's voice broke.

Jessica shook her head in disbelief, her tone incredulous. "Are you saying you only see him *once* a year?"

Magdalena wiped her eyes. "The bastard only allows me weekly video calls and one visit per year. Yes."

Jessica's gaze narrowed. "But how can he do that? It's not up to him! Hector's your son."

CHAPTER 48 — LITTLE THINGS

Magda frowned. "No, unfortunately he can. When you're Esteban Enrique Delgado, you can do whatever the hell you want."

"Not in England, you can't!" Jessica felt indignant.

Magdalena glanced around surreptitiously. Her voice took on a low urgency. "Listen, Jess, he's *very* powerful. There are stories of things that happen to people who cross him."

Jessica leaned in closer. "I don't understand. How did Hector end up with him in the first place?"

Magdalena sighed heavily. "When things started, it was wonderful. Esteban was so passionate about everything. Then, after Hector, he changed. Women. Drugs. He hit me countless times."

"He what?!"

She nodded. "One day, when Hector was two, I found the courage to run away… back to Spain, to Barcelona this time. For almost four years we were fine, and I assumed he'd given up on us. *Four years*, Jess. I was living a different life, teaching yoga again, we were happy. But by this point, Esteban had become a powerful politician in Venezuela. I thought we were safe, but one day," her voice trembled, "I go to Hector's school to pick him up and… he's gone. They said his father had collected him." She smiled bitterly. "*Four* years and not a peep from that man and then bam. Yet, when he was little, Esteban never even played with him! He claimed he couldn't bond with a whiny, wimpy brat. Now, he wants a relationship? Huh!"

Jessica listened with empathy.

"In court, he called me 'unfit to be a mother' – and falsified evidence against me; said I have a history of mental illness and drug abuse. All lies! He acted like the perfect father, but later told me Hector needs to be shown how to be a 'real man' and that he would beat the wimp out of the boy."

"Hah?!" Jessica gasped.

Magdalena continued, her voice rising. "The bastard kidnapped my son and got away with it!" Her eyes flashed. "The ju-" She stopped speaking mid-sentence to let a group of runners pass, before carrying on in a harsh whisper, "The judge was totally on his side even though he made up bullshit stories about my state of mind."

"But you're his mother! Dammit, Magda, we've got to do something!" Seeing Magdalena's resigned expression, she quickly added, "No, seriously. A nine-year-old boy shouldn't be exposed to that lifestyle. We must rescue him before it's too late."

Magda stared blankly at the scenes of families having fun. Her voice was barely audible when she spoke. "How?"

Jessica sounded quietly confident. "I don't know yet. But we'll find a way. I promise."

CHAPTER 48 — LITTLE THINGS

"She doesn't need to go out again, Joseph, really! She's been at camp all day... outdoors. If she'd rather be home this afternoon, we should allow her to stay."

Joseph had returned to their family nest in a foul mood, probably because she hadn't answered his earlier call and he couldn't bear to be ignored. Jessica had long since dispensed with using any term of endearment for her husband. Even the overused "darling" was too much.

Not that she disagreed with the importance of outdoor play, but his manner – his bully tactics, disbelief, and dissatisfaction with anything not pre-approved – was exasperating. Determined to avoid a row, she moved into the kitchen, busying herself with preparing supper.

With her dad out of earshot, Sophie followed her mother into the neutral-zone kitchen, twiddling her fingers. "Maybe you should just take me to the park, Mummy," she said morosely.

Jessica glanced at her daughter and placed the knife on the cutting board. Wiping her hands on her apron, she knelt in front of her.

"Why? Do you *want* to go to the park, darling?"

Sophie shook her head emphatically. "No... I'm tired."

"Okay then," she kissed her child on the forehead, "I'm going to run you a lovely bubble bath with your toys and you can relax. Would you like that?"

Sophie nodded but looked worried. "But Daddy..." her voice faltered.

Jessica smiled reassuringly. "Leave Daddy to me, darling." Seeing Sophie's dubious expression, she continued, "I promise we won't argue. Are you a little scared of him?" she pressed encouragingly.

Sophie's nod was almost imperceptible.

Jessica pursed her lips tightly, her eyes glistening as her heart ached for her child. "Well, you should *never* be scared of Daddy, my angel. He loves you so much and you don't need to win his love. So that's why you sometimes don't show him your actual feelings – you're afraid he'll get angry?"

Sophie looked bewildered. "I don't want to be the reason you and Daddy fight."

Jessica hugged her tight, her voice catching. "You could never be the reason we fight, darling. Mummy and Daddy disagree over silly things and it's really nothing to do with you. I promise I'll try hard not to fight with Daddy, okay?"

Especially not over little things.

CHAPTER 49

Searching for Answers

Muffled male voices grew louder and more animated, seeping through the door.

"Lord knows, we won't get such praise from our wives…" The tone held a snigger.

"No, just nag, nag, nag, all day long!" Jessica recognised Joseph's voice. She frowned and pressed her ear more firmly against the door. Did she really nag him? These days she tried so hard to avoid arguments, tiptoeing around issues with deliberate vagueness. *Nag?*

"Yes." That was Edwin's lazy drawl. "Moments of self-congratulation are crucial for a man's ego. If *we* don't say 'well done' to ourselves, who the hell will?"

Clinking of glasses and more laughter ensued. Jessica had always pegged Edwin as one of those unsavoury friends – the type no wife wants for her husband. And although Joseph was mostly his own man, who knew what he might be capable of these days?

"Ah, what are we complaining about?" The first voice again, one Jessica couldn't quite identify. "After all, we get the required praise from our girlfriends." He placed undue emphasis on the word 'praise' and a loud guffaw followed.

Jessica could make out Joseph's distinct laugh; a sound she rarely witnessed these days. Presumably, something he reserved for his mates. She shook her head in disappointment. She hadn't meant to eavesdrop but curiosity had gotten the better of her. Maybe it really was the end of the road for them. If he felt half as dissatisfied as she did, why on earth were they still together?

She crept away from the closed door, a little disheartened and wishing she hadn't overheard their conversation. That he was joking with his friends about what they were going through caused her some discomfort. She thought she'd stopped caring, but clearly not. Huh! *This is more serious than Joseph realises. He's made himself redundant to me. I started off needing him so much; desperate to please him and wanting his approval.*

CHAPTER 49 — SEARCHING FOR ANSWERS

Jessica wiped away a tear, lest it smudge the ink on her journal. She sniffed and continued writing.

And now, I couldn't care less! I'll do what I must and move on with my life. Right now, I need to figure out how to help Magda get her son back. Focusing on someone else's problems might take my mind off my own.

Here they were, with Sophie away for the weekend, staying with her grandmother in North London. This would have been a great opportunity for her constantly bickering parents to rekindle their dying love. Instead, Joseph had invited his boisterous friends over for a boys' night.

Jessica blinked rapidly to stem the flow of tears that threatened to spill once again. Tears of self pity, no doubt.

It'd been a month since they'd made love, but strangely she didn't miss it. (Or so she'd told a sceptical Annabel during their last trans-Atlantic call.) Well, she missed 'it', but not from him. She felt relieved he wasn't doing his usual predictable thigh stroke routine – the pre-curser to intercourse. Quite boring. It seemed rehearsed, almost like he was following a manual – going through the motions knowing he'd get his desired result every time. Such a jaded view, Annabel had been quick to inform her. But truth be told, Jessica never said "No". It just wasn't in her to deny sex, especially given she enjoyed it so much. Aargh, so frustrating! Earlier in the day, she'd glanced at him descending the stairs and had reluctantly admitted he was a handsome man. Yes, she'd give him that, but he was becoming increasingly repugnant to her.

She'd begun to dislike him so much that the idea of him touching her made her skin crawl. *I find him repulsive.* And by the looks of things, the sentiment was mutual. Her tears spilled over.

☙

Freida was on loudspeaker. "Been meaning to ask… did you ever confront Debbie after it happened?"

"Nope," Jessica stated, manoeuvring her Mercedes into a parking space. "Didn't want to give her the opportunity to gloat."

"To gloat? Over *what?*" Freida's tone was scathing. "She's a complete loser, Jess. Someone needs to tell her to her face."

"Oh?" Perplexed by Fifi's sudden indignance, Jessica asked, "What's brought this on? It's been years!"

"Yeah, well, I bumped into her the other day. She tried to behave as though she hadn't seen me, of course, but I'm certain she did. Stupid, cowardly girl."

"Hmm, maybe you're right. Perhaps I should've confronted her – and if I ever see her again, I will." She mused, "Fifi, I think my inability to confront the ugly truth of betrayal stems from a subliminal fear of rejection; of not being enough. Even with my dancing, I want to give my best but, sometimes, I fear my past failures will resurface and reveal to

CHAPTER 49   SEARCHING FOR ANSWERS

my audience I'm not the real deal. Just a wannabe. A fake. Like Madame Travers said all those years ago, my body isn't classical – not ideal for ballet – so I've had to bend it, almost to breaking point, just to achieve today's success."

"Don't be silly, Jess. As Africans, dancing is in our DNA. You love it and you're great at it!"

"True. It's all I've ever wanted to do. But honestly, Fifi, even as a little girl, when I'd watch that famous prima ballerina on TV, remember? I suspected some aspects of dance would always elude me. I felt it, even then. That I'd never be enough. And to top it off, the only appreciation I got came from the one person I never should have trusted."

"Hey, don't go there…," her sister warned.

"No, seriously. It's time I faced the truth. I have been a terrible judge of character. Kofi – Debbie – TJ – all poor judgements. Could it be that Joseph is one, too?"

"Now you're being ridiculous!" Fifi chided. "Shall I tell you what I think?" Her tone was firm. "I think Joseph is a good man – he's not William, and you need to stop expecting the same type of love. He's different; less demonstrative from what I can see, but he loves you in his own way. He adores Sophie and is a brilliant father."

Jessica was silent.

Freida continued, "What *you* need is a solid dose of self-confidence.

Find yourself again, darling. Stop expecting Joseph to affirm the old Jess. Who is Jess today? Figure *that* out."

"Yes, but… things are different. Joseph is leaving a week earlier for Summer because of business and I've got to say, I can't wait for him to go. In the early days, I'd literally mourn his absence; missing him even before he left. And now, it's like… puuhh! His aura is so oppressive I look forward to him travelling so I can be free to be me."

Freida chuckled. "I'm sure there are loads of wives who feel the same way about their husbands, Jess, that doesn't mean you don't love him."

"You're right," Jessica conceded. "I admit I do care for him. But increasingly, life is about keeping promises to myself and not about anyone else, or what others think. It's about being honest about my feelings and taking ownership of everything I do; for example, doing chores because I choose to."

"That's called growing-up," Freida stated laughingly. "Sounds like you've been doing some soul-searching, which is a good thing. Being true to who you are. Only *you* can decide what you want."

"I realise that. Hey, remember I told you about my friend Magdalena? I really want to help her, Fif. Just need to figure out how. She's been amazing to me over the years, and I can't believe she never once hinted at her problems. Well, maybe she did once, but I didn't press. It was all me-me-me."

CHAPTER 49 — SEARCHING FOR ANSWERS

"Listen to yourself! I like what I'm hearing, little sis!"

"Seriously, it's clear to me now. I need to give something back. This is an opportunity for me to step out of myself; see things as they really are." Jessica's voice rose with excitement. "My focus has been on what's lacking, which means I receive more of that lack. I expect Joseph's love to be imperfect and fleeting, so that's exactly what I get. But it's love, regardless."

"Precisely," Fifi agreed. "I know he loves you, Jess. He's just a very practical man who's a little less tolerant of your BS."

"Hey!" Jessica feigned hurt feelings. "What d'you mean, BS?"

Fifi giggled, "You know what I mean!"

"Yeah, I do. It's no-one's fault I'm bloody stressed all the time. I'm doing this to myself."

"Exactly! And, another thing, darling. All these arguments you mention you and Joseph keep having…"

"Yes…" Jessica prompted warily.

"You know what I'm gonna say, right?"

"That *I'm* to blame?"

"No, not at all. That it always takes two. I was listening to this preacher guy who said… no, don't hang up. I share your allergy to American preachers, but this one was good. He said, 'Don't fight battles that are not between you and your destiny.' What it means is before engaging in an argument, ask yourself the question: Will this simply satisfy and fuel my ego or will it make a difference to my destiny? If it doesn't affect what matters, let it go."

〰️

Jessica stood by the master bedroom's big bay windows, looking down into the communal gardens below. Children were playing a joyful game of hide-and-seek and, from her vantage point, she could spot all their ingenious hideouts. She smiled at the scene, then turned her attention back to the phone call.

"Thank you for waiting. Mr Cortez will speak with you now."

"Thanks."

"Hello, Miguel Cortez here. How may I help you?"

"Hi, Mr Cortez. I'm interested in hiring a private investigator and hear you're the best in the business."

"That, I am," he affirmed with no hint of humour. "Can find dirt on anyone, anywhere, anytime. So, shoot. What d'you need?"

〰️

They were at their Summer House in Ville Franche-Sur-Mer on the Cote D'Azur and Jessica stepped onto the terrace to enjoy the view. She took slow, tentative sips of her delicious, but scalding, freshly brewed coffee and gazed out to the horizon. The aquamarine sea was dotted

CHAPTER 49 — SEARCHING FOR ANSWERS

with sailing boats, and the sky was an expanse of azure blue without a cloud in sight.

Then, she heard it! The loud bellow seemed to come from somewhere below, crashing rudely into her serene morning. She couldn't pinpoint the exact location of the voices – the dense foliage which served as protection from the prying eyes of neighbours obscured her view – but she could tell they were Italian. The female was screaming "*Smettila*" which means "Stop it!" and the man was spewing a tirade of unrepeatable abuse, words which should never be exchanged between people who profess love for one another.

Jessica cringed. This must be how we appear to our neighbours in London – like an out-of-control, crazy couple who shouldn't be together. What was the purpose of shouting and arguing, anyway? So pointless and exhausting, not to mention embarrassing.

Shaking her head at the memory of some of their less-redeeming interactions, she closed the French windows to block out the cacophony of indignant outrage, moving to the quieter side of the villa where father and daughter were frolicking happily in the infinity pool. This view never grew old and was an aide-mémoire to how fortunate they were. It was a beautiful sight to behold, and Jessica smiled as they beckoned her.

"Come in! Join us… it's so lovely."

"Yeah, Mum, it isn't cold at all…"

She laughed and simply waved. The post-pool palaver of washing her bouffant afro provided enough incentive to keep her where she was, perspiring from the heat but content to remain chlorine free.

Seeing them like this warmed her heart and reminded her that they should cherish their time together as a family, and not just for Sophie's sake.

It's really up to me, Jessica conceded in a wave of awareness. *I am the peacemaker in our home. I need to count my blessings and be thankful for the good things in my life. There's so much to be grateful for, and yet I keep focusing on what I don't have.*

She pulled out her laptop. Her current self-help book encouraged participants to write and submit their "truth". The online analysis she received read: The tragedies and betrayals which struck early in your life have knit a tight vest of fury and disappointment which you slip on daily; the donning of which entitles you to remain a victim; leaving you little room to manoeuvre the nuances of effectively grieving one storm before being whacked by the next. Barely enough time to recover and stand upright again. A shadow of yourself. Unhappy. Seeking a reason to be infuriated with your circumstances. Blame someone else. Blame Joseph.

Jessica stared at the screen. This analysis was incredibly accurate.

The scars were still there. Not fully healed. Knitted into a vest of regret. And each day, she made an excuse to put it on. The hurt. The pain. The grief. The anger.

But these were excuses.

CHAPTER 49 — SEARCHING FOR ANSWERS

Reasons to remain stuck.

She was so busy being angry and wallowing in the self-righteous position of taking offence, she'd forgotten how to just… be. Live and let live. No expectations. No disappointments. No *wahala*.

PALM TREES IN THE STORM

CHAPTER 50

Rescue Plan

"I've got it!" Jessica exclaimed, her eyes lighting up with determination. "I know exactly how we can make Esteban give you full custody of Hector."

Magdalena seemed sceptical. "How?"

"By hiring a private investigator," Jessica asserted, raising a hand to halt Magda's predicted objections. "No, listen. I spoke with this PI, who sounds like the perfect guy for us. He's South American, so he's familiar with Venezuela and its different states. He has offices here and in Miami, and wasn't at all fazed when I told him who the target is." Jessica looked pleased with herself.

Magdalena rubbed her nose with a forefinger, eyes narrowing thoughtfully. "But it would cost an arm and a leg, Jess. I don't have that kind of money."

Jessica hugged her friend's hunched shoulders. "Don't worry about it. I've got this covered." Magda's eyes widened and Jessica smiled. "Consider it handled," she promised.

And true to her word, the next time they met for their regular walk, Jessica whispered urgently, "Cortez discovered something big. Remember, you mentioned he used to cheat on you and maybe do drugs?"

Magda shrugged. "Yeah. And?"

"There's more. I'm talking serious sexual deviance. Revolting stuff. Stuff that would absolutely ruin his political career if it ever came out."

Magda's face flashed with a glimmer of hope. "Ok, but these things are difficult to prove, especially with a man like Esteban." She was already shaking her head.

Jessica's amber eyes glowed. "No, we have proof. Photos. I can't show you here, but let's go back to mine and you'll see for yourself. They reveal everything. Unbelievable. This is our ticket to justice, Magda."

Magdalena cupped her cheeks with both hands and took two

CHAPTER 50 — RESCUE PLAN

deep breaths. When she glanced up, she was weeping silently. "Thank you. For your strength. For not giving up. You're a good person, Jess."

Jessica pulled her into a hug. "No, *you've* been incredible. Right from the start. This is the least I could do. I'm indebted to you, Magda. I wouldn't be here if it wasn't for you. You're the best friend a girl could wish for and all this time I had no clue what was going on in your life because all I ever talk about are *my* problems. Darling, this is my chance to make it up to you and I promise I will fight tooth and nail to get your son back." She choked on these last words, and the two women hugged even tighter.

***

Several weeks had passed since their dreadful argument, the one where Joseph told her, point blank, she wasn't an asset to him. This was the reason she'd become so focused on proving her worth – 'liability' had been his exact choice of word, and the connotations in her mind were endless. He had also recently given her six months "to make something of herself". He'd said it in anger and, although outraged by the ultimatum, she was already working harder than before, needing to prove, mostly to herself, she could do it! She could be successful again. She wasn't "getting too old", as Joseph often reminded her. Thirty-nine, *too old*? What planet was he on! Yes, she accepted things had shifted for her as a dancer, but she was still a kick-ass choreographer. Besides, she had so much more to offer the world. Her time wasn't up by any stretch of the imagination. *Jessica Sokari Brown is no-one's liability!*

She had the television on full blast and the voice ringing through its speakers resonated with conviction.

"Whatever's got your name on it cannot go to anybody else. God," *(pronounced 'Gaad,' in his Southern drawl)* "has enough favour for you."

Jessica found Fifi's recommended preacher's words captivating. He said life has a way of burying dreams – they're buried under disappointment, under heartache, under discouragement and past mistakes. We wake up one day and find ourselves living in mediocrity, even when we once had amazing dreams. The key is to remember that the vision *Gaad* put into your heart is still there. Focus not on the pain, or your past foibles, but on those dreams. (Gosh, her mother would love this man!)

Yes, when aspirations become hidden under low self-esteem, it's easy to settle for mediocrity even though you were destined for greatness. This sounded exactly like her life – she'd settled for a decidedly ordinary existence. But this handsome American preacher was saying that just because *you* gave up doesn't mean *God* gave up. Your dream is still alive and can still come to pass.

Jessica found herself nodding idiotically at the television and giggled. Thank goodness no one could see her. Ok, Jess. Time to dig up some dried-up bones! She switched off the TV with a renewed sense of hope and vigour. This fresh approach to life was a work in progress. Albeit at a snail's pace, she was definitely moving forward. She glanced at her

CHAPTER 50 — RESCUE PLAN

watch and dashed out the door.

Magdalena entered the café just as Jessica was beginning to think she wouldn't show.

"Sorry, I'm late. I missed my train and had to wait for another." She draped her jacket on the back of her chair and sat.

A server approached. "What can I get you Ladies?"

Jessica gestured for Magda to go first.

"An oat milk cappuccino, please. With very little foam."

"I'll have the same, thank you." Jessica was eager to begin.

"Anything to eat?" The waiter smiled politely.

"No, thank you," they both said in tandem, waiting for him to leave.

"Esteban called me last night," Magdalena began without preamble, "to say that because he cancelled the usual July trip, he'll be coming to London at the end of August instead. With Hector," she added, beaming with hope, and Jessica's chest tightened.

"That's wonderful news, Magda! You'll see Hector sooner than you thought and we can start making arrangements for custody. Cortez has…," Jessica paused as their coffees were placed on the table, then lowered her voice to a whisper and continued, "he found more proof… that he's receiving cartel funding. This strengthens our case."

Magdalena pursed her lips, biting her inside cheek. "You don't know Esteban, Jess. He can bury *any* evidence."

"Not here, he can't," Jessica countered, undeterred. "And now he's scheduled to be in London, we should set our plan in motion."

"Which is?"

Jessica leaned forward. "You play nice with him." She grinned when Magda scowled. "Arrange a dinner, inviting me. Make sure to look stunning. Entice him; anything to bring his guard down. You mentioned he's volatile and I don't want any *wahala*, so I'll have security agents placed strategically to ensure our safety. Let's get him feeling relaxed and comfortable, then wham! He won't expect it when I present him with all the evidence."

"What if he doesn't take the bait?" Magdalena squinted with concern.

"He'd be a fool not to. I've already contacted his nanny service, hired the best lawyers, and have the media on my side. He'll take my threats of exposure seriously, I guarantee you."

"You think it'll work?" Magdalena sounded unsure.

"I'm certain it will," Jessica declared confidently.

※

The uplifting sound of instrumental jazz pervaded the vibrant atmosphere of the Mayfair restaurant, and Esteban Enrique Delgado was in a celebratory mood. Magdalena Maria Gonzalez was dressed in an emerald green halterneck top, paired with a form fitting, knee-length leather skirt,

CHAPTER 50 — RESCUE PLAN

which highlighted her viridescent eyes.

"You look *stunning*," Jessica whispered encouragingly to her friend, before they followed the host to the secluded table where Esteban was waiting.

An hour into dinner, Jessica observed that Magda was positively glowing. Her face was alive with excitement and interest, making Jessica wonder whether she might still love the father of her child. Esteban laughed at something Magda had said, and Jessica knew the moment was right. She excused herself to the cloakroom, where she retrieved a large, brown envelope she'd left there for safekeeping.

When she returned to the table, Esteban was still gazing into Magdalena's eyes, his oily, slicked-back hair gleaming in the candlelight. Jessica furtively leaned the envelope against the leg of her chair and cleared her throat. That was Magda's cue to head to the Ladies' Room.

"I can see you're a good friend to Magdalena."

Esteban initiated conversation, but Jessica stilled him with an impatient gesture. "Please. No need for small talk. As lovely as this dinner was, I'm here for an entirely different reason."

Esteban's eyes squinted dangerously, and he leaned back, taking a slow sip of his wine.

Jessica looked him dead in the eye. "I'll keep this brief. Magda told me everything. About how you abused her in Venezuela, the prostitutes, the drugs…"

"Hah!" The sound was a snigger. "*That's* what you wish to talk to me about? Lady, mind your own business."

"The kidnapping, the lies…"

His chin rose imperiously. "Where is that bitch, anyway?" Esteban continued as though she hadn't spoken. "Why isn't she here to confront me herself? Stupid, cowardly woman."

"Magdalena is anything but a coward," Jessica defended. "She left me to speak with you for this very reason. Your vicious insults and name-calling! Your way of browbeating her into doing whatever *you* want. But that ends today."

Esteban sneered, "So you are her bulldog, eh?" He laughed nastily, then added, "What a waste of my time." He rose and picked up his jacket.

Jessica stood too and moved closer, whispering in his ear, "I have proof of your cocaine habit and your links to the cartel. It'll ruin you, and any chance you have of winning the state elections." Her peripheral vision told her his bodyguards had also moved closer.

Esteban scoffed and put an arm through his jacket.

Jessica's tone hardened. "And evidence of your appetites." She pulled the brown envelope from beside her chair.

Esteban's gaze turned dagger-like. "What the f- what are you talking about?" He spoke through clenched teeth, his voice dripping venom.

CHAPTER 50 — RESCUE PLAN

"Sit!" she ordered, spreading the envelope's vile contents on the table.

He glanced at the images, then glared at her. "*What do you want?*" he growled, a tic pulsing in his jaw. He gestured for the guards to stay back.

Jessica matched his angry gaze. When his eyes darted back to the photos, she knew she had him cornered.

Her tone became acerbic, filled with disgust as she dictated the terms. "From this day forward, Hector will live with his mother. You shall never again breathe a word about Magdalena's state of mind, or try to regain custody under any jurisdiction." She handed him some printed documents and added, "This deal is non-negotiable, Mr Delgado. If I don't hear from you within 24 hours, it's cancelled, and I go to the press."

Esteban clasped and unclasped his hands, his pulsating, brick-red face a frightening spectacle of rage, and Jessica wondered what his constituents would say should they see him now.

Magdalena returned to retrieve her shawl. Esteban half rose, his arm poised as though to strike her. Then his eyes darted around the crowded restaurant, and he sat back down slowly, mumbling instead, "Bitch!"

"You are truly loathsome!" Jessica spat in disgust. She pointed at the photos, her tone quietly menacing. "This is only the beginning, Mr Delgado. You may keep these copies as a reminder. You should know that the authorities have been told where to look should anything happen to either of us. Enjoy the rest of your stay in London," she added sarcastically, then followed Magdalena to the exit.

As she walked towards the door, she couldn't resist a smile of triumph.

Esteban Delgado didn't show for the exchange. His representative met Jessica and Magdalena and handed them the signed papers. Hector waited anxiously in the car. Jessica watched as both mother and son clung to each other and wept.

It was still Summer, but she had goosebumps all over.

CHAPTER 51

This is Who I Am

"Be right here if you need me," Joseph promised. His gaze, soft yet intense, brimmed with empathy.

Jessica slowly eased her hand from his, her fingers lingering for a moment. "I'll be alright," she murmured, although her eyes began to mist over. "This is something I must do on my own."

She trudged through the cemetery gates, each step heavy, toward the two graves standing silently side by side in the pristine, well-kept yard. The air was thick with the scent of damp earth and fresh-cut grass.

Kneeling before the headstones of father and son, she whispered, "It's been years since I visited you both. I've blamed myself for your deaths, but it wasn't my fault. Your time was up. I still feel the pain and will always remember you."

Large, silent teardrops fell, unrestrained, dripping from her chin to the cold, wet ground. She sat cross-legged in the sombre quiet, lost in her thoughts, oblivious to the minutes passing by. When the drizzle began, Jessica rose to leave, dabbing her streaming eyes. She spotted Joseph still standing by the cemetery gates, his bald head shining with droplets of rain. His stalwart, comforting presence triggered immense gratitude within her, and she trotted the last few steps towards him.

As she flung herself into his arms, he held her tight and whispered, "I'll never let you go, sweetheart. You've got me."

"We did it, Fifi! Wiped the smug smile off that bastard's face. Oh, you should've seen his surprise when I brought out those disgusting photos. Hah! Still can't fathom he might actually become a Venezuelan governor one day. He's shameless."

"At least you helped Magda gain custody. Which is amazing, Jess. Well done."

"She deserves it. Imagine not living with your son for *three years*! I had no clue she was suffering. Hmmm. Thank Goodness I could help. That's

CHAPTER 51 — THIS IS WHO I AM

the only way we could beat him at his own game. With money."

"The agreements he signed are watertight, right?"

"Completely. He can't worm out of this one. We've got him."

Freida chuckled softly, a sound that always signified happiness, and Jessica asked, "What's so funny?"

"You. You're so stubborn in your pursuit of justice for another. It's sweet. You know, that's always been your true nature – to help people."

Jessica gave a self-deprecating grunt. "Yeah, me who's so wrapped up in my issues. I can't see beyond my nose."

Freida tutted, "Not true, darling. You've always been the girl who wants to save others. Even when you were a child. Remember how you and Debbie became friends? How you almost broke your neck rushing to her aid?"

Jessica pressed the handset closer to her ear.

Freida continued with a smile in her voice, "It's who you are, Jess. Compassionate. Kind. Helpful. Giving. You just lost your way for a while, but now you're back on track."

Jessica's eyes flooded. "Thanks, Fifi." She felt oddly happy.

"Ok. Tell me. How are things with Joseph?"

"Oh, let's not talk about me…"

"No, I want to know. The last time we spoke, you were threatening to walk away."

"Nah. That was a moment of major self-pity. Temporary insanity. Things are much better since the summer hols. He came with me to visit Will's grave yesterday."

"You went! That's great, Jess. You needed to make peace with that. And good on Joseph for supporting you."

Jess admitted, "It was Magda who talked some sense into me. And seeing her turmoil made our petty complaints and arguments seem pathetic. I even telephoned Will's parents."

Jessica could hear Freida applauding her from across the Atlantic, and she giggled. "Stop mocking me, Fifi."

Freida laughed. "Hey, no-one's mocking anyone here. Everything I'm hearing today is just wonderful. My little sis has finally grown up."

"Aged thirty-nine!" Jessica added with a shake of her head.

Freida chuckled. "Well, better late than never!"

Oh, my goodness, I'm becoming my mother, Jessica considered with amusement, as she wiped down the kitchen counter whilst humming to herself. No longer resentful, she recognised that taking responsibility for keeping the house in order was simply something she'd seen her own mum do. It was neither a big deal, nor a thing to despise. It was a choice

CHAPTER 51 — THIS IS WHO I AM

that she, Jessica, made entirely of her own free will.

Pick your battles – that's wisdom.

After his initial scepticism, even Joseph seemed impressed by her tenacity for hard work. She appeared less concerned with his opinion and more focused on how she felt about herself. A little older and wiser, after so many instances of being bitten, Jessica was deliberately vague in her responses to his probing queries.

"You're up early. What are you so busy writing all the time? Your memoirs or what?"

Joseph's mildly mocking tone was met with a serene smile from Jessica. She glanced up from her computer, aware he was fishing and choosing not to take the bait. It would be foolhardy to sow the seeds of her precious dreams onto such unfertile ground. He wouldn't understand and might even try to dissuade her from pursuing these ideas. No. She would keep this baby close to her chest until it was successfully birthed and had legs of its own.

Could it be happening? Was the "I" in her finally becoming a little more authentic? She no longer behaved like a puppet on a string, always dancing to the tune of her master; constantly striving to please him and prove herself worthy of his attention.

Dear J, the "I" in the question "Who am I?" is no longer linked to the affirmation of others.

"Welcome to this very first episode of *'Can You Dance like Me?'* Thank you for tuning in to the show where our contestants are required to replicate my choreography to the letter and prove they can 'dance like me'."

Explosive applause ensued.

"Thank you. Before we begin, I promised I'd respond to media speculation about why I created this new program about dance, rather than revive my previous show 'Chocolate and Vanilla'."

An enthusiastic audience member called out, "Yes, Jessica. You'll always be our preferred brand of dark Chocolate."

Jessica chuckled. "Thank you, Sir. I'm sure you meant that as a compliment. I should ask you to remove your mask so we can see your cheeky face."

Everyone laughed. Jessica continued, "Well, first, let me say how truly excited I am to grace your television screens once again. But this time, doing what I was born to do. 'Chocolate and Vanilla' is a fun highlight of my past; a period I remember fondly, but the past nonetheless. And, yes, I *do* miss my dear friend Annabel, who's out in LA living *her* dream; meaning Chocolate and Vanilla is well and truly over."

The sound of disappointed mumbling rumbled through the audience.

Jessica lifted a stilling hand. "I'm at a new phase of my life, and

CHAPTER 51 THIS IS WHO I AM

I know you all wish me well."

Several nods. Her eyes scanned the faces in the room, seeking further confirmation and a glimmer of approval. They landed on the fourth row, on Joseph, who smiled encouragingly. Jessica beamed.

"… A stage where I realise it's not about how famous I am or what I've achieved or how people see me – but more about… my legacy. If I were to die tomorrow, what would everyone say about me? How much of the true Jessica did I leave the world? What lasting impression did I give you?"

Silence. Everyone watched her intently. Emily Dunn, who moved back to London recently, stood in the wings, clipboard in hand, probably nervously holding her breath, trying to gauge the mood of this bizarre, socially distanced studio audience. It was difficult to tell what they were thinking with those bloody masks hiding their expressions.

They were a vocal bunch, that's for sure.

Jessica's voice rang with confidence. "Every day, I ask myself the question: 'What do I want out of life?' We often regard the word 'I' as selfish – but it isn't. It's simply a recognition of one's essence, of one's state of being, one's intrinsic value to the world. Once you acknowledge and understand you've been created for a specific purpose, that you're unique, you place a higher value on your person and see the bigger picture of the reason for your existence. A lot of us don't rate ourselves. Not really. Not deep down – and it shows. I used to be one such person. Once upon a time, I had no real belief in my talent and even hated my body for the longest period."

Murmurings of surprise rippled through the audience.

"It was a tough lesson to learn; that people rise to whatever expectations you have of yourself. So, I say to every young person out there, never do things based on what others think of you. The question is, how do *you* see yourself? Accept yourself and the world will embrace you."

Magdalena was first to stand to her feet and Jessica's eyes glistened with gratitude. The applause was rapturous. The enthusiasm unanimous. Jessica had the unwavering attention of everyone under the sound of her voice.

She glanced at Emily, who closed her eyes and visibly sighed with relief. The gamble had paid off. Jessica was born to be on stage in one form or another. This speaking thing came so naturally to her.

"It's about the bold choices I make, every day, to ignore how anyone else might view my 'non-classical' ballet body, or my assertive personality, or my unique dance style. It's about letting go of my past drama and having the boldness to re-invent the wheel, rather than trying to fit into the mould of what's traditional or expected. Tragedies may come, but life goes on."

Jessica uttered this last statement in an airy and somewhat hubristic manner, as though she had it all figured out. This raised a few eyebrows

CHAPTER 51 — THIS IS WHO I AM

in her discerning audience, most of whom were die-hard Jessica Brown fans and well aware of the trials and triumphs of her story. Their eyes widened in anticipation and empathy.

She switched her tone to one more earnest. "Yes, there has been great tragedy in my life, but I can't change history. None of us can. There's such freedom in recognising the past as just that. What we all must do is work on the present... live in the present... accept what's happened and move on. That's what I've done. My first love is dance. Yet, when I started out, I didn't believe I was built for it. But this is who I am. It's what I was born to do. And I would love to help countless others do it, too. So, tell me, *Can You Dance Like Me?*"

It began as a murmur of approval that mushroomed into ecstatic applause.

Her heart-felt introduction had convinced all her sceptics of her authenticity and rendered her elated fans vociferous with praise. The new show was on.

PALM TREES IN THE STORM

CHAPTER 52

The beginning

J essica closed her eyes and inhaled the crisp, cold air, her sigh one of pure contentment. Wrapping her sheepskin coat more snugly around her, she pressed the red record button on her dictaphone and spoke in a clear, conversational tone:

"I adore this time of year when the purchasing panic has ceased and we focus on what matters most – family, love, and a few indulgent, non-essential gifts I might even enjoy. This season always reminds me to be grateful for the myriad of blessings in my life."

She paused, breathing in the peaceful silence of the frosty morning. "I've started taking solitary walks every day. They're not lengthy, but seem to do me a world of good. When I walk, it's as though each stride guides me deeper into the recesses of my mind, allowing me to think. It feels like a luxury to be able to focus on no one if I so choose – just my thoughts, my feelings, my hopes and dreams."

Jessica's eyes sparkled with a soft light as she spoke. "Joseph and I made love this morning. The moment he awoke he reached for me, and I'm convinced he'd been dreaming about it all night! Well, I suppose after the last few days, who'd blame him?!"

She laughed softly at the memory. "Ok, let me put this into context. Growing up, what struck me most as I watched my mum and dad was how close they were – almost like they were one being. Us kids couldn't breach that wall of intimacy, no matter how hard we tried. And believe me, all eight of us tried!"

Her voice took on a reflective tone. "It was kind of weird, and I didn't understand it until recently. Now that they're here for Christmas, I've been observing them and realise nothing's changed. Albeit much older and not as randy and demonstrative as they used to be (thank Goodness!), their closeness is impenetrable. It makes me see where I've gone wrong. I was so bent on maintaining my independence that I failed to recognise that giving myself to another human being doesn't mean I cease to exist as an individual."

CHAPTER 52 THE BEGINNING

She sighed deeply. "Although my parents appear as one entity, they couldn't be more different in personality and behaviour. I always thought marriage meant there's no more you and me, only us. Yet, even with William, my first love, I questioned whether this was true. Do the two really become one flesh, as stated in the Bible?"

Her tone grew softer, more introspective. "It now strikes me I've been short-changing myself (and the men I married) by keeping secrets from them in a way a spouse never should. Boyfriend and girlfriend are 'you and me,' but husband and wife are definitely an 'us.' 'Us' doesn't mean 'I', as an individual, disappear. In fact, a strong 'I' makes for a stronger 'us'. Secrets shouldn't exist between a married couple – not even the tiniest ones – because if they do, then the 'us' ceases to exist and it becomes the separate 'you and me' once again. Look at what my secret did to William and how it broke his heart, and mine. No. Secretive behaviour is wrong and forms a callus on your hardened heart."

She nodded to herself and took a swig of her water bottle. "But I digress – back to Joseph and our passionate lovemaking this morning and what led to this moment of rare intimacy. For several years, I've observed my husband oscillate between dutiful hard work and self-loathing and, after our lovely summer in the South of France, I broached the subject. I asked him what he'd rather be doing with his life and he replied without hesitation, 'Creating beautiful clothes for beautiful people.' No surprise there. So, I encouraged, 'Do it,' and let the cat out of the bag. Told him about my 'inheritance' and how I used a portion to finance my successful Magda mission. I think Joseph was surprised, but impressed. Remarkably, after his initial probing, he hugged me, said he was pleased for me, and was relieved he could pursue his dreams with a free conscience. He rarely says anything he doesn't mean, so this is a big deal. He even clarified he was okay for me to contribute to the upkeep of the family as I saw fit, but wouldn't want a penny of my money. Noble.

It felt like we drew a line in the sand that day, and although nothing changed outwardly, I noticed the shift. He now looks at me differently and moves as if a tremendous weight has been lifted off his burdened shoulders. He's opened the eyes of my heart and I can now see him; can see that his intentions are honourable - that he means no harm. He is just a simple man, wanting to live an uncomplicated life. And he loves me."

Jessica's voice grew gentler, imbued with warmth. "So, three or four days ago, I woke up early as usual to enjoy a quick coffee before my morning walk. When I popped back into the bedroom, Joseph had moved to my side of the bed, which has always been his way of saying I want you. As he lay there, he must have sensed my gaze because his eyes flickered open.

He wanted to make love – I could tell from his cheeky squint, but… alas! The wafting scent of baking muffins reminded me breakfast was in danger of burning.

I leaned in and kissed him with a breezy, 'Good morning, darling,' then immediately dashed from the room. His sigh told me he was disappointed.

CHAPTER 52 — THE BEGINNING

Ordinarily, Joseph doesn't take rejection well, but this time there was no hint of irritation. He merely rose and followed me. As I bent over the oven to rescue said cinnamon-banana-muffins, he grabbed my behind and thrust his pyjama-clad hips towards me. Naughty boy! Then he pulled me into an affectionate, lengthy hug and I felt it. I really did. I felt his love.

We shut the kitchen door and this morning's amorous activities ensued, after which I murmured, 'You don't think Sophie heard us, do you?' Joseph chuckled and responded, 'Well, she didn't hear *me*.' Cheeky sod!"

Jessica chortled at the memory, before concluding, "This could be the beginning of something new, but only if I grasp it with both hands and hold on tight. It's up to *me*. I'm the one who defines the dynamics of every relationship I'm in."

She pressed the stop button on the recorder and placed it inside her coat pocket. Tracing the imprint of her winter boots in the muddy ground, she hummed all the way back home.

～

Sophie's eyes widened in terror at her father's raised voice. Jessica glanced away, **maintaining** her razor-sharp focus on her computer screen.

She'd chosen to sit this one out and let Sophie glimpse just how unreasonable her father could be.

"Ok, time for bed, darling." Joseph's cheery tone sounded forced, showing he was tired after his long day at work.

Sophie tried negotiating for an extra ten minutes, then five, then two – all to no avail. Like his refusal to give her more than a fist-sized portion of popcorn, he was in no mood to be lenient on the bedtime front.

Sophie whined, but shuffled to her feet.

"Good night, darling." Jessica felt relieved she could get an hour to concentrate on the treatment for the show.

"But *you're* putting me to bed, Mum!" Sophie declared petulantly, clinging to her mother.

"No, my love, Daddy is. I put you to bed last night *and* the night before." Jessica tried to keep her tone light and kissed her daughter on the cheek.

"Awwww!" Out came the bottom lip, and she somehow stomped and dragged her reluctant feet in tandem, slouching up the stairs.

Jessica exchanged a conciliatory smile with Joseph and shrugged.

A mere three minutes later, Sophie was down again, tiptoeing into the kitchen. Jessica watched in surprise as her daughter grabbed a large handful of popcorn from the bag her dad had discarded on the counter, then glared defiantly at Jessica as she popped them one by one into her mouth.

Amused by how much Sophie reminded her of herself, Jessica grinned and raised an eyebrow.

Sophie sounded defensive. "Well, it didn't make sense! He prepared

CHAPTER 52 — THE BEGINNING

the whole big bag... I didn't even ask for any... and then... and then he gave me the tiniest amount and expects me to be happy. And all this..." she took another handful, "will be thrown away."

Jessica nodded, trying not to smile.

"Such a waste, Mummy! What's wrong with salty popcorn, anyway?"

Some questions have no answer. She kissed Sophie on the forehead and said, "Ok, darling. You've had your fill, now off to bed you go!"

Sophie and Hector were playing a game of counting baubles on the tree. It was Christmas Eve and the Ofosu/Brown battle had begun in earnest – the battle of Ghanaian versus Nigerian *jollof*. As Jessica later explained to a bemused Emily and a fascinated Magda, *jollof rice* is a big deal in West Africa and these two nations have a long-standing tradition of competing about which tastes better – although Nigerians will always tell you there is zero competition as Ghanaians are tantamount to their poor cousins and therefore not up to par.

As a Nigerian married to a Ghanaian, Jessica found this feud ridiculous, but also wonderfully entertaining because watching her mum and mother-in-law attempt to win the men over with their cooking prowess was hilarious.

The self-appointed judges were Sokari Brown and Joseph Ofosu, and little Sophie would be the tiebreaker.

If nothing else, it lightened the mood and put everyone in a festive spirit. Regarding the *jollof*, if you asked Jessica, she thought her mother had the upper hand because, as a Nigerian woman living in Ghana, she benefitted from understanding both cultures and used the best aspects of each cooking method to her advantage.

Christmas came and went, and even Josephina seemed to enjoy herself. "If I didn't know better, I'd say she was warming to me; or at least to the fact that I seem to make her son happy," Jessica whispered to Edith Brown with a giggle.

For their customary long walk on Boxing Day, Jessica positioned herself alongside her father for most of the afternoon.

They walked in companionable silence for a while and then he revealed what was evidently on his mind. "Jessica…" His voice was gruff.

"Yes, Dad?" she inquired, smiling.

He cleared his throat. "You're a warrior – you know that, don't you?" He glanced at her expectantly. She nodded, and he continued, "Promise me you will persevere, eh… re-ignite that fighting spirit of yours…" He linked his arm through hers. "This life… it's a journey. Trust the process – that whatever happens is already written." He stopped to give her an intense stare. "If you lost something or someone, it was *meant to happen*."

Jessica swallowed. "I know, Dad. I'm trying to…"

He nodded. "I understand. As my grandmama used to say, we all

CHAPTER 52 — THE BEGINNING

are palm trees that must bend with the wind. So, when the storm comes, we do not break. When the crisis is over, the palm bounces right back to its upright position. It's wonderful to see you bouncing back, Jess."

She nodded, chuffed to see her father pleased with her progress. Yes, that's what she was – a palm tree that remains standing even after the storms of life.

They resumed walking; the others were way ahead of them by this point.

"Some people are not content because they do not yield to the natural flow of life."

He's referring to Joseph, Jessica mused. Or… maybe to me as well.

"Stubbornness leads to a lack of fulfilment. You know what's kept your mother and I happy all these years?" He paused, then answered his own question. "Our flexibility and willingness to adapt. In other words, our resilience. It means we can weather any storm."

Jessica looked at her mother, who somehow sensed their gaze and turned at the same moment. Her father's eyes lit up, and he smiled at the woman who still brought him such joy after so many decades. Edith grinned back at him, before suddenly bending over to do a little *Tu Seki* booty dance, causing him to chortle heartily. Jessica thought with amusement, my parents are something else, honestly!

Her dad's tone switched from serious to almost jovial. "Life isn't meant to be a constant struggle, you know. You young folk need to stop going against the grain of your natural talents and gifts. Living is much simpler than you make it. When you do what you were born to do, it's easy and you're happy." He gazed adoringly at his wife. "After fifty plus years, I still love her craziness."

Jessica chuckled and slipped her arm through his. "Thanks, Dad. I needed to hear this… if I'm honest, it hasn't been easy. But I'm getting there."

"I know you are, my dear. You've endured a great deal and come through. This business of living is a work in progress, eh?" Sokari Brown let out his signature laugh. "They say you've got to fake it till you make it, right?"

"Right." She hugged him back.

And the words she'd subconsciously been awaiting all her life, came once again.

"I'm proud of you, Jessica. You've come a long way."

~

Joseph and Jessica spent 31st December 2020 alone, allowing Sophie to stay up late and usher in the New Year with them. They played games, ate popcorn and chocolate and watched the fireworks on TV. Throughout the evening, Joseph kept throwing glances at Jessica, his eyes glistening with love and something else. Desire? Perhaps it was the champagne? Whatever it was, she wasn't complaining. Midnight came,

CHAPTER 52   THE BEGINNING

and they all cheered, Sophie cheering the loudest and sneaking another sip of Jessica's champagne.

"Hey you!" Jessica chided, swiping the glass out of her child's grasping reach with a merry laugh. Joseph was also in a high-spirited mood. He tugged his wife into his arms in a movement so swift they both almost toppled over. They fell into fits of giggles, like two naughty children, about to be caught doing something they shouldn't.

And for the first time in a long while, he kissed her. *Really* kissed her, deep and passionate, then gentle and teasing, their bodies fusing together as one.

Sophie's little voice sounded disgusted. "Eewww, yuk! Gross! Stop... you're gonna make a baby, I know it!"

They pulled away from each other laughing, looking down at their beautiful daughter and drawing her into the hug.

Father and daughter had gone for a walk, leaving Jessica alone at home. As her eyes took in the room, she spotted a lone bauble, a forgotten remnant from the box of Christmas decorations now safely tucked in their basement for resurrection the following year.

Grateful for the wonderful memories it conjured, she sighed and picked up her journal one last time.

Dear J, unexpectedly, things have begun to turn and it would appear God is smiling down on us. The impossible has been made possible. I can view my husband with feelings akin to love, sometimes mixed, washed and tumble dried with a myriad of other emotions, but love nonetheless. And, thankfully, my little teenager of a daughter is acting like a child once again. It's true that if you take care of yourself, you have the bandwidth to care for others. And Daddy's right. We are palm trees – and it's my dancer's flexibility that has enabled me to manoeuvre the storms of life, and ultimately embrace who I am. Despite daily and inevitable ups and downs, the future looks bright.

This is where my story begins.

CHAPTER 52   THE BEGINNING

PALM TREES IN THE STORM

EPILOGUE

In shadows cast by starlit dance,
A silent cry for one last chance,
Through whispered dreams and love's embrace,
Within the storm she finds her place.
Tempest winds, they howl and tear,
Yet steadfast roots defy despair,
In tender arms of hopes reborn,
She weathers night to greet the morn.
Beneath the weight of time and pain,
Each tear a trace, each scar a stain,
Amidst the wreckage, beauty's grace,
She bends, not breaks, in life's embrace.
Her heart, though worn by trial's hand,
Awakens strong, a guiding brand,
Through weary paths and skies grown dim,
She rises tall, where light feels thin.
As palm trees bow then stand anew,
In every gust her strength shines through,
With every storm, a tale retold,
In simple truth, her spirit bold.

WWW.GENAWEST.COM

The author, Gena West, is an award-winning singer/songwriter and performer, with four critically-acclaimed albums to her credit, a number 1 hit single *"Joy"*, and accolades for numerous high-profile events around the world, including the Olympic Games. As the daughter of a United Nations diplomat, she has travelled the world extensively and, coming from a diverse background, Gena is an avid agent of change, as exemplified in her TEDx talk and in her cutting-edge television chat show, *"A Different View with Gena West"*. Gena studied law at the London School of Economics and Political Science and is a qualified Barrister and member of the Honourable Society of Lincoln's Inn. As a motivational coach and speaker, she is a great believer in the gift of empowering others, and this is reflected in her writing. Gena is of Nigerian heritage, was born and educated in the UK, and has lived in London, Accra and New York.

Printed in Great Britain
by Amazon